COFFEE TEA THE
GYPSY & ME

CAROLINE JAMES

RAMJAM PUBLISHING COMPANY

FOREWORD

Coffee Tea The Gypsy and Me is my debut novel. The book where it all began. I'd wanted to write from an early age but never thought that I was good enough. Finally, I sat down and wrote this book and to my joy, it was a huge success. More books have followed and my writing dream has come true.

Thank you for reading my work
and I sincerely hope that you enjoy it.

With love
Caroline James.

COPYRIGHT

DEDICATION

For my precious family

With love

THE BEGINNING...

Jo's romance with the gypsy began with his first kiss.
She never forgot it...

New Year's Eve 1987

Jo stood at the door of the hotel and gazed out at the inky, snow laden sky. In the distance, the band struck up Auld Lang Syne and she imagined the revellers joining hands as they sung their hearts out and promised eternal friendship tonight and evermore.

The beginning of 1987 had been life-changing and now, as it rolled over into a new year, Jo made another monumental decision.

It was freezing. She should have put a jacket over her gown but Jo was unaware of the cold as she watched the snow begin to fall. She wondered where her gypsy was, what night sky would he be watching?

The snow came down in a sudden flurry and Jo held her face up to the heavens as the giant flakes caressed her skin. She closed her eyes and remembered the most tumultuous year of her life...

1

January 1987

Jo SAT by the window of her rented house and stared out at the view. An icy wind whipped a squall of sleet against the windows which ricocheted like bullets.

The television in the corner of the room was tuned to a game show and as the opening music for Strike It Lucky ended, Jo heard the host call out to the audience, "Awight!"

She stared at the hostile stone walls of Butterly Castle, an imposing building in the valley below the window. Built in 1092 when William II reigned over the county of Westmarland, it had resolutely deterred marauding Scots, the walls were covered in creeper and its bony branches clawed destructively at the masonry.

Jo clutched her throat and shuddered. There were hardly any holiday makers in January but a few brave souls undaunted by the bitter winds, entered the Norman Keep and climbed the steep stone steps. They emerged at the top to admire the magnificent view.

Jo hated this house.

A recent build, in a cul-de-sac called Castle Close it formed part of a modern housing estate. She sat with her chin on her knuckles and contemplated her life, Jo knew that she looked terrible, face puffy and hair a mess, but she didn't give a damn.

Greg, her husband of eight years had left her.

He'd run off with their sixteen-year old Spanish nanny and the hurt and scandal were too much to bear.

The house was still. Baby Thomas slumbered in his cot, the pale blue quilt rose with his gentle breaths. Jo glanced at her son and felt a wave of sadness; tears trickled down her cheeks. As the River Bevan thundered by below, Jo watched the deep muddy water and wondered what the hell she was going to do with her life.

The phone rang and the shrill bell startled her. Jo spun around to turn off the television and knocked a Cabbage Patch Doll from the table. It fell to the floor.

She kicked the ugly toy to one side and grabbed the receiver, fearful that Thomas would wake. The doll was a gift to Thomas from Greg and Jo felt like stamping on its face.

"Yes?"

"Is that you, Jo?" A man said. "Robert Mann here, how are you?"

"Oh you know, busy," Jo lied. What did Robert from Mann & Co Estate Agents want? The last call had been to invite her to lunch, to celebrate the sale of the pub she'd owned with Greg.

"We've a property in the area that might be of interest to you," he said. Jo held the heavy black melamine phone to her ear and wiped her eyes. She tried to concentrate as Robert continued.

"It's about six miles north of Butterly, in a lovely village with the River Bevan at the back and fells to the front. It's a bit neglected. Been a guest house in its time and the chap had plans to turn it into a nursing home, but it seems all these new regulations and safety laws are putting him off."

Robert droned on and Jo wondered what he was banging on about?

"What's it called?" she asked.

"Well, it's quite a large place and the owner seems to think he could get a good price if a hotel chain bought it. Thinks it's perfect for a country house hotel - that sort of thing, it doesn't need planning permission."

"What's it called?" Jo repeated as the image of a familiar building began to take shape.

"Of course he knows bugger all about catering. Bit of a shark if you ask me, wants to make a quick buck."

"What's the name of the place?" Jo chewed the skin round her thumb nail.

"I think it'll haemorrhage his money if he doesn't move it on soon. It's a biggish place and needs a lot of work."

"Robert, what is it called?" Jo shouted, no longer able to contain herself.

"Kirkton House, in the village of Kirkton Sowerby."

Jo dropped the phone. It bounced off her knee to the floor and she stared at it in disbelief, then scrambled to pick it up. Her heart hammered and she felt excited for the first time in ages. She took a deep breath.

"Jo, are you there?"

"I'll have it."

"What Jo? I can't hear you, what did you say?"

"I said I'LL HAVE IT!'"

"You don't even know the price. Are you mad?" Robert shouted back.

"I know the place and I know you'll do the best possible deal." Jo smiled, her tears forgotten. "Arrange a viewing and we'll finalise everything as soon as possible."

She slammed the phone down and jumped up then punched the air and spun around, tripping over the Cabbage Patch Doll. Unable to stop herself she stumbled and fell to the floor. Eye to eye with the creature, it stared soullessly. Jo leapt to her feet and with a determined kick sent the vile object spinning across the room.

"Stuff you Greg!"

She watched the doll hit the window, momentarily splayed out under a hail of icy bullets before it dropped to the floor. Thomas woke up and began to cry and Jo reached into the cot. She tucked the quilt around his body, cradled him in her arms and rocked him.

"I'll show your daddy how to run a business," she whispered as she kissed the baby's soft downy head. "Only this time it will be all on my own."

2

Jo swung her car through the gates of Kirkton House and skidded to a halt by the front door. Robert Mann jumped back. Gravel flew from under the tyres and threatened to pebble-dash his gleaming black Volvo estate. He scowled and rubbed the body work with his sleeve.

"Morning, Robert," Jo said as she sprang out of her car. It was a cold and frosty day and she knotted a scarf around her throat, then reached for Thomas and tugged a bright yellow bonnet over his ears.

"You look like a banana." Jo smiled at her son, encased in a custard coloured fleece suit.

"Go to Uncle Robert for a moment while I inspect our new home." Jo thrust the baby into Robert's arms.

"I say Jo, um … what do I do?" Robert was horrified. He held the wriggling fleece well away from his Harris Tweed overcoat. Jo ignored him and walked across the drive, then stood by the gates and stared at Kirkton House.

The familiarity of the lovely old building wrapped itself around her like a warm hug. She remembered the house from a viewing some time ago with her husband Greg, who'd disapproved of her scheme. He didn't think a hotel would work in the area and the house was too run down. Jo tingled with excitement. Today she would make plans for the building that was to become both her business and home.

Jo gazed at the dark, deserted property. Tall, gracious pillars rose protectively around the Georgian porch and windows either side reflected branches of a huge oak tree that had stood there for centuries.

"Let's get cracking." Jo sprinted across the gravel and took Thomas.

"At least it's a good distance from Butterly and you won't have the Fair to contend with." Robert reached for his clipboard and dug into his pocket to select a solid brass key from a large bunch, then unlocked the front door. "The gypsies would wreak havoc with this place."

On the second Thursday of June, Butterly hosted a Gypsy Horse Fair, an annual event which attracted up to ten thousand gypsies and travellers. They camped on a hill outside the town, appropriately named Fair Hill and thousands of visitors poured into the area for the week-long occasion.

"We didn't have much trouble with gypsies at the pub," Jo said. She remembered the large sums of cash that Greg had banked after the fair each year.

The horse fair was a tradition dating back over 300 years, protected in a charter granted by James II. The local population loathed it and wanted it banned. Few businesses stayed open, but those that did made a fortune. Vast amounts of alcohol were consumed which always led to trouble, generally amongst the inebriated visitors. The gypsies had their own way of dealing with discord and the police left them to it, much to the disdain of the very perplexed and frustrated locals, who hated having their civilised country lives disturbed.

"I suggest you close in Fair Week." Robert shut the door. "Better to be on the safe side." Jo ignored him. Her only concern at that moment was to ensure that the sale went through.

"Is Mr Sullivan joining us?" She asked and stood on a wide staircase that curved around onto a gallery. A tall sash window over-

looked the large oak tree. Robert shook his head. He'd suggested a price to the owner and with very little bargaining, it had been accepted. Mr Sullivan's debts were mounting and he was keen to move on. Jo stepped into the hall as Robert opened a heavy oak door.

"As long as your finances are in place and the survey's ok, things should go through quickly," Robert said.

Jo was confident that she'd get support from the Westmarland Trust Bank in Butterly.

Mr Knight, the manager, had enjoyed overseeing a flourishing account when the pub traded.

Robert followed Jo into a large room, it smelt dank and dusty. Jo walked over to the bay window where a white sheet covered sparse furniture. She yanked it to one side and dust caught in a shaft of sunlight flew up, creating a sparkling fog that floated through the room.

"I've always dreamt of having my own hotel," she said. "When Greg and I came to view this place, I knew it was the property I'd always dreamt about. But we'd got the pub and Greg said this was too posh, it was impossible to have both."

Robert watched Jo. He smelt her heady perfume - Beautiful by Estee Lauder and his gaze travelled to the copper hair that fell to her shoulders. Tall and slightly heavy, but with soft round curves, Jo had sea-green eyes that sparkled as she spoke. Dressed in country clothes, she wore a sensible pleated skirt and pumps with a ruffle-collar blouse in the style of Princess Diana. Her confidence captivated Robert, despite his wife Miriam's acidic comments.

"How can a young girl run a business and have a child?" Miriam had argued. Robert had been angry. What the hell did Miriam know? She'd never run anything more serious than a coffee morning. They'd often had a bar meal at the pub with local solicitor Peter Gavmin and Greg flirted outrageously with Miriam. Charmed, Miriam convinced herself that Jo had driven Greg away.

Robert sighed and put thoughts of his wife out of his mind. After twenty years in a monotonous marriage with the stick-thin Miriam, he allowed himself day dreams and Jo was his fantasy. Robert let his imagination run wild. He replaced Miriam's bony body, encased in flannelette, beside him at night, with visions of Jo. Voluptuous in silk, her full milky white breasts poured out of a lace negligee as she enticed him to pleasurable delights way beyond the daily grind of Robert Mann & Co, Estate Agent for Country Living...

"Wake up." Jo nudged Robert and walked across the hall to another musty room. "We'll soon have this old place rocking," she declared.

ROBERT TRAILED behind Jo for the next two hours. He held and pacified Thomas while Jo climbed stairs and opened doors and cupboards. From the cellar to the attics she worked her way through the building and planned the layout.

In a low-ceilinged room, she ran her fingers over solid dark beams. "This will make a great cocktail bar," she said and stepped into an adjacent room with wood panel surrounds and knelt in front of a cast iron fireplace. "It'll be perfect for log fires, on cool days." Jo stroked the grate.

The next room overlooked the garden. French doors stood either side of an Adam style fireplace. Jo turned a key in the lock and tugged the frame. The sharp movement disturbed a bird's nest and the ancient shell crumbled onto an outside terrace where a long conservatory was covered in moss and weeds, the windows streaked with mildew.

They gazed up the garden where the sky, as blue as a Robin's egg, peeped between slow-moving clouds. The frost-covered lawn glittered. High stone walls circled the whole garden and dense herbaceous borders lay beneath. Foliage trailed over paths. They climbed steps alongside a frozen fountain and traced a gravel path that weaved between unkempt lawns. At a set of rusted wrought iron gates, they paused.

"It's more beautiful than I remember," Jo said. She walked through an overgrown meadow and looked out to the Westmarland Fells.

"Tourists will love it. Imagine waking to this every day, Robert."

"You're taking an awful lot on." Robert was daunted by the amount of work to be done. He stared at Great Gun Fell, part of the Pennine Way.

It was a magnificent backdrop and Robert suddenly caught his breath. Bathed in a pinkish and mauve light, the house stood proudly under the wintry blue sky and he realised - she was right, it was magnificent.

Jo walked ahead and picked her way amongst the decay of a greenhouse. Panes of broken glass mingled with dozens of old clay pots and gardening debris.

She stepped over lead pipes, which indicated a Victorian heating system and opened a door, hidden in the wall. It led to a pebbled courtyard surrounding a stone cottage.

"More bedrooms," Jo smiled.

Robert made notes. Jo's enthusiasm was infectious and with his agent's mind he began to form a sales guide of the property five years on...

Formerly the principal residence of the village, Kirkton House dates back to the 17th and early 18th centuries with an elegant front wing added in the 19th century. The resident owner has carefully renovated the property and created an award winning, stylish country house hotel. The property has en-suite rooms and a fine dining restaurant.

He calculated his potential commission and grinned.

"Robert," Jo called. "Let's have a look at the kitchen." They entered through a side door and Thomas woke up. Jo sat on the kitchen table and fumbled about in her bag for a bottle of juice.

"Look at that." She pointed to an arched recess where the date 1720 was carved into the sandstone lintel. "When I viewed before, I did some research." She propped Thomas on her lap and pushed the bottle into his eager mouth. "The family who lived here were yeoman farmers. They owned the house and a lot of land in the valley and made mega bucks from the local tanning industry." Thomas guzzled happily.

"In the early 1800's they had sugar plantations in the West Indies and traded through the port of Whitehaven." Jo paused, "Do you know what they sold?"

"Slaves," Robert said. He knew his local history.

"Can you believe it?" Jo looked at Robert and shook her head.

"It was perfectly normal and respectable. They shipped the poor blighters, kidnapped in Africa and sent them to make rum on plantations in the Caribbean."

Jo put Thomas on her shoulder and jumped off the table. She rinsed the bottle under a tap. "Will you talk to Mr Sullivan and get a completion date? I'm off to the bank to sort out a loan with Mr Knight and then I'm going to instruct Peter Gavmin." She walked out of the kitchen. Robert reached for his set of keys, locked the back door and followed Jo into the hallway.

"It's been a good day today, Robert." Jo turned. "Thank you." She stood on her toes and pecked him on the cheek. Robert watched her walk away. With the baby balanced on one hip, her bottom swayed suggestively in perfect motion with the pleats of her skirt. He touched his cheek.

"But get a move on." Jo called over one shoulder.

Robert fumbled for the large brass key. A move on indeed! He locked the front door and climbed into his car, then engaged reverse gear and drove towards the gates. As he looked back at the house, the weak sun had fallen beyond the fells and a cold chill emanating from the darkening sky, left the house once again empty and in shadow.

Robert remembered Jo's enthusiasm. She'll bring this place to life! He thrust his car into gear. Robert was going to enjoy the reincarnation and grinned as he drove off along the main road.

3

"Five o'clock. By heck I'm late," Hattie mumbled. "I'm off, Mam."

Hattie's mother sat in the living room in a smoky haze. She had a child on each knee and watched The Magic Roundabout on television.

Hattie looked at her two young sons who gazed in awe at the characters.

"For goodness sake, your fag ash is falling on the kids," Hattie yelled. A smouldering cigarette hung limply from her mother's lips.

"Aw get on your way our Harriet and stop moaning." Her mother flicked the ash into the fireplace. "And don't forget to tell 'er how you ran your own place."

Hattie grabbed her parka coat from a hook in the hall and wriggled into it. She slammed the front door of the terraced house and hurried out to her car on the busy street. She unlocked the Opel Kadett and gripped the steering wheel, then closed her eyes and whispered a prayer.

"God or whoever you are, please help me make an impression on this Jo Edmonds, who's probably a snotty bitch and looking for someone with a grammar school accent. I promise not to swear and to keep me blouse buttoned up and smile sweetly, no matter what she asks about that bastard Italian Stallion and his tart. I need this job..." Hattie pushed sticky sweet and crisp packets to one side and placed her handbag on the passenger seat, alongside an untidy file of paperwork from the employment office. She cranked the ignition into life. The traffic was heavy and the car jerked as she approached the main road out of Marland. Hattie glanced at the fuel gauge - the tank was empty.

"Bloody 'ell," she mumbled and disengaged the gears to freewheel down the hill to the nearest garage - Pete Parks Autos. The car lurched across the forecourt, faltered and cut-out yards away from the nearest petrol pump. "Shite." Hattie sighed and looked around.

Pete Parks ambled across the tarmac, his hands shoved into the pockets of an old leather jacket.

"Now then Harriet, running on empty again?" he said. "Let your hand brake off and we'll glide you in." Pete bent over the rear of the car and gently pushed it in line with the pump.

Hattie jumped out and straightened her tight black skirt over ample hips.

"You're always a gentleman." Hattie smiled suggestively. "Stick us a fiver in."

"And you're looking as lovely as ever, Harriet." Pete winked. "Got a date?"

"Piss off, Pete. Save your charm for those that need it. I'm after a job at Kirkton House." She unbuttoned the top of her blouse and pulled a crumpled five pound note from her bra. "Keeping it warm for you," she teased. "I've heard that's how you like it."

"Warmer the better." Pete's deep blue eyes flickered as he looked her up and down. "What are you after there?"

"That new place, the hotel that's opening - I'll take whatever's going, Pete." She fiddled with her buttons as he put the petrol nozzle back on the pump. "I can't be choosy, got the kids to feed and bills to pay."

"No help from Mr Cornetto by the sound of things?" Pete screwed the petrol cap back into place.

"No, not a bean." Hattie squeezed past Pete and climbed back into her car. "I'll see you," she called out as she pulled away.

The road was impossibly busy for the time of day and Hattie began to panic that she'd be late. She drummed her fingers on the steering wheel and tried to remain calm as the traffic crawled along at fifteen miles an hour.

She thought about Pete Parks. No wonder his garage did so well every female in the Northern Lakes clamoured for a test drive. Hattie'd heard that he played away from the marital home but was discreet; no one seemed to come forward with any juicy gossip. His wife had horses, but didn't they all round here?

Most of them look like their horses... Hattie thought bitchily. She recalled a photo in the Westmarland Tribune recently of Mrs Parks in full riding apparel, smiling at the camera from under her hat as she received a rosette from the local dignitary Lord Crowther, for first place in dressage at the county show.

Hattie knew Pete had a hobby too - he raced motorbikes. He'd won a race at the TTs on the Isle of Man, a year or two back. Race circuits must be a hot bed of lust Hattie decided. There'd always be somewhere to engage his throbbing engine...

She could see a gap in the oncoming traffic and as she went past, noticed that the cause of the hold-up was several old fashioned, horse-drawn, gypsy caravans that meandered along the main road. Bloody hell, not the gypsies already.

Hattie watched the pretty caravans as they plodded along, the gypsies called them Vardos.

Some were horse drawn but most sat on trailers attached to a variety of vehicles and charabancs. Surely the hotel won't open with this lot about to descend? The Fair fascinated Hattie and she remembered sneaking out to the hill with her friends, her mam would've been furious if she'd known.

"Keep away from them gypsy men, they'll 'ave you in trouble." Hattie could hear the reprimands but was fascinated by the colourful comings and goings and all the fancy goods on sale, with fortunes to be told by wizened old women behind thick curtains. The gypsy boys loved a fight and Hattie knew many a tale of bare knuckle brawls to establish the hierarchy. Few visitors ventured up on the hill after night fall and in the day Butterly was over-run, despite an influx of police from all over the county. There was little law and order.

Hattie sighed, she was late! She put her foot down and once past the entourage, soon approached the village of Kirkton Sowerby where the Templars pub looked deserted, the car park empty.

There didn't seem to be much going on anywhere. She drove past the village hall and school, then along the main road that ran through the heart of the village and slowed down as she saw a large house loom before her. A sign had been erected beneath a huge oak tree and proudly announced in gold lettering: Kirkton House Hotel.

Hattie parked on the gravel driveway, climbed out and approached the front door. This is posh, she thought and turned the handle but the door was locked. She pushed a brass button and waited. Several moments passed and Hattie wondered whether to press again.

"Hang on I'm coming." A woman rushed down the hall. She flicked hair out of her eyes and dug in her pocket for a large brass key, then fumbled with the lock, opened the door and invited Hattie in.

"I'm Hattie Salerno," Hattie began nervously. "Sorry I'm late."

"Don't worry, I'd completely lost track of time. I'm Jo Edmonds, do come in." She ushered Hattie into the hallway. "We'll have a seat by the fire in the Red Room. Would you like some tea?"

Hattie nodded and sat down in a leather armchair. She vaguely remembered Jo coming to her restaurant with a good-looking man, whom Hattie assumed was her husband. She'd heard that he'd run off with the nanny. Another two-faced shite who couldn't keep his hands off the hired help. She looked around the room. It had a high ceiling and a log fire roared in the grate.

Deep vermillion walls contrasted with an oak dado rail, white picture rails and wooden window shutters and a dark green carpet matched floor length curtains. It was classy. On one wall, a glassfronted recess contained a magnificent dinner service on tiered shelves. Soft lights lit the display and enhanced elaborate tureens and chargers. Hattie thought there must be over a hundred pieces.

Coffee Tea The Gypsy & Me 15

"I see you're admiring the porcelain?" Jo placed a tray of tea on a side table. "Astonishing what you can pick up these days, isn't it?" Jo placed a cup and saucer in front of Hattie.

"Robert Mann bought it in the salerooms at Marland. No one else bid and he got it for a song. We think it came from Crowther Castle." Hattie watched Jo pour the tea. She used a strainer.

"So Harriet, tell me about you."

Hattie felt she'd better come clean. Jo had eaten at their restaurant and Hattie had no doubt that the rumour mill had reached Kirkton Sowerby and beyond. When she'd finished, she sat back and waited anxiously for Jo's reaction.

"It's difficult Hattie. May I call you Hattie?" Jo asked. "My husband went off with a much younger model. You think you can't live with the shame, but somehow you do, if only for the kids. I've got a little one too."

Hattie began to relax.

Jo seemed friendly and maybe her circumstances helped. Hattie visualised herself in a smart uniform moving around these rooms, dispensing drinks as she discussed the history of the porcelain. She'd chat with weary travellers, who'd stop for a night's rest. Hattie was warming to the post and didn't hear what Jo said.

"So when can you start. I take it you want the job?"

Hattie looked at Jo in amazement – she was offering her a position!

"I'm not sure what your role will be, but you seem able to do most things. Shall we start with reception and see how things go?"

Hattie lurched forward. Her hands trembled as she put her cup on the table. "Sorry Mrs Edmonds, I'm taken aback." She looked up. "Yes of course I'd love to work here. It'd be fantastic. I've done accounts and things and know how to run a restaurant," she rambled.

"Great. I want to open in June and the sooner you get here the better. Shall we say nine in the morning? Are you alright with child care?"

"Oh yes. I've good neighbours and a school and nursery nearby and me mam, sorry my mother, will help."

Hattie stood and followed Jo into the hallway.

"Call me Jo by the way, let's not be formal."

Hattie ran across the driveway to her car and urged the engine into life. Wait till I tell Mam! Hattie beamed as she drove away.

4

"That's the one, Mrs Brough." Jo sat on the floor of the cocktail bar with the proprietor of Brough's Interiors. They were surrounded by swatches of fabric. "We'll have a dozen assorted cushions to match the seat covers."

Mrs Brough nodded her head. Her tightly curled, rigid blue hair bobbed up and down and as Jo ran her fingers through her own tousled hair, she made a mental note to avoid A Cut Above in Butterly, run by Mrs Brough's daughter-in-law.

Jo looked at Mrs Brough's neatly tailored suit and sighed. She needed some new clothes. Old skirts and tatty jumpers wouldn't suffice once the hotel was open. At the pub, Jo kept behind the scenes while Greg played 'mine host' and her clothes hadn't mattered.

It'd been different when she'd met Greg in London. In those days, she was a girl-about-town and loved to be fashionable. Their eyes had locked over a drink in the Chelsea bar, where Greg mixed cocktails. Jo was smitten and they'd married six weeks later. Their dream of running a pub came true when they sold their terraced house in Clapham and made enough profit for a deposit. With Jo's parents acting as guarantors, they secured a loan and moved to Butterly on Bevan. The pub, an old temperance inn, sat on the main street of the bustling market town just yards from Butterly Castle.

Jo was thoughtful as she matched the swatches. How had she become Mrs Frumpy Country Wife?

She'd rarely been seen in anything other than chef's whites or housekeeping overalls during the punishing hours she'd worked at the pub. No wonder her wardrobe was scruffy and boring. Her weight bothered her too. She'd spent too much time in the kitchen constantly grazing and during the months of unhappiness after Greg left, the weight had piled on.

"Will you have everything ready in time?" Jo referred to her mammoth order.

Mrs Brough and her team had worked night and day to finish mountains of curtains, bedspreads and drapes. The blinds and cushions for the conservatory were the final job.

"My lasses are all taking work home and I promise we'll be on schedule." The blue perm bobbed up and down. "I've told my Ivan, he's to bring me here for a meal when you're open." Mrs Brough packed the samples away.

"You're an angel," Jo said.

They left the bar and wandered out through the conservatory, where the windows had been repaired and gleamed in freshly painted frames. Lloyd Loom furniture in polythene packing was stacked against pale cream walls. Jo stood in the courtyard and waved as she watched Mrs Brough drive off in her shiny Mercedes Estate.

Jo turned and looked at the garden and thought about everything that had happened in the last few months. What would Greg think of it all? Despite her anger, Jo's heart ached whenever she thought of him. She knew he'd have loved it here.

Once the paperwork had been done, completion took place on the agreed date.

Mr Knight from the Westmarland Trust Bank visited the property with his surveyor and true to his word, arranged the loan in record time.

Jo looked at the hotel. The side wing was a perfect home and she

luxuriated in the space after the confines of the tiny rented house and cramped flat at the pub.

Someone waved from a window on the first floor. It was her mother. Jo smiled and waved back. Her parents had arrived from their home in Wiltshire and taken up residence. Jean loved looking after Thomas and he adored his doting grandmother. George liked the spacious garden and spent happy hours pruning trees and clearing the greenhouse with Nipper, his Jack Russell at his heels. Jo bent and plucked a weed from the gravel then stopped at a wooden bench and paused, the sun was warm and the bench inviting. She sat down and thought about the weeks of hard work.

Hattie had joined them the day after her interview. The Marland Employment Office sent though paperwork and asked if Jo needed references. Jo didn't see much need. She knew that Hattie's husband had cleared off with one of the waitresses at Salerno's Taste of Tuscany and now ran a chip shop on the Costas. Jo recalled a tall, arrogant man who screamed orders to and from the kitchen. Hattie needed a break and Jo was going to give her one.

Jo gradually put a team together. A local girl called Judy was now restaurant manager and general help. Judy came from The George Hotel, in the busy market town of Marland. At twenty-three, she was petite and pretty with blonde hair and a broad Westmarland accent.

Judy's best friend was Sandra – a robust and jovial cook who'd worked for Jo in the pub.

Sandra blossomed when Jo took over the pub and taught her to bin the boil-in-the-bags and make good, wholesome food from local produce. Their food had been a huge hit with the locals and Jo had no hesitation in employing her again, but could she create a more refined cooking style? There was so much to be done.

Jo was determined to have the hotel open in June. What had first seemed impossible was fast becoming reality, as the former guesthouse was transformed. Skilled tradesmen moved heaven and earth to keep to Jo's deadline. Robert knew every furniture auction and house-clearance in the vicinity and worked tirelessly to accumulate the pieces that now graced the public rooms and bedrooms. At a bankrupt sale near Windermere, he'd bought carved Victorian dining chairs and tables and a mahogany serving cabinet. A cushion mirror over the fireplace in the Green Room came from the castle in Butterly, in a job lot with twelve framed prints of Lakeland scenes that now graced the walls in the panel room restaurant.

Ladies from the village came forward and sixth-form youngsters were keen for evening and weekend work. They'd advertised for a chef to assist Sandra and after several interviews, chose Michael Haggity. He was twenty-seven, single and had references that suggested a creative chef. Jo bought a second-hand static caravan to accommodate him and Michael settled in immediately. He'd made a start by digging the herb garden and setting seedlings in the greenhouse. Jo prayed that the kitchen would be busy enough to support both their wages. Local suppliers offered deliveries to the hotel. Trevor Pigmy had the finest meat in the area and knew the history of every animal that ended up on the slab of his shop in Butterly.

His Westmarland sausages were notorious - thick, meaty and juicy and all spiced with his secret ingredients.

Jo was deep in conversation one morning with plumber Arthur Harrison and looked up when Judy interrupted them. Jo had a visitor. Delighted to be relieved from the complicated plumbing arrangements for the bathroom in Room Two, Jo turned from her crouched position under the toilet system. A tall sandy haired man held out his hand.

"Need a lift up?" he said and bent forward, then tugged her to her feet.

Jo looked at his weathered face.

"I'm Alf and I'm 'ere because I'm a game man."

What on earth was he talking about? Jo certainly didn't need any game men on the premises with all the female staff about.

"Rabbits, hares, birds of any description, the finest venison from the Crowther Estate - whatever you want." He smiled. "For cash of course."

Jo breathed a sigh of relief.

"Well that's wonderful Alf," she said. "Do you think you could manage some samples?"

"Follow me." Alf ushered Jo out of the bedroom and down the stairs to the front door, where his battered old Land Rover was parked at an angle. Jo tried not to notice the lumps of mud on the carpet as she followed his Wellingtons. Alf reached into the back of his vehicle and pulled out the inert bodies of two rabbits and a haunch of venison.

"See what your Sandra can do with this lot and I'll be round for an order in a couple of days." He thrust the dead animals into Jo's hands, climbed into his Land Rover and roared off in a cloud of diesel fumes.

Jo heard a bell and looked up to see her mother by the conservatory door. Jean held a large brass school bell in her hand and steadied Thomas on her hip with the other.

"There you are," Jean said. "I found this old bell in a packing case upstairs. Shall I put it on the hall table for your guests?"

"I hope they don't ring it as loudly as you." Jo reached for Thomas. His plump little body oozed out of a pale blue romper suit and he chortled as she scooped him up and kissed his pink cheeks. "This suit Thomas is wearing cost more than I've spent on clothes in a year," Jo said as she straightened the hand-stitched smocking.

"Well it's time you considered investing in something decent." Jean shook her head. "You look a mess and won't attract respectable clientele looking like that. Even the gypsies on Fair Hill out-class you." Jean stared at Jo's old skirt and shapeless jumper.

"I know, but I have to get this place sorted first."

"By the way, this was in the post." Jean handed Jo a card. An embossed picture showed a sunny beach decorated with colourful parasols. Jo flicked it over. Her heart missed a beat as she recognised Greg's handwriting. She handed Thomas to Jean.

"Greg wishes me luck with the business."

"You'll need a lot more than luck if you don't start to look the part." Jean returned the child to her hip and marched off to give Thomas his lunch.

Jo read the card again. Her heart knotted in anger. Greg hadn't even asked after Thomas!

Holed up in some Spanish bar no doubt, overlooking a sun kissed beach with his nubile mistress in attendance.

Jo ripped the card into tiny pieces and stuffed them in her pocket.

She stomped through the hotel and caught sight of herself in a mirror. A tired expression stared back from under tousled hair. Get a grip Jo. She whispered to the forlorn face. He's never coming back – get over it. Her mother was right. This new start needed a new image. She felt the scraps of paper in her pocket and glared at her reflection. Watch this space Greg!

5

Four days to go. Jo's head spun with last minute details as she poured herself a mug of coffee and hurried to reception. Hattie was on the phone and looked up as Jo sat down.

"All booked." Hattie replaced the receiver. "I've made appointments at Camille's in Carlisle at twelve o'clock today then Dorothy

Osborne's at two." Jo

sipped her coffee.

"Tomorrow, you're booked into The House of Beauty from nine o'clock, and you'll be there most of the day."

"Are you mad, Hattie? I can't have two days out now."

"I'm completely sane." Hattie smiled. "As your mam says, we want a boss who doesn't look like the cleaning lady. Put your cheque book in your handbag." She stood up. "Do you want something to eat?"

"I do, but I don't," Jo replied. She glanced at her hips and pulled a face.

"Well I could do with a bacon buttie to keep me going, we've a busy day."

Jean had been insistent that Hattie accompany Jo, to ensure she purchased several new outfits and Hattie was looking forward to the trip.

The phone rang.

"Table for four on Saturday, Mrs Parks?" Hattie spoke with her best voice. "Yes of course. What time would suit you? Eight o'clock. Perfect. We'll look forward to seeing you then." She replaced the handset, as Jo leaned over the desk and flicked through empty pages of the restaurant diary.

"Don't worry, it'll fill up." Hattie wrote the reservation down. "Pete Parks hasn't wasted anytime. That was his wife booking a table."

Jo glanced at the accommodation chart. Only two rooms booked for Saturday, visitors to the village for a family party, the rest of the chart was blank.

"I'm surprised you want to open so close to the fair." Hattie murmured.

Jo was worried too about the practicalities of opening her beautiful country house days before the gypsies and travellers descended on Butterly. She knew she'd need to be vigilant. The fair officially lasted for a week but trouble often began long before.

Most pubs closed and barred their windows and doors during Fair Week, but Jo and Greg had stayed open. They had doubled their staff and worked all hours. Jo had enjoyed the atmosphere as gypsies and travellers flocked from all points of the compass. This was the main event of the year for them, a time to show off and catch up. Dressed in their finest clothes, they traded horses, bet on trotting races, got wildly drunk and wickedly promiscuous. They loved to eat, drink and be merry and had the time of their lives. When trouble occurred, the locals blamed the gypsies and the gypsies blamed the visitors.

In the kitchen at the pub, Jo and Sandra had manned the stoves hour after hour, and grilled steaks as the orders poured in. Always hungry, the gypsies wanted the finest local meat and had the money to pay for it. Greg worked the bar and restaurant and took orders late into the night.

The staff knew that a big cash bonus would be in their pay packet at the end of the week.

The pub had stayed trouble free - grateful for good food and service, the gypsies had soon sorted any problems out.

Jo knew she couldn't possibly let the gypsies near the hotel. The affluent locals would never cross the threshold again if they saw charabancs and vans outside and they wouldn't like Jo for encouraging 'that sort of trade.' Best to keep the doors locked and only answer the bell to residents...

AN HOUR LATER, Hattie and Jo began their journey to Carlisle. Jean watched from the doorway with Thomas in her arms. She held his hand and waved it at the departing car. "Look at mummy, you won't recognise her soon."

Jo forced a smile.

She wasn't looking forward to the shopping trip and doubted that they'd find anything suitable in her size. She stalled the engine and the car lurched across the gravel. Muttering obscenities under her breath, she tugged on the choke and the car bunny hopped out of the driveway.

"I don't know why you're so grumpy." Hattie finished her bacon sandwich and bounced about on the passenger seat. "Most women would be ecstatic to spend a bit on themselves."

Jo concentrated on the road ahead. She knew she was frumpy but hadn't a clue what look she should be aiming for.

It was easy to keep up when she lived in London; where it was imperative to look great to attract a man, but Jo was slimmer then and had buckets of confidence. She never socialised in Westmarland and had no need for sophisticated clothes.

Hattie held her bag on her knee and reached for a toffee as the countryside whizzed by. "You should change this car." She said as she un-wrapped the sweet and popped it in her mouth. "Even your dad says 'to be prosperous you have to look prosperous.' She sucked on the creamy caramel and thought about George's comments on his daughter's battered old car.

"I don't really think a Fiat Uno is cutting it on the drive do you?" Hattie crossed her fingers and hid them beneath her bag. She knew she was wading in deep. Jo was after all, her boss but someone had to tell her.

"Well Greg went off with the Rover and I haven't thought about a car," Jo said. "This was cheap and gets me around." Jo knew Hattie was probably right but she felt loathe to part with money.

"Get yourself glammed up and go and see Pete Parks. A bit of cleavage and a wiggle and you'll have a BMW on the gravel before you can say How Much?

"He has got very blue eyes hasn't he?"

"And wandering hands I've heard, but you can cope with a grope round the gear stick if it gets you a decent discount."

"Hell Hattie, I wouldn't know a grope from a gear stick, it's been so long." Jo looked miserable as she turned off the motorway and followed the road into Carlisle. "I don't even think I want to remember. I'm not sure that I'll ever get over Greg."

Hattie smiled. All this was about to change and she knew she'd enjoy being around to witness it!

"Is she one of us?"

Jo tentatively opened the door of the lingerie shop and peeped at the woman who'd made the comment. Hattie gave her a shove and Jo fell forward over the threshold, plunged into a luxurious room filled with exquisite silk and lace lingerie.

"Ah, who have we here?" the woman said. She peered over the top of gold lorgnettes and held her head at an angle, as though an obnoxious smell had entered the room.

"This must be Mrs Edmonds, your twelve o'clock appointment, madam." A nervous assistant came forward.

"That's right love." Hattie took Jo's arm and walked her to a brocade-upholstered chaise. "You must be Mrs Camille? Mrs Edmonds is the new proprietor of Kirkton House Hotel." They sat down and Hattie continued. "She hasn't got much time, so we'll begin with a glass of bubbly and a selection of your finest support wear for daytime and evening."

"It's Mrs Sherwin, madam.," the assistant whispered to Hattie.

"Sherwin, Camille, whatever... pink bubbly will do for both of us to start with." Hattie put her handbag on the floor. "Shove up," she said to Jo, who appeared stunned by her surroundings.

"She's the biggest cow in the North West," Hattie whispered. "Her hubbie deals in diamonds and whores in Hatton Garden, but she knows her underwear."

Jo was white faced and clutched her old gillet tightly around her body. "Do I have to take my clothes off?" she asked. "I'm terrified, Mrs Sherwin is so elegant and so thin."

"What do you think the champagne's for?" Hattie giggled. "Half a bottle and you'll be ripping your vest and drawers off and telling the old bat to Sex Me Up! You won't get this in Debenhams."

Two crystal flutes of pink champagne appeared on the coffee table, beside brochures with shiny covers. Slim, toned models in the briefest bras and tiniest knickers taunted Jo.

"When Mrs Edmonds is quite ready." Mrs Sherwin appeared. "Shall we start with daytime garments?" Tall and still with her hands clasped together, she wore a beautifully cut, grey wool dress. Her jetblack hair was swept into a severe chignon, the narrow face powdered and cheeks rouged. Her lips were shiny with red gloss. Mrs Sherwin held her bony fingers together and tapped long scarlet nails impatiently.

Jo was reminded of a crow about to attack.

"Marie will take you to the changing room - when you're ready."

Hattie held Jo's elbow and helped her up. Jo felt like a lamb to the slaughter and knew she was being mentally undressed and sized. No tape measure required - this woman knew her business.

The next hour flew by. Marie was discreet and helpful. Stripped down to her plain white pants, Jo was manhandled into an array of structured undergarments that pushed and pulled her into shape.

She looked at herself in the mirror and was amazed - she had a waist! Her bust was hoisted into an under-wired bra and by some miracle, she had a cleavage and her hips had shrunk at least two sizes.

Faces intermittently appeared around the curtain.

A stern Mrs Sherwin nodded approval and a red-cheeked Hattie, who'd consumed the remainder of the champagne, grinned.

"Now something to get the mortgage paid off," Hattie suggested. She looked at Marie and winked.

Marie held out a wisp of scarlet lace.

"I can't wear that - it's no more than a handkerchief." Jo gasped.

"If Madam would be so kind and slip it on." Marie adjusted the silk ribbons as Jo eased the fabric over her body.

"Holy smoke..." Hattie roared. "Jo, you look amazing."

Jo stared at her reflection in disbelief. The figure in front of her looked wonderful and the body suit was divine. It was cleverly constructed - enhancing every curve and hiding every bump. Even her legs went on forever.

"Don't look at the price tag," Hattie hissed.

Marie pursed her lips and shook her head. "Mrs Sherwin never puts prices on the garments, madam."

HATTIE AND Jo left Camille's laden with carrier bags and giggled like schoolgirls as Jo fanned herself with her cheque book.

"I just signed a cheque without looking at the amount."

"You'd better get used to it today." Hattie held Jo's arm and guided her over the road. "I fancy some dainty sandwiches and I'm sure Dorothy Osbourne will oblige."

"Did you see Mrs Sherwin's face?" Jo said. Hattie steered Jo, she knew exactly where they were going.

"She never moved a muscle as she handed me the bill. Not a word of thanks or a good luck wish." Jo shook her head. "The woman's an absolute cow."

"She certainly is." Hattie agreed. "But she knows her stuff, and you might be surprised to find you'll start getting custom from those that can afford her prices. She'll recommend you. She knows how to keep you coming back. What you've just spent is an investment for both yourself and your business."

Five minutes later, they'd reached their next destination. Hattie rang the bell and pushed Jo forward into the ladies-wear shop.

"Mrs Edmonds and Harriet?" Dorothy Osbourne greeted them warmly. "Come on through and make yourselves comfortable."

She gestured towards two velvet covered sofas and Jo and Hattie sank gratefully into the deep pile and sat back and admired the décor. The walls were covered with a William Morris paper and hunting prints hung from chains on a high picture rail. Dorothy stood before them, she was immaculately groomed in a two-piece cream coloured silk suit. Good tailoring disguised her ample shape.

"I'm sure you must be ready for some refreshments, ladies?" Several rows of pearls bounced across her bosom. Hattie and Jo nodded and watched her glide away. Dorothy's strawberry blonde hair flicked up on her shoulders but stayed rigidly in place.

"Is that a wig?" Jo whispered. "It looks like a helmet."

"She's had four husbands," Hattie replied. "Anyone would lose their hair."

Dorothy returned with a younger version of herself who carried a tray laden with sandwiches and cake.

"This is my daughter Vicky. Would you ladies like a soft drink or something stronger?"

"Tea for me Dorothy," Hattie leaned over to take two plates from the tray and handed one to Jo. "These butties look good. I'll have a bit of cake too."

Jo put her plate on the table and looked around. She was mystified, there didn't appear to be any garments? The room was very oldfashioned. She'd never experienced shopping like this and wondered how Hattie knew what to do.

"Perhaps Mrs Edmonds would like to make a start?" Dorothy said.

"Yes that will be grand." Hattie dusted crumbs from her blouse.

"Now as I said on the phone, Mrs E needs to look the part. She's running a country house hotel and needs some smart daywear and cocktail outfits suitable for a hostess."

"I understand perfectly," Dorothy said. "We'll be ready for you shortly." Vicky followed her out of the room.

"Hattie, how do you know about this place?" Jo whispered "I've never seen a set-up like it. There's not a dress to be seen and she doesn't even know my size."

Hattie was enjoying her sandwiches and was not going to be rushed. She selected a slice of fruit cake.

"The ladies who lunch round here all come to the likes of Camille and Dorothy Osborne's," Hattie began.

"You'll come across Jinny Atkinson soon. Billy, her husband, owns a construction company. He started with a wheelbarrow and a bucket of tar and laid driveways," Hattie bit into her cake.

"Billy went on to build most of the motorway up here. His company is Westmarland Manufacturing. You must have heard of it?" Jo looked puzzled.

"Well, Jinny was an accounts clerk and Billy got her pregnant so they had to marry. Now she's Lady Muck living in a huge house at Stainton. Billy loves the horses and has taken to buying Jinny a racehorse every birthday. They've a son called Young Billy. Golden balls just like his dad. Got local lass, Eileen, pregnant and had a shotgun wedding."

"How do you know all this?" Jo was fascinated.

"I'm coming to that," Hattie continued. "Young Billy's a bit wild and was out on the lash all the time. Naturally Eileen wanted out, so Jinny and Billy bought her a flat opposite me on the new estate. She's lonely and we've become good mates over litres of Lambrusco. I hear all about the racing world and Eileen says this is one of Jinny's favourite shops. If Jinny isn't shopping in London, she comes here. Dorothy knows her customers personally and you'll never meet anyone in your set wearing the same outfit."

"It wouldn't bother me if I did," Jo said as she sipped her tea.

"Might not bother you but you'd never see Jinny or her cronies again and at these prices I think you'll change your opinion."

Dorothy returned and scrutinised Jo, whose shabby old clothes were not in keeping with a country house and affluent clients. Vicky guided Jo through to a curtained changing area.

"You've booked her in at The House of Beauty?" Dorothy raised an eyebrow and whispered to Hattie.

"Aye I have, first thing in the morning," Hattie replied. Dorothy nodded approval.

"This way ladies, please."

"Don't hurry, Hattie," Jo said.

Hattie followed with a cup in one hand and cake piled high on the saucer. Hattie gathered her bag and followed the procession. She smiled sweetly at Vicky. "Lead on!"

HATTIE DROVE them back to the hotel.

"I've never spent so much money on myself. Not just in a day, but ever," Jo said.

"Well you won't have to do it again for a bit." Hattie glanced sideways at Jo's worried face. "You should be grateful that you can."

"I know you're right, Hattie, but it feels strange." Jo looked out of the window. "Greg was so mean when it came to spending anything on me." She fiddled with her watch strap. "I haven't had any decent clothes for years, other than the occasional Laura Ashley blouse or a Jaeger skirt. It seems strange to think that in London I wore bespoke Hardy Ames suits to work." She sighed. "What happened to me in the married years?"

"You became a product of your husband," Hattie said.

"Safe and boring, not a chance anyone else should find you attractive." She studied the road. "It happens to women, including me. Lots of husbands want their wives that way, but in the process you lose your confidence." She glanced at Jo. "I think you're going to make up ground pretty quickly once you get that lot in your wardrobe." Hattie nodded towards the carrier bags on the back seat.

"It was fun wasn't it?" Jo allowed herself a smile.

Dorothy had chosen a selection of outfits to take Jo through her working day. She'd begun with a smart black suit by Vera Mont that looked plain and ordinary on the hanger. Jo had her new scaffoldinglike underwear in place and tried it on. Fabric covered buttons fastened the jacket and the knee length skirt skimmed her hips. It was simple but chic and Jo adored it. "I love shoulder pads." She brightened up as she thought about the outfit. "They give such a good shape."

"I wear them with everything, even me vest," Hattie said. "Slims you down a treat."

Vicky had produced a succession of daytime dresses by Betty Barclay and Joseph Ribkoff in lovely colours and sexy stretchy fabrics that hung beautifully and flattered Jo's figure. For evening, Dorothy chose Dusk by Frank Usher. Jo initially rejected them, insisting that the dresses and black suit would be enough.

"Do you want to look like your restaurant staff?" Hattie was annoyed. "Stand out Jo, you're the boss! Tell her Dorothy."

"Mrs Edmonds will be more comfortable when she's tried one on." Dorothy helped Jo into a black and white jersey dress. A slim strap, tied with a soft draping bow left one shoulder bare. Jo twirled in front of the mirror.

Between them, Mrs Sherwin and Dorothy Osbourne had cleverly chosen garments that knocked two sizes off her size and transformed her figure.

Jo was thrilled.

Hattie drove the car through onto the drive and parked at the front of the hotel.

"Is the world ready for the new me, Hattie?" Jo reached for the door and hesitated.

"Are you ready for the world, Jo?" Hattie replied. They climbed out of the car and reached for the carrier bags on the rear seat.

They both began to giggle.

"There's only one way to find out!" They cried in unison and ran into the hotel.

6

The next morning Jo set off again. She had appointments all day at The House of Beauty in Marland and despite her protests, Jean and Hattie had persuaded her that the hotel would still be standing when she returned.

Everyone was working hard in preparation for the trial run of the restaurant the next day. They officially opened the day after, but Jo wanted to give Sandra an opportunity to test her menu. The staff, their partners and family were to be guinea pigs and so far, there were twenty four guests.

Jo made plans as she drove. They hadn't done any advertising yet and she hoped they wouldn't have to, but the charts and diary were empty. Jo was nervous. Surely bookings would come once the doors were open?

Jean was interviewing a nanny on Friday - the nursery in Marland had recommended a girl from Stainton who'd recently gained qualifications. The thought of leaving Thomas with a stranger added to Jo's worries.

She parked her car behind the church and paid for a ticket from the machine, then walked along the cobbled lanes to find The House of Beauty. The morning was clear and fine and the sun warm on her face. The wind however, was brisk. It whipped hair into her eyes and as Jo tucked it behind her ears she wondered what style she'd have in a few hours time, maybe just a trim so she could tie it back?

The cherry trees in the vicar's garden had blossomed late this year. Their fluffy pink blooms swirled in the breeze, reminding Jo of soft pink confetti, as it fell to the ground around the church. There was a market today in the covered walkway and the smell of fresh fish was strong. Jo looked over to the corner of the building where a large marble counter lay beneath a green and white striped canopy. Fish of all varieties were displayed on the slab.

"Delivering to you tomorrow, Mrs Edmonds." Dougie Cannon called out. An ex-trawler man, Dougie was son in D. J. Cannon & Son – Fresh Fish Daily. He was as gnarled and wizened as the elements he'd faced and knew the provenance of all his fish from coast to counter.

"Thanks, Dougie. We're officially open on Saturday."

"Aye, the missus is booking a table."

Dougie leaned over and straightened lines of plastic grass that separated rows of mackerel and salmon. "Our Annie doesn't get out much. She's faddy about her food."

"We'll be happy to see you, Dougie. Give my best wishes to Annie."

"Aye I will, I'll have your order there first thing."

Jo continued her walk past the Westmarland Trust Bank and turned into an alley running parallel to the town.

Marland was full of tall buildings and narrow passages that went on forever, behind the façade of the town. Jo wondered if they were to deceive invading Scots in days gone by. She studied the numbers Hattie had given her, precise instructions to look for a brass plaque, on a dark blue front door.

Jo found the plaque halfway down the alley, engraved with the words The House of Beauty. She crossed her fingers and climbed the steps then raised the heavy brass knocker and tapped once. A

moment later, the door opened and a young girl wearing a clinical white tunic ushered Jo in.

"Have a seat." The girl motioned to a chair then glanced at a leather-bound appointment book, which lay on a Regency desk. She traced Jo's appointment with a polished nail and ticked it off.

Jo studied her surroundings and gripped her bag. The hair salon was on a raised gallery and Jo looked up at the large gilt mirrors and ornate coving that surrounded swivel chairs and counters.

"Would you like a drink?" The girl stood next to her.

"I'd love a black coffee, please." Jo thanked the receptionist.

For the next three hours Jo tried hard to enjoy her experience in the salon. Naked, but for disposable paper pants, she lay face down on a table while Peruvian pan pipes played softly in the background. The haunting whine annoyed her. A tiny oriental lady introduced herself and proceeded to pummel and push Jo's pressure points as she massaged her back. Her probing fingers irritated Jo and she longed for the treatment to end but worse was to come. She was plucked and waxed in places she didn't realise hair grew and silently cursed Hattie as she endured the pain and embarrassment.

At long last, wrapped in a fluffy white towelling robe and slippers, Jo was led up the stairs to the gallery and seated in a comfortable cream leather chair. She glared into the mirror.

Her blotchy face stared back and as she slumped miserably, she yearned for something stronger than coffee.

A flurry of activity made her sit up. A tall thin man glanced over the gallery rail and clapped his hands.

"Ellen get off your arse!" he shouted to the receptionist. "Get some champagne up here pronto." He spun Jo's chair around. "This lady's gasping after all she's been through."

Jo recoiled. Male piercings were a rare sight in Marland and the stylist had a large diamond stud in his left lobe with a tiny silver bar through his eyebrow. They matched the huge diamond in his signet ring.

He stroked Jo's hair.

"Mrs Edmonds." he smiled. "Are you ready for me?" He wore a colourful Versace shirt and drainpipe jeans, tucked into cowboy boots.

A heavy chain bounced off his waxed and tanned chest. The receptionist appeared with a laden tray and placed champagne and two glasses beside Jo.

"Call me Paulie," he said and popped the cork with finesse.

"Here's to success in your new venture." Paulie knocked back the drink and topped up his glass, then ran long fingers through his closely cropped hair and glanced in the mirror to tweak a blonde streak of hair on his forehead.

"We've heard all about you, Robbie and I can't wait!"

He spun Jo round to face the mirror and plucked a comb from his pocket. "Somewhere decent to dine... Now what are going to do with this lot?" Paulie lifted strands of Jo's hair and pulled a face.

The hair fell limply to her shoulders.

"Are we going to be brave today and let your Uncle Paulie transform you?"

The champagne had mellowed Jo, she could feel her aching muscles relax as she stretched her legs, wriggled her toes and held out her glass for a top up.

"I'm in your hands Paulie, make me beautiful."

Paulie beamed and swung into action. A glossy magazine appeared as a manicurist slid into place and dunked Jo's fingers into bowls of warm fragrant water. Paulie reached over to a hi-fi system and flicked a switch. The salon reverberated to Annie Lennox and Aretha Franklin as they belted out, Sisters are doing it for themselves!

Paulie spun around and punched the air as he joined in the chorus. "I just love this song!" he exclaimed, then separated Jo's hair with large clips and began to cut.

FOR THE NEXT forty minutes Jo buried herself in the magazine. She feigned an interest in Caroline of Monaco's latest escapade and Princess Diana's fabulous outfit at the Cannes Film Festival. Jo was terrified of looking up as Paulie's scissors whirled around her head and chunks of long hair began to pile up on the floor. Jo was wheeled

around the gallery from backwash to blow dryer until the final stop, by a counter of makeup.

"Nearly there." Paulie stroked her arm encouragingly. Fifteen minutes later he whisked her gown away.

"Close your eyes," Paulie whispered. "Eh Voila!" He spun her round to face the mirror.

The face that stared back at Jo was unrecognisable.

THE WIND BLEW ROBUSTLY as Jo stepped onto the cobbles in the alleyway. She patted her hair and hoped that Paulie had used plenty of spray to keep it in place.

The change was dramatic.

Jo felt like an overexcited child and wanted to run and jump through the alley, such was her joy in her new look! Instead, she braced herself against the wind and hurried along, but stopped as she caught her reflection in the market hall windows.

A striking image stared back.

Cropped hair framed her face and emphasised the high cheekbones, subtle copper shades warmed her skin and she glowed from all the treatments. Her makeup was perfect and shades of green and brown shadow matched her eyes and made them look huge. She wore a long-line suit that Dorothy had recommended for the day. It had three quarter sleeves and two gold buttons.

Jo was mesmerised.

"Beautiful!" A voice called out and Jo spun round. Pete Parks leaned casually against the wall of the Westmarland Trust Bank and grinned. He had one hand in the pocket of his leather jacket and the other held a battered briefcase.

"Suits you," he said.

Jo blushed. She was tongue-tied and couldn't think of a thing to say. She gripped her bag, gave him a wave and ran back to her car.

"Be seeing you Saturday." Pete flicked the heavy black fringe off his forehead and admired her retreating bottom in the tight-fitting skirt. "Make sure you've got steak on."

As Jo drove home she glanced at her reflection in the rear-view mirror, she could hardly believe her new image. She skidded her car onto the driveway and parked under the trees, then ran across the gravel to the side door.

Hattie and Judy were in reception, deep in conversation.

"Bleedin' hell." Hattie looked up.

"Mrs E, you look amazing." Judy clapped her hands together.

"Well, that gentle soul certainly knows how to cut hair, I'll hand it to him. You look great." Hattie poked at Jo's short crop. "Just lose a stone and I think we're in business."

"You could have warned me about Paulie." Jo darted away from Hattie's probing fingers and thrust her bag on the desk.

"Anyone who can make you look like that in a couple of hours can be as camp as Christmas in my book. He deserves a medal," Hattie said.

"He knows what he's doing, but this cut will be high maintenance." She postured in front of the mirror. "I'll have to go back every month." She pouted her lips and turned from side to side. "I do like it though."

"Well you better come down off planet-pose pretty sharp. The phone's never stopped ringing." Hattie flicked her pencil. "Restaurant's full on Saturday and I've had to turn bookings away in case the bedrooms fill up."

"Crikey, Hattie, are you sure?" Jo gasped as she looked at the diary. A long list of names and telephone numbers filled the page. A birthday cake was ordered too. "Wow, we really are in business. Girls you're brilliant!"

7

Friday morning and Jo woke early. It was rehearsal day today and tomorrow they'd be open to the public. She took a quick shower and rubbed her hair with a towel. Very gently, she blow-dried the style and watched with pleasure as it fell into place. Determined to recreate her new look, she carefully applied make-up then wriggled into Mrs Sherwin's firm foundation wear and added silky hold-up stockings, a red lace camisole, the black suit and court shoes. Jo stood in front of the mirror and sucked her tummy in as she posed. The suit fitted snugly over her hips and the jacket accentuated her shape. She tucked a lipstick into her bra and ran up the stairs to the playroom where Jean sat on the floor, balancing Thomas on her lap as they studied a book of nursery rhymes.

"Look at Mummy, Thomas, doesn't she look smart?" Jean smiled as Jo leaned down and scooped Thomas into her arms. "You look like a different girl." Jean nodded approval. "Don't forget to show your father."

"Thanks, Mum, I will. See you later." Jo left them to their rhymes and skipped down the stairs. She stopped at the guest bedroom and knocked gently.

"Dad?" Jo opened the door.

The room was quiet and dark. She crept across to part the curtains and a beam of sunlight lit the room. George was asleep. A lump under the covers bobbed up the bed and Nipper appeared on the pillow, her eyes bright.

"Morning Kiddo." George yawned and turned over. He opened his eyes. "My, don't you look grand." He shuffled into a sitting position. "I like your get-up."

"Go back to sleep, Dad, it's still early." Jo kissed his forehead. "I'll get you a cup of tea and let Nipper out."

Nipper bounded off the bed and shot past Jo on the stairs. Jo opened the side door that led to an enclosed yard and Nipper flew out.

"Behave yourself, Nipper. Stop yapping!" The terrier raced happily round the raised flowerbeds. Jo left the door ajar and opened the concealed door that accessed the hotel from her home. She stepped through and closed the door.

"Morning, Mrs E," Judy called out.

She stood by the mahogany cabinet and dipped cutlery into a jug of boiling water. "I'm so excited about lunch today, are you?" Judy polished the silverware with a soft cloth. Jo thought she was going to be sick with nerves but smiled at Judy and went through to the kitchen.

Michael rinsed pots in the deep sink under the window and looked around as Jo reached up and took a file from a bull-dog clip on the wall.

She studied the dinner menu.

Brandy Pate with Caramelised Onions and Melba
Toast
Roasted Red Pepper Soup with Sesame Seed Bread

Sole Veronique
Fillet Steak with Rich Brown Sauce

Sandra's Sticky Toffee Pudding & Vanilla Ice-cream
Lemon Panacotta

* * *

Coffee, Fudge & Tiffin

"You need to be organised," Jo spoke to Sandra and looked around the kitchen. "I know it's a simple menu today, but it'll be three times that size tomorrow."

"We won't let you down," Sandra assured her. She glared at Michael. "Michael needs a rocket up his arse, mind."

Jo prayed that Sandra would cope. She desperately wanted to put her chef's whites on and get behind the stove, but her role was front of house and she was going to have to get used to it, no matter how much she longed for the security of the warm kitchen.

"Thanks, Sandra." Jo said. "Could you ask Judy to take my dad a mug of tea?"

The front door buzzed. Jo left Sandra to her chores and went to reception. She poked her head over the desk and saw Hattie bustle down the hallway.

"Suppose I should be using the tradesman's entrance now, eh? By heck you look good."

"Good morning Hattie, you look pretty tidy yourself."

Hattie shrugged her coat off, hung it on the back of the door and pushed her handbag under the desk. She wore a black skirt and a white blouse with pretty lace edging.

"You need to button up a bit." Jo looked at Hattie's blouse. The top four buttons were open and large amounts of creamy cleavage burst over the top of Hattie's push-up bra.

"It's got a life of its own this shirt." Hattie shoved her wayward bosom into the constraints of the blouse and fastened two buttons. "Right, shall we start with a coffee and get cracking?"

As THE MORNING wore on Jo paced around the hotel, she tried to reassure herself that she'd be better once the lunch was underway.

The hotel looked lovely. Bees wax polish mingled with sweet smelling logs that crackled welcomingly in open fires. Jo flicked table lamps on and for the umpteenth time, plumped cushions as she checked every detail.

The florist had created a stunning arrangement of tall tiger lilies on the hall table and their heady fragrance wafted through the rooms.

The restaurant shone and crystal and silver sparkled on crisp white cloths with fan-shaped serviettes. A single yellow rose in a clear vase had been placed in the middle of each table. Jo joined Judy in the wine cellar and carefully selected wine for the lunch.

"There's a visitor for you," Hattie called down the steep steps. Jo checked that Judy had the correct white wine chilling and knew when to decant the red, then ducked her head under the low ceiling and ran up the steps. Robert Mann stood by the door with a huge bouquet in his arms.

"Hello Robert, how lovely to see you." Jo beamed as she saw the flowers.

Robert stared at Jo, he was lost for words. She'd cut her hair and looked striking! Her hourglass figure was elegant in a smart suit and heels and he was mesmerised by the red lace that peeped out of the suit jacket. She was positively seductive!

"I wanted to wish you luck," he muttered. "I thought you might like these but can see you've plenty." He remembered all the flowers he'd passed as he came through the hotel.

"Good Lord no, I can never have too many flowers." Jo took the bouquet. "You're naughty to spend your money on me." She kissed him on the cheek. Robert smelt her perfume, it was heavenly and her hair soft against his cheek.

"Will you stay and have coffee?" Jo asked.

"I will, but I don't want to be in the way," Robert said. "We've booked for dinner tomorrow, with the Gavmins. I'm looking forward to it." God she was ravishing. "I just wanted to wish you luck." He found it difficult to look Jo in the eye. "Make sure you keep your wits about you too, the gypsies have settled in Butterly." He'd passed countless horses tethered to the roadside and hundreds of caravans were already on Fair Hill.

"Thanks, Robert, but I think we're a bit pricey for the travelling folk."

"Well, be sure to be on your guard."

"Make yourself comfortable by the fire and I'll have Hattie bring you some coffee. Or would you like something stronger?"

"Coffee's fine." Robert turned reluctantly and withdrew to the lounge as Hattie swung though the kitchen door with a tray in her hand.

"Don't tell me you've only just clocked it?" She nodded at Robert's retreating figure. "He's mad about you. He's got such a hard-on seeing you in that get up, he can barely walk." She grinned. "Coffee for one in the lounge was it?"

"Hattie, you're terrible, whatever makes you say such things?" Jo watched Hattie gather a lace liner and place it on the tray, then add a coffee pot, creamer and sugar bowl. "He's right about the gypsies though, we'll have to watch out."

Hattie picked up the tray and disappeared in the kitchen. Jo remembered the expression on Robert's face. Did he have feelings for her? In that instant, Jo realised that Hattie as usual, was probably right.

THE FRENCH ORMOLU clock on the hall table struck noon. It was a wedding gift from Greg's mother and Jo was reminded of her husband. She thought about him relaxing on a warm sunny beach, far away from the responsibility of a baby and business. Her heart ached as she thought of him with Estelle. She must pull herself together. Greg had forgotten about them and Jo had a business to run.

If only her stomach would calm down. She smoothed her suit jacket and tugged at the camisole, then whipped a lipstick out of her bra and leaned into the mirror to apply it. She took a deep breath and walked to the front door where she turned the brass key then wedged the outer door back with a heavy granite curling stone. Here goes!

Lunch was booked for one o'clock.

Jo hoped that her guests would appreciate being 'guinea pigs' and not be too demanding. She closed the porch door and went for a final check.

In the restaurant, Judy gave last minute instructions to two waiters, twin brothers from Saltby Farm. In smart black trousers, crisp white shirts and black bow ties, Simon and Steven were drop-dead gorgeous.

Jo gazed at their dark curly hair and olive skin and wondered if one of their ancestors was a slave who somehow found his way from Whitehaven to Westmarland?

They were so handsome! Their sister Suzy was as lovely as her brothers and studied music; she was to play the piano in the restaurant.

"All ready?" Jo said.

"Yes, Mrs Edmonds." Simon twisted a white cloth in his hand.

"Don't screw up your serving cloth Simon." Jo folded it neatly over his arm. His bow tie was crooked and as she straightened it, she was tempted to smooth the shirt across his muscular torso. She tore herself away and headed for the kitchen where delicious savoury smells wafted through the doors of the still-room. Gerald Harrison wiped down stainless steel surfaces and checked the temperature of the water in the deep metal sinks.

"How are you getting on, Gerald?" Jo asked.

Gerald was Arthur Harrison's son and Jo half expected the plumber to don a rubber apron at any moment and join Gerald at the sink. She'd been warned by locals that Gerald 'wasn't all there' but Arthur had begged her to give Gerald a job.

"Hello Mrs Edmonds." Gerald wrung a dishcloth and his heavy fringe flopped over his eyes. Gerald's mother had died in childbirth and Arthur never remarried. In school, Gerald was slow and the other kids teased him. He'd helped on farms and stacked shelves in shops but his vagueness irritated employers.

In desperation Arthur had turned to Jo and she decided she'd give Gerald a chance.

Today was a trial shift and although not required until noon, Gerald had been in since eight with Arthur by his side, showing him how to operate the dishwasher. Arthur was joining the lunch party and had gone to tidy himself up.

"I'm sure you'll get along fine, Gerald." Jo smiled encouragingly.

"Where's Michael?" she asked Sandra.

"He's checking his herbs in the greenhouse. He potted some up t'other night and checks them at least three times a day. He's got the furnace working. Seems determined to have them on the menu soon, bit much if you ask me."

"Nice that he's keen. Are you ready?"

"We'll soon find out Mrs E." Sandra said.

"Are you having a bracer?" Hattie carried a bucket of ice and placed it on the counter. The bar sparkled with every optic polished and bottles of liqueurs gleamed above shelves stacked full with mixers. Hattie held a glass under a beer tap and pulled a pint. "Better make sure it's drinkable." She filled the glass and held it to the light.

"I hope you're not thinking of supping that," Jo said.

"I'll taste it then tip it, much as it grieves me to do so." Hattie sipped the beer and poured it down the sink. "You look nervous. Here, get your laughing gear round this." She poured a shot of Cointreau into a crystal glass and handed it to Jo.

"Don't be daft, Hattie. I can't possibly breathe alcohol fumes over the guests."

Hattie pulled a packet of extra strong mints out of her pocket. "Stick one of these in the side of your mouth."

"You're leading me into bad ways." Jo picked the glass up and tossed the clear, syrupy liquid down her throat. It exploded in her stomach.

"Better?" Hattie grinned.

"Christ that's strong!" Jo grimaced as Judy appeared in the bar.

"Shall I light the candles?" Judy asked.

The front door buzzer sounded and Hattie and Judy turned to Jo. Hattie crossed her fingers and held them up.

"Go get 'em Tiger!" Hattie winked.

The alcohol had a calming effect on Jo. She smiled and with purpose went to greet her guests.

8

Thomas lay snuggled in the crook of his mother's arm and sucked hungrily on his bottle. Jo kissed the top of his head. She breathed in his soft baby smell and stroked her face against his silky crown.
Outside the sun was rising, it was going to be a glorious day.

Jo wondered where Greg was.

She lay still and listened to an early morning chorus as the birds brought the garden to life. Thomas finished his bottle and in the warm, drowsy surroundings his eyes drooped and he fell asleep. Jo looked at his little face and thought about his dad. Greg would be waking up next to Estelle, probably in a posh hotel as they journeyed through Europe. He'd always wanted to see Europe. Jo cursed the day that she'd let the Gavmins introduce her to Estelle - here on an exchange visit to learn English. It had seemed ideal to employ her as a nanny, as she'd cared for countless younger siblings at home in Spain. Estelle wanted to learn and Jo needed help. She imagined Greg in Estelle's arms, making love to her on a balmy Mediterranean morning.

Jo's heart ached. She climbed out of bed and walked to the window. Yesterday the grass had been mown and the damp mulchy smell wafted up. Jo gazed at the garden. She knew that Greg would have loved all this but it was no good dwelling on things, Greg was gone. She sat on the window seat and cuddled Thomas.

"Morning, Jo, I thought I heard you." Jean was dressed and carried two mugs of tea. "Here have this, big day today." "Thanks, Mum." Jo took the tea and sipped it.

Yesterday afternoon Jean had interviewed Ann. She was nineteen, with good references from the nursery in Marland and wanted a livein position.

"Ann can start straight away." Jean sat on the bed and watched her daughter.

"I'll stay until I feel confident that she's right, but it's my gut feeling it won't be long."

Jean waited. Jo seemed miles away.

"Your dad and I need to get home to see to the garden" She added. "We'll be back, don't think I'm abandoning you."

"I know Mum." Jo thought about Ann as she gazed at Thomas. "It'll feel odd having a stranger in the house." She sighed. "I sometimes wonder what the hell I am doing taking all this on."

"Stop it." Jean was brusque. "It's your choice and you have to make a living to keep a roof over the child's head, so don't start feeling sorry for yourself." She held her hand out. Chastised, Jo drained her tea and handed the mug to her mother. Jean was right. No time for regrets or feeling sorry for herself - she had a hotel to run!

Jo left Thomas with Jean and showered quickly. She dressed in her black suit and added a cerise vest. She called out to Jean that she'd catch her later then knocked gently on George's bedroom door.

"Morning, Dad," Jo whispered but George was dressed and sat in a chair in front of the open window.

"I'm admiring the lawns." George looked down the garden. "Do you know the rules of croquet?" He held the empty barrel of a pipe and placed in his mouth. Nipper lay asleep on his lap.

"Thank God that thing isn't lit, Dad. I wouldn't see you for the fog it used to make." Jo remembered the smell. Her father's pipe had been notorious for its terrible aroma no matter how good the quality of tobacco, but tobacco was a thing of the past on his doctor's orders.

"First day, Jo, are you ready?"

"Yes. Ready as I'll ever be. Will you come and have a look round when you've had breakfast."

"I'll start with that croquet lawn and work back. Don't worry about me, just get stuck in." George held out his hand and Jo took it.

It felt warm and strong.

"Don't worry, love. It'll be grand."

Nipper raised her head and nudged George's hand away. George looked at the dog and shook his head. "Always gets jealous, little sod. Now get off and get some work done." He sucked the empty pipe and returned his gaze to the garden.

Jo walked down the stairs. She glanced at her watch, it was still very early. She went over to the window in her lounge and looked out to the gravel drive where her battered old car stood. She'd have to change it at some point. Hattie and Dad were right. It didn't really suit the image of the hotel. She sat down and thought about the lunch the day before.

YESTERDAY THE DRIVE was almost empty. Most folk had walked over from the village and left their transport at home. Jo greeted her staff and their family members warmly.

They'd all turned out in their smartest clothes for the occasion and even Old Johnny, who'd oversee the garden, wore a shirt and tie. In his youth he'd been head gardener at Kirkton House and was keen to see things back to their former glory. With a couple of strong lads labouring under his instructions, he'd already made it respectable and tidy.

The twins led the guests through the hotel to the restaurant. They stopped to explain the layout and areas of interest and pulled out chairs for the ladies, then shook serviettes for waiting knees. Arthur Harrison tucked his into his shirt collar, he was anxious about Gerald. Judy poured wines and conversation became animated.

The lunch had gone well.

Sandra had poached Dougie Cannon's lemon sole and served it with a creamy sauce and grapes. Trevor Pigmy delivered his best steak and everyone said it was sensational. Individual dishes of vegetables amused the diners, who were used to sharing stainless steel dishes of limp, overcooked produce at the Templars pub.

Jo wandered around the tables as they finished their desserts and asked if anyone would like to have a look around, before retiring to the lounges for coffee.

She took them out to the garden and one or two had a stab at croquet, where George discussed tactics and Nipper snapped at the heavy balls as they rolled over the lawn.

Jo led them across the courtyard and they admired the four bedrooms in the coach house. In the kitchen, Sandra and Michael donned clean aprons and stood to attention as Gerald stacked the dishwasher in an effort to contain debris from the restaurant, which was stacked high.

Guests climbed the stairs behind the conservatory and admired the garden from the gallery. In the bedrooms, they noted Mrs Brough's stunning drapes with matching counterpanes. Each room had a welcoming basket of fruit, copies of county magazines, folders of tourist information and fresh flowers beside a decanter of sherry and glasses. Jo guided them down the front staircase where they returned to the reception rooms and enjoyed coffee and chocolate tiffin, a special recipe of Jo's.

In the evening, Jo and Hattie had kicked off their shoes and sat by the fire with a glass of wine. George and Jean joined them. George sat in a wing-backed chair and enjoyed a whisky, while Jean cuddled a sleeping Thomas and sipped a gin and lime. Ann was due to move in next day.

The house was quiet, the staff long gone and the front door locked.

"Make the most of this," Hattie sighed. The phone had been ringing all day and the local paper wanted to run an article next week.

"I wonder if Greg gets the Westmarland Tribune in Spain?" Jo stared into the flames.

"Oh who gives a shite?" Hattie snapped. "Sorry, Jean," she added. "Greg's toasting his flesh and flashing his cash with the Spanish Madam and hasn't even called to ask how Thomas is. I doubt he'll be giving you any thought." Hattie was angry. Greg reminded her of her own errant husband.

"You'll probably never see him again,Jo." Jean nodded.

George rolled the whisky round the glass and Jo decided to change the subject. Mention of Greg sent George's blood pressure soaring.

"I need to keep my eye on Gerald," Jo sighed. "I thought Arthur was going to have a fit when he heard the glasses break during desserts."

"Well so he should," Hattie said. "That was a dozen of your best claret glasses - it sounded like a car crash. Sandra's mother nearly fainted."

Jo poured herself another glass of wine. She'd have to keep her eye on Gerald.

Jo STIRRED. There was traffic on the road outside. The village was waking up and commuters and holiday makers drove past her door. She put thoughts of Greg and Gerald to one side - she was about to open to the public! The familiar knot of anxiety tightened her stomach and she tried to ignore it as she went to her desk and took out a large bunch of keys. She must unlock the hotel and get ready.

Jo headed to the conservatory.

Selecting the correct key, she placed it in the lock. Something pushed her shoulder! Jo stumbled and fell forward into the door as it hit her again... It felt fleshy and cold. What the hell was that?! Fear sliced through her body. The room felt icy and Jo couldn't move. She gasped for breath and forced her paralysed body to turn but there was no one there. Her heart hammered and beads of sweat trickled down her cold brow. Was that a shadow? Jo shook. With trembling hands she forced herself to unlock the door then threw it open.

Warm air gushed in and Jo fell onto the terrace with relief.

When she turned, the conservatory was empty.

Convinced that someone had pushed her, she forced herself to go back and search the hotel.

Four croquet mallets stood by an urn of umbrellas and Jo grabbed one. With trepidation, she went through to the Panel Room - it was empty, as was the Rose Room and bar. The kitchen was in shadow and reception exactly as she'd left it last night. Jo flung doors open and searched furiously. The cloakroom was dim and she poked about with the mallet but nothing lurked in the shadows. She moved quickly to the front rooms, opening curtains and shutters to let the morning light in.

Gradually she began to feel calmer.

Had she imagined it? Was it just in the conservatory? Jo caught sight of herself in the hall mirror. Her face was white. She took a tissue from her sleeve and wiped perspiration from her forehead she must pull herself together! She walked down the hall to reception and told herself not to be so silly and to focus on the day. Jo sat down. She must've been dreaming in the conservatory, there was nothing there - she mustn't be so paranoid! But as she rubbed her shoulder she realised that it was sore.

The phone rang and she jumped.

"Anything you want on me way in?" Hattie shouted.

Jo sat back and breathed a sigh of relief. "Just your lovely self and pick up some change from the Post Office." Jo gave Hattie instructions and put the conservatory episode firmly out of her mind.

9

"You can put a bit of that pie up and I'll take it as me bait." Alf pointed to the venison pie on the kitchen table. He looked at the crisp, golden pastry with succulent layers of meat and smacked his lips.

Sandra cut a large slice and placed it before him. She watched Alf eat with enthusiasm, grunting approval with each mouthful. A few crumbs remained on the plate and Alf picked it up and pressed it to his face, then licked every last morsel of pie from the smooth white china.

"Get your big gob off that plate and leave it for the next person. Don't you get fed at home?" Sandra scolded Alf but hid a smile. It was good to see a man appreciate his food, especially if she'd cooked it.

"Here get a spoon and try this hare. It's been braised overnight in red wine, probably a bit posh for you." Sandra pushed an ovenproof dish towards Alf. He picked up the largest spoon he could find.

"What's this hard stuff on top?" Alf tapped at the crumble and pushed it aside.

"It's pistachio nut crumble. Bet you won't have tasted that before." Alf tentatively put the mixture into his mouth. "It's horrible, the meat is grand but you can leave out the crap on top." He wrinkled his face in disgust.

Sandra grinned. She hadn't expected Alf to like the recipe, which would be on the menu this evening alongside several other new dishes. She was enjoying this kitchen. Unlike the pub there wasn't a great long menu that required constant attention. At Kirkton House the menu was fixed price and consisted of six choices on each course. Sandra could adapt this daily, depending on available produce.
Tonight they were going to experiment with tasters between courses.

She had a long day ahead.

"Come on. Shift yourself! I've got work stacked up. Get on your way and give that lazy sod Michael a shout, he's late." Sandra wrapped a large slice of pie in greaseproof paper and handed it to Alf. His eyes lit up.

"You'll find him in the greenhouse," Alf said and buried the pie deep in his waistcoat. "Least ways he was when I came down the yard."

Earlier, Alf had part unloaded a trailer of freshly cut logs and stacked them in an outhouse. Jo had promised cash on delivery and he wanted to get a move on. There was a pint of warm beer with his name on at the Templars. No doubt the locals would be asking all about the hotel and he knew he could certainly fuel the gossip.

JO FINISHED her bedroom checks and took one final look at Room Two. It was perfect. The four-poster bed stood invitingly and a glass chandelier hung from an intricately carved ceiling rose in the centre of the room. Jo loved the Georgian rooms, with their original features and high ceilings and she'd enjoyed furnishing them with large gracious antiques. She gently closed the door. Linda knelt on the stairs and polished the banisters.

"Smashing meal yesterday Mrs Edmonds. My hubbie said his steak was the best he's ever tasted."

"Thank you, Linda, let's hope tonight's guests say the same." Jo hurried down the stairs as the front door opened and Hattie lumbered in, weighed down with a heavy post office bag, full of silver and bronze coins.

"Hope you need all this lot, Mystic Myra on the counter tutted as she counted it all out," Hattie grumbled. "She's a miserable cow that one. Anyone would think she was forced to be there, when we all know she's knocking off Jim in the sorting office and can't wait to get her fat bum on his swivel chair at break time."

Jo shook her head. She wasn't going to ask who Mystic Myra was nor ask after her relationship problems, it was time to open the doors.

"Stick it in the safe, Hattie and you can start by putting the Aboard out." Jo watched Hattie put the bags down then trudge across the drive. The board, advertising morning coffee and afternoon tea, was heavy and Jo went to help her.

"Well this is it - we're open," Jo said. She picked up one side and they deposited it on the verge by the road.

"Hurrah!" Hattie beamed. She nodded over to the Templars Inn, where the landlord stood on the doorstep and watched them. He was the only person who'd voiced his objection to Jo opening the hotel. Several charabancs were parked beside the pub and two cob ponies, tethered to the fence, grazed alongside.

"He's serving the gypsies," Hattie said. "I think you need to keep the door locked. Leave it open and you'll be wiped out."

"I will when the Fair starts," Jo said. "I'm not locking it on our opening day." A car pulled onto the driveway and Jo and Hattie simultaneously turned and collided.

"I'm having the first one," Jo whispered as they ran into the hotel.

The phone rang.

"Ah, saved by the bell." Hattie reached reception. "Good morning! Kirkton House Hotel, Harriet speaking. How may I help you today?" Hattie winked as Jo went to greet the couple in reception.

"Good morning Sir." Jo said.

"Your sign says you're serving coffee, could we have coffee for two?"

"With pleasure, would you like to sit in the lounge by the fire? Or make yourselves comfortable in the conservatory overlooking the garden. The cloakrooms are on the right." Jo beamed. She was in business!

THE MORNING PROGRESSED as customers took coffee and locals called in to wish Jo well.

At mid-day, the front door opened and a man stepped into the hallway. He checked his appearance in the mirror and fingercombed dark wavy hair. At six foot, he was good looking and knew it. He saw the brass bell, picked it up and gave it a shake.

In the kitchen, Jo heard the bell ring and ignored it. Hattie would see to whoever was there. Jo watched Sandra tuck a tea towel into the band of her crisp white apron, then spoon thick creamy mixture into a confectionery bag, and expertly pipe pale vanilla custard into two dozen glazed mille feuille pastry cases. Jo picked one up and bit into it. The light flaky pastry crumbled like a soft falling snow as she tasted the delicious dessert.

The school bell rang again. Jo wondered where Hattie was and hurried to reception.

The man watched her approach.

"I'm sorry to keep you waiting," Jo said. She felt him scrutinize her appearance. He was gorgeous! Jo was conscious that she must look a sight, all hot and sweaty from the kitchen.

"No worries," he said.

Jo straightened her shoulders and wished she'd put some lipstick on. She sucked her stomach in and looked him in the eye.

"Can I help you, sir?"

"Like school playtime," he nodded towards the bell.

"Yes, we certainly hear it when guests give it a good old swing up and down." Jo was mortified - she sounded like a complete nerd!

A smile twitched the corners of his handsome mouth as the man examined the flecks of pastry glued to Jo's cleavage. Flustered, Jo felt a blush tingle up her throat. "How can we help you?"

"Have you got a room on Friday?"

"Erm, I'll just check." Jo looked into his brilliant blue eyes and felt her knees buckle. Her limbs refused to function and she was rooted to the spot. She visualised his naked body spread across Room Two's four poster bed and her blush, like a tidal wave, engulfed her face. Horrified, Jo forced herself to turn and almost ran down the hall to reception, where she thrust the door open and flung herself into the office.

What the hell was she doing? She brushed the crumbs off her chest and groped for a lipstick, then smoothed the warm wax over her lips.

The action soothed her. She didn't need to check the accommodation charts to see if there was a room free next Friday - she knew the whole hotel was empty. She took a deep breath and stepped back into the hall.

The stranger had one hand in the pocket of his well-tailored trousers and the other straightened the collar of a pale blue cotton shirt. Jo smelt his aftershave. Polo by Ralph Lauren.

"Room Two's free," she blurted out. "Would you like to make a reservation?"

"Room Two it is," he smiled.

"Will that be single or double occupancy?"

"Single to start."

His mischievous eyes bored into her and Jo felt her face burn yet again as he pulled a wad of notes out of his pocket.

"Doherty's the name. People call me John," he smiled. "Stick this on the account."

He moved towards her.

Jo sensed the warmth of his body like an electric current as he thrust a parcel of notes into her hand.

She was paralyzed.

John reached out and placed a finger under her chin, tilted her head upwards and leaned forward, then brushed her lips with a warm kiss. "You've got flour on your nose," he whispered and with a cheeky smile he winked, turned and walked out of the hallway.

Jo watched him open the front door and slide into the seat of a gleaming red sports car.

He roared off across the gravel.

Dazed, Jo turned to the mirror, touched her fingers to her lips and traced his kiss on her mouth.

Her reflection showed a long white floury streak across her nose and cheek.

"Fuck!" she exclaimed and dabbed furiously at her face. The notes in her hand fell to the floor and lay in a pile at her feet. Jo scrambled to pick them up. It was a fortune.

She wondered how long John Doherty intended to stay.

"How much?" Hattie was astonished. "A stranger gives you a grand, says his name is John and you stand there like a nerd and don't even get a phone number?"

Hattie shook her head and tried to hide the smile that threatened to break across her face. Jo sat on the office chair and swung nervously from side to side, as she tried to explain that she didn't know how long to reserve Mr Doherty's room.

"He seemed like a very nice gentleman and he was in a hurry. Anyway, we've got the deposit, so I don't see that there's a problem." Jo couldn't meet Hattie's eyes and blushed as she remembered John's kiss.

"None of my business I'm sure but it's just a little odd, when you've drilled in reservation procedures to me and Judy for the last month and don't even get an address. Are you sure he's not a gypsy? We could have half Fair Hill in here by Saturday night."

The thought had crossed Jo's mind and she prayed that she hadn't screwed up. She felt a tingle in her stomach as she remembered John.

"Was he good looking?"

"I couldn't tell you." Jo looked away.

"How old?"

"I've no idea Hattie. He just wanted a room and seemed very pleasant."

Jo remembered his cheeky face and lovely blue eyes. He'd smelt gorgeous too and she was having feelings that she'd totally forgotten existed. She thought about running her fingers through the dark curly hair on his well-toned chest. Her cheeks burned, she kept her head low and fidgeted with a pencil.

"I detect a crush," Hattie laughed out loud "Well I never."

"Hattie you're talking rot." Jo stood up and pushed the chair back. She bristled with annoyance, both at herself for her lack of control and with Hattie for her persistence. The reception door flew open and they both turned as Judy burst in, oblivious to the atmosphere.

"Who on earth was that man?" Judy exclaimed.

"I was taking Old Johnny a cup of tea when I saw a red sports car pull out of the gates. It stopped to wait for the traffic and the driver winked at me. He's bloody handsome."

She was very excited. "Oh sorry Mrs E, I didn't mean to swear, but it's not often we get dishy blokes in Ferrari Testarossas racing around the village. Even Old Johnny looked up from his sweet peas. Blinking amazing car. My dad dreams of them, but says they cost twice as much as our house." Hattie smiled.

"Just a cast iron guaranteed booking that Mrs E here has fortunately managed to secure us for a few days," Hattie said. "Lucky she was around eh?"

Jo DECIDED to have a break and spend an hour with Thomas. She needed some fresh air. As she changed into jeans and a fleece, she thought about what she'd done.

Was she mad? She'd taken a booking on their first day, from a man who could easily be associated with the fair and every tinker in the vicinity.

There was a good chance trouble lay ahead. Jo sighed as she peeped around the spare bedroom door and saw Jean having a nap on the bed. George was asleep in his chair by the window. Nipper looked up and thumped her stubby tail. Jo closed the door and left them to it, then climbed the stairs two at a time. She knocked gently on the playroom door. Ann and Thomas were on the floor with a miniature farm. Ann made animal noises and held up a carved figure while Thomas grunted his own version.

"How are you getting on, Ann?"

"Hello, Mrs Edmonds. We had a walk around the village today and I showed him the sheep and cows on Winderwath farm." Ann stood up. "Are you going for a walk?"

Jo nodded as she picked Thomas up. She liked Ann and hoped she'd settle in.

"I'll have his tea ready when you get back." Ann waved goodbye to Thomas as Jo whisked him down the stairs and out into the fresh air.

SIX O'CLOCK. Jo felt nauseous. The walk with Thomas had done nothing to stop her anxiety. The restaurant had forty-eight guests booked in.

She knew they could do more but this was the first night and would test the staff. Her hand shook as she tried to put her make up on. Dear Lord don't let me make a fool of myself, please may it all go well. Jo prayed, as she pulled on black tights and promptly laddered them. Fuck!

The phone rang. She grabbed it, hooked it under her chin and flung the contents of several drawers onto the floor while searching for a new pair of tights.

"Yes," Jo growled.

"Everything ok with the hostess-with-the-mostest?" Hattie said. "We're filling up here and I've let three more rooms – two of which want dinner, so you're up to fifty two now."

"Oh Jesus Christ, Hattie, does the kitchen know? For God's sake don't take any more bookings!" She ripped open a new pair of tights.

"Calm down, it's all in hand. I've got the bookings staggered and the staff can cope." Hattie knew that weeks of hard work and continual preparations were all about to be put to the test. But the biggest test of all was Jo who was terrified of being out front with the guests. Hattie wondered if Jo was about to lose the plot.

"What are you putting on?" Hattie asked carefully. "Wear the black and white like we planned, get your slap on and calm down, I'll be up in a mo."

Jo had laddered a second pair of tights.

Hattie found her in her underwear sitting on her bed, as she tried to hold back the tears that threatened. She hung her head when Hattie entered the room.

"Hey now, come on Jo," Hattie said gently and sat beside her. "You're just a bit nervous that's all."

"Oh, Hattie, what have I done? Greg's laughing at me from some Spanish bar. Whatever made me think I could do it? You know I hate putting myself in the spotlight and I feel fat and tired." Jo held her head in her hands. "If it all goes wrong I'll be a laughing stock, I can't believe I've got to go and stand in front of Robert and the Atkinsons, even Pete Parks and his cronies. I just want to run away." Jo was distraught. She seemed to be falling apart.

Hattie took a deep breath...

"Ok, there's your dressing gown and a magazine by your bed, you climb in and get your feet up." Hattie held the covers back. "I'll cope with everyone downstairs. You stay up here and feel sorry for yourself," she nodded towards the bed.

"I'll just pop next door and let Jean and George know that you are having a bit of a breakdown and then I'll tell the staff that you won't be coming down to celebrate opening night. It's fine. You wallow in

self-pity and we'll get on with what you pay us for, come on, get in."
Jo sat with her head bowed.

"Of course you could always get a bleedin' grip of yourself." Hattie
picked up the ruined tights and put them in the bin. "There are people
down there, me included, who are really looking forward to tonight."
She shook out the cocktail dress and began to tug it over Jo's head.
"As I speak, your mum and dad are discussing how proud they are of
you. And that little lad upstairs needs someone strong to make
a good life for him, unlike that dick of a dad he's got."

Jo stood up and Hattie pulled the dress over her hips.

"Do you know how bloody lucky you are?" Hattie rambled on.
"You've got everything – a future and a life in a job that you can do.
So, get your face on and strut your stuff." She thrust a new pair of
tights towards Jo. "People down there are paying for the privilege of
eating here tonight and you've taught us all for weeks on how to run a
restaurant. We know it backwards. Now for goodness sake get your
arse down there and give us all something to remember!"

Jo wiped the tears from her face and nodded. She picked up the
tights and walked to the dressing room. "I think I've got some lacy
hold-ups somewhere, sod the passion killers." Jo threw the tights to
one side. "I might as well go all out. Pour me a large Cointreau, you
old battleaxe. Let's get this show on the road!"

10

Jo walked through the restaurant and looked around, she was anxious to ensure that they were ready. Everything twinkled and gleamed.

The Panel Room was bathed in a soft glow from a fire in the cast iron grate and in the Rose Room the evening sun cast dancing shadows across the tables. Discreetly placed lights under tall herbaceous plants in the garden, lit up the pale pink and lime-washed walls and as Jo looked out, the sun descended from an ochre sky and slowly faded into the valley beyond the paddock.

A couple enjoying the sunset strolled hand in hand and stopped by the fountain. The man reached into a pocket and handed his partner a coin. She tossed it on the shimmering water.

Jo heard a rustle of fabric. Suzy stood in the doorway.

"You look lovely," Jo said. Suzy wore a dark red prom dress with a full skirt and puffed sleeves. Her glossy black hair was scooped up and tied with a matching ribbon. She sat by the piano and selected sheets of music.

In the conservatory, candles glowed on the windowsills. Jo flicked a switch and water in the fountain outside cascaded over rocks and tumbled into the pool below, to the delight of the couple, still lost in the magic of the garden.

Jo stood in the open doorway and gazed out.

But a sudden chill made her shiver. Icy tentacles began to claw at her skin and she spun around as something crashed against her shoulder. Jo stumbled back and grasped a chair. What the hell was it? Fear raked through her body. What on earth was in this room?

The door crashed shut.

"Steady, you'll break the glass." Hattie held a glass of Cointreau. "You want some water with this?"

Jo felt her pulse drum in her ears but the room was suddenly warmer.

"My, don't you scrub up well." Hattie admired Jo's appearance. "Are you ok now? You look a bit peaky."

Jo felt the pain in her shoulder. What had hit her? She forced herself to smile and slowly let go of the chair. Whatever was in this room must be dealt with later. She had to carry on.

"Just checking the garden." Jo willed her legs to work and took the drink. She knocked it back. "Mmn that's better," she said as the alcohol hit her veins. "Are the first guests in?"

"Robert is suited and booted and leering longingly at the door, waiting for your bewitching arse to sashay around the frame." "Better not keep him waiting…"

"AND I SAID, 'He must be with the enemy,' and do you know what? He was!"

In the Rose Room, Peter Gavmin perched his portly figure in a winged armchair and entertained his wife Isabel alongside Robert and Miriam. Jo found them grouped by the fire. In his role as local solicitor 'the enemy' referred to a rival practice and their clients.

"And here's our hostess." Peter rose with difficulty.

Jo greeted the party.

"My dear this is credit to you." Peter waved his chubby arm around the room. "It's marvellous to be here on your opening night." He puckered his pouting lips and kissed Jo on the cheek. With a tight hold on her arm he turned to the rest of his party.

"You know my lovely wife Isabel."

As stout as her husband, Isabel heaved herself forward and warmly embraced Jo.

Jo remembered Isabel from Butterly where Peter's office was on the main street, opposite the pub. They'd often called in for a bar meal.

"And of course you know our property expert Robert and his beloved, The Lady Miriam."

'Lady' Miriam remained still. She feigned annoyance at Peter's reference but secretly preened herself. She hoped Jo would appreciate her assumed status and nodded curtly as she calculated the cost of Jo's off-the-shoulder cocktail dress. She crossed one long thin leg over the other and wrapped bony fingers around her flute of champagne.

Robert stood as Jo extricated herself from Peter's grip.

"None of this would have been possible without this man." Jo said and took Robert's hand. She kissed him fondly on each cheek. He was immaculate in a dark wool suit. "You're a very lucky lady," Jo told Miriam.

Miriam fumed. How dare this tarty girl be so familiar with her husband!

Miriam considered Jo to be way above her station and shouldn't be so intimate with the guests.

"Fetch the menu," Miriam ordered. Her glare bore holes into Robert's back as he sat down.

"Just doing my job." Robert mumbled. "It was a pleasure to help a client."

He reached for his glass and took a large gulp, fearful that Miriam would sense his true feelings. Jo looked absolutely stunning. The change from a shabby abandoned wife to the striking confident woman with an amazing cleavage, unsettled him in more ways than he cared to think of. He retreated deeper into his chair.

"I hope you enjoy your evening." Jo handed out menus and placed a wine list on the table. She threw a dazzling smile in Miriam's direction and left them to select their meal.

Hattie appeared with a tray of champagne. "You've not selfcombusted then?" She shot a glance in Miriam's direction and hurried into the Green Room, which was now full of animated guests. Jo caught sight of Dougie Cannon.

He wandered up the hallway from the bar looking very smart in a jacket and tie, but he seemed uneasy.

"Dougie, it's lovely to see you."

"Aye, Annie's in the bar, erm…" Dougie hesitated and looked around.

"The gentleman's cloakroom is on the left," Jo said and Dougie disappeared. Jo found Annie buried in a chintz chair in the cocktail bar. She was a tiny woman with salt and pepper hair. Her stick thin, mottled limbs were childlike and protruded from a short-sleeved floral dress. Fortunately, the white knitted shawl that framed her face stopped her from blending into the chair.

"Dougie'll be back in a minute," Annie said, clutching a glass of mineral water. "That champagne doesn't agree with him, I told him not to have it." Her worried frown furrowed across her forehead.

"I'll pop back and take your order when Dougie's ready."

Jo smiled then raced to reception and found some indigestion tablets. She placed two on the desk as Dougie re-appeared.

"It's lovely to see Annie." Jo beamed. "Your scallops are going to be popular tonight." She pushed the tablets towards him. "I don't know about you, but champagne bubbles always give me indigestion," Jo whispered. Westmarland men were proud and Jo didn't want to embarrass Dougie. He picked the tablets up and disappeared again.

Jo went into the kitchen where there was a flurry of activity. Hattie pinned an order to the board and Sandra barked orders at Michael.

"First residents are seated and dining," Hattie told Jo. "By heck that Peter Gayman doesn't half go on and the Lady Miriam must be the sourest woman in Stainton."

"It's Gavmin," Jo corrected Hattie.

"Hmn, well he's odd. Never trust a fat man with small round eyes, my mam always said, and he grabs onto you when he's talking. My arm's sore!"

"Shall I take over the orders for a bit?" Jo reached for the pad and rapped Hattie's fingers with it. "Stop picking." Hattie had a canapé in her mouth and Sandra bore down on her with a heavy metal spoon. Jo winced as the spoon swung in the direction of Hattie's head.

In the stillroom, Gerald was buried under the hood of the dishwasher.

"Is everything alright, Gerald?" Jo asked. Gerald's face appeared through the steam and he nodded. The swing door opened and Simon came though. He deposited two soup bowls by the dishwasher and rolled his eyes in Gerald's direction.

"Get on with it, Simon, call the next course!" Jo snapped.

She had the urge to grab an apron and join Gerald at the sink but instead, said a silent prayer to the guardian of the stillroom and left him to it.

The sound of piano music was delightful as Suzy's deft fingers skipped over the keyboard to Scott Joplin's The Sting. Hattie and Steven danced around each other in the narrow corridor where Hattie's chest almost impaled Steven.

In the Panel Room, the couple from the garden sat at the corner table by the fire and stared lovingly into each others eyes. He stroked her arm tenderly as they waited for their next course.

"Honeymooners..." Hattie whispered.

Jo headed for the Green Room and noticed a pint of beer on Simon's tray as he led Dougie and Annie through to the restaurant. Dougie nodded at the pint and winked at Jo.

"Enjoy your meal." She stood back to let them pass.

Hattie led more new arrivals into the bar.

"Brace yourself! Pete Parks has arrived," Hattie said. "I've put him in the Green Room well away from Peter Gayman who hates him – Pete's 'with the enemy'..."

"Gavmin" Jo corrected Hattie again.

She gripped her order pad to stop her hand shaking and forced herself to go and greet the Parks party.

The group sat on matching Chesterfields in the bay window and as Jo walked towards them she felt Pete study her, from her court shoes up.

"Good Evening everyone," Jo said. The ruddy, weather-beaten faces smiled back. Simon offered champagne and the ladies giggled and made remarks about getting tipsy. Mrs Parks removed her coat.

"Let me take that for you." Jo held out her hand.

Pete slipped his jacket off. With his back to the others he stared at Jo's cleavage. "You can have mine as well." His blue eyes bore through her clothes and Jo blushed as she took the jacket.

Hattie appeared with menus and handed them round, she remarked that the steak was especially good, Mr Pigmy's best, no less.

Jo almost ran from the room. She flung the cloakroom door open and hung Mrs Parks tweed on a hanger but found herself holding Pete's jacket to her face. The smell of soft, expensive leather with a trace of aftershave was delicious. She closed her eyes.

"Bleedin' hell, let's hope that wears off soon." Hattie peered around the door and rolled her eyes. "Not The Parks Effect - I warned you."

"Oh bugger off Hattie. I'm just smelling real quality, that's all." Jo was embarrassed and changed tack. "I wonder where he gets his jackets from?"

"Who cares? We're filling up out here." Hattie held the cloakroom door ajar. Jo dodged past and wondered if Westmarland men were always so randy? Even Dougie had winked at her and the night had only just started...

"Look lively! The Bentleys just pulled up." Hattie gesticulated to Steven and, following precise instructions, he began to open car doors and usher the guests into the hotel.

Jo hurried to greet the Atkinsons.

"I've put them in the Red Room," Hattie whispered as she bustled past under a mound of fur. "Jinny's done up like a dog's dinner, who the bloody hell would wear fox in June?" Jo
entered the room.

Billy Atkinson stood by the fireplace and spoke to Peter Gavmin.

The atmosphere was clearly strained and Jo wondered if Billy was with 'the enemy'. Peter's podgy little face looked distinctly relieved when Simon called his party through for dinner.

"Enjoy your meal," Jo said cheerily as Peter and Robert stood back and let their wives go ahead of them.

Jinny Atkinson scrutinised Jo. The two women cast a calculated eye on the others apparel, both seeing Dorothy's work at first hand. Jinny was immaculate in a black cocktail dress with long gloves.

Frank Usher Jo thought, pleased that she knew.

Jinny placed a cigarette in a tortoiseshell holder and glared at Jo. Billy flashed his Dunhill lighter. Jo prayed that Jinny wouldn't light up in the dining room - Kirkton House was one of the few restaurants in Westmarland to have a no-smoking policy.

"So you're the female version of Tom Tovey eh?" Billy smiled and sipped his champagne.

"It's sweet of you to put me in the same league." Jo acknowledged the reference to a successful hotelier west of the county.

"Call me Billy. Looks like you've done a good job here, lass." Billy looked around. "You've worked hard. I remember this place when we built the main road."

Jo remembered Hattie's reference to Billy's work and wondered if the road outside was in his wheelbarrow days.

"This is my son and my good lady, Jinny," Billy said and young Billy stepped forward and shook Jo's hand.

Like his Dad, young Billy was handsome in a rugged way, both dapper in designer suits.

"I'm very pleased to meet you all," Jo said. "It's lovely to have local support."

Jinny stubbed her cigarette out and looked bored. She flicked a compact open and repaired her lipstick. She'd no intention of being friendly to this girl, who'd hardly been in the area for more than five minutes and needed to know her place. Several ladies from Jinny's Luncheon Club had expressed an interest in arranging their next meeting at Kirkton House and Jinny was determined that Jo would work hard for their business. Jinny watched her husband as he finished his glass of champagne and ordered a bottle of Krug. His eyes never left Jo's shapely figure. Furious, Jinny looked away as Jo explained the menu and took their wine order.

Jo was relieved to leave the room. Jinny was pure venom and the Atkinson men far too forward.

Had young Billy brushed his hand up her leg? She hoped she'd imagined it. She hurried to reception and collided with Hattie who came out of the kitchen with a plate of canapés.

"Look out! Shite I nearly lost them!" Hattie cursed.

"You've got pastry on your mouth," Jo snapped. She was reeling from the degrees of warmth and hostility she'd just encountered.

"She's a sour cow eh?" Hattie nodded at the beautiful silver fox fur coat piled on the office chair.

"Don't you think you should hang that up?" Jo began but stared with horror at the coat.

Two of the canapés were face down on the silk lining. Oily pesto oozed over the fabric creating a dark stain.

"Fuck, Jinny will kill us if she sees that. For God's sake, Hattie, do something."

"Well I'm not licking it off. It's nothing that can't be fixed with warm soapy water." Hattie disappeared to the kitchen as Jo stared with dismay at the expensive coat.

"How's it going, babe?" A man's voice whispered. Jo spun around and in an effort to hide the damage, plonked herself on the coat. Pete Parks placed his hands on the counter and leaned over. Jo felt trapped. She also felt a warm oily mess penetrate the back of her dress.

"Oh, hello there..." Jo said nervously. "Did you want something?" God, he has got incredibly blue eyes!

"You know what I want babe."

Jo felt like a rabbit trapped in the headlights. Cornered with no where to go. The reception door flew open and caught Pete on the forehead. He reeled back from the blow. Oblivious, Hattie hurried through with a dishcloth in her hand.

"What in God's name are you sitting there for? You'll look like you've shit yourself!" Hattie tugged the coat from under Jo.

"Oh hello, Pete, can we help you?" Hattie saw Pete steady himself. Dazed, he held his hand to his brow.

"Have you tumbled?" Hattie asked "Not used to the champagne eh?"

"Hattie," Jo hissed, "Mr Parks was looking for the lavatory."

Hattie rolled her eyes heavenward. She threw the dishcloth at Jo then guided Pete away.

"Well the lav is on the left, you'll not find it in here."

11

Jo and Hattie sat in the conservatory and mulled over the events of the previous night. The evening had been a success. Guests who'd departed that morning had been full of praise and assured Jo that they'd return. Diners in the restaurant had left handsome tips and many compliments, even Gerald had got through the night without any breakages.

"Hattie, is it me or do most men around here seem to have the urge to stray, or at the very least flirt like hell at any given opportunity?" Jo sipped a mug of coffee.

"They don't get out much in Westmarland. You're a challenge to them." Hattie dunked a shortbread biscuit in her tea. "It's only natural that every man with a pulse in his penis is gagging to be the first to conquer the New You."

Jo drained her coffee and took Hattie's mug. Crumbs clung to the side.

"Another one?"

Hattie shook her head. She leaned back and stretched her legs, then circled her feet. They were swollen and bulged over her kitten-heel shoes.

"My bloody feet are agony. They look like pigs trotters." Hattie complained.

"Well get off home and have a Sunday with your boys, I can manage." Jo's parents were leaving that morning and Ann would take responsibility for Thomas.

"Judy's here all day," Jo said. Judy was staying in the hotel, in a small en-suite staff room by the linen room.

It was a lovely day and bright, warm sunshine brought the garden to life. Jo looked out and saw Michael in the greenhouse. He bent over a tray of seedlings and potted his precious herbs and plants.

Old Johnny sat on a stool close by.

"Michael puts a lot of time into that greenhouse," Jo said. "You'd never think he was a keen gardener would you?" "Nah, he's a lazy bugger." Hattie yawned.

"The plants must be his relaxation," Jo said as she picked up an accounts ledger.

"You must be pleased?" Hattie nodded at the first day's receipts. "Billy Atkinson spent a fortune on wine; you'll need to re-stock the Barolo."

"I didn't have Pete Parks down as a Muscadet sort of man," Jo mused.

"Nope, more of a house white, not that his Mrs would know the difference." Hattie shook her head.

"She's not what you'd expect is she?"

Jo remembered the shy and giggly Mrs Parks, who'd turned into quite a party animal as the night wore on and the wine flowed.

"Aye, she certainly wasn't what Peter Gayman expected!" Hattie chuckled.

"Gavmin," Jo corrected. "He was quite upset when she sat on his knee." Jo remembered the look of absolute horror on Peter Gavmin's face as the drunken wife of the enemy plonked her rotund bottom on his lap, removed his glasses and told him to 'giddey-up!'

"By heck did you see Lady Miriam's face?" Hattie said. "She was apoplectic. She nearly burst when she told Robert to 'Take that horse-faced woman away!',"

The girls giggled as they remembered the night's exploits. Jo was sure she'd heard Annie Cannon throwing-up in the ladies loo after picking her way through dinner.

The vomiting would explain her emaciated appearance.

Dougie was hopelessly drunk and had to be led out by Hattie and Simon via the back door, into a waiting taxi. He'd accompanied his departure with a loud rendition of "Show me the way to go home!"

74   CAROLINE JAMES

Annie had run after him as Gerald and Arthur respectfully stopped their pot-washing.

"Evening, Annie," they'd politely acknowledged as she flew past. Jo wondered whether to send the bill on, or knock it off the fish account...

"I wouldn't worry about Jinny's coat," Hattie said. She stood up and stretched. "I got most of the pesto off. I heard her asking you about Ladies Lunches – are you on for that?"

"I'm surprised Jolly-Jinny wants to frequent this humble establishment with her charity committees, but a litre of Krug probably helped," Jo replied.

"Don't forget to have your dress cleaned..."

"Go on home, Hattie, and get your feet up." Jo gave Hattie a half push out of the conservatory door.

"Do you feel something cold just there?" Hattie looked at the door. "It's weird. I've noticed it before but thought it was the wind. It's icy when you stand in that doorway."

Hattie shivered. "You want to get yourself a dog, anyone might be lurking. Get a guard dog - you'll need it with Fair Week coming up."

"Get off Hattie, you're imagining things." Jo shook her head. Hattie had felt something too! "And as for a dog, I've never heard anything so silly. Like I have time for a dog?" Jo shooed Hattie away.

"There's a phone call for you, Mrs E," Judy appeared in the doorway.

"Thanks Judy," Jo left the conservatory and went to reception. She picked up the receiver.

"Jo Edmonds, can I help you?"

"Room Two all ready for me?"

Jo nearly dropped the phone. John Doherty's voice was rich and suggestive. She tried to compose herself.

"Mr Doherty, thank you for confirming your booking," Jo looked up, Hattie stood by the desk. She raised an eyebrow.

"We wondered how long you'd be staying with us." Christ she felt such an idiot! Jo was sure John was smiling.

"Still got flour on your nose?" he asked.

"I'll put you down for five nights." Jo felt Hattie scrutinize her every word.

"I'm looking forward to seeing you again," John teased.

"And we'll look forward to welcoming you to Kirkton House." Jo wanted to die. Why did she sound such an idiot when she spoke to him? Hattie's overbearing presence didn't help.

"Keep the bed warm for me," John whispered. Jo turned scarlet. She mumbled goodbye and hung up the phone.

"Glad to see you got all his details this time." Hattie nodded towards the blank note pad. "You could fry an egg on your face! See yah tomorrow," Hattie waved as she waltzed off.

"Shite!" Jo stamped her foot and rocked back in the chair. She held her face in her hands in an attempt to stop the burning. But a tingle had begun in her fingers and toes and as she stared at the chart, she began to count the days off until Friday.

GEORGE SLAMMED the boot of the overflowing car and climbed in. Nipper bounced up and down on the back seat and yapped furiously when Jean thrust the car into gear.

Jo stood in the doorway and balanced Thomas on her hip. She waved goodbye to her parents. "Love you Mum, bye Dad, thank you for everything."

"Watch out for those gypsies," George warned. "Promise me you'll lock every door during the Fair." George didn't want to go but Jean had her garden to attend to and the bedding plants needed to go in.

"I promise, Dad, I'll be fine," Jo assured him.

George fastened his seat belt and closed his eyes. The car lurched forward, mounted the kerb and careered into the road and he held his hands in prayer as they disappeared into the distance. Jo turned to Ann who stood alongside.

"Take Thomas for a nap please." Jo handed her wriggling child into Ann's outstretched arms.

Jo sat in reception and began to compile the staff rotas, the fair would start in a few days and she must be prepared.

Judy had taken a booking for two double rooms - the Hunts from London. Jo smiled. Harry Hunt and his brother were guests from the pub days and had managed to find Jo at the hotel. She was delighted that the East End boys were staying with her. The brothers had a chain of green grocers and market stalls and always travelled to Butterly for the fair.

No doubt their own origins had Romany roots but they were East End boys 'done good' and knew how to spend their hard earned cash.

Jo wrote over Judy's pencil booking with ink.

"Morning Mrs E," Phillip Campbell stood by the desk and courteously removed his trilby hat. Jo looked up and beamed at the retired army major.

"Hello, Mr Campbell, I didn't hear you come in."

"Sneaked in the back way m'dear, been having a trot around your garden. I say, you've got things ship-shape, that young fellow in the greenhouse looks keen."

"That's Michael our chef. He wants to get fresh herbs on the menu as soon as possible."

"Very commendable, I like to see initiative."

Phillip Campbell lived in Bevan House, a stunning period property that had been in his family for generations.

"Thanks for looking after our lot at the weekend," Phillip said. "Helen sent a thank-you." He handed Jo an envelope.

"A pleasure, Mr Campbell, did you have a good party?"

"Marvellous, but there are some sore heads this morning. Not for the lucky blighters staying here though, after your breakfast they're set for the day. Who came up with the porridge recipe?"

Jo grinned. Hot porridge with whisky was her idea and despite Sandra's horror that Jo was 'ruining good oats,' nearly all the guests had enjoyed it.

"We'll be back." Phillip gave Jo a salute and greeted Judy as they met in the hall.

"Busy on coffees," Judy called to Jo and hurried by.

THE MORNING WENT QUICKLY and in the afternoon Jo took a break to enjoy a brisk walk around the village with Thomas. They stopped at the children's playground and Jo sat on a swing with Thomas on her knee gently rocking to and fro. Honey-coloured stone houses and quaint cottages nestled around the village green. Jo thought they resembled gingerbread houses with their little windows and colourful doors. Ducks nesting in the reed-edged pond waddled out as a child threw bread on the water. Jo felt happy to be part of the chocolate box village; all she had to do was make a success of it...

Thomas cooed with delight as they rocked. He's so like his dad. Every expression reminded Jo of Greg. Would he have been happy at the hotel with them? Jo knew he would have loved it. But he'd chosen the Spanish One. Jo felt sad as she watched her son. His father was far away on some sunny beach, laughing with the lithe bikini-clad Estelle, wandering hand in hand as they paddled in warm seas without a care in the world. Jo wondered if she'd ever stop loving Greg. Does a broken heart ever mend? She gathered Thomas up and secured him in his buggy. Villagers enjoying Sunday in their gardens waved as she passed.

The pub garden was busy and Jo saw Alf, he was sitting beside a wooden bench with a pint of ale.

"Havin' one with us?" Alf called out.

"Go on then, but only if I'm buying," Jo said.

"Get away with you." Alf disappeared into the darkness of the bar.

Jo sat down and rocked Thomas back and forth.

"Cider for the lady and a lemonade and pork scratchings for the lad."

Alf plonked himself beside Jo and opened the bag then handed Thomas a piece of salty dried skin.

Thomas grabbed the stick and Jo winced, she wanted to tear it out of his hand but didn't want to offend Alf.

"I grew up on them," Alf nodded at the pork stick.

"They didn't do you any harm," Jo smiled.

"How's it going?" Alf nodded in the direction of the hotel and Jo followed his gaze.

"Well the first weekend is nearly over and it's been good." The car park was half full and she hoped that Judy had let some rooms. "It has to get busy though, I've invested everything. There's no margin for quiet times."

"You'll be alright." Alf took a long swig and looked at Jo. "Your man must 'ave been mad." He shook his head then finished remainder of his beer in one gulp. Jo didn't know what to say.

"Don't worry about the gypos. I'll be 'ere, you'll come to no harm." He put his glass on the bench and thrust out his hand. Jo took it - it was warm and calloused, but very reassuring.

"We're friends thee and me."

"Thank you, Alf."

Alf's face broke into a huge grin and he threw his head back and laughed. "There'll be some right gossip t'nite after this." He gathered Jo's glass, ruffled Thomas' hair then picked up his own empty glass.

"I'll see thee!" Alf shouted and disappeared into the depths of the 17th century pub.

Jo released the brake on the buggy and set off. Everyone was warning her about the fair and images of marauding, pillaging gypsies ransacking the hotel raced through her mind. She crossed the road to her house where Ann waited in the small kitchen.

"Good walk, Mrs C?" Ann asked. She lifted Thomas from his buggy and guided his legs into his high chair. "What have you got here little man?" She touched the soft gooey mess that was smothering his fingers and mouth.

"Don't ask, Ann," Jo warned "You'll have the authorities in if you knew what he's eaten."

"I'm sure he'll have a lot worse, whatever it is," Ann rubbed a warm soapy flannel over his face.

Jo kissed Thomas then hurried through to reception to see what had happened in her absence.

"I've sold four rooms," Judy said excitedly as she greeted Jo. "They're all eating in and the kitchen knows."

"That's brilliant, Judy - we won't be empty tonight after all."

"We've been manic with afternoon teas too." Judy pushed a metal money box across the desk.

Jo counted the notes with pleasure and smiled. There's nothing like the feel of cash! She thought as she locked the box in the safe.

12

Monday morning. Jo set about breakfast preparations with Michael and felt like she'd been up for hours. There were ten residents due, another room had checked-in late evening and with the morning calls already done, there would be signs of life in the dining room soon.

Jo endeavoured to be patient but Michael was driving her mad. He was so slow. She made a start with the porridge and watched the chef leisurely place breads in the oven. The bacon needed racking and sausages cooking, plus a dozen other jobs. Simon had already made fresh coffee, set the tables with milk, butter and pots of homemade marmalades and jams.

"Come on, Michael, get a move on," Jo scolded the chef. She was frustrated and wanted to shove him out of the way, put her apron on and got stuck-in behind the stove. "Breakfast is the easiest duty of the day. You should be prepping-up for tonight now."

She took the menu off the board and noted that Sandra had left precise instructions for Michael. He looked weary and his eyes seemed bloodshot. Jo wanted to sniff his breath but felt it would look too obvious. She'd wait for an opportune moment; Sandra would be in at ten o'clock.

Jo had made her mind up that she'd wander over to Marland later to ask Pete Parks about another car, she knew it was time to put something a bit more in keeping on the drive.

But in the meantime, she'd Michael to supervise through breakfast.

ALF STOOD at the side door of Jo's house. He knocked hard and hoped that Ann would hear him, he didn't want to go through the hotel or kitchen. There was no sign of life as he walked around to the garden, then looked up at the lounge window on the first floor and shouted out.

"Ann, open the door!" Alf picked up a pebble and tossed it against window pane. It bounced hard on the glass and he heard it crack.

The sash window flew open and Ann's head thrust through the gap.

"Jesus, Alf, What the bleedin' hell do you think you're doing? You've broken the glass."

"Get down 'ere, I've something for the missus," Alf hissed back. He glanced nervously. He didn't want to be coughing up for a broken window.

A few moments later Ann unbolted the door. She held Thomas on her ample hip. Thomas recognised Alf and waved his hands. "Alf, Pig, Pig." He held out a pink plastic pig.

"All right little fella, I've got something grander than that." Alf said and strode past Ann into the small kitchen. He led an unkempt and sorrowful looking creature behind him by a thick length of dirty rope.

Ann was aghast.

"What on earth have you got there?" she said.

"She's called Pippa. She needs a good home and the Missus needs a dog."

Alf deposited the dog in the middle of the floor, then turned to Thomas and tickled him under his chin.

Alf began to explain to a dumbfounded Ann that he didn't think the dog was very old and he'd found her wandering around a farmyard up on Gun Fell. The farmer didn't know where she'd come from and didn't want her, so Alf had put her in the back of his old Land Rover and brought her down here.

Ann thought that Jo would have a fit.

Thomas was wriggling out of Ann's arms and as she bent down to put him on the floor, he crawled towards the dog.

Pippa sat meekly on the stone slabs and trembled. Thomas stopped and pushed his plastic pig towards her. He poked at the dog's paws and tentatively touched Pippa's fur with his fingers. With complete wonder, he looked up into her fearful brown eyes as the dog bent her head and sniffed his hair curiously then gently licked his cheek.

Thomas pulled her ear.

"Doggie, uff uff." Thomas chortled between licks and strokes.

Alf and Ann watched the child and dog bond. Ann smiled. The dog was a collie mix with some Labrador retriever; by nature it would be gentle with the child.

"That's that then." Alf nodded at the floor. "I'll see thee!" he grinned at Ann, turned and left the house.

Horrified, Ann stared at his retreating back.

"Uff uff." Thomas poked happily at the dog "Ippa, Ann, Ippa."

Jo was relieved that breakfast was over and hurried through to her house to get changed. She'd ended up doing most of the cooking and now smelt like a greasy spoon fry-up. Sandra had come on duty and weighed-up the situation immediately, noting that Michael seemed to be hung-over. Jo left Sandra to sort him out and climbed the stairs to her bedroom.

"Uff Ippa."

Jo stopped. Thomas was calling out and his voice seemed to be coming from the bathroom.

"Uff uff."

She realised that he must be in the bath playing with a toy dog from his farmyard, his treasured pig no doubt floating in the bubbles.

Jo took the stairs two at a time, pleased that she had a distraction. "Woof woof, Thomas." Jo called and threw the door open.

Thomas was strapped in his rocking cradle perched on a linen chest, while Ann kneeled over the bath. Ann was shocked to see Jo, but Thomas grinned and kicked his legs.

"Holy Moses, what in God's name is that?" Jo stared at the bedraggled, wet and foamy animal.

The dog sat in a foot of dirty water and hung her head. She cowered as she heard Jo's raised voice and began to scramble backwards out of the bath. Ann threw the soap to one side and leapt to catch the dog, but fell as it wriggled and squirmed out of her grip. It showered Ann and Thomas with white frothy bubbles and soaked Jo's skirt as it sped past and made a bee-line out of the bathroom.

Ann jumped to her feet. She was drenched and her t-shirt clung to her.

She began to try and explain the situation but Thomas squealed with delight and threatened to rock wildly onto the floor at any moment.

"I can explain …" Ann began.

"Shall we catch the creature first?" Jo turned and ran after the trail of wet paw marks, catching up with it in the first floor lounge. Pippa had leapt onto the window seat and was hell-bent on making her escape through the window.

"Oh no you don't…"

Jo lunged forward and grabbed the dog. She held it tightly, as Ann, complete with Thomas in his cradle, thrust out a large towel.

The dog shook uncontrollably, it was terrified.

"There, there, old girl it's alright," Jo picked up the towel and as she slackened her grip, she caught sight of a large crack in the window. "Crikey it must have hit the window, it's broken." Jo gently

wrapped the dog in the towel and began to rub. "What a good job I caught you."

"Ippa Mumma," Thomas gurgled. Jo raised her eyebrows and looked at Ann.

"Er, it's been abandoned," Ann said.

She sensed that Jo was softening. Ann's arms were full of Thomas and the cradle contraption. She placed him down on the floor and crossed her fingers behind her back.

"You see," Ann began, "Alf turned up and said that you needed a dog and this dog needed a home. And I thought it was ok with you and that I ought to get it cleaned up before you saw it and then you might like it a bit…"

She trailed off, still squeezing her fingers together. Her face twisted into a plea as she watched Jo.

It wasn't looking good.

"Oh I understand," Jo said as she stared at Pippa. "Alf thinks he can dump the dog on me, does he? Well he better think again. I've absolutely no time whatsoever to be looking after any waif and stray he gets his hands on. You'd better call him and tell him to get straight back and find some other poor unsuspecting bugger to provide board and lodgings for his cast-offs." Jo turned to the dog.

Pippa still trembled, but she began to lick Jo's hand. Her ears had dried into soft little dreadlocks where Jo had towelled the fur.

"What is she, Ann?" Jo asked as she watched the dog, the warm tongue on her hand was not unpleasant.

"Bit of an allsorts I'd say," Ann replied. "Mostly Labrador but those ears could be anything. Should I look after her 'til we get Alf back? Thomas seems to like her." Her fingers hurt, they were still tightly crossed.

"What's her name?"

"We think it's Pippa - she seems to respond to that."

"Go and see if Sandra has got anything to feed her, she's as thin as a rake. I'll see if Hattie can track Alf down."

Jo rose to her feet and folded the towel. "How old is she?"

"Alf didn't know, thinks she's quite young though." Ann's fingers were killing her.

"Hmn. Alf's got a lot to answer for." Jo leant down and kissed Thomas, who rocked excitedly and pointed at Pippa. "Ippa Mumma! Ippa!"

Jo looked from the child to the dog and back again.

"Oh, bloody hell, Ann. You know I can't turn the poor thing out," Jo sighed. "Sod it. Sod it… Sorry Thomas - Mummy means sausages or something. Have we got a blanket anywhere that we can put her on?

And get her somewhere warm when she's had some food, she looks frozen. I'll bloody murder Alf when I see him."

Jo turned away to stop herself falling to her knees to cuddle the animal. She thundered out of the room.

13

Jo parked the car behind the car wash. It was an upright unit with two huge yellow brushes that looked like crazed gallows for naughty vehicles.

A gormless youth stood beside it. He held a plastic spray with cleaning chemical in one hand and a large sponge in the other, he stared at Jo as she got out of the car. Jo wondered if she was about to get a rub down too and moved around to the rear door. She encouraged Pippa to jump out.

"Come on dog. I can't leave you. Lord knows what you'll do." Pippa had barked furiously at every oncoming vehicle they'd passed on their journey to Marland.

Jo bent down and picked up the rope that Alf had knotted into a loop to form a lead. She pushed it over Pippa's head and the dog trotted obediently beside her as they walked to the car showroom.

Jo glanced around for a salesman and hoped that Pete Parks was out. She stood in front of the large glass doors and tried to slide them apart. They refused to budge and she began to feel foolish. She peered beyond the gleaming vehicles, to an office area where Pete sat behind a desk. He was speaking into a telephone and as he saw Jo he waved in a circular motion, indicating that she use the side door.

"Sod it," Jo mumbled. She wiped her finger marks off the immaculate glass with her sleeve, then tugged the dog's rope and walked briskly to the side of the building where she entered the showroom and moved cautiously along the wall. She hoped that Pete would leave her be while she looked at the cars on display.

Pippa's claws clicked on the tiled floor.

"Now then, what have we got here? My, this is a pleasure on a Monday afternoon." Pete came towards them. "Are you on your way to the animal shelter?" He looked down at Pippa.

The animal was unsure of the tiled surface and trembled as she waited for Jo's next move.

"Have you found it wandering about?" Pete rubbed the dog's head. "It will have been abandoned by the gippos, she looks half starved."

"She's mine. She needs a new collar and she hasn't had her dinner yet," Jo blurted out. She suddenly felt protective.

Pete looked at her and smiled.

"Aye, that's it, that's all she needs." He made a serious face. "Let's see if we've any biscuits in the tin. I'll stick the kettle on and you have a look around. Hattie said you'd be in to change the Fiat and I've got just the vehicle for you, over there..."

Pete nodded across the room and went back to his office. Jo watched him walk away. Hattie! She must have phoned ahead. Jo pulled Pippa over the tiles to see what he'd been pointing at.

"Like it?" Pete asked. They stood by a gleaming dark blue BMW. He handed Jo a mug of coffee, then dug into his pocket and bought out a rich tea biscuit. Pippa gobbled it down and sniffed the tiles for fallen crumbs.

"It's only just come in. One careful owner and low mileage, bit like myself." He winked and gave Pippa another biscuit. Jo walked round the soft top saloon.

"Want a little test drive?"

Jo looked up. The last thing she wanted was to be confined inside a car with Pete and his wandering hands. "Erm, I'll have a think about it."

Jo handed her coffee to him and opened the driver's door.

"Have a sit in, get a feel for things. It's got two litres under the bonnet so you'll fly around the lanes."

Jo sat behind the steering wheel and moved the gear stick gently. She liked the polished wooden trim and the leather seats were gorgeous, very up-market. She caressed the soft hide.

Pete admired her legs.

"Come and drink your coffee and I'll get Michael to get her out of the showroom."

Without waiting for an answer, he waved at the car-washer who put down his sponge, rubbed his hands down his jacket and ran over. Pete tossed him a set of keys, then placed his hand on the middle of Jo's back and guided her into his office. Jo looked uncertainly at the car and the man who dragged the large glass doors open.

"Don't worry. He may look daft but he knows what he's doing. That's our Michael, my sister's lad, he knows more about an engine than I do." Pete installed himself at the large desk as Jo sat opposite.

A large framed image of a motor bike and rider travelling at speed, hung on the wall behind Pete. Jo looked at it with curiosity.

"TT races at the Isle of Mann three years ago. I won it." Pete leaned back in his swivel chair and laced his fingers over his chest.

"You must've seen the bunting out in Butterly. They went mental when I got back," he smiled. "I had to ride up and down the main street, did a few stunts too for the locals." He looked thoughtfully at the photograph.

Jo remembered the commotion in Butterly when rider and bike had triumphantly returned home.

Pete had proudly displayed his winner's medal and everyone turned out to wave and cheer as the local lad-made-good rode victoriously through the town. Jo had been stuck in the pub kitchen, cooking with Sandra. When they heard the roar of the bike, they ran to a guest bedroom at the front and hurled the window open to lean out and watch the display.

"You must be very brave. Isn't that one of the hardest courses?" Jo stroked Pippa's head.

"Aye, it's a tough one. You have to be mad to do it, there's nowt brave about it. Where there's no sense there's no feeling," he spoke modestly.

Jo watched his face as he talked about the race. His eyes were so blue! Like pools of tropical water, they made you want to dive in.

"So how's it going?" Pete leaned forward. "Food was great t'other night. You've made a lovely place of it."

"Thank you." Jo met his gaze. "People are being supportive, but we need to get the holiday makers in and build up bookings. We should be full, at this time of year."

"Aye, it will come once folk know you're there. Mind, with this Conservative government, things will be rough if they don't shake themselves up."

Jo looked away. She didn't want to get into a political discussion and had tried to ignore the shaky economy. Tourism had been hit and she hardly dare think about it. The last thing she needed was the government increasing interest rates. People would stay at home and save money. She'd already had to increase her overdraft facility as costs had escalated by the time she'd opened the doors. She needed working capital to keep wages paid and suppliers happy.

What the hell was she was doing here looking at a new car?

She remembered her father's words and focused her attention back to Pete. She wouldn't buy it outright. The monthly repayment could go through the business.

Pete leaned forward and stared at Jo.

"I don't want you to be worried by what I am going to say," he said.

Jo felt alarmed, whatever was he going to tell her?

"You know I think you're a grand lass. In fact I fancy you something rotten. I'd do anything to get you into bed and you'll have to forgive me if I keep trying." He smiled wickedly and Jo felt herself blush as he continued.

"I've always thought that prick of a husband was a bloody fool when he left you. But life goes on and he'll come to regret it. I told him at the time that he was making a big mistake." Pete shook his head. "So here you are and you're doing well. I want you to know that I'm your friend and if there is anything..." He leaned forward. "I'll always be here, you've only to ask."

Jo stared at Pete. She was embarrassed but felt humbled by his words.

"You don't need to say anything, but just remember I'll always be there for you." Pete scraped his chair back and stood up. "Let's get you in that motor and on your way." He waited by the side of the desk as Jo stood up.

"Thanks Pete." She could smell his aftershave and wanted to reach out and touch his soft black sweater. Hell, Jo, get out of here!

She gathered the rope, pulled Pippa to her feet and walked out of the office. She seemed to be accumulating 'friends.'

Both John and Alf had assured her of their loyalty in the last twenty four hours!

Michael was polishing the bonnet of the car with a soft yellow duster. He looked up and smiled. More blue eyes! Jo concentrated on the vehicle. The top was down and the elegant car beckoned.

"I've put a cover on the back for t'animal." Michael glared at Pippa. Pete laughed and opened the driver's door for Jo.

"Sure you don't want me to go with you?" Pete asked as he settled Jo in the front and Pippa in the back. But Jo had already turned the engine over and engaged the gears. He closed the door gently and bent down alongside the open window.

"Mind how you go. There's plenty of lead under that pedal. Not that you can't handle it I'm sure." He winked salaciously, stood back and put his hands in his pockets. "Give us a shout when you get home. If you like it, I'll sort the paper work out."

Michael watched the car move off and twisted the duster in his hand.

Pete waved as Jo pulled away, then sighed and walked back to the showroom.

Jo took a long route home. She left Marland and headed out on the bypass then turned off on a side road. The car was divine to drive. It hugged the road round bends and sped smoothly away as she accelerated.

The wind felt wonderful in her hair.

Pippa sat on the back seat and ignored the oncoming traffic as she sniffed the passing countryside, her ears flapped in the breeze.

Jo smiled to herself, the car was glorious! He's a clever sod, she thought. He knows no one in their right mind would go back to the Fiat after a couple of miles in this.

She pulled up by the castle at Hough and parked in the visitor's car park. She felt like stretching her legs and wanted to see how Pippa reacted to being in the countryside. Jo led the dog through the turnstile, to a wide-open field where the River Bevan flowed alongside. Pippa walked beside Jo and glanced up for reassurance while Jo looked around to make sure there were no sheep or people to worry about. She loosened Pippa's lead and let her off. The dog stood still. "Come on, sweetheart. Have a run." The dog was rigid.

"Come on, Pippa. It's ok" Jo bent down to stroke her and Pippa began to shake. Jo patiently encouraged her until suddenly, as if realising that she was free, Pippa took off and hurtled past Jo, knocking her off balance. Jo scrambled to her feet in panic and watched the dog race off and run around the edge of the field, barking like a maniac as she sped away. She loped across the grass, graceful in her movement and there was something else - she was happy! The dog was expressing joy and delight and Jo felt herself welling up. How stupid to feel emotional, it's only a dog! But it's a lovely dog and it needs a friend... Jo thought and as she seemed to be accumulating friends, she determined to become one.

"Pippa, Pippa!"

The dog slowed and trotted over, wagging her tail. She flopped down and licked Jo's hand.

"We'll be fine, old girl," Jo whispered.

She bent down and cupped Pippa's head, then took the rope from her pocket and slid it in place. In perfect step, they strolled back to the gleaming vehicle on the car park.

"FRIGGING 'ELL, I told him to look after you but this beggars belief! What have you promised him?"

Hattie paced round the gleaming BMW and admired the sleek body work as she stroked the paintwork and peered through the windows.

"Did he throw the dog in as well?" Hattie looked disapprovingly at Pippa, who sat on the gravel wagging her tail and looked adoringly at Jo.

"It's a business deal, nothing more, he'll be paid appropriately," Jo snapped back. "Pippa needs a good home and I've decided to give her one so don't be horrible, she's lovely." She patted Pippa affectionately.

Hattie shook her head. "I'm saying nowt," she mumbled. "You've done well with the car though. Your dad will be pleased."

They walked to the side door of the hotel where Judy rushed to greet them.

"Mrs E, the photographer's here from the Westmarland Tribune," she said excitedly. "He wants you and all the staff outside the hotel for a photo."

Jo and Hattie's eyes met.

"Shite!" They flew past Judy to reception and hurled themselves on their handbags then frantically began to apply make-up.

"Morning, ladies."

A pimply face leered around Reception.

"It's Peter Pigmy, Trevor's nephew," Hattie said. "Westmarland's answer to David Bailey. It'll be all teeth and tits in the photo. He's a slimy little devil." Hattie pushed her handbag to one side and nudged Jo.

"Morning, Peter," Hattie smiled. "You're looking as handsome as ever."

"Got you down as centre-spread Harriet." The photographer licked his lips and gazed at Hattie's cleavage where her breasts tumbled out of a tight white shirt.

"Best mind where you put the staples." Hattie reached out and tickled him under his chin.

"Have you stopped using that cream the doctor gave you?"

Hattie frowned and looked pointedly at his acne plagued face. Peter flushed and started to fiddle with the lens of a large camera slung around his neck.

"Mrs Edmonds, the paparazzi await." Hattie grinned. "Where would you like us, Peter?"

"In front of the hotel." He stormed down the hall.

"You're heartless, Hattie." Jo looked in the mirror, puckered her lips and applied lipstick.

Judy gathered the staff and everyone met in the porch. Linda and Kath from housekeeping chatted excitedly with Sandra and Michael. They were joined by Simon, Gerald and Old Johnny. Jo and Pippa stood in front of Judy and Hattie and Jo removed the rope from the dog's neck as Peter took charge.

"Say SEX!" he called out and began clicking way.

"Not with you," Hattie said loudly.

"Thanks, Mrs Edmonds." Peter glared at Hattie. "It'll be in the paper on Friday, if the supporting adverts are ready," he threw an angry glance at Hattie.

"I'll be on my way." He jumped in his car and sped off.

"Hardly the Sunday Times," Hattie grumbled.

"You could have been pleasant, offered him a cup of coffee or something," Jo said.

"Nah, he's like a leech, you'll never be rid." Hattie disappeared in the kitchen where Sandra was experimenting with a new taster course for the evening's menu – a warm asparagus soup served in a shot glass.

Jo left Pippa with Ann and Thomas and went to see how preparations for dinner were coming along. As she opened the kitchen door, Hattie and Michael spun around. Michael had a ladle in his hand

and Hattie held an empty shot glass. Her top lip was covered in green froth.

"Turning into the Incredible Hulk?" Jo asked.

Hattie wiped her mouth with the back of her hand. "It's my duty to taste everything."

"Absolutely Hattie, we don't want you wasting away." Jo turned to Sandra who shook her head. "Is everything alright, Sandra?"

"Aye, the soup is really good. Especially with some of Michael's coriander blended in, just gives it a bite."

The phone rang in reception and Hattie disappeared.

"Thanks, Sandra, I'll see you later." Jo left them to it and made her way to the house. She found Thomas crawling around the floor.

"Uff Mumma," Thomas chortled.

Ann's well-built behind stuck out from under the stairs as she folded a blanket into a large dog basket, she sat back and pulled Thomas onto her lap.

"That looks inviting," Jo stared at the box.

"I asked my brother to drop it off," Ann said. "None of our dogs use it."

The box fitted under the stairs perfectly and provided a safe, warm refuge where Pippa could watch the daily comings and goings.

"Pippa, in your box." Jo pointed at the box and Ann patted the blanket.

The dog trotted over, took a sniff, then climbed in and plonked herself down. Thomas wriggled free and snuggled himself beside her, he stroked her fur as Pippa nuzzled him in a motherly fashion.

"God, my mother would have a fit if she saw Thomas in a dog box," Jo said.

"Best make sure he's out of it when she visits then," Ann looked up, relieved that the dog had been so easily accepted.

Alf had been right.

14

The Westmarland Tribune featured a double page spread on the opening of Kirkton House. A photograph of Jo and her staff outside the hotel sat alongside the editorial, surrounded by supporting adverts from businesses that supplied the hotel.

Jo was flattered, everyone had wished her well including Mrs Brough who'd placed a large advert:

Swags & Tails of Westmarland
Wish Kirkton House Success
Proud to Supply Soft Furnishings

The photograph was pinned to the notice board in the kitchen and someone had drawn a plant on Michael's head and tassels on Hattie's bulging breasts. The article was doing wonders for bookings and the phone rang constantly with reservations for dinner.

But first there was Fair Week which was now officially underway.

Jo sat in Reception and tickled Pippa's tummy with her bare feet as the dog slumbered happily under the desk. Jo munched on a slice of toast as she worked through the bookings. Another guest who'd stayed at the pub in Fair Week had tracked her down. Jo looked at the chart and read 'Big Ken from Rye?' scrawled across four days. Judy had taken the booking. 'Says you know him...' She'd added in pencil. Jo smiled and put a confirmation tick across the reservation. Ken would require a decent bed, he was six foot four and huge. Room Nine would be perfect with its king-size bed and generous armchairs.

The kitchen door nudged open and Alf peered cautiously round the frame.

"Morning Alf," Jo didn't look up. "Have you got another mongrel tucked up your trouser leg that needs re-homing?" Jo pushed her plate away as Alf cleared his throat.

"What can I do for you?" She tapped her pen on the desk.

"Is she alright?"

"Are you referring to the dirty, half starved mongrel you left in my kitchen?"

"You need a dog."

"I don't know what makes you think I need a dog or that I can afford another mouth to feed." Jo was harsh. "I'm pleased you've come in – you can take her back with you."

She fiddled with the pen and tried to look severe but a warm tongue was gently licking her ankle. Alf heard the motion and as Pippa peeped out of her dark shelter, she recognised him and squeezed past Jo's knees to wrap round his legs then roll over, wagging her tail excitedly.

"She's settled in I see." Alf leaned down and scratched the long silky fur on Pippa's pink tummy. The dog sniffed his Wellingtons.

"She can stay for a bit, we'll see how she gets on," Jo glowered.

"Aye, alright." Alf straightened up. He was relieved that Jo had accepted the dog and nodded curtly. "Your venison's in th'out house and Sandra knows it's there." He took a last look at Pippa and disappeared through the door.

Jo set about her daily round of the hotel. Fresh flowers were arranged in large vases and sun streamed through open windows.

The smell of summer was heady.

Linda and Margaret methodically changed beds and cleared debris from the night before. They greeted Jo as she moved through the rooms and checked each detail, ready for a new batch of guests.

Sheets and towels tumbled out of the laundry room and Simon appeared on the back stairway with armfuls of table linen.

"Morning, Mrs E."

Simon dumped the napkins and cloths on the floor and grinned at his boss. "Are we going to have a busy weekend?"

"I hope so, Simon, although I don't think the gypsies will come this far out. Are you going up on the hill to have a look?" Jo reached for a laundry list.

"I'm taking my girlfriend on Sunday to have her fortune told." He began to load a large canvas bag. "She's never seen the fair before."

"Make sure you keep a tight hold on her. The gypsies love a pretty girl."

"I'll not let her out of my sight," Simon said as he secured the bag and stacked it, ready for the daily collection from Culgarth Linen Supplies.

Jo went to Room Nine and pulled out a chair. She sat down at the desk. Taking a pen and a sheet of headed notepaper from the stationery folder, she wrote a welcoming note. Big Ken would find it propped on the decanter of malt whisky. He had a farm in Rye and bred cart horses. A seasoned visitor to the fair, his interest was mainly in the trotting races.

Jo hurried through the corridor to check Room Two. She held a crystal glass to the light and wondered who'd be drinking from this tonight? Would John Doherty get lucky? She remembered his handsome face and put the glass down with a sigh. There'd be a string of local girls vying for his attention once that amazing car hit town.

The car park was full and the staff busy as they served sandwiches and drinks in the garden. Jo went to check the courtyard rooms. She stopped by the herb bed and plucked a leaf of sage. It was strong and pungent.

"Be sticking that in some stuffing later," Michael called out as he crossed the yard to the dry stores. Kirkton House was embroidered on his crisp white jacket.

"Will you make some sage bread too?" Jo asked. "Maybe with olives?"

"Aye, that'll be grand," Michael nodded.

In the coach house Kath was singing. She was on her hands and knees cleaning a bathroom.

"Morning, Kath. It's warm in here." Jo said and opened a window.

"Dunno what the guests were up to, but there's enough empty bottles to sink a ship."

Jo smoothed the counterpane on the freshly made bed. She was proud of the coach house conversion. A few months ago these dilapidated rooms had been over-run with mice. The four oak beamed rooms now had en-suites and created generous accommodation, full of character. Jo leaned out and watered the window boxes on the upstairs sills. Old Johnny had planted tubs and baskets and set them around the courtyard, where they made a colourful display.

Jo closed her eyes. Delicious cooking smells wafted over the cobbles.

"Mrs E, there's someone here to see you." Judy stood by the kitchen door, "well several people actually, the Hunts from Essex?"

"Be right down."

Jo reached for lipstick and turned to a mirror. She smoothed the velvety pink colour over her lips and looked at her reflection. Dorothy had assured her that the cerise jump suit was bang on trend for daytime and Jo loved it. Shoulder pads shaped the buttonthrough top and a wide belt made her waist look small. The trousers tapered down to her ankles and she wore matching suede pumps.

She turned to check her reflection.

Jo still wasn't used to seeing her slimmed-down figure and said a silent thank you to the competent ladies in Carlisle who'd given her confidence.

"This is it," she whispered to herself. "Fair Week starts here."

Two men sat on wrought iron chairs and admired the garden as Judy placed pints of foaming beer before them.

They saw Jo approach.

"DARLIN'!" Harry Hunt exclaimed and leapt to his feet.

"By Christ you're lookin' good." Harry opened his arms and wrapped Jo in a bear hug.

"You remember Elvis?" Harry released Jo and turned to his brother, who embraced her with the same enthusiasm.

"How are you, Elvis?" Jo said. She was delighted to see the Hunts again.

Heavy gold necklaces glinted on Harry's dark tanned chest and chunky bracelets jostled alongside a jewelled watch.

"You tracked me down." Jo smiled.

Harry grinned and flashed a gold tooth. Elvis, the image of his namesake, looked her up and down.

"She's a right peach now eh, 'Arry?"

Harry shot him a glance. "Be a bit respectful, Elvis."

"Can't think what Greg was doin' up and leaving you." Elvis shook his head, raised his glass and downed the contents.

"Business good, boys?" Jo took the empty glass. "You look like life's treating you well."

Their casual clothes reflected money and wealth. Elvis wore a cashmere jacket, designer jeans and hand-made crocodile skin shoes.

"Can't complain, darlin'," they replied.

A commotion began to spill out of the conservatory.

"Gawd, 'Arry! Thought you'd 'ave got the bubbles out by now."

Two blondes, with copious amounts of tanned flesh in tight white blouses and denim shorts, stumbled onto the patio. Their white stilettos clacked across the terrace.

"This gorgeous boy's helping us," they sniggered.

A red-faced Simon followed. He carried a bottle of Verve Clicquot in a silver ice bucket. Judy spread a linen cloth on the wrought-iron table and placed flutes beside a wine stand. Simon popped the cork and it flew across the lawn.

The girls squealed and Pippa raced to find the cork.

"Meet the gals, Jo."

Harry introduced Tracey and Stacey as Simon returned the bottle to the ice bucket and bolted for the conservatory.

Tracey and Stacey grabbed their drinks and fell about laughing.

Harry shook his head.

"Leave the boy alone. You're old enough to be 'is muvver," he said.

"It's not 'is muvver I was thinking of being," Tracey nudged Stacey. "Gawd he's handsome." She pushed Stacey onto a chair and flopped down beside her. They kicked off their shoes and flexed long legs, smothered in St Tropez Bronzing Gel.

"Watcha, Jo!" Tracey raised her glass in acknowledgement. "You can keep this coming." She downed the glass in one. Harry and Elvis rolled their eyes.

"We'll get some recliners so you girls can relax after your long journey." Jo fussed over her guests as Judy went off to find Simon, to set up the garden furniture.

"Could murder a plate of chips?" Harry and Elvis looked hopeful.

"Couple of eggs with it?" Jo smiled.

"Magic." They beamed. Jo knew that Sandra would have a fit and point at the pub over the road.

She left them to it and went into the bar.

Judy had checked another guest in and was pouring a pint of bitter. The new arrival introduced himself, his name was Bertie O'Reilly.

"I'm very pleased to meet you." Jo shook his hand. "Are you here for the fair, Mr O'Reilly?"

"Call me Bertie, won't you," he had a strong Irish accent. "Yes, I got the early ferry. I'm here for the trotting."

The horse trotting was one of the attractions of the fair and took place on the large showground by the river in Butterly.

The main event was held on Monday evening - nine heats and a final. People gathered from all over the country and huge sums of money changed hands. Carriages with two wheels harnessed to a horse, were driven by a single occupant and sped dangerously round the course. It took considerable skill to compete without mishap.

Jo asked Bertie if he'd been to the fair before.

"No, madam. Not this one, but there's plenty of trotting back home."

"Where's home Bertie?"

"I've a little place south of Dublin, overlooking the sea."

"Do you have horses?"

"I've one or two." Bertie picked up his pint and looked at Jo.

"I understand this is a busy fair?"

Jo pushed a bowl of nuts towards him. "Yes it is," she said. "The field on the outskirts of Butterly was originally known as Gallows Hill, now it's known as Fair Hill. Over the next three days you'll see horses everywhere – in the River Bevan, on its banks and roadsides or tethered outsides pubs and shops in Butterly. It's quite a sight." "And bloody dangerous!" A voice rang out.

Hattie slammed the door to Reception and joined them in the bar. Bertie munched on a handful of peanuts and looked up as Hattie entered. He smiled and held out his hand.

"Harriet Contaldo, sir." She shook his hand. "Sorry about the language but I'm not over fond of the travellers. Takes twice as long to get anywhere and the shops double their prices." She raised the hatch and stood behind the bar.

"I'm very pleased to meet you, Harriet." Bertie sipped his pint.

"Call me Hattie."

Hattie busied herself with a tray of dirty glasses. Her breasts threatened to bounce out of her tight blouse as she leaned over to place a coaster under Bertie's drink. He was mesmerised.

"Hattie will look after you, please make yourself at home," Jo said and left them to it.

Guests were ordering afternoon tea and Judy and Simon hurried about. It was an idyllic afternoon and the sun became warmer as the day progressed. The walled garden created protection from any wind and everyone relaxed in the sudden heat. Water cascaded over rocks in the fountain and glistened in the sunlight as it poured into the pool below. Plates of fluffy scones, dainty cakes and sandwiches on pretty china were relayed steadily from the kitchen to expectant guests.

The Hunt brothers ate their egg and chips, smothered in tomato sauce and the girls munched on cakes and sipped champagne, as they lay on comfortable recliners. Stripped to tiny bikinis, their skin gleamed with oil and the coconut aroma gave a continental smell to a perfect English afternoon. Harry and Elvis removed their shirts. They wore matching aviator sunglasses and supped their beer happily.

Hattie took Bertie into the garden and introductions were made. The Hunts insisted that he join them and a lively conversation about horses and fairs ensued.

The afternoon wore on.

Taking advantage of the lovely weather, Ann had set up a paddling pool on the top lawn by the fruit trees.

Shaded by a large umbrella, Thomas sat in the warm water and splashed about with his plastic pig. Pippa lay alongside. Jo decided to join them and as she sat down, she slipped off her shoes and rolled up her trousers, Thomas chortled with delight when she dunked her feet next to him.

"I've put plenty of sun cream on him, Mrs E." Ann leaned over and stroked the child's pale skin.

"He's so fair, Ann. Just like his dad." Jo thought of Greg's pale skin and hoped it was burning as he lay on a Spanish beach.

"Is there any room for a little one in there?"

A deep voice boomed up the garden and Jo spun round as Big Ken descended. His massive frame obliterated the sun.

"Ken!" Jo scrambled to her feet and threw her arms round him. "How are you?"

Ken was exactly as she remembered with a shiny bald head and large round face, his pudgy fingers were covered in gold sovereign and horse-shoe shaped rings.

"Obviously not as well as you, young lady. This place does you proud."

Ken looked around the garden. "Is this the little fella I've been hearing about?" Ken crouched down. He steadied himself and levelled his gaze at Thomas who looked at him with curiosity. Pippa sniffed Ken's legs as his huge hand engulfed her head and he scratched the dog affectionately.

"He's a grand fellow, image of his dad." Ken said.

"I'm afraid so, Ken." Jo stared at Thomas. "But how are you? How was your journey? Have you been to Butterly yet?" The questions tumbled out. Jo was so pleased to see him.

"I'll have a wander over there in a bit once I've had a pint with the lads." Ken nodded towards Harry, Elvis and Bertie who waved back and held up their glasses.

"One waiting for you," Harry called out.

"Are you ok, girl?" Ken looked at Jo with concern. He remembered her at the pub and the endless hours she'd worked. He wondered why on earth Greg had left her, with a baby too.

"Yes, I'm fine thanks. It's so good to see a familiar face."

"Always knew you were a survivor." Ken heaved his massive bulk upright. Lawn clippings clung to his moleskin trousers.

"He's a grand little lad, Jo," Ken smiled.

He flicked the clippings with his handkerchief and wiped the perspiration on his brow. "Now where's my pint? I'm gagging." Ken lumbered down the garden.

Tracey and Stacey were well into their second bottle of champagne and called out to him. Jo picked up her shoes, smoothed her trousers and bent to kiss Thomas on his wet head. She smiled at Ann.

"It looks like we're going to be busy," she said. "See you later, byebye, Thomas."

With a wave, Jo ran barefoot over the garden to take care of her guests.

15

Friday night was hectic. The restaurant filled with casual bookings and the staff re-set tables to accommodate everyone.

The Hunt party were late sitting down to dinner. Earlier, they'd taken a taxi to Butterly and joined Ken and Bertie to have a few pints with the locals. By the time they all returned, famished and very tipsy, they threw themselves on prawn cocktails and Mr Pigmy's finest steaks and ate with relish.

"Good job this menu is temporary," Sandra grumbled to Jo after she'd grilled the umpteenth steak. "Anyone would think we were back in the pub. Are they eating this late every night?"

Michael worked his way through piles of dirty pans in the pot sink and Gerald clattered about in the still room.

"Probably," Jo snapped. "You'll all get massive tips, so let's just get on with it."

"Tell her to stop moaning," Hattie washed glasses in the bar, she'd overheard the conversation. Jo straightened cushions and poked the fire then added another log. The flames leapt into life.

"Take them all a drink will you, Hattie, they've had a long day, no wonder they're grumpy." Jo looked at her watch. It was nearly midnight. The Hunts would drink till the early hours, if they ever came out of the dining room...

"I'm not complaining," Hattie filled a pint. "The tips are bloody fantastic. Every time anyone has a round, they buy one for us. They love her grub," she nodded towards the kitchen.

Jo sat down. She'd been so busy that she'd hardly eaten in the last few days and the Cointreau diet was certainly working! The black lacy dress she wore fitted her perfectly and the backless design flattered her figure. Hattie had been despatched to Mrs Sherwin's to pick up a suitable bra to wear under the dress and had returned with a complicated garment with straps that crossed at the waist. Jo didn't think the dress was suitable for work but Hattie was insistent.

"Stand out. You're not a waitress - you own the place."

Jo had given in.

Simon appeared with a tray of coffee cups and placed it on the table beside the fire. The residents in the dining room wanted coffee in the bar.

"Thanks Simon, I'll see to it." Jo arranged the cups alongside dishes of chocolate tiffin. She glanced at her watch.

"Still got one room to arrive?" Hattie asked casually as she busied herself, conscious that John Doherty hadn't shown up yet. Jo had been up to Room Two at least three times to check it, unaware that Hattie noted her absences.

The front door buzzer sounded.

Simultaneously their eyes locked. Hattie reached for a glass, poured a large Cointreau and pushed it towards Jo. They could hear loud guffaws and laughter as guests approached from the dining room and Harry and Elvis led Ken, Bertie and the girls through to the bar.

Jo downed the drink in one. She shoved the empty glass back across the bar and grimaced as the fiery liquid hit her stomach.

"I'll get the door, you see to Harry," Hattie said and disappeared.

"Finest meal I've ever 'ad," Harry bellowed. "This way ladies and gents, get comfortable, the party's just starting."

Tracey and Stacey flopped into low armchairs and Ken and Bertie settled on a sofa by the fire.

"Ease up, 'Arry, I'm knackered, I've been up since dawn."

Tracey put her feet on the table whilst Stacey tucked into the tiffin.

"Liqueurs, anyone?" Jo asked.

"Brandy all round, on me," Bertie said. "Make them large ones to be sure."

Jo slid behind the bar and searched for six brandy goblets. Where was Hattie? Who'd come in?

"Courvoisier?" She asked.

"Perfect," Bertie nodded.

"The poor lamb's tired." Hattie said as she returned to the bar. She reached for the tray of brandies. "Mr Doherty's had a long day. He's gone straight to bed, says he'd like his breakfast at ten o'clock, if that's alright with the kitchen?" Hattie raised an eyebrow and watched Jo's face fall.

"Who's for a big one?" Hattie leaned over and brushed Bertie's arm with her chest as she placed the glasses on the table.

"Be Jesus, Harriet. I'll be having a heart attack if you do that again." Bertie's face was flushed. His eyes never left her chest as he knocked back his brandy. "You can fill this up and steady me nerves."

Bertie thumped the glass back on the table and reached up to slap Hattie's bottom but she wriggled past and he slapped thin air, much to everyone's amusement.

"Whatever it takes to increase the bar takings…" Hattie whispered.

Jo shook her head. "I'll make a start on the bills."

"Fine with me unless you want to take a cocoa up to Room Two?" Hattie winked.

"Oh bugger off, Hattie. I've got work to do and this lot will see the sun up." Jo turned and flopped down in Reception.

What was wrong with her? Why was she feeling miffed that she hadn't seen John Doherty? She knew she looked good in her new dress but no doubt he'd turn up tomorrow, when she'd been mucking the fire out or sweaty from the kitchen. She flung the ledger open, reached for receipts and with a sigh buried herself in the book work.

For the next hour Hattie was hectic as the Hunts attempted to drink the bar dry.

Jo locked the safe and joined them. Bertie had fallen into a deep sleep and Ken's eyes drooped. The girls, curled up in their chairs, snored loudly.

"One each, gentlemen?" Hattie asked.

Harry lifted Tracey into his arms as Elvis scooped up Stacey and Ken took Bertie by the shoulder and wrenched him to his feet. Hattie held the fire door and watched the wobbly procession climb the stairs and disappear.

"I'll be off too, are you alright to lock up?" Hattie said as Pippa appeared in pursuit of her mistress.

"Yes go ahead. I'll not be long."

Jo watched Hattie turn the lights off and go through to the guest room in the house. She kicked off her shoes and stroked Pippa.

"You want to go out?"

Pippa scampered through the bar then disappeared in the conservatory. Jo followed her.

Suddenly, the dog started to bark.

Jo grabbed the door frame and stood still. Someone was in there!

She heard Pippa whine piteously and Jo's heart lurched. She felt sick with fear as she groped for the light switch.

Brightness flooded the conservatory and Pippa skulked towards her with her head down and tail between her legs. The dog was clearly disturbed and shook as she leaned heavily against Jo's knees.

Jo felt a cold and clammy perspiration trickle down her neck.

The air in the conservatory was icy. She flicked another switch and light poured over the garden, illuminating the still pond and silent trees.

What had scared the dog? Who or what, was in this room?

"Bit late for a moonlight walk?"

Jo gasped and spun round with her arms raised to lash out.

John Doherty stood in the doorway.

"Steady on." He raised his hands in surrender.

"Oh Christ, I'm sorry." Jo faltered. "I thought there was someone there. I was locking-up and the dog barked."

She took a deep breath and ran the back of her hand over her forehead.

"You look like you've had a shock." John stared at her pale face, her hands were shaking. "You need a drink," he said and led her through to the bar.

Jo succumbed and as she sat down Pippa, sensing security, settled by the fading fire and went to sleep.

John searched through bottles of spirit on the bar and poured a large Cointreau, then held a glass under the vodka optic and shot two measures into it then flipped the top off a tonic water and put the drinks beside Jo.

"Drink up." He splashed tonic into the vodka.

"Sorry," Jo began.

"Old places are spooky at night." John sipped his drink.

"Did you need something?" Jo wondered why he was up.

"I couldn't sleep."

"Why Cointreau?" Jo looked at her drink. How did he know she drank it?

"All girls love it. It's strong – hits the spot." He took another swig and sat back.

Jo sipped the Cointreau. Christ, he was handsome! She felt her heart pound. He wore a white shirt with the collar open and a shadow of dark hair peeped out. His neatly groomed hands cradled his drink and rested on expensively cut trousers. Jo tore her eyes away.

"Did you have a good journey?" she mumbled. She felt foolish.
John smiled and nodded. His blue eyes bore into her.

"Is your room comfortable?"

"Lovely, thanks."

She stared at his fingers curled around the glass and imagined them caressing her skin.

"I was just locking up when you startled me…"
She didn't finish her sentence.

John put his glass on the table then reached for her hand and drew her to her feet, their bodies inches apart.

She could smell his aftershave and feel his warmth. His hand was strong and as he touched her naked back, he pulled her into an embrace and kissed her.

Jo melted, any resistance drained as the kiss became harder and more urgent. She ran her hand through his thick curly hair and caressed his powerful body through the crisp cotton shirt.

John broke away. He kept a tight hold of her hand and led her through the hallway to the Red Room. It was dark, the shutters closed and as he pulled her into the room she heard the key turn in the lock. Instinctively, he led her to the largest Chesterfield and they flung themselves on it. Kissing her neck, he cupped her face whilst his other hand confidently lifted her dress over her hips and slid her lacy knickers down to toss them to one side. His hands eased her out of the top of her dress and Jo prayed he wouldn't get whiplash from the complicated fastenings on her bra, but soon forgot all concerns as he scooped her breasts and kissed them. She wanted to rip his shirt off, but restrained herself as she remembered the expensive cotton.

John pulled away and she heard a rustle of clothes. When he returned he was naked and his warm body felt wonderful as he lay beside her.

Jo closed her eyes as John's hand slid between her legs. She thought she would die as he gently stroked and discovered her secret places. She heard him sigh with pleasure as he slid into her and they moved together as one. Jo felt exhilarated as they pounded against each other and as they climaxed he cried out.

It seemed to last forever. Every inch of Jo's body felt alive and tingled as she melted into his arms.

"That was beautiful," John whispered. "I've longed to do that, ever since I kissed your floury face." He cradled her body and nuzzled into her neck.

Jo felt like the cat that had got the cream as they drifted into a deep and satisfied sleep.

Jo's BACK ACHED. She opened her eyes, suddenly aware that a faint light penetrated through the shutters.

Shit! What time was it?

John murmured and held her tightly.

Jo began to panic. What the bloody hell was she doing? Anyone could find them! She pushed him away and grabbed her clothes, then began to dress. Her stockings were laddered and her knickers lay abandoned on the rug by the fire.

"John. Wake up!" She shook him. John opened one eye and smiled. He reached out to caress her leg.

"Stop it. I've got to get dressed," Jo protested as he pulled her back into his arms and began to kiss her.

"I'm serious John. The staff will be here soon." "Let's

get in my bed." He held on but Jo wriggled away.

"Please, get dressed," she urged.

Reluctantly John stood and gathered his clothes then reached for her. Jo longed to embrace him but pushed his naked body away and peered tentatively around the door. She crept into the hall and signalled for him to hurry. At the foot of the stairs he locked her in a clinch and caressed her naked back. It felt delicious.

"See you later," he whispered as she pulled away.

Jo stopped.

"Why are you here?" she asked.

"For the fair of course." He winked.

Mesmerised, Jo watched his naked bottom bound up the stairs.

16

Two empty glasses stood beside a tonic bottle on the table in the bar. Hattie picked one up and sniffed. The dregs were sticky but there was no mistaking the smell of Cointreau.

She looked around. The lights were on in the conservatory and the fire door wedged back. Hattie opened the door to Reception and tripped over a pair of patent court shoes. She smiled and placed the shoes neatly under the desk.

Michael clattered about in the kitchen and the delicious smell of bacon reminded Hattie that she was hungry. She decided to grab a bacon sandwich before starting her shift. Hattie looked at the diary and wondered if Room Two was down for an early morning call?

Jo sᴛᴏᴏᴅ under the shower and let the hot water pummel against her skin. She raised her face to the jet and alternated the pounding stream with hot then icy spray. Her thoughts were frantic but the shower helped.

She reached for a towel and wrapped it around herself, then walked into her dressing room and picked up the dress she'd discarded moments ago.

Thank God Hattie was opening up today! It would give Jo time to clear her head and convince herself that the Red Room Romp had never happened.

What the hell was she playing at? Shagging the guests! It was unthinkable.

Jo shook the crumpled dress, reached for a padded hanger and placed it in the wardrobe. She must compose herself - she had a hotel to run! Perhaps he wouldn't remember if she didn't refer to it. Furious with herself for being so stupid, she pulled on ski-pants, leather boots and a t-shirt and went to find Thomas.

"THAT'S THE LAST BREAKFAST, MICHAEL." Hattie thrust the order for porridge and a full-house on the stainless-steel kitchen table. A very hung-over Bertie Carrington sat in the Panel Room, tucking into bread rolls and lashings of tea.

"Are you sure?" Michael said. "I'm still one short on the room list."

"That'll be Room Two. I don't think we'll be seeing him for a bit." Hattie arranged toast in a rack and handed it to Penny.

A bell rang.

Hattie told Penny to finish serving breakfast and went though to Reception, where a florist in a smart uniform placed an arrangement of flowers on the desk.

"Delivery for the Boss."

"Blimey." Hattie stared at huge bouquet of white lilies and gerberas and reached for the card. It contained a sachet of crystals but no note.

"I've just seen her pushing a pram round the village," the florist said. "Make sure you keep them cool till she sees them."

"Aye alright." Hattie snapped. She knew what to do with flowers! She wondered why Jo was out so early? Walking off a hangover or guilt?

Hattie took the flowers through to the still-room and looked around for a large vase. She filled it with water and thrust the flowers in. Ann hurried past with a basket of washing. It overflowed with small colourful socks and bibs.

"I'm going to hang this lot out in the sunshine," Ann said.

"Where's Thomas?" Hattie feigned ignorance.

"Out with his mam." Ann replied. "She looked a bit tired, said she was going to get some fresh air to wake herself up. You must've had a late night."

"Some of us did," Hattie retorted and left Ann to her laundry.

Laughter came from the Panel Room where Harry Hunt was finishing his breakfast.

He wiped bread over the bacon fat on his plate and licked his fingers with pleasure. Tracey and Stacey sat either side of Elvis who wore dark glasses and quietly sipped strong, sweet tea.

The girls were dressed in velour track suits, Tracey's bright red and Stacey's a deep emerald green.

"You look light a set of traffic lights," Ken bellowed as he stuck one of Mr Pigmy's finest Westmarland sausages into his mouth. "Elvis is the colour of piss."

"Could you speak a little lower?" Bertie whispered. He rubbed his forehead.

"Hangover, Bertie?" Hattie crept up behind him and slapped his back. Bertie's eyes popped as he thrust forward.

"Jeysus, Harriet, have some sympathy for a man," Bertie groaned, much to everyone's amusement.

"Hair of the dog and you'll be back on form." Hattie said and bustled about removing plates. "More toast anyone?"

"Only if you'll sit on me knee and feed it to me."

Bertie looked longingly at Hattie and licked his lips as he watched her move around the tables. Her breasts bounced in a white lace blouse that strained to contain them.

"I'd lose you down me cleavage and you'd never be seen again. We don't like to lose guests," Hattie smiled sweetly. "Well not before they've settled up."

Hattie left them to finish their meal and went through to reception. They'd all be heading to Butterly for the fair after breakfast, with any luck she could get up to date with office work.

The phone rang.

"Good morning, Kirkton House, Harriet speaking, how may I help you?"

Jo DRAGGED the buggy over the gravel as Pippa ran ahead. She opened the side door of the house and headed to the kitchen.

Surely she was wrong? The figure she'd just seen in a black tracksuit, jogging down the main road, was a dead ringer for John and Jo prayed that he hadn't seen her. She ran her fingers through her untidy hair as she thought about him. John had hardly broken into a sweat and Jo was amazed at his energy. She felt like she'd been run over by a bus.

Ann stood by the sink folding washing.

"Enjoy your walk? Come here my lovely little 'un." Ann reached down and lifted Thomas into her arms as Jo battled with the empty buggy. It refused to be folded.

"Yes thank you," Jo snapped as she thrust the buggy up and down. It wouldn't collapse. In frustration, she kicked it.

"Why do they have to make them so complicated?" Jo slammed it to one side.

Ann pulled a sympathetic face and made herself busy. Jo had a grump on and they'd be better off out of her way.

"Would you like a coffee, Mrs E?"

"No thanks. Sorry, I've got a headache." Jo kissed Thomas and ruffled his hair. "Would you tell Hattie I'm going to get my hair cut, I'll be back in a bit." Jo grabbed her handbag and keys from the hook behind the kitchen door. "See you later."

Ann and Thomas waved goodbye and watched the car reverse at speed as Jo headed off to Marland.

"I KNOW I haven't got an appointment and I know you're very busy, but it's only a trim, can you ask him?"

Jo pleaded with the Ice Maiden on reception at The House of Beauty. She could see that the appointment book was full but tried her hardest to get a slot with Paulie.

"He's very busy, people book months ahead. You'll have to book for another time."

The Ice Maiden dismissed Jo and turned away.

Jo felt like an idiot but she was desperate to get her hair done. She looked up at the gallery where Paulie was engrossed. In his multicoloured shirt, he strutted like a peacock as he engaged in gossip with an elderly lady.

He plucked pins from the metal rollers shrouding her head and shelled them like peas onto a trolley. Jo coughed to try and attract his attention but realised his music was playing and he couldn't hear her. In desperation she grabbed a pen from the desk and hurled it towards the gallery. It skimmed the head of his client and landed on his trolley.

Paulie spun around.

"Darling heart!" he yelled down. "Your hair's frightful, get your arse up these stairs immediately."

The Ice Maiden looked murderous. Jo grinned smugly and ran up the stairs.

"Fuck Me Sideways sweetie! What have you been doing?" Paulie called out. "You look like you've been tumbling in the hay."

A deep blush burned across Jo's face and Paulie laughed.

"Angela will finish you off, Mrs Hendry. I've an emergency to attend to." He shoved Jo into an empty chair. "Who is he?" He whispered in her ear. "Is he hot?"

"I haven't had time to come back in and see you," Jo spluttered.

"Obviously, darling." Paulie tugged at her hair. "Give me the gossip later; let's get this mess sorted first. Gown her up!"

He clapped his hands and an assistant ran forward to engulf Jo in a gown. She tucked a towel round Jo's neck and whisked her off to the back wash.

Two hours later Jo emerged from the salon and stepped out into the cobbled mews. Her hair was lustrous and shone in the sunshine.

Jo felt very indulgent and slightly guilty as she hurried back to her car.

Paulie had booked a table for dinner that night and as Jo ran past Dougie Cannon's fish counter, she made a mental note to write the reservation in the diary.

Dougie looked up and waved as he saw Jo.

"Remember me to Annie," Jo called and reminded herself to ask Hattie if he'd paid his dinner bill.

JUDY HAD LEFT a note in reception and Jo scanned the message pad as she sat at the desk. Jinny Atkinson wanted Jo to call her as soon as possible to discuss her Luncheon Club.

Jo dialled the number. Mouth-watering smells wafted in from the kitchen and reminded Jo that she was hungry.

"Hello?" Jinny answered.

"Good afternoon Mrs Atkinson, Jo Edmonds here. I understand you rang about your Luncheon Club?"

"Let me just pull over so I can hear you." Jinny made it clear to Jo that she was using a car-phone.

Ground-breaking technology! Jo thought sarcastically and yawned.

"Yes, we meet on the last Friday of the month," Jinny said. "We'll be with you in two weeks, at twelve thirty for one o'clock lunch. You can send menus to my home for approval and our club secretary will confirm numbers two days before," Jinny barked her orders.

"Thank you for the booking." Jo replied but Jinny had hung up. Jo pulled a face and replaced the receiver. She wrote it in the diary.

"Christ these are good," Hattie appeared from the kitchen.

"You've got chocolate all round your mouth."

"Better than sex these truffles," Hattie licked her lips. "Not that sex is on the menu here of course," she raised her eyebrows. "Your hair looks nice. In fact, I would say you're glowing."

"Bugger off, Hattie." Jo felt herself blush. It was typical of Hattie that she'd sussed Jo out.

Jo was damned if she was going to admit to anything.

"Nice flowers."

Hattie nodded towards the huge arrangement on the side of the desk. Jo was silent and Hattie sensed Jo's unwillingness to confide details of her nocturnal exploit. Hattie gave a shrug and went off to prepare the bar and rally the staff for the evening ahead.

Jo could only think of one person who'd send flowers. John had been out early, pounding the village roads. She felt a glow of pleasure and leaned over to smell the lilies. He hadn't turned up for breakfast but Judy had reported that she'd served John afternoon tea in the Green Room. She told Jo that he'd had a meeting with a man who'd arrived in an amazing top of the range Mercedes and they'd been deep in conversation.

Jo checked the diary to see if John had booked dinner. Nothing, he'd probably stroll in when he felt like it.

She put her pen down and went through to the bar. Her stomach growled and she thought that she should eat something. Jo caught her reflection in the mirror over the fireplace and tweaked the collar of her halter-top. She decided to apply a fresh coat of lipstick and as she reached into her pocket she realised that Hattie and Judy were gossiping in the panel room, unaware that Jo could hear them.

"No, it was Pete Vardy from Leeds" Hattie said.

"Doesn't he have car dealerships all over the country?" Judy asked.

"He's got more money than you and I can imagine. It seems our Mr Doherty does business with him," Hattie rattled the cutlery drawer.

"He's driving a Roller this time."

"Aye, there'll be some bent deal and I've got doubts about him. He might look the part but you can tell a gypo a mile away." Hattie banged cutlery onto the tables. Jo sighed as she applied the lipstick. Hattie was convinced that John was up to no good. She stepped into the Panel Room.

"Don't gossip about the guests," Jo said as Judy scurried away.

"I wasn't," Hattie replied. "Judy wanted to know about Pete Vardy." She finished laying the tables.

"Who is he?" Jo was intrigued by Pete Vardy.

"I recognised his car plate 'V 1' - I used to live in Leeds, remember?"

Hattie and Jo walked through to the bar and Hattie raised the hatch.

"Everyone knew about Pete Vardy, he's into all sorts of deals." She poured Jo a drink. "He owns most of Woodhaven, a rich residential area full of posh new apartments. Judy says he was talking to John about a property deal."

Jo felt her stomach tense nervously at the mention of John's name, all thoughts of hunger forgotten. She reached for her drink.

They heard the front door buzzer and Hattie hurried to greet new arrivals. Jo drank the Cointreau and shuddered. She loved the surge it gave as it dulled her anxiety.

"Where's our Heavenly Hostess?" A voice squealed from the hallway. Jo put the empty glass on the bar and went to greet Paulie.

"Darling! You look divine!" Paulie admired Jo's halter-neck catsuit with its tuxedo style top. "Better than the rags you wore to the salon today." He air-kissed her cheeks and introduced his partner.

"Robbie say hello to the most glamorous hotelier in the county."

A good looking man in an expensive but conservative suit bowed slightly and took Jo's hand.

"I'm very pleased to meet you," Jo said.

"The pleasure's all mine," Robbie smiled.

"Well it's usually mine actually..." Paulie spun around. "Love the threads, darling." He tweaked Jo's collar.

"That's a great suit." Jo traced the bold yellow check on Paulie's worsted jacket.

"Robbie says I look like a circus act, but I say if you've got it flaunt it and I can see you agree." He took her hand and twirled her round.

"Come and have a seat." Jo led them into the Red Room and Paulie fell onto the large Chesterfield.

Jo jack-knifed away as she thought of her nocturnal exploits and bumped into Steven, who appeared with chilled champagne.

"To your success." They raised their glasses.

"Oh my God, I never tire of champagne," Paulie smiled. "It tastes of everything wicked." He eyed Jo up and down and smirked.

Simon appeared with canapés and handed out napkins. Paulie reached blindly towards the tray, his eyes glued to Simon.

"God Almighty, Jo, where did you find those two!" Paulie whispered and strained forward to watch Steven and Simon leave the room.

"Twins! My ultimate fantasy..." He sighed, fanned himself dramatically with a serviette and leaned back.

"The staff are off the menu," Jo smiled. "With a partner as gorgeous as this why would you want to look elsewhere?"

"Don't worry, Jo, he's all talk," Robbie nibbled a canapé.

Paulie was a talented stylist but Robbie was the brains and finance behind the business.

Hattie appeared with menus and described each course. She recommended the pork tenderloin which was stuffed with fresh herbs from the garden.

In the bar Harry, Elvis and the girls enjoyed pre-dinner drinks, joined by Ken and Bertie. They cheered as Jo entered and Elvis wolf whistled.

"Have you all had a good day?" Jo fussed around removing empty glasses as she handed out menus.

"We most certainly have darlin'," Harry said. "Ken lost his shirt on an 'orse and the racing don't start till Monday." Jo smiled and began to explain the menu.

"The pork tenderloin is delicious with herb stuffing and if you want a real treat, we've hot buttered lobster with lemon hollandaise. Then there's Sandra's delicious roast duck with kumquat liqueur that melts in the mouth."

The men looked anxious.

"Of course we have chef's special, which isn't on the menu," Jo continued. "Mr Pigmy's finest twenty-four ounce T-bone steak, served with a sauce of your choice - peppered, chasseur or rich brown gravy."

The men thrust their menus down.

"Peppered and rare for me," Ken said.

"Brown gravy and medium," Harry and Elvis agreed.

"Well-done and chasseur," Bertie added.

"Lobster and chips." The girls slugged back their gin and tonics and called Simon over. "Still as 'ansome as ever." Tracey teased as Simon fled to replenish their drinks.

Jo took the order to the kitchen. She watched Sandra slap t-bones onto the stainless steel table.

"I can guess," Sandra said. "So much for the pork."

"It'll fly out as soon as the orders start. Don't worry," Jo assured her. Gerald polished glasses in the still room.

"Evening, Gerald, how's your dad?"

"All right thanks." Gerald glanced through the window where Arthur sat in his car, discreetly parked beside the coach house. He read a newspaper and Jo knew he'd be stepping in to help Gerald as things got busy.

"Are you happy in your work, Gerald?"

"Aye, I am," Gerald looked at Jo. "I love it, Mrs E."

Simon thrust through the swing doors and slapped a tray of dirty glasses down. He tutted when he saw Gerald and Jo restrained herself from kicking Simon in the shin.

"You're doing a great job, Gerald." She spoke loudly. "You're an important part of my team and I'm very pleased that you're working here."

Gerald looked up, his eyes wide.

"You'll cope without your dad soon," she whispered. "Don't worry if he helps you till then."

Gerald beamed. "Is this all you got?" He took Simon's tray. "Some of us likes being busy, you know." He flung open the dishwasher and began to load it.

Jo glanced heavenward and mouthed a thank you as she left the stillroom.

At last - Gerald was finding his confidence.

17

Hattie steered her car onto the garage forecourt and waited patiently for the queue of charabancs and four wheel drives to get their fuel. Sunday morning was normally quiet, but not today. Pete Parks must be raking it in, Hattie thought as she watched the colourful characters head off to the Fair at Butterly.

She pulled up alongside the pumps.

"You busy, Michael?" Hattie watched Pete's nephew undo the fuel cap.

"Aye, Pete's got me on the pumps. Too many of these gypos fill up and drive off or cause confusion so they can rob the shop." He returned the nozzle and took the money from Hattie.

"Hang on, Harriet," Pete ran towards her. "Got your fancy clothes on, not working today eh?"

"Just having a couple of hours on Fair Hill with the boss, I'm working later."

"Well don't believe anything Gypsy Rose tells you," Pete sneered. He was no fan of the fair. His eyes darted to the stream of vehicles. Hattie started the ignition and began to pull away but Pete leaned in through the window. He didn't want Michael to hear.

"Did she get the flowers?" Pete asked.

Hattie stopped dead.

"Did you send them?" She glared at him.

"Aye, I'm quite romantic when I want to be," Pete winked.

"You're also bloody married, Pete Parks." Hattie was furious. "She'll set her sights higher than a frolic and a fumble with you, just because you're bored at home."

Hattie revved the engine and pumped the clutch then sped away leaving Pete in a cloud of blue smoke.

Bloody men. Hattie cursed. John Doherty should have sent the flowers and Pete Parks had no right to. She'd need to be diplomatic but Jo had to know.

Right now, Jo was in La La Land, thinking that lout from Leeds was Mr Perfect. Hattie accelerated and overtook two caravans. She almost ran them off the road and an oncoming vehicle hooted and flashed its headlights at her reckless driving. Hattie responded with a two-finger gesture and put her foot down.

"I'M OFF NOW, Judy, I won't be long." Jo put her head around the kitchen door. "Make sure you keep the doors locked."

Jo wasn't taking any chances with casual visitors over the next day or two. She'd had a terrible experience last night and was resolute the guests would have to ring the bell during the Fair before being allowed in.

Jo hurried through to her house to change. Hattie would be here shortly. They were going to Fair Hill to have their fortune told, maybe they'd wander down to Butterly too and watch the gypsies prepare their horses for the trotting races.

As she dressed, Jo thought about her harrowing experience the night before…

THE RESTAURANT HAD BEEN PACKED by eight o'clock with extra tables in the conservatory. Everyone seemed to be in a holiday mood and the drinks flowed.

The menu was a success and Sandra's pork dish was the most popular main course.

Mrs Brough and her husband Ivan dined in the Rose Room. She was in a very light-hearted mood and giggled throughout her dessert and coffee.

Ivan looked bewildered.

"Never seen her so happy, by heck she enjoyed that pork," he told Jo. "My steak was excellent, but I wonder if I should've had the pork."

Peter and Isabel Gavmin had also chosen pork, followed by two portions of chocolate parfait.

As Jo served coffee, they both lunged forward and munched their way through a dish of fudge and chocolate tiffin. They seemed to think this hysterical and Isabel asked for more.

What was the matter with everyone? Jo wondered. Paulie and Robbie sat in the Rose Room and as Jo poured their wine she saw Paulie nod towards Mrs Brough.

"Blimey. She's cheerful - I'll have whatever she's having." Paulie gave Mrs Brough a little wave and she shrieked with laughter and waved back excitedly.

"That would be the pork medallions with a lovely sage and apple stuffing, served on a bed of creamy fennel potatoes," Jo said as she watched Ivan. His jaw dropped as he observed the exchange between his wife and the flamboyant hairdresser. A Cut Above had competition...

"Perfect." Paulie raised his glass and saluted the room. Robbie ordered lobster.

In the Panel Room, the Hunt party noisily told stories and cracked jokes. Ken collected the remnants of the t-bone steaks and insisted that Steven put them on one side for Pippa to enjoy later.

The evening flew by and with the last order safely in the kitchen, Jo headed for reception. She careered headlong into John.

"Table for one?" he asked. "Nice outfit." John stroked Jo's naked shoulder and smiled seductively. He leaned in and kissed her neck. Jo felt an electric shock pass through her groin and her legs began to give way. Flummoxed and terrified that anyone should see them, she waved him to a seat in the bar and thrust a menu on the table. She ran into reception.

"Hattie, please will you take that order?" Jo pleaded.

"Is there something wrong with your pen?" Hattie teased. She moved bills to one side, stood up and slowly smoothed her skirt over her hips.

"You know exactly what's wrong." Jo whispered frantically. "I can't face him, please go and see to him."

"I think he's already had a good seeing to..." Hattie picked up her order pad and disappeared.

"He's having the lobster," Hattie said when she returned. "No doubt he'll be getting something special for dessert?" She raised her eyebrows.

"No he jolly well won't." Jo felt her face burn.

"Well it's not for me to judge, but you want to be careful. He's dodgy if you ask me."

Hattie was about to elaborate but a commotion in the bar summoned them. They hurried to see what had happened. Bertie was shouting.

"Jeysus, will you look who it is!" He grabbed John and pulled him into a bear hug. "How the devil are you? Feck, but it's many a year since I last saw you." Bertie was delighted to see John. "You're doing well for yourself?"

"Can't grumble Bertie," John beamed at his old friend and reached for his drink. "Will you join me?"

"I will, I will... but why don't you join us?" Bertie looked at Hattie.

"No trouble, Bertie. I'll set a place for Mr Doherty right away." Hattie said.

For the rest of the evening Jo deliberately avoided the Panel Room, but Paulie wanted a dessert wine and Jo was summoned to assist.

He too seemed to have caught the infectious giggling bug and like the Gavmins, Mrs Brough and several residents, could barely control himself.

"Sweetheart," Paulie said as Jo approached, "something sweet for my sweet."

Robbie shook his head. "The lobster was delicious," he told Jo. They both watched Paulie who shrieked at a joke being exchanged with the next table. "He'll enjoy the Pineau des Charentes."

Jo gave the wine order to Steven and hurried away but Harry had seen her and yelled across the Panel Room.

"Come and join us, darlin'. Have a glass of John's Chablis and get the weight off your feet. Doesn't she look gorgeous in them trousers?"

Jo wanted the ground to open and swallow her. John sipped his wine; his blue eyes sparkled in the candlelight as he watched her.

"Perhaps later Harry," Jo said and fled from the room. Christ she needed to pull herself together! She may as well have 'shagged' imprinted on her forehead. She hurried to oversee the guests having coffee and busied herself making conversation before wishing them goodnight as they departed for home or retired to their rooms.

She was in the Green Room rearranging cushions when the front door opened. She realised that she'd forgotten to lock it after she'd bundled the giggling Gavmins into a taxi and hurried into the hall. Two men stood by the door.

"Can I help you gentlemen?"

The scruffy individuals swayed slightly. Both stank of sweat, stale beer and cigarettes.

"You certainly can, Mrs."

The older man lunged forward and Jo jumped back in panic. Everyone was busy in the restaurant and had no idea of her situation. She eyed the heavy brass bell on the table and wondered if she could reach it, but the man had seen her glance and grabbed her arm. He shoved her into the Green Room and slammed the door behind them.

"Get off me!" Jo shouted and tried to free herself.

"We heard you ran this on your own," he said. "Now be a good gal and get us something to see us on our way." He tightened the grip on her arm. "Something really valuable..."

Jo was terrified. Frantic, she glanced around looking for a means of escape.

"My mate has itchy fingers..."

The younger man reached in his pocket and Jo glimpsed a flash of steel – a knife! He laughed as he wandered around the room then picked up a vase, turned and threw it against the fireplace. The vase crashed against the tiles and shattered. "Hurry up. I've got clumsy hands," he looked for another object.

"Leave it out." Distracted, the older man loosened his grip.

Jo seized the opportunity and pulled herself free but both men had their backs to the door and she had no way of escape.

Oh Lord, please don't let them hurt me! She thought of Thomas and his angelic face as the two brutes came closer, their foul aroma made her cringe. Jo realised that they were enjoying themselves. She reached out blindly and prayed that she'd connect with something to hurl at them.

"Looking for something, lads?"

Ken's deep growl pierced the room. The men spun around and Jo saw the knife gleam. She screamed. Ken leapt forward and with a sickening crack, grabbed the man's arm and knocked him down. The knife fell and the man cried out as his partner bound over a chair to make his escape but crashed headlong into Harry, Elvis, Bertie and John. They pinned him to the floor in a flash.

"You've broken my arm!" the older man howled. Elvis kicked him and he writhed in agony.

"Let's get you on your way," Ken said. The men were wrenched to their feet and shoved through the hall then thrown out onto the drive.

"Don't come anywhere near here again!" Ken towered over them. "D'you hear me?" he bellowed. The men were terrified and realised they'd made a terrible mistake. "You're not welcome and you'll be best advised not to come back!" Ken stood firm. Harry, Bertie and John made a formidable wall beside him.

"Sorry, mister, sorry!" The men scrambled to their feet. Elvis ran forward and aimed a kick, but missed and fell flat on his back as the men sprinted away.

"Still got a pint on the table haven't we lads?" Elvis lay on the gravel and grinned while Ken tugged him to his feet.

"Bleedin' hoodlums," Ken mumbled as they all returned to the hotel. He stooped to pick up the abandoned knife and buried it deep in his trouser pocket.

Hattie stood in the doorway.

She hurried everyone inside and locked the door. John held Jo in his arms and soothed her, she was shaking.

"You alright, darlin'?" Harry asked Jo. "That bastard hurt you?"

"I'm fine, Harry." Tears threatened but Jo didn't want to cry. "I don't know how to thank you all."

"They won't bother you again," Ken said. "I can assure you of that." He glanced at John. Their eyes locked and John nodded.

"I think we all need a drink." Bertie took control. "Set them up Harriet." He ushered everyone into the bar but stopped and shook his head when he got there. In the middle of the floor, Pippa crunched her way through a t-bone. Her tail thumped against the carpet when she saw them.

"Some guard dog you are." Ken smiled and leaned down to tickle the dog's ears.

"Have we missed something?" Paulie appeared. He was linked to Tracey and Stacey and as they fell into the bar, they hooted with laughter. Harry shook his head. Robbie followed with the remaining guests and they all sat down.

Seeing a full bar, Hattie rubbed her hands and positioned herself behind the counter.

"Ok, what's everyone drinking?" she beamed at Bertie, who fell over Pippa in his hurry to order a pint...

Jo SHUDDERED as she remembered the attack. It was a stroke of luck that Hattie had heard the front door and when she saw the men push Jo into the Green Room, Hattie had raced to fetch Ken.

Make-up was strewn across the table and Jo stared at the array of bottles and tubes. She turned when she heard a knock on the door and Hattie bustled in.

"Why are you knocking?" Jo asked.

"Never know what I might find." Hattie thrust her bag down and wrestled her arms out of her jacket.

"There won't be further shenanigans with Room Two if that's what you mean." Jo selected a tube of foundation. "After witnessing the silent code that passed between them all last night, it makes me wonder who the hell I've got staying under my roof."

"He's a gypsy, make no mistake." Hattie flopped down on the window seat and put her feet up. She stretched her legs. "He'll have got word to the boss man on the Hill about the trouble last night."

Jo stared out of the window. John's expensive car gleamed in the sunshine.

Hattie was probably right.

John had slipped out last night when everyone was drinking in the bar and Jo didn't know what time he'd eventually come back.

"He's obviously made good but you wonder what it took to get him there?" Hattie mused as she watched Jo put her make-up on. "They're thick as thieves," Hattie said. "The Hunts, Ken, Bertie and certainly His Lordship can all trace their roots back to Romany stock, they've a bond."

"The unwanted visitors realised that too," Jo said and knew that word would have spread on the Hill that Jo had protection from their own.

"You'll not have any more trouble." Hattie yawned and folded her arms.

"I can't fathom why Pete Parks sent me the flowers." Jo felt Hattie's grim mood and changed the subject as she smoothed foundation over her skin, then rummaged around the make-up and found a compact.

She flicked it open and dabbed translucent powder on her nose.

"Because he's a stupid twit who thinks he can always get what he wants," Hattie said crossly. She remembered Pete's bemused face as she'd left him choking in diesel fumes.

A mini bus pulled onto the drive and Hattie watched Harry, Elvis and the girls climb into it. Harry patted Tracey's behind, clad in tight white jeans. Bertie and Ken joined them and the vehicle set off for Butterly.

"Are you alright, Hattie?" Jo asked cautiously.

"I'm fine," Hattie snapped. She watched Jo apply lipstick.

"You weren't too late last night?" Jo had left Hattie to lock up.

"Not if you can call two o'clock early," Hattie shrugged.

"What is the matter?" Jo had never seen Hattie so grumpy and wondered if she'd upset her.

"Oh I don't know. It's hard to fathom men, isn't it?"

"Are you referring to any particular man?"

"No one ever pays me so much as a glance."

"Bertie would give his right arm to get a kind word from you." Hattie stared incredulously at Jo.

Bulls Eye! Jo smiled. Hattie was smitten with Bertie.

"He's always too pissed to notice me." Hattie looked desolate.

"He's probably pissed because you're so horrible to him."

Jo gathered her make-up and stuffed it into her bag. "Come on. Get your miserable arse in gear. Let's get up to the Hill and see what Gypsy Rose and her buddies have to say, we could both do with a look into the future."

Hattie picked up her jacket.

"You won't need that," Jo said. Get your buttons undone and strut your stuff."

Hattie glanced at her neckline.

"Aye, you're right," she said and looked Jo up and down. "You look like a bleedin' gypsy in that get up."

"Is that a grin I see on your miserable face?" Jo smiled and slipped her feet into gold high heels.

"Dorothy would have a fit if she saw you."

"Dorothy is the last person we'll see on the Hill." Jo tweaked the tight, animal print Capri pants with matching top. "I couldn't resist, Hattie, it cost a fortune." She twirled and put her sunglasses on her head. "I feel so sexy in it."

"Hardly a Country House Hotelier." Hattie shook her head.

"Oh come on, loosen your buttons and get in the car. Let's escape from here for a couple of hours."

Jo pushed Hattie out of the door.

The sun was shining as they ran across the gravel to the BMW. Jo climbed in. She pressed a button and the canvas roof folded back.

Someone tapped on a window and Jo looked up to see John in Room Two, his knuckles poised on the glass. She was tempted to abandon the car and rush up the stairs into his arms but looked away and revved the engine.

"Come on, get in." Jo yelled to Hattie, who gripped her bag and flung herself onto the passenger seat. Jo thrust the car forward and narrowly missed John's gleaming vehicle as Hattie slammed the door and the car gathered speed.

Jo roared out of the drive.

"See you!" She waved in John's direction and they both giggled like school girls as they hurtled off along the main road to the Fair.

18

Hattie wriggled uncomfortably on a plastic-covered floral banquette. She sat inside a large chrome caravan, surrounded by cut glass ornaments and gleaming chinaware.

"I see a man from over the water. He speaks in a different way but you'll know what he means." Gypsy Rose spoke.

The wizened old lady cradled a crystal ball in her gnarled hands. Hattie stared at the translucent skin, blue veins like ribbons of ink bulged beneath the aged membrane.

On the other side of the caravan, Jo sat by the door and made a face as Hattie shot a nervous glance towards her.

The old woman put the crystal ball in a velvet pouch and pushed a pack of playing cards across the table. "Shuffle these an' give me three. Make a wish on yon last un."

Hattie gently moved the cards up and down between her fingers. She was useless at shuffling and half the pack fell to the floor. As she leaned under the table to pick them up, she made a rude gesture at Jo, who giggled and turned away.

The windows in the caravan were closed and the atmosphere was dim and stuffy, it smelt of camphor. Hattie felt hot and uncomfortable as she wiped her brow and returned the cards to the table.

"Gypsy Rose sees your sadness," the old lady began. "But he was a wrong 'un and you'll find love again."

Hattie leaned forward and focused. The Italian Stallion was certainly a wrong 'un and Hattie wondered what was coming next.

"He's gone. You'll not see him again. There's no money from him but money don't make you happy girl and you can earn your own way."

Hattie wished there was less emphasis on her earning her own way and sighed as she watched Jo lean forward, suddenly interested in the reading.

"You've bonny boys," Gypsy Rose continued. "One will stay close, he's like his mammy. T'other will work with flames but he'll come home safe."

The old lady sat back. She was tiny against the large pieces of Crown Derby displayed in a glass cabinet, the rich red and gold tones of the smooth china warmed her deathly pale skin. Hattie fiddled with a lace runner on the arm of the banquette and passed Gypsy Rose another card.

"I see lots of folk, eating and drinking." The gypsy held the card up. "You work hard but there's one who has the eye only for you." She gazed at the King of Clubs. "He loves only you and there'll be money."

Hattie handed over the third card and made a silent wish. Gypsy Rose's expression changed. She stared at the card then pushed it back in the pack.

"What does it say?" Hattie asked. The old lady had moved the cards off the table and seemed to be in a hurry.

"Nothin', it don't say nothin', your reading's over."

Hattie was puzzled but reached for her purse. Gypsy Rose looked at her watch and reached for Hattie's hand. She gently stroked it and shook her head.

"That'll be twenty." She took the money then dismissed Hattie and nodded to Jo to take her place.

"I'll come back later," Jo stood up. She couldn't wait to get out of the caravan.

It was hot and oppressive and she wasn't comfortable with Hattie's reading.

Hattie hurried ahead and ran out into the sunshine.

"Take care of 'er, she'll need it," the old lady whispered and Jo felt a chill run down her spine. "An' you watch for the one with the blue eyes!"

Jo clattered down the metal steps towards a queue of people waiting to go in. She spotted Simon with his girlfriend.

"Got the winning pools numbers Mrs E?" Simon called out.

"It's all a load of nonsense," Jo told him. She forced a smile and gripped Hattie's arm.

"Well you're all gas and gob." Hattie pulled a face. "What's with the sharp exit, too near the knuckle?"

"You could say that." Jo steered Hattie past a group of children who held out bunches of lucky heather for a pound a piece. "At least you've got love and money to look forward to." Jo pushed her sunglasses on. "I should've asked her about the strange atmosphere in the conservatory, but I'm not sure I want to know."

"Aye, there's something odd in there." Hattie replied. "And it's no surprise that you've got to watch out for blue eyes..."

"Oh Hattie every man in Cumbria seems to have blue eyes, she's hardly Miss Marple is she?"

There were travellers, traders and tourists everywhere. Hundreds of caravans shimmered in the heat as the girls wound their way through the colourful crowds. Fair Hill was dry and dusty from endless hordes of traipsing feet but everyone seemed to be enjoying themselves.

The fair attracted up to thirty thousand visitors each day and was loud and chaotic. Children chased each other and shouted out, some were barefoot. Goods of every size and description were for sale lucky brass horse-shoes, lace table cloths, fancy china and glassware, pottery, gifts and crafts. Several old-fashioned horse-drawn caravans clustered together around a camp fire. Brightly painted utensils – kettles, dishes, troughs and mugs were displayed and folk haggled until a deal was done.

Hattie and Jo soaked up the atmosphere as they strolled down the hill and headed towards Butterly.

"High heels were a mistake," Jo complained. She wished she'd worn something flat.

They reached Flashing Way on the main road to Butterly. It was closed to allow sellers to display their horses to potential buyers, by trotting them back and forth along the busy roadway in front of groups of men who discussed the merits of the finest piebald and skewbald gypsy cobs.

"Watch where you're walking." Hattie jostled Jo around mounds of dung which littered the tarmac.

They watched in fascination as the sellers enthused over the quality of their horses, all talking excitedly about the markings and grace of the beasts that clattered up and down the road.

"I can't understand a word they're saying," Jo whispered as they watched a handsome young man roll up his sleeves to begin trading formalities with a bare-chested older man, who wore moleskin trousers and braces. The men bartered over a fine black and white mare. Both looked hot, sweaty and intent on a deal.

"It's Romany," Hattie explained as they listened to the fast, harsh dialect.

The men eventually agreed a price then slapped each others hands several times before exchanging a pile of notes. The younger man handed back twenty pounds.

"That's luck money,'" Hattie said. "It's part of the deal and has to be returned to the seller, to ensure good luck for the horse."

A procession of horses trotted down to the banks of the River Bevan, which flowed in a u-shape around the town.

There were horses everywhere - in the river, on its banks, along the roadside and tethered outside pubs and shops.

Men and boys, naked from the waist up, stood in the deep muddy river and groomed the horses ready for trading. Mothers with children sat in the sunshine and groups of young women paraded up and down, dressed in their finest, most colourful clothes.

The gypsy girls wore short skirts, tight leggings and skimpy tops, teamed with high heels and an abundance of gold jewellery. They flirted outrageously with the men, who preened and showed off their horses - riding bareback at speed down the road as tourists leapt out of their way.

The fair was a huge courting arena for unattached gypsies and many met their future partners there.

Outside the Blacksmith Arms a noisy group supped pints of cold beer.

"Well bugger me, look whose over there," Hattie said. She looked over the road where Ken, Bertie and the Hunts stood in the sunshine and enjoyed the vibrant atmosphere. Jo lifted her sunglasses and squinted in their direction.

"Come on, I fancy a beer."

Jo grabbed Hattie's arm and looked in either direction then jostled them through the mass of people and horses. They ran as a horse and rider thundered down the road, oblivious to the mayhem he was causing.

"Bleedin' hell!" Hattie screamed. She narrowly avoided a collision, lost her footing and stumbled.

Bertie heard her cry and spun around. Seeing Hattie career towards him, he opened his arms and caught her as she fell. He scooped her up and plonked a kiss on her lips.

"Jeysus, Harriet," Bertie cried out. "Will you take care of yourself, feck you could have been killed." He pulled her roughly into his arms away from the horses and held her tightly. Hattie, shocked by the kiss, pulled back. A blush burned up her neck and spread along her cheeks.

"But you look even prettier when you blush, so you do." Bertie smiled and proceeded to kiss her again. Jo watched with amusement as Hattie hesitated then returned the kiss, to a roar of approval from Ken, Harry and Elvis.

"Bout bleedin' time." Tracey and Stacey squealed and clapped their hands.

"That calls for a drink. What are you having, girls?" Harry asked then disappeared into the crowded bar.

Bertie held his arm protectively around Hattie and turned to Jo. He looked her up and down.

"Dear God, you'll be driving these fellas crazy in that get up." He admired Jo's outfit and looked longingly at Hattie's cleavage.

"Did your mammy never tell you girls to wear a vest?" Bertie sighed and shook his head.

Hattie wasn't listening. She was mesmerized by a magnificent horse coming toward them. The crowds parted as it was led down the road.

Jo turned to see what Hattie was staring at. John Doherty's eyes were shaded by expensive Ray-Bans but he wore a cocky grin as he held the reins of a beautiful dapple grey mare.

The horse held her head high, she was aloof to her surroundings and walked arrogantly beside her master.

They stopped in front of Jo.

"Fancy a ride?" John lifted his sunglasses. Jo felt her heart miss a beat as his blue eyes met with hers.

"I don't ride," she replied and instantly regretted her words.

"Not what I've heard..." Hattie whispered. She extricated herself from Bertie's embrace and took a glass of ice cold lager from Harry.

John and Jo gazed at each other and he stroked the bruise on her arm.

"You won't have any trouble at the hotel again," John said and brushed his fingers gently along her cheek. Jo wanted to lean forward and kiss him, the rhythmic stroking aroused her and she had to stop herself from reaching out. Her heart banged in her rib cage as John's fingers traced a path around her neck...

"Fine beast you've got there," Ken interrupted. He ran his hand over the mare's back, appreciating the strong muscled body as the horse sniffed curiously around his face. "Selling her?" Ken asked.

John reached took Jo's hand and gave it a squeeze.

"No, she's not for sale and never will be." He looked at his horse with pride. "She'll be racing tomorrow. Make sure you bet on her." He spoke with quiet confidence.

"What's her name?" Jo asked.

"Mirabelle the Magnificent," John smiled. Jo felt her whole body turn to jelly and she longed to kiss him. Hattie sensed the electricity and nudged Bertie.

"That didn't touch the sides, are we having another?" Hattie held out her glass. Bertie was engrossed in the horse.

"It's my round I think." Bertie tore himself away. He gave Hattie a kiss on the cheek and laughed as she blushed.

Bertie collected their empty glasses and headed to the bar.

Harry and Elvis patted the horse too and John turned to answer their questions. Hattie shuffled Jo to one side.

"Why don't you just shag him standing up against the horse?" Hattie hissed.

"Oh you can talk, Bertie can barely bloody walk he's got such a hard on," Jo snapped back.

"I didn't know he was going to make a grab for me."

"You hardly shoved him off - sure you didn't fall on purpose?"

"Listen to the kettle calling the pot." Hattie raised her eyebrows and nodded towards John. Hattie and Jo glared at each other then both began to giggle. They huddled over as their laughter became uncontrollable.

"You couldn't write this lot could you." Hattie shook her head and punched Jo on the arm. "Just be careful with him."

"I should say the same to you." Jo winced and rubbed her arm. "But somehow I feel you're safe with Bertie."

Bertie returned with a tray of beer, his face deep in concentration as he endeavoured not to spill a drop. Hattie looked at him with affection.

The men turned from the horse and reached for their drinks.

"Will you be having one, John?" Bertie asked.

"No, maybe later."

John tucked his sunglasses into his shirt pocket and locked eyes with Jo. He raised his eyebrows and smiled. Jo sipped her drink and spattered the foam as his innuendo registered. She'd swallowed the wrong way and began to choke. Bertie rushed to slap her back and take the glass from her. Bent double from

Bertie's slap, Jo grabbed Hattie by the arm and hurried to the ladies room.

"Jesus, you've got it bad." Hattie rubbed Jo's back as she stood over the sink.

"Have I ruined my make-up?" Jo stared at the cracked and misty mirror.

"Nah, you're perfect – just horribly besotted with a bad 'un. It'll pass when he's gone. It's the getting there that bothers me."

"You're right, Hattie. I'll never see him again after the Fair and I've got a business to run. I'm being stupid. I think I should get back to the hotel and see what's happening."

Jo rinsed her hands and ran her fingers through her hair as Hattie leaned into the mirror and applied a lipstick.

Jo reached out and took it off her then smoothed it over her own lips. They stood back and assessed themselves.

"Not bad for two down trodden divorcees," Hattie said.

"We'll pass muster," Jo replied. "You stay a while and enjoy yourself with Bertie. I'm going to head back." Jo picked up her bag.

They pushed through throngs of inebriated bodies in the bar and stepped out into the sunshine.

John had gone and Bertie beamed as he watched them approach.

"See you all later," Jo called. She thrust her shoulders back and swung her handbag onto her shoulder, then walked purposefully off to find her car in the field beyond the hill.

"She'll never get there in one piece," Harry and Elvis said in unison, eyes glued to Jo's retreating bottom.

Bertie nodded as he watched Jo disappear into the crowd.

"Greg was an idiot." Ken shook his head.

"Must be my round, lads?" Elvis rubbed his hands together and gathered everyone's glasses. "All the fun of the fair, eh?"

Jo wandered back to her car. She was troubled for she knew that Hattie was absolutely right.

John was completely unsuitable and would only cause her anguish. But she couldn't help the way her heart ignited and sent shock waves to every part of her body whenever she saw him and was certain he knew how she felt.

It was so long since she'd felt like that and she realised that she'd stopped thinking about Greg. Just as well, Jo thought as she doubted that she'd ever see Greg again.

She looked around. It was such a glorious day and she would have liked to stay with the others at the pub but she must get back and focus on the business of running a hotel. The Fair would be over in a couple of days and life would return to normal.

John would be gone. She mustn't make a fool of herself. It had been a stupid mistake.

She mustn't repeat it!

Jo made a resolve to ignore his advances and focus on her work. She quickened her pace. She'd had a narrow escape last night and must make sure that the doors remained locked during the Fair.

Thank God Ken and everyone had been there, who knows what might have happened! But somehow she knew it wouldn't happen again – John had reassured her of that today.

Jo pushed through the crowds. She was jostled as men shouted and called out as they paraded their horses and looked for buyers. They laughed and swore in the searing, dusty heat and made suggestive remarks as Jo passed.

No wonder the locals disliked the fair so much, Jo thought, the town was completely disrupted. Their idyllic country life was turned upside down by this mass invasion of a culture very alien to the day to day comings and goings of Westmarland folk.

With relief, Jo found her car and threw herself into it. She opened the top and started the engine, then slowly edged off the field. Life will soon be back to normal she assured herself.

Simon and Penny served afternoon teas to new residents while guests enjoyed drinks on the patio, in the sun-drenched garden. Judy sat in reception and made a list for the dining room that evening. She looked up as she heard Jo come in.

"Good time on the Hill, Mrs E? By heck your outfit's a cracker, I'm surprised you're back in one piece." Judy admired Jo's outfit.

"I left Hattie in the arms of an amorous Bertie," Jo said and leaned over the desk to look through the diary.

"Well I never," Judy said. "Good old Bertie."

"Let's just hope she comes back, she's on duty at six."

They could hear a man talking in the kitchen and both turned to investigate.

"And I said 'that's no gypsy – that's my mate Jo.'" Alf had his back to the door as Jo stepped into the kitchen. Oblivious to her presence he continued. "By heck you should have seen her outfit; she looked like a sexy snake winding down the Hill."

"And she will start hissing if you don't get your backside out of here and let Sandra get on with some work." Jo looked stern as Alf spun around.

"You want to be careful in that get up. I hear them gypos were about to smuggle you away." Alf shook his head.

"The only smuggling round here is your illicit contraband. I have to convince myself it started life honestly."

Jo looked at a haunch of venison lying on the stainless-steel table.

Four large salmon gazed lifelessly alongside - their silvery blue bodies plump and shimmering.

"I expect you'll want cash for that lot?" Jo asked. She nodded to Judy who went to find some notes.

"Very kind, Ma'am," Alf touched his cap and bowed. "I'll be on me way, mind how you cook that beast," he reprimanded Sandra. "You buggered it up with that crumbly crap, leave it be this time." Alf took the money from Judy's outstretched hand and folded it into his pocket.

As he turned to leave, Michael appeared with a large basket filled with herbs.

He set it down by the sink and separated the foliage, then placed a bunch on the table while Sandra poked the venison.

Alf picked up some of the leaves.

"The venison will have a sauce of juniper, red wine and Dijon mustard," Sandra announced as she planned her recipe.

"Delicious and will you add some of Michael's lovely herbs," Jo said.

With a clatter, Sandra lifted a large roasting tray from under the table and thrust the salmon towards Michael.

"Stop fanning around with them herbs," Sandra told Michael. "Make yourself useful with a knife and get filleting these buggers." She swiped out with her tea-towel and Michael dodged away.

Alf, meanwhile, held a bunch of herbs to his nose and pinched the leaves. He sniffed and wrinkled his brow.

"You'll be sending folks to the funny farm if you cook with these." Alf made a face and thrust the leaves back in the basket.

Jo felt the hairs on the back of her neck stand up as comprehension dawned. Her mouth went dry and she felt her forehead pulse. Visions of the giggling Gavmins flashed through her mind as they scoffed chocolate tiffin by the plateful. She could see Mrs Brough falling around the dining room in hysterics with Paulie and numerous equally hysterical residents.

The tick from the clock on the wall sounded like oncoming thunder as the kitchen fell silent.

They turned to Michael. His eyes darted nervously from one to the other, then quick as a flash, he lunged forward and grabbed the herbs to thrust them into the waste disposal unit, snatching frantically at the switch to crunch them down the drain.

But Alf got there before him and wrenched Michael's hand away. He twisted his arm behind his back.

"God Almighty!" Sandra roared.

She held the venison haunch in one hand and blood dripped onto the kitchen floor. Michael's face was contorted in pain as he tried to wriggle from Alf's grasp, but Alf held firm and looked at Jo. "Out..." Jo uttered. "Everything out... NOW!"

Alf held Michael and with his feet barely touching the floor the chef was manhandled through the kitchen and marched up the yard to his caravan. The three women watched in silence, stunned by the realisation that Michael had been growing marijuana and unknowingly they had drugged their guests with his home-grown weed!

Jo closed her eyes and gripped the kitchen table. When she opened them Judy's face was white and Sandra looked like she was about to explode. They looked up the yard and watched Michael remonstrate furiously. Alf had flung the contents of the caravan to the ground and hurled suitcases at Michael's feet.

Sandra bit her lip. She wrenched the knife drawer open and picked up a machete then threw the venison onto a chopping board and swung the knife in a wide arc. It smashed the haunch in two. Blood splattered and two specks landed on her nose. She looked up.

"If he comes in here again, it'll be his head on this board," Sandra said. "Not a word to anyone, Mrs E. And you too, Judy." She glared at Judy.

"We'll say he's gone 'cause of the drink." Sandra shook her head in disbelief. "I blame myself - I should have known he was doing something stupid, spending all that time in the greenhouse."

"The only person to blame is me," Jo said. She began to make plans. "Judy, can you step in here for now?"

Judy nodded and reached for an apron. She thrust it over her head and tied the strings around her waist. The reception bell rang and the women looked at each other.

"Not a word," Sandra said. Each nodded and made their pact, then moved swiftly about their business.

19

Jo glanced at the clock on the hall table. Panic clutched vice-like across her chest as the clock struck seven o'clock.

Where on earth was Hattie?

A couple approached in search of pre-dinner drinks and Jo guided them into the Red Room and settled them in a corner by the window. She took their bar order and drummed her fingers on her order pad, as they chattered about their day at a Beatrix Potter Exhibition and their huge collection of Peter Rabbit plates.

The front door sounded as more guests arrived for dinner. Jo extricated herself politely and went in search of assistance.

The place was filling up. She gave the bar order to Steven and looked around for Simon. He appeared from the garden with a large tray of dirty glasses.

"Simon, can you see to Reception please?"

"I'll just put these down."

He disappeared into the kitchen and seconds later, Jo heard a monumental crash and curses as the bell on the hall table rang and the front door buzzer sounded again. Harry Hunt came in from the garden and held out two empty beer tankards.

"Are you busy, darlin'?" he asked.

Jo was unsure what to do first. Angry voices could still be heard in the kitchen and guests approached from the hallway.

"I'm never too busy for you, Harry." Jo took the tankards from his large beefy hands and indicated to Steven to take over as a red-faced Simon appeared from the kitchen.

"Sorry, Mrs E," he rushed to assist Jo. "Judy's all over the place and that idiot Gerald knocked into me." Jo forced a smile.

Poor Judy had been plunged in at the deep end, but the guests came first and Jo motioned to Simon to attend to reception.

Where the hell was Hattie?

Jo took a couple of orders through to the kitchen and didn't linger. In the absence of Michael, Sandra was struggling to cope with a multitude of tasks and Judy was struggling to keep up.

Bertie strolled into the bar. He seemed very pleased with himself and whistled as he looked around, then asked where everyone was. Jo pointed to the garden, where the Hunts sat on the terrace with Ken, enjoying drinks in the evening sunshine.

Bertie politely thanked her and disappeared through the conservatory. Jo wanted to call after him and ask if he knew where Hattie was but restrained herself. She'd a damn good idea! Starting with Bertie's bedroom... Jo sighed and went to take more orders.

As she hurried through the panel room, Jo noticed the door to her house slowly creak open and Hattie peeped through. Unaware that Jo was watching, Hattie checked to see if the coast was clear then slipped into the room. She closed the door and smiled at the seated diners.

Jo stopped in her tracks.

Hattie was wearing Jo's black two-piece suit and her chest spilled out of the jacket, while the skirt strained across her hips. She wore a pair of Jo's court shoes and wobbled precariously as she moved through the room. Jo stepped forward and Hattie ricocheted into her.

"Shite, didn't see you there..." Hattie mumbled. Jo glared at Hattie's chest - a strawberry-coloured bruise marked her creamy skin.

"Been bitten?"

Hattie coloured.

"Only two hours late and you've found yourself a lovely new outfit?" Jo looked Hattie up and down. "It's like a bloody knocking shop in here. Do you think you could join us? We could do with a hand."

"I left my uniform at home, I didn't realise I..." Hattie's voice trailed off.

Jo placed her hands on Hattie's shoulders and turned her in the direction of the garden, then shoved her forward.

"You didn't realise you'd be shagging all afternoon? The Guests!" Jo hissed, but smiled as Hattie tottered away on unfamiliar heels. Jo wasn't in the least angry with her - she was grateful that Hattie had turned up. The bell rang in reception and with much relief Jo went to attend to it.

BOTH DINING ROOMS had filled up as the evening wore on and guests were animated. There'd been an almighty fight on Fair Hill that afternoon and everyone discussed the gypsy brawl. The sons of two disputing families had vied with each other and in time honoured tradition, the only way to sort the matter out was by bare knuckle fighting until either party gave in. But the fight had brutally escalated and the police had no control over it. Tourists stood aghast as limbs were broken and body parts severed.

It was only resolved when the head of the gypsies stepped in and fought until the opposing families could fight no more. The fight left a trail of carnage - much to the delight of the fair-goers, who were thrilled to lay claim to being there and would discuss the matter for years to come.

Hattie had got her act together and worked hard alongside Jo as the guests enjoyed Sandra's delicious drug-free food accompanied by plenty of wine. Whilst the contented diners sipped coffee and afterdinner liqueurs, Jo and Hattie sat in reception and went through the bills.

"I thought you were mad at me." Hattie ate a chocolate dessert and handed Jo the bar receipts.

"Hardly, I was relieved to see you, even though you look ludicrous in my suit. You'd better not burst the stitching." Jo glanced at Hattie's thigh where the fabric strained.

"I can't believe Michael had everyone stoned." Hattie shook her head.

"We must keep it to ourselves. Sandra would kill me…" Jo looked at the diary. "I see Mrs Brough has booked a table for next week and the Gavmins are in again tonight."

"They're back for more feel-good-fayre," Hattie giggled. "I hope you've destroyed all the plants?" She finished her dessert and pushed the plate to one side. "Where've you packed Michael off too?" She asked as she examined her chest then dabbed at the love-bite with make-up.

"Alf packed all Michael's stuff up and drove him to the station."

Jo watched the mark on Hattie's neck disappear.

"I gave Michael a month's wages and Alf made sure he was on the first long distance train," Jo said. "Alf's dug all the plants up and put them in the incinerator. He's a saint."

Hattie brushed translucent powder over her bruise, taking care not to get any specs on the lapels of the black suit.

"Are you and Bertie an item?" Jo asked.

"Oh I don't know. More like two lonely folk in need of a good shag." Hattie was blunt. "I do like him though, he's kind and thoughtful and so soft spoken, unlike that Italian bastard." Both girls nodded, the bills pushed to one side.

"He'll be going back to Ireland the day after tomorrow," Jo said. "Has he asked if you can get together after that?"

"Nah, he never mentioned it." Hattie replied.

"But I don't suppose the love rat you've set your sights on mutters about Life-After-Fair-Week does he?"

They hadn't seen John Doherty since that afternoon.

"He's never mentioned it, and I don't trust myself on my own with him." Jo rocked on the office chair with her back to the desk.

Hattie sat on the stool and stared at the wall.

"There'll be no repeat of that night," Jo sighed "You're right, he's bound to be a complete shit and not one you'd ever rely on. He'll have a string of women up and down the country all impressed with his fancy cars as he flashes the cash." She studied her finger nails. "I'll never sleep with him again or take any of his shifty money." "If there's any left I'd like a vodka and tonic please." Jo and Hattie spun around.

John watched them collide into each other as Hattie fell backwards off the stool.

"Fuck," Jo said.

John moved away into the bar.

"No not me, don't make me go!" Jo pleaded with Hattie, who had grabbed the stool and struggled to her feet, but as she straightened up she felt the lining of the skirt rip.

"I'll see to it," Hattie said and reached around her waist. The lining hung below her hem in shreds and she gave it a tug. Jo hadn't noticed and Hattie darted through the door before she did...

Jo's cheeks flamed. Oh Christ! She closed her eyes to try and compose herself. The door opened and Hattie silently held out a large glass of Cointreau. Jo snatched it and swigged the contents back. Fuck, fuck, fuckety fuck!

The liquid coursed through her body. She grabbed a lipstick and ran it angrily over her mouth, then threw it on the desk and watched it clatter to the floor. The door opened again and Jo braced herself. Hattie waved a note. Conscious that John might hear, she indicated that Jo should read it.

He's going to have a club sandwich in his room. Wants a bottle of Chablis with it...

Jo read the note. She knew she owed John an apology; he was a guest for goodness sake. She took a deep breath and forced herself to move then crossed her fingers and stepped into the bar.

It was empty. John was nowhere to be seen. Jo looked around in disbelief – he'd been here a moment ago.

She put her head into the Panel Room and the conservatory but there was no sign of him.

As she passed the back stairs she heard the fire door close on the landing. He'd gone back up to his room.

Hattie met her in the corridor.

Jo's face said it all. Hattie took her by the arm and guided her back into the bar.

She poured another Cointreau and stood back as Jo sipped the drink. She looked devastated.

"There's a good chance he didn't hear you," Hattie began.

"Like hell. He can't get away from me fast enough - he even took the back stairs to avoid me." Jo looked miserable and downed her drink.

"Well, looking at the state of you there's only one thing you can do." Hattie placed the empty glass on the bar. "Get that lipstick off your teeth and look lively. You're going to do a room service order and you've got about five minutes." "I can't!" Jo was horrified.

"You can." Hattie poured another Cointreau.

Jo rubbed her finger across her teeth. The red wax left a smudged imprint on her skin. She gulped the drink.

"Don't have any regrets, Jo. You may never meet another man who makes you feel like this."

Jo was astonished. Hattie had certainly changed her tune.

"Oh what the hell..." Hattie smiled. "Better to die with the memory... I'll cover for the rest of the night."

The kitchen door swung open and Simon clattered through. He carried a tray with a silver dome covering a multi-layered club sandwich. He placed it on a table and added a cold bottle of Chablis.

"How many glasses?"

"I'll see to it, Simon, thank you."

Hattie placed two glasses beside white linen napkins then reached down and lifted the tray. "Come on." She put the tray in Jo's hands.

They scurried up the back stairs and into the corridor. John's room was at the front. Jo gripped the tray. The corridor seemed to go on for ever.

"See yah later," Hattie whispered and gave her a gentle shove. Jo took a deep breath and willed her feet to move forward in measured steps.

At the door of Room Two she balanced the tray on her hip, freed one hand and tapped gently on the door. Her heart pounded. "Room Service," she called out.

"Come in, it's open."

Jo turned the brass handle and pushed the door gently. Her feet felt like stone.

John sat by the bureau and looked up as she entered the room. Jo's face burned and she dipped her head, frantically looking for a table. John put his drink down and stood up. Silently, he took the tray and placed it on the bureau.

He stared at her.

Apologies screamed through Jo's head but she couldn't speak. Mortified, she reached for the door but in a flash John got to it first. He held on tight to stop her from opening it. Inches apart, their eyes met and John gently lifted her hand. He wrapped his arms around her and Jo felt as though she was drowning as he kissed her. Her legs buckled as she kissed him back.

"You took your time," he whispered.

Jo stared into his beautiful eyes and her heart melted. She was weak as she felt his warm skin, while he nuzzled her neck and roamed around her body with his eager hands.

She began to reply, but John silenced her lips with a kiss then guided her to the four-poster bed.

Their clothes seemed to melt away and he expertly unwound the laces of Jo's red lacy basque and watched it fall to the floor.

He peeled back the thick quilt and lay on the cool cotton sheets, as he guided Jo across him and held her waist. She straddled him and watched him gaze longingly at her breasts. He kissed her gently as she leaned into his face, he smelt so warm and masculine, so delicious!

Jo breathed him in and felt every nerve in her body react to his touches, as he traced her skin with his fingers and explored each inch. She took control of their love making and John responded passionately. Jo astonished herself with her power, as she slowly guided him into her and gently moved up and down. John groaned with pleasure as he reached for her breasts and pushed more urgently; she felt herself explode as he cried out.

The world seemed to stop for one long, glorious and unimaginable moment before Jo collapsed, then snuggled into his arms. John sighed contentedly, his hand caressed her thigh and as he opened his eyes he smiled.

"Wow," John pulled her to him again. Without unlocking their limbs or extracting himself, he rolled her over till she lay on her side, her leg wrapped tightly as he stroked and caressed her.

Jo felt him grow firm again and responded, allowing him to penetrate. She felt like a wild animal! Thrusting and gasping with exertion they rode against each other furiously, the quilt and pillows scattered.

Locked together they were oblivious to anything but each other. Jo heard a cry and realised that it was her own, as John gripped her hard and spent himself, his fingers digging deep into her flesh.

The room was silent, the storm abated. John stroked her hair and kissed her face.

They may have slept, Jo didn't know but when she opened her eyes John was sitting on the bed with the tray beside them. She watched him pour cold wine into a glass, the pale amber liquid looked like nectar as he held it out. Jo sat up and reached for the pillows then bunched them behind her head.

John unfolded a serviette and began to eat. "God I'm hungry, want some?" he asked.

Jo shook her head. She gazed at his naked body and sipped her wine. His limbs were toned and tanned, soft dark hair covered his chest.

"Have I got you for the night or have you guests to look after?" John munched on his sandwich and stroked her leg as his eyes wandered lazily over her body.

Jo felt like the cat who'd got the cream.

He dabbed at his mouth with the napkin, placed the tray on the floor and raised an eyebrow.

"Well?"

"All night," Jo whispered.

She placed the wine glass on the bedside table, as his fingers walked slowly up her legs and came to rest between her thighs.

Jo groaned and reached for him.

"All night," she sighed.

20

The crowd went wild! Mirabelle the Magnificent had come from nowhere in the fourth race at the Harness Racing in Butterly - she was a rank outsider in the betting, but out of the blue had won.

Jo sat in the stands at Colne Farm Arena and watched the celebrations below. Harry and Elvis congratulated themselves and Ken beamed with delight. Tracey and Stacey leapt up and down, their short skirts bouncing above endless tanned legs as they teetered precariously on spiked heels.

On John's advice, they'd all placed large bets and now reckoned up their winnings. It was considerable, with the odds at eleven to one.

Bertie danced around the stands in an Irish jig. He held Hattie and as they spun, her breasts threatened to bounce out of her blouse. She was ecstatic, Bertie had placed a hundred pounds on Mirabelle just for her! Hattie couldn't believe that she'd won so much money.

Jo smiled as she looked around, she was thrilled for Hattie. The evening was warm and the place buzzed with spirited chatter. Tall leafy trees surrounding the arena swayed in the breeze. Jo watched John as he stood by his driver in the arena below. A young boy, wearing the same colours as the driver, towelled Mirabelle down. He patted her gently as he dried her steaming coat. Jo saw John rub the horse's nose, he whispered in her ear, then gave instructions and Mirabelle was led away to prepare for the final.

A man stood next to John and as they spoke, John reached down and picked up an oblong case by his feet. He opened the lid and pulled out a portable phone.

Jo was fascinated. She'd heard of mobile phones but had never seen one. John handed the phone to the man.

Hattie watched too. "Who's the man with the phone?" she asked Bertie.

"Vincent Scott," Bertie replied. He's a leading racing pundit and a representative of the British Harness Racing Club. He's come up from Cheshire and seems to be well in with our man." Bertie watched Vincent return the phone, shake John's hand, then disappear into the crowd.

"All very interesting," Bertie said and sipped his beer. Froth clung to his top lip and Hattie wiped it away with her finger.

Another man appeared and congratulated John.

"Isn't that Pete Vardy the car dealer?" Hattie asked.

"Aye," Bertie said. "And the fellow in the camel coat is his minder."

"Christ. What do you have to do to have a minder?"

"Ask our man himself. He normally has one." Bertie watched John. A man with red hair was speaking to him and picked up the case.

Hattie looked around for Jo and spotted her in the stand. Jo gave them a wave and hopped over the benches.

"Having a good time?" Jo asked.

"Couldn't be better," Hattie smiled. "Hope you had a decent bet on old Mirabelle, I've won a bloody fortune."

"Oh hell," Jo said and nodded to the arena. "Look who's just arrived."

Below them they could see Jinny and Billy Atkinson arm-in-arm as they walked ahead of an entourage of family and friends.

"Quite an entrance," Hattie said as Billy acknowledged everyone and was soon surrounded by racing cronies. Jinny seem distracted and searched the crowd, she saw John and letting go of Billy's arm, she rushed forward and grabbed John by the shoulder. As he turned she kissed him on the cheek.

"Shite," Hattie whispered and reached for her drink. It was empty. She looked around for Bertie who told her that Jinny had a horse, Westmarland Prancer, in the next race.

Jinny was immaculate as usual in a stunning gold dress, the silk gathered at one side and fell in a waterfall to her knees. Jo felt out of place in her Mondi outfit.

Hattie nudged her. "She thinks it's sodding Ascot, not the harness racing in Fair Week. Don't let her get to you."

Bertie returned with a bottle of champagne and Hattie grinned as she took the glasses. "Get this inside you." Hattie held a glass for Jo and Bertie poured.

Jo watched Jinny, who held onto John's arm. He leaned his head to one side and listened when she spoke in his ear. John moved back and Jinny's hand fell away. He looked up and caught Jo's eye, then glanced at his gold Rolex watch and broke away from Jinny to run up the steps and join Jo.

"Got a glass of bubbly for me?"

"More than a glass my Man," Bertie poured him a drink. "Jeysus, Mirabelle's a fine horse so she is." He raised his glass to John. Harry and Elvis joined them and were vociferous in their thanks as Tracey and Stacey sang 'For he's a jolly good fellow.'

"To Mirabelle the Magnificent!"

"And may she win in the final!" Elvis added.

John embraced Jo and kissed her, which set off another round of cheers.

"Mmn, I'm having a good day," John whispered in her ear. "You look nice." His hand wrapped around her bottom. "What's on the room service menu tonight?" Jo giggled as he nuzzled into her neck. She looked over his shoulder and realised that Jinny was glaring at them.

"I didn't know you knew Jinny Atkinson," Jo said.

"I don't really. I've done some work with Billy though."

"She seems to be taking a lot of interest in you."

Jinny glowered in Jo's direction, then spun on her heels and stomped off. She grabbed Billy's arm and pushed him in the direction of the champagne bar.

John gave Jo another lingering kiss then told her that he'd people to see and moved off into the crowd.

"Fuck me you're not making any friends." Hattie took Jo's arm and nodded in the direction of the Atkinson party.

"I'm amazed she's here," Jo replied. "I wouldn't have thought trotting races were her style."

"There's an awful lot of money to be won tonight, Jo." Bertie had overheard their conversation. "Westmarland Prancer's a fine horse and should clean up in the final."

Hattie was thoughtful. She knew the Atkinson's loved racing and Jinny had several successful horses. It was clear that Jinny knew John too. Perhaps he held other attractions than racing for her?

The next race was about to start and there was a flurry of last minute betting as Bertie, Ken and the Hunts placed large amounts on Westmarland Prancer.

The impatient horses thrashed about as their drivers trotted them to the starting line and manoeuvred into position. The starting pistol fired and they were off!

The vehicles sped around the course in a cloud of orange and brown dust as the horses thundered past.

The drivers gripped harnesses in one hand and held whips high in the other, wheels spun and the yelling crowd went mad.

Westmarland Prancer lay in second place. She'd had a good race but was too far behind to win. As she headed for the final furlong her driver whipped her repeatedly; he stood on the running board and yelled as he leaned to one side. The horse thrust forward, the whites of her eyes huge as foam trailed from her mouth, she'd caught up! With a crack of the whip that drew blood, her driver wrenched the harness back causing the carriage to crash into the side of the leading horse. It toppled over onto the white railings and Westmarland Prancer flew past to the final post.

Angry cries went up, surely she would be disqualified?

But the protests were drowned by Westmarland Prancer's supporters.

Jinny shrieked with joy and Billy popped a bottle of champagne and showered his friends.

Hattie and Jo watched the performance and felt sickened. Surely that shouldn't have been allowed? Bertie reassured them that the horse that had toppled was fine and that's how trotting races are sometimes won. He rubbed his hands together - another windfall. Jo looked at her watch and wondered how they were coping back at the hotel.

"They'll be alright. Stop worrying," Hattie said. "Everyone's down here, there'll be few folk wanting a meal."

The heats continued and Jo hardly saw John. He seemed busy and moved around the arena talking to different groups of men. As the final race approached he returned with Vincent Scott by his side. Hattie rushed forward to be introduced. She was delighted with her winnings and intrigued by the betting. She wanted to ask the racing pundit how the bets were worked out and what Mirabelle's odds were. Vincent explained that it all depended on how good the other horses were in the race. Mirabelle was well fancied for the final as she'd won the qualifier easily, the odds would probably be three to one but they mustn't forget the favourite Westmarland Prancer, whose odds were currently two to one.

"Are you having a bet Jo?" Hattie watched the bookies wave their arms around and call out the odds. "I could take to this, it beats work!"

"I can't understand a word they're saying," Jo replied. She hadn't placed a bet all night and toyed with the idea of backing Mirabelle. She reached into her bag to find her purse.

"You don't need that," John appeared and put his hand out to stop her. He dug into his pocket and handed a wad of cash to Ken. "Put this on the nose for Jo.

Ken took the money and headed off to his favourite tout.

"You don't have to do that..." Jo began but John put his finger on her lips and silenced her.

"Enjoy it," he began but was distracted. "Hello, Robert," John said and held out his hand.

Jo turned and came face to face with Robert Mann. "Robert," she exclaimed.

"Jo." Robert stared at Jo. He saw how close she stood to John and comprehension dawned as he acknowledged them.

"John, my dear fellow, how are you?" Robert took John's hand. Jo was glowing and Robert knew why.

"I didn't know you liked harness racing?" Jo leaned forward to kiss Robert on the cheek.

"You look well," Robert replied. "I like your outfit."

John watched their exchange and raised an eyebrow. He looked to Jo for an explanation.

"Robert found Kirkton House for me," Jo began. "He was an absolute angel. I don't know what I'd have done without him."

"But you and Greg did so well with the sale of the pub," Robert gazed at her.

"The 'forced sale' you mean," Jo added quickly. The last person she wanted to discuss in front of John was her errant husband Greg. "How are you, John?" Robert regained his composure.

"Oh you know, trying to earn a crust, and yourself?"

"I'm thriving on jobs like Kirkton House." Robert smiled at Jo.

"Obviously," John said. "Excuse me. I need to speak to my driver." He politely extricated himself.

"Good Luck!" Robert called out as they watched him disappear into the crowd.

"Is he staying at the hotel?"

"Yes, how do you know him?"

"I knew his father," Robert said.

"What did he do?" Jo was intrigued.

Robert sighed, he was reluctant to enlighten Jo but could see that she was eager to learn something of John's past.

"The old boy began with a rag and bone cart," Robert said. "He did well on his rounds and began to deal in antiques. He was a true Romany and always came up here for the auctions, and the Fair of course. Quite a character if I remember, all the family travelled with him. He refused to move them into property and they all lived in caravans."

"Is John an antique dealer?" Jo asked.

"No. Not to my knowledge," Robert shook his head. "Property's his main interest. I've sold him one or two large places which he's converted and sold on. And cars of course, he's made a fortune." He trailed off. Jo was eager to ask more but Hattie was calling her. The final race was about to start.

Robert looked longingly at Jo.

"I have to go," she spoke softly.

"Of course, you must," Robert stood back. "Good luck in the race. I hope John's horse wins," he sighed. "We'll be over for dinner again soon."

Jo touched his arm. For a moment, their eyes met and Jo could see the adoration in his eyes. She turned and ran to join Hattie and Bertie. Robert watched as she disappeared in the crowd and with a sigh, returned to his colleagues.

THE FINAL RACE was about to begin and the carriages paraded around the arena, before heading off to the starting line. Clouds of dust from pounding hooves merged into the haze of the sultry evening. The impatient horses sensed the tension and drivers struggled to keep control. Last minute bets were placed and punters jostled for a clear view of the track.

Jo stood in the stands that overlooked the finishing line.

She was surrounded by the Hunt party who were animated and excited as they waited for the race to begin.

John stood alone, several steps higher, where he had a clear view. He scrutinised the field then focussed on Mirabelle as she trotted into the arena.

The horse stood out, composed and elegant. John checked his watch and turned to look for Jo. Their eyes met and he smiled. Jo wanted to run to his side but Hattie held onto to her.

"It's about to start!" Hattie shouted and linked Jo's arm.

Nine carriages lined up. The crowd cheered as the race and runners were announced.

Jo sensed the anticipation. A great deal of money rested on this race. Mirabelle stood a head above her rivals. Jo had heard people say the horse was unsuitable for harness racing – she was too big and ungainly. But as the light faded and a dusky sun caressed Mirabelle's sleek grey coat, Jo thought that the horse was just like her name truly magnificent.

Westmarland Prancer lined up some distance away. The jet-black horse snorted with impatience and banged her hooves on the hard ground. The starter raised his pistol and they were off! Jo crossed her fingers and Hattie clutched her arm. They hopped up and down to try and see the horses as they rounded the first bend. The race was a blur of colour as the spirited crowds shouted and waved.

A few minutes in and it was a two-horse race. Mirabelle and Westmarland Prancer pulled away from the rest of the field and pounded furiously alongside each other. Whips cracked as their drivers urged them on.

Jo looked at the stand above and searched for John. He stood very still with his arms folded, his gaze never leaving his horse. Hattie wrenched Jo's arm.

"She's pulling away!" Hattie screamed. The cheers and shouts reached fever pitch as the horses rumbled along the back straight. On the last bend, Mirabelle gained a lead and looked certain to have a clear route to the finishing line, but suddenly Westmarland Prancer lurched forward. Her driver dragged the harness to one side, lashed out with his whip and careered Westmarland Prancer into Mirabelle. Mirabelle's carriage squealed and teetered as it lunged towards the railings.

The crowd was hysterical. Hattie fingers dug into Jo's flesh as the girls witnessed the carnage. Jo dragged her horrified gaze from the frenzy to look for John. He stared, not moving a muscle, as he watched his beloved horse stumble and begin to fall.

"Cheat!" the crowd screamed.

The track was almost obscured by the dust that flew up in the fracas. With Mirabelle tearing into the railings and blood pouring from her injuries, Westmarland Prancer began to romp home. John's driver stood at an angle, every muscle on his body strained as he pulled on the harness and tried to drag his floundering carriage back up. Mirabelle was almost down, her legs buckled as her grey coat turned red.

The crowd gasped and Jo flung her hands over her eyes.

"Look, Jo, look!" Hattie screamed.

Jo opened her eyes to see Mirabelle right herself!

With gargantuan strength the horse had pulled the cart from the railings, whilst her driver clung on for dear life.

Somehow Mirabelle gained pace around the bend. She headed in a straight line for the flag, but Westmarland Prancer had the edge. The two wild-eyed horses surged alongside each other; nose to nose, and with a final massive effort Mirabelle pulled ahead and cleared the line by inches.

The crowd went ballistic, their roars, cries and cheers were deafening and Hattie and Bertie jumped up and down and hugged each other.

Jo pushed through the mass to find John, but he'd gone. Frantic, she turned to see if he was in the stand but Harry and Elvis grabbed her and Ken tried to tell her how much she'd won.

"By heck, Cumbrian Prancer should have been disqualified," Hattie said angrily. "Poor old Mirabelle got a pounding – is every final like that?"

"No," Bertie replied. "In any other horse race there would be a disqualification, but this is trotting…" He trailed off and Hattie shook her head in disgust.

A loud-speaker announced the winner and the cheers went up again.

Jo managed to climb higher in the stand and looked down on the arena. She easily picked John out as he pushed people aside. Everyone wanted to congratulate him and some slapped his back while others tried to hug him but he ignored them and fought to reach his horse. As he approached the paddock, the crowd stood back.

John tore at the buckles on Mirabelle's harness and together with his driver, wrenched it away.

Jo saw his hands tenderly caress Mirabelle, blood from her wounds seeped through his fingers as he calmed his beloved animal. A vet reached them and threw his bag on the dust, then began an inspection of her injuries.

Jo winced as she looked on.

"She'll be ok." Ken appeared. "The cuts aren't deep. Probably be scarred for life though." He gave Jo's shoulder a squeeze. "Come and have a drink."

They all trooped off to the champagne bar, where Billy and Jinny were surrounded by friends who consoled them with second place. Jo didn't want a drink. She needed to get back but wanted to see John before she went.

"I'm off," Jo turned to Hattie. "You stay here and enjoy yourself." Jo realised that Hattie wasn't listening.

Hattie's attention was focussed on the Atkinson party.

John had entered the bar and Jinny stopped him. He wore a jacket but blood was clearly visible on his white shirt. Billy turned from his cronies and walked over to John. The two men glared at each other. Billy said something and held out his hand. After a moment, John took it. They shook and John walked away, but Jinny ran after him and pulled him back. She spoke earnestly and John leaned in to listen. Billy had his back to them and laughed and joked with his friends, oblivious to their conversation.

Jo dragged her gaze away and with a sigh said goodbye to Bertie and Hattie. She hurried off before they could stop her.

Bertie put his arm around Hattie as they watched Jo disappear.

"What was all that about?" Hattie nodded towards the Atkinsons but Bertie shook his head. He smiled as John approached.

"She'll have her heart broken with this one." Bertie said softly. He kissed the top of Hattie's hair then moved to greet John, who was surrounded by well-wishers.

Quite a party had begun.

21

Jo walked briskly along the busy high street in Marland. It was a lovely sunny day and as she pushed Thomas along in his buggy, he chortled happily and kicked his chubby little legs out.

The Fair was over.

Jo thought about the week and what a weird few days it'd been. She felt as though she'd briefly existed in another world and now stepped back into her real one. There was no obvious change - the hotel was the same with everything as before and the staff all going about their business.

But Jo felt different. Her heart was doing things she'd forgotten it could do. Every time she thought about John Doherty, it jumped about in her chest and tears pricked her eyes. She told herself that she mustn't think about him, the Fair was finished and so was her fling. For that's all it was – a fling. Something that had ended as abruptly as it had started.

A colourful display of tennis gear in a sports shop reminded Jo that Wimbledon week approached. Strawberry teas in the garden.

Pippa tugged on her lead and stopped by a lamp-post. She began to sniff.

"Ippa Mumma, Ippa," Thomas pointed at the dog. Pippa looked up and Jo tugged her away from the scent.

They stopped at a newsagent on the market square to buy a paper. Jo had no idea what was happening in the news and there'd been no time to watch the television. She ought to catch up. The headlines announced that Van Gogh's Sunflowers had sold for twenty-four million pounds at Christies Fine Art Auction.

Jo shook her head - a few daubs of yellow paint on a canvas!

Thomas leaned forward. He'd spotted some miniature toys on a shelf and reached for them. Rabbits, bears and mice stood to attention. Jo picked one up and read the label - Sylvanian Families. She held the rabbit out and Thomas took it eagerly.

Jo dug into the pocket of her jeans to search for a note and remembered that she had a large carrier bag stuffed with money, hidden under Thomas' seat. She must get to the bank. She paid for the toy as Thomas pulled on the rabbit's ears and began to suck them.

Jo dragged the buggy up the steps of the Westmarland Trust Bank and pushed hard on the door with her bottom, then manoeuvred into the marble vaulted lobby.

At the counter, she reached for the carrier bag.

"Good morning," Jo spoke pleasantly to the cashier. "I think the paying-in book is here somewhere." Jo rummaged about in the bag. Mr Knight stood beyond the counter and waved.

"Mrs Edmonds, you've survived Fair Week?" He came forward to greet her and noted the considerable sum being counted.

"Yes we did," Jo said. "It was a bit different to the pub days but the takings were just as good."

Thomas flung his rabbit across the polished floor. As Jo turned to rescue it, Pete Parks entered the bank and the toy skidded to a halt by his feet. He picked it up and handed it back to Thomas.

"You're a grand little lad, the image of your daddy." Pete smiled. Mr Knight stood behind Jo and grimaced at Pete, who quickly changed the subject.

"Had a good fair, Jo?" Pete nodded at the cash.

"Not as good as you."

Jo stared at Pete's bulging briefcase. She thanked the cashier and said goodbye to Mr Knight, then turned and pushed the buggy out of the bank. Pete caught up with her and touched her arm.

"When are we going to have a drink?"

"I'll pretend I didn't hear that, if you remind yourself you've got a wife."

"Oh come on, Jo," he said and leapt to hold the door open. Jo removed his hand.

"You know you want to, no one will know, that hotel of yours is a big old place with lots of room," Pete pleaded.

"Don't flatter yourself, Pete. I'll see you around."

"Aye you will one day. I won't give up," he called after her, admiring her bottom in tight blue jeans. Jo wore shiny red pumps and a red cashmere jacket with animal print panels that hugged her figure. Pete shook his head and smiled as he watched her hurry up the street to the car park.

"Did you place the advert in the Caterer?" Jo threw herself on the stool in reception.

"Yes it'll be in this week," Hattie replied. "But can't you look closer to home? There must be someone local who can train under Sandra?"

"Well maybe you should put it in the Westmarland Tribune too. Give your mate Peter Pigmy a call."

"That slimly little devil will be round here in a shot, if he thinks there's a coffee and a cleavage shot up for grabs," Hattie sneered.

Jo collected the post from the counter. She sighed, there were a lot of brown envelopes.

"You can't be busy and not have bills," Hattie peered at the post.

"Oh look - there's a card here from Ireland." Jo held the card and scrutinised the writing. "To my Darling Harriet..."

Hattie made a grab for the card but Jo held it high and continued to mimic Bertie's accent.

"I miss you terribly and wish you were here with me, looking at the meadows and sea..."

Hattie snatched the card out of Jo's hand and turned it over. Her face lit up.

"Time you got yourself on a plane," Jo poked Hattie in the ribs. "Go and spend some of that cash you won at the trotting races."

"No way, I couldn't leave you." Hattie turned the card over and gazed dreamily at the picture on the front. "The place will fall apart if I go off gallivanting."

She tucked the card into her pocket and picked up a telephone directory.

"You must go Hattie." Jo was serious. "Take your boys over there for a week or two. Don't worry about this place, I can manage. It's not as if I have anything to distract me."

Hattie dialled the number for the Westmarland Tribune.

"I mean it, Hattie, get a holiday booked - enjoy it while you can." Jo watched Hattie flick through the directory.

"But what about you?" Hattie asked and Jo and knew by her expression that she was about to start asking questions about John Doherty.

Jo hadn't mentioned his name since the night of the trotting and didn't want to discuss him now. She pushed the envelopes to one side and walked away.

"Classified ads please," Hattie spoke to directory enquiries. She picked up her pencil and as she waited, began to doodle on a blotter. A hangman's gallows appeared on the page, beside a gypsy caravan with a matchstick man standing beside it.

The lead in the pencil snapped as Hattie etched a noose around the figure's neck.

JO WANDERED INTO THE GARDEN; she needed to clear her head. She thought about the night that Mirabelle had won the final trotting race. John hadn't come back to the hotel.

The restaurant had been busy and the Hunt party drank late into the night as they celebrated with other residents. It was almost two o'clock when Jo locked up and went to bed.

The following morning Hattie had noticed that the key to Room Two was still on its hook in reception, she'd tried to make conversation but Jo hadn't been in the mood.

"I'll crack on with breakfasts then," Hattie said.

Harry and Elvis had appeared and asked for their bills. They were fresh and alert despite their party the previous night. Ken and Bertie followed shortly afterwards, they'd all got long journeys home and were keen to get on the road.

Jo was checking the bills when a man appeared at the desk and asked to settle John's account. He explained that he worked for John and his name was Rory. He apologised and said that John had been unexpectedly called back to Leeds.

Jo handed Rory the key for Room Two.

She knew she should check his credibility, but decided against it and as Rory disappeared upstairs to pack John's things, she made up the bill. There was a credit from the cash deposit, which she put in an envelope and handed to Rory when he returned the key. He opened the envelope, took out fifty pounds and asked her to put it in the gratuity box.

"John sends his regards." Rory smiled politely. Jo forced herself to smile back. Rory left no forwarding address or number for John and Jo was determined not to ask. She watched him leave by the side door and carried on with her work.

"Mrs E!" Judy cried out as she ran down the hallway. "There's a Bentley convertible on the drive."

Hattie appeared and hurried down the hall with Judy, they watched Rory open the driver's door and get behind the wheel.

"Come on," Hattie called out to Jo, "your guests are leaving."

Jo joined Hattie outside as Rory started the car. The interior was upholstered in smooth cream leather with red piping and a polished wood dashboard. Harry and Elvis whistled in admiration as the Bentley purred into life.

"When you gonna get us one of them?" Tracey and Stacey watched the car speed away. They both wore dark glasses and complained of monumental hangovers.

"Wouldn't suit you, darlin'." Harry hoisted the girls into his Cherokee pick-up and threw their cases in the back.

He turned to say goodbye and Jo hugged and thanked him, then turned and hugged Elvis too. She promised to keep their rooms for next year and leaned into the truck to say goodbye to the girls.

"Mind how you go, Jo." Tracey and Stacey chimed. The girls winced and held their heads as Harry started the engine.

Bertie turned to Hattie and pulled her to him. They held on to each other and she was completely engulfed by his embrace.

"It's not goodbye, my dearest Harriet - I'll phone you as soon as I get back," Bertie assured her. "Now you look after yourself," he gazed at her with longing.

"Taxi for O'Reilly!" Ken shouted and tooted his old motor. Bertie had accepted Ken's offer of a lift to the station in Marland, where he'd catch a train for Holyhead then a ferry to Dublin. As they all drove away they sounded their horns and Hattie blew kisses to Bertie while Jo waved until the vehicles had disappeared down the road.

Hattie longed to ask about John, but as she began, Jo shook her head. Hattie was seething and told Jo that she'd shoot the bastard if he ever put a foot in the place again. But Jo was adamant. She wouldn't discuss him. There were a hundred jobs to do with new guests arriving later.

Hattie stomped back to reception and Jo went up the stairs to Room Two. She opened the door and locked it behind her. The room was neat and tidy with a couple of drawers open on the bureau, where Rory had removed John's things. She opened the wardrobe door. An empty dry-cleaning bag hung limply from a padded hanger, the label read Platinum Cleaners Leeds.

There was an imprint of a suitcase on the thick quilt. Jo pulled it back and reached for a pillow then buried her face in the soft Egyptian cotton. It still smelt of John. Jo's heart ached as she breathed in and she sank to the bed, hugging the pillow.

After a while she sat up.

What was the matter with her? She punched the pillow and threw it back on the bed, then went over to the mirror. She stared at her unhappy face. Why was she allowing a man to hurt her again? A couple of nights of casual sex and she was a wreck.

Jo knew she needed to pull herself together. She ran cold water in the bathroom sink and splashed her face, then patted it dry with a towel. His smell was on the towel too. She flung it angrily into the bath tub and marched over to the window where she pulled the curtains apart and flung the windows open wide. The sooner this room was aired the better. Jo propped the door open with a wooden wedge and took one last look, as Linda rattled down the corridor with a bucket of cleaning materials.

"Give it a really thorough going over," Jo called out as she ran down the stairs. "We need to get the Fair out of this place."

22

Jo hated interviews. The applicants for the position of chef to assist Sandra had been a dismal lot and she didn't seem any nearer to finding a replacement for Michael.

The caravan had been thoroughly cleaned and was ready for a new occupant and a mountain of empty beer bottles had been disposed of. Any traces of plants living, dried, or smoked had been removed and destroyed.

"What do you think?" Jo asked Sandra. She nodded at a pile of CVs that lay on the table beside them in the conservatory. Sandra settled her broad backside into a wicker chair and sipped a mug of tea.

"Not a lot."

"Me neither," Jo agreed. "Do we employ someone for the sake of it or wait for the right applicant?"

"I'd sooner wait than have a wrong 'un," Sandra nodded. "Judy's coping ok. She's no fine skills but she does a lot of prep and Gerald's been doing the vegetables. He seems to want to do more and asks lots of questions."

"Gerald asks questions?"

"Oh aye, he's really come out of himself. Arthur only helps if it's very busy. Gerald runs the stillroom like a military operation these days."

"Well I never," Jo shook her head. "Well we must make some sort of decision. Hattie is about to go off to Ireland and we'll need Judy front of house." She looked up as Penny interrupted them.

"Mrs Edmonds, the gentlemen in reception are asking for their bill."

"I'm on my way, Penny, thank you." Jo stood up and left Sandra to go through the CVs again, there may be possibilities that they'd missed.

In reception, two guests waited to check out.

"Sorry to keep you," Jo said. "I'll just total your bill, has everything been alright for you?"

The men wore suits and had briefcases beside their feet.

Jo lifted their bills out of the rack and read the telephone meter. As she calculated the amount, the taller man leaned over the counter.

"We've had a very pleasant stay, thank you." He pulled a chequebook from his briefcase and reached for a pen. "Do you have facilities to run small conferences?"

Jo thought quickly, she had two restaurants – one could easily be converted for conferences.

"Yes we do," she smiled and handed him her business card and a brochure. "Give me a call and I'll put a package together for you."

The man turned the card over, examined it and tucked it in his pocket. He studied the bills and settled both accounts.

"Thank you, Mr. Pucker, it was a pleasure to meet you," Jo said and Mr Pucker beamed. Jo thought he was quite a decent looking man, if you ignored his battered ears. She smoothed the bodice of her dress and fiddled with a button.

Mr Pucker noticed and glanced down.

Jo's red lacy bra was just visible under her tartan print dress. She whipped her fingers away.

The men said their goodbyes.

"Mr Pucker? That's a corker," Hattie said.

She placed a mug of coffee on the desk and watched the men walk over the gravel, where two identical company cars stood alongside each other. "Rhymes with all sorts of things, did you see his ears? Rugby player." Hattie sat down.

"He wants to book small conferences. What do you think?"

"I think you can do anything and conferences would be great, despite his cauliflower ears." Hattie sipped her coffee. "He works for a tobacco company, plenty of money. Old Pucker there is Northern

Sales Manager, no less."

"How do you know?"

"His mate was boring the arse off me last night, while he nursed a warm G & T and told me all his sorrows," Hattie yawned. "How miserable his wife was, how much his boss earns, the usual rubbish. You'd gone to bed."

"Amazes me, how men pour out their troubles and think you're interested," Jo mused.

"Then go off to bed and thank you for being such good company, when you haven't said a word," Hattie shook her head and finished her drink.

"That's the art of being a good hotelier," Jo smiled.

"You can say that again, something you need to put into action pronto." Hattie looked at her watch. "Are you braced for Her Highness? She'll be arriving in about an hour," Hattie pulled a face.

Jinny Atkinson's Ladies Luncheon Club was meeting at the hotel today. Two weeks had passed since the trotting races and Jo hadn't spoken to Jinny. Menus sent to her home had come back approved, the numbers confirmed by her club secretary.

The weather looked promising for the luncheon and Jo decided that they would serve drinks and canapés on the terrace, followed by lunch in the Rose Room with the doors open to the garden.

"I shall be politeness itself and enjoy taking their money," Jo told Hattie then went to check the table arrangements.

In the Rose Room she looked around with pleasure. Laid for lunch, the garden room looked delightful. Big pink cabbage roses spilled from vases on the mantelpiece and tables, their old-fashioned perfume heady in the sunshine.

The twins polished glasses.

"Morning, Mrs E." they both smiled. Tanned from the summer sun and handsome in their uniforms, Jo said a silent prayer of thanks to their mother. The Ladies of Westmarland would be well and truly charmed today.

"Is everyone okay with the menu?" Jo asked. Judy stood alongside the twins and they all nodded.

"Battle stations!" Hattie yelled. "They're here."

A procession of vehicles pulled onto the drive as husbands arranged times to collect wives and taxis disgorged well-heeled ladies. Those guests who'd driven to the hotel found spaces and parked carefully.

"Westmarland's finest fillies," Hattie said as Mrs Parks climbed out of her friend's Volvo and crossed the gravel. They wore outfits from Country Casuals and Jaeger and were met by friends in similar attire. Ruffled blouses and pleated skirts by the yard were the order of the day as they swept over the driveway to congregate in the hall.

The twins stood by with trays of pink champagne and there was a jaunty atmosphere as well-upholstered bosoms and stout, corseted figures mingled and chatted.

A chauffeur driven saloon came to a halt by the front door and Jinny Atkinson stepped out of the car. She dismissed the chauffeur, patted her hair then tucked her bag under her arm and strode confidently into the hotel. Like the parting of the Red Sea, the ladies fell over themselves to move out of her way as she sailed past.

"Moses I presume," Hattie whispered.

"Good afternoon, Mrs Atkinson, how nice to see you," Jo forced herself to smile but Jinny walked past without a word. She snatched a glass of champagne and swept down the hallway.

"Count to ten," Hattie said but her attention was suddenly diverted. "Christ, look who's just arrived."

A Mercedes Coupe screeched onto the drive.

Gravel flew as it narrowly missed the gate post and came to a halt by the front door, careering into a stone urn. Brightly coloured geraniums and lobelia toppled to the ground. The driver's door opened and to their amazement, Mrs Sherwin tumbled out. On the other side of the car a well-set coiffure wobbled into view. Dorothy Osbourne eased her considerable weight out of the sports seat and rose to full height. She slammed the door and glided around to join her companion. Reaching down, she took hold of Mrs Sherwin's elbow and guided her unsteadily across the gravel. Mrs Sherwin gripped Dorothy's arm for support.

"Is she pissed?" Hattie whispered in astonishment.

Jo stepped forward and welcomed them.

"Hello, dear," Dorothy said. "What a lovely day." She levered Mrs Sherwin over the threshold.

Mrs Sherwin stared at Jo. She had one eye half closed and attempted to focus with the other.

"You remember, Mrs Edmonds, Vera dear, don't you?" Dorothy said.

"Of course I do. The large shupport pants and shwilky red bashque…"

Dorothy flashed a smile over lipstick-stained teeth and hoisted Mrs Sherwin into the hall. Simon offered champagne.

"Vera?" Hattie and Jo whispered. They tried not to laugh out loud.

"Bleedin' hell I thought she was at least an Esther or an Abigail – never a Vera." Hattie shook her head. They watched Simon lead the guests through to the terrace as Mrs Sherwin polished off two glasses en-route.

"Well I never," Jo grinned and followed them.

She distributed menus to the guests on the sunny terrace and Suzy struck up a lively recital on the piano.

The meal was a great success. The ladies sighed over the daintiness of the canapés, as the twins encouraged them to try the tasty offerings. They giggled and told themselves they mustn't, but took two portions of everything. Once seated in the Rose Room, they were served the first course, a delicate crab soufflé with warm granary bread. It was a hit, as was the main course of tender veal escallops with citrus dressed leaves and a minted potato salad. Fresh summer berries, with white chocolate sauce, completed the meal and an air of well-being oozed, as chilled Chardonnay flowed. On Jinny's instructions, coffee was served at the table. Jinny stood up and chinked a spoon against a glass.

Her audience snapped to attention.

She addressed the group and attended to formalities, various fund raising events required volunteers and leaving no room for argument,

Jinny commandeered helpers. A nervous club secretary scrawled the minutes across a notepad.

"How does the bossy cow get away with it?" Hattie shook her head. The girls stood in the doorway and watched the proceedings as Jo sipped a glass of wine.

"Money? Power? Shagging other people's lovers?" Jo replied sarcastically.

Jinny wound the meeting up and the party began to disperse.

"You can't let Vera drive home, she'll never get out of the gates," Hattie said. They watched Dorothy support her friend. She lost the battle and Mrs Sherwin's head flopped to one side as she fell asleep and slid down her chair.

"I'll sort a room and call a taxi for Dorothy," Jo said.

As she turned to head for reception, she bumped headlong into Jinny. Both women froze. Jinny looked Jo up and down and her cold grey eyes glared, as they alighted on the wayward red lace bra peeping out of Jo's cleavage.

"Is everything alright for you, Mrs Atkinson?" "Send the bill on," Jinny snapped.

"I'm sorry your horse lost at the trotting races."

"What would you know about racing?"

"I know she ran a very controversial race," Jo held Jinny's glacial stare.

"She was unlucky," Jinny spat the words out and with a ram-rod back, walked angrily out of the room.

"That's put paid to the next Ladies Luncheon Club," Hattie said as she watched Jinny retreat.

"Actually, I don't think it will. I think that madam wants to keep her eye on me." Jo was thoughtful.

"Well you'd better give her something to think about eh?" Hattie raised her eyebrows. "He'll be back, mark my words. Bad pennies always turn up."

Jo gulped the contents of her wine glass and banged it down on the table. She was not going to discuss John Doherty under any circumstances.

Two ladies in twin-sets, with pearls bouncing on their broad bosoms, grabbed Jo's arm and gushed praise for the meal. Jo chatted amiably as she walked them to their transport.

They assured her several times over that they'd be back with family and friends and unsteadily climbed into waiting cars.

As the last guest left, Jo wearily closed the front door.

"Christ, everyone's three sheets to the wind," Hattie said as she watched the vehicles pull away. "I've called a taxi for Dorothy and Vera's snores are raising the roof in Room Eight." Jo
looked up as Steven hurried down the hallway.

"Call for you, Mrs Edmonds."

"Thanks, Steven, who is it?"

"Sounded like a Mr Fucker?" Steven said.

Jo winced. "I'll be right there."

23

A distinguished grey haired gentleman sat in the bay window of the Green Room and savoured his morning coffee. Beams of July sun streamed through the windows and highlighted the faded pile of a Persian rug beside the fireplace. He shook the pink pages of the Financial Times and smiled as Jo approached.

"Would you like more coffee, sir?" Jo picked up a bone china cup and poured carefully. The man leaned forward. He ignored the silver tongs, hooked on the rim of the Georgian sugar bowl, and put two lumps of crystallized sugar into the steaming brown liquid.

"Are you the proprietor?" he asked.

Dressed in a tailored Harris Tweed jacket with smart blue shirt and monogrammed cufflinks, Jo recognised the light blue stripe of his woven silk tie - Old Etonian. A hotel brochure lay face down on the table before him.

"Yes, sir, what can I do for you?" Jo replied.

The man indicated that she should join him, then laced his elegant fingers together and crossed one leg over the other. Red silk socks flashed above handmade leather loafers. Jo made herself comfortable on the opposite chair.

"I've secured some shooting rights nearby and I need a venue to entertain my top clients." He looked around the room. "I run a cider company. It's for the Glorious Twelfth and we need exclusivity."

Jo did a quick calculation. August 12th was less than a month away.

"My guests are very important and I want them to have anything they require to make their stay comfortable. Do you think you can cater for a shooting weekend?" He picked up a gold case, snapped it open and placed a pair of tortoiseshell spectacles carefully in the holder.

"We'd be delighted to accommodate you, sir." Jo replied. She'd crawl across a zillion broken cider bottles to secure this! "Would you like to have a look around?"

"No need, m'dear. You come recommended. I always trust my game keepers and young Alf said you'd look after us."

He reached into his pocket and handed Jo a business card. Jo studied the gold embossed writing - Henry Mulberry MBE, Managing Director, Mulberry Cider, Tinerton, Somerset.

"Excellent, my secretary will be in touch." Mr Mulberry bent to retrieve his briefcase and tucked the hotel brochure into a side pocket.

"I'm salmon fishing on the Tay and my ghillie says they're biting, must be off." He held out a hand. "You take dogs of course?" "Of course, Mr Mulberry." Jo shook his hand.

"First class."

Jo watched Henry Mulberry crunch across the gravel to a waiting vehicle. A chauffeur held open the rear door of a silver Rolls Royce and Henry disappeared into the luxurious interior. Jo's head spun. Dogs? Where the hell would she put a brood of well-bred hunting dogs?

In her own bed if she had to.

She picked up the coffee tray and raced to the kitchen. "Sandra, start thinking about game menus. Shooting parties here we come!"

"Now get off and enjoy yourself," Jo stood by the departure gates at Newcastle airport and pushed Hattie forward. Hattie's boys were dressed in neat new outfits and both gripped their mother's jacket as they stared excitedly at the plane standing on the tarmac.

"You'll have a brilliant time," Jo ushered them all forward. "I'm sure Bertie is pacing up and down in the arrivals lounge." She imagined an anxious Bertie in Dublin.

"We'll see you in a week then." Hattie looked lovely in a soft pink jacket and pale blue jeans, her hair curling softly around her face. She leaned forward and gave Jo a hug. "Don't do anything daft while I'm gone."

"Bring me back a rich Irish farmer - Bertie must have lots of friends." Jo grinned as she watched the departing trio.

Hattie handed over boarding passes and jostled the boys ahead of her. They disappeared through the gate.

Jo's car was in the short stay car park. She paid the exit fee and drove out into bright sunshine where the traffic was heavy. It began to thin as she left industrial areas behind and headed along the route home, crossing the country from east to west through lush valleys and open moors.

Jo was pleased that Hattie was having a holiday but wondered how Bertie would cope with two young boys. His only daughter Siobhan had left for America some ten years before, after her mother Oonagh died of cancer. Bertie had nursed Oonagh at home and told Hattie that it was the lowest point of his life.

He'd felt guilty that he hadn't given Siobhan the time she needed and it was no surprise when his daughter up and left.

He'd insisted that Hattie bring the boys to Ireland and now, they all headed for his coastal farm fifty miles south of Dublin, a dairy farm on a hundred and fifty acres with a full pedigree herd. Bertie adored his horses, he was a keen rider and as she drove, Jo visualised Hattie bursting out of a blouse as she bounded along beside Bertie.

Jo flicked the radio to a classical station and made plans for the weeks ahead. The glorious weather in July had improved business and Jo had taken on extra part-time staff. A widow called Marian, who lived in the village, was helping in the kitchen. She'd cooked in hotels all her life and got on well with Sandra. Gerald now worked as a trainee chef – who would have thought it? The shy and clumsy boy had blossomed. Summer students stood in for him in the stillroom and he oversaw them with army like precision. But his passion was cooking and he thrived alongside Sandra, quickly learning basic skills. With everyone agreeing to keep an eye on him, he'd moved into the caravan. Arthur too was a changed man. He no longer seemed fraught with worry about his son and often dropped by the kitchen for a coffee and chat with Sandra.

Jo was however, worried about business going forward. No one wanted to commit for autumn and bookings were sparse. The daily news bore grim forecasts about the economy and the government warned of austere times. Jo knew it was affecting holiday trade and was thankful that Mr Mulberry's shoot would help the takings in August.

Cases of wine had already arrived and Jo would charge corkage on vintage wines from the Mulberry cellars.

ALF HAD BEEN COMMISSIONED to create kennels. He was busy at work on the outbuildings and had segregated two sheds into kennel arrangements, with warm sleeping quarters and an open run.

"You could eat your dinner off the floors," Alf had announced as Jo watched him brush up a pile of wood shavings.

"I'd sleep in there myself," she'd told him, ever grateful for his input.

Alf had told Jo that he looked forward to the shoot too. As chief beater he was responsible for all the arrangements, including the line of beaters who would drive the grouse for the waiting guns across the miles of moors that the shoot would cover.

It was a responsible position. Mr Mulburry had paid a fortune for the shooting rights.

Alf was to ensure that they got their money's worth – even the weakest gun would go home with several brace of birds.

Jo MADE good time and as she pulled onto the car park, she saw her parents' car by the entrance to her house. George and Jean were visiting for a few days. Jean sat at the kitchen table and spooned mashed potato and gravy into Thomas' eager mouth. He sat in his high chair and banged a plastic spoon on the tray, while Pippa positioned herself below and waited for any falling scraps.

"Hello, Mum." Jo embraced her mother.

"Your dad's in the garden stretching his legs," Jean said. "The place looks lovely Jo, you've been busy."

"This glorious weather helps," Jo replied. "Has Ann left?" Ann had a few days off and was spending it with her family in Marland.

"Yes she's long gone," Jean replied. "Now go and find your father and tell him all your news."

Thomas had potato all around his mouth and spat blobs in Pippa's direction. Jo kissed the top of his head then went in search of George. She found him in the garden, on a bench by the fountain where he chatted happily to Old Johnny. Both men sucked on pipes – Johnny's billowed smoke but George's was empty. Nipper lay quietly beside them but began to bark as Jo approached.

"Hello, Dad." Jo leaned down and hugged her father. "Has Johnny been filling you in with all the gossip?" She crossed her fingers and prayed that it wasn't cannabis burning merrily in Johnny's pipe.

"Aye and it sounds like you've been busy. I hear the garden's been getting plenty of use." George looked around at the fountain cascading over a rocky ledge as it flowed into the pond below. The croquet lawn was smartly cut in defined stripes and sprinklers gently watered the rich turf. Teak steamer chairs with thick padded cushions invited guests to relax and wrought iron tables with colourful umbrellas gave shade from the hot sunshine. The walls on either side of the garden were thick with clematis and climbing roses and tubs of bright red geraniums tumbled over the patio, where hanging baskets overflowed with pink and white trailing fuchsias.

George nodded his head with approval and looked further up the garden. The throb of a ride-on mower hummed as one of the village boys, stripped to the waist, cut the top lawn which led to the meadow.

Pippa hurtled across the lawn and Nipper rose to greet her. They wagged their tails and pranced round each other.

Nipper licked potato off Pippa's head.

"Yoo hoo!" Jo heard a squeal. Two men stepped out of the conservatory and crossed the garden.

"Excuse me, Dad. I need to greet those guests."

George and Johnny resumed their conversation and Jo ran across the lawn to Paulie and Robbie.

"Look at you two," she exclaimed.

Paulie wore a baseball cap, Bermuda shorts and leather sandals. Robbie was immaculate in pressed linen trousers, a cotton shirt and Panama hat. He carried a novel.

Paulie ran his fingers through Jo's hair and pulled a face.

"You need more high-lights," he said and flicked the fringe off her face as Simon approached with a laden tray. Steven followed with a bucket of chilled champagne.

"Be still my beating heart," Paulie whispered as he watched the twins cover a table with a cloth. He feigned a swoon. Steven placed a vase of pink garden roses on the table and unloaded plates of dainty salmon and cucumber sandwiches, a china stand of fancy cakes and dishes of strawberries and cream. The twins arranged steamer chairs and an umbrella and with polite nods retreated.

Jo picked up a napkin.

"I hear you've been having a tryst?" Paulie said.

"You shouldn't listen to gossip," Jo popped the cork and poured champagne into crystal glasses.

"You shouldn't create the gossip."

"The hotel's been too busy; I don't have time for trysts."

"What nonsense!" Paulie said. "A gorgeous girl like you, the more trysts the better. You must have men falling over you."

"Well there's a sales manager who seems very interested," Jo grinned.

"Ah, but has he any money?"

"I am sure he's very comfortable." Jo thought about the call she'd taken from Mark Pucker. He'd invited her out to lunch.

"We don't do comfortable, darling, only stinking rich. We want to get your mortgage paid off." Paulie whipped a bottle of Hawaiian Tropic out of his back pocket.

"Will you join us, Jo?" Robbie held a glass of champagne.

"You're very sweet but I must get on. Hattie is away in Ireland," Jo said as she folded the napkin around the neck of the bottle.

Paulie kicked his sandals off and sat down. He poured oil onto his palm and rubbed it over his chest and arms, then lay back and turned his face to the sun.

He extended one leg and dangled his toes in the sprinkler, playfully flicking water over Robbie who sat in the shade. Pippa settled beside him with her head on his knee and eyed the sandwiches.

"Don't worry about us," Paulie called, "just keep those twins coming with the fairy cakes."

As more guests wandered into the garden to enjoy afternoon tea in the sunshine, Jo placed a cushion under Paulie's head. "No naked romps in the fountain," she ordered.

"Oh don't spoil my fun, darling." Paulie pulled a face. "Is that your father?" He squinted over his designer shades. "I've always fancied older men." He gave George a little wave.

"Behave yourself. He'll have a heart attack." Jo fussed with the plates on the table.

"Ah, but what a way to go." Paulie held out his hand and Jo tucked a glass into his fingers.

"Off you go. You remind me of the grim reaper." Paulie waved her away. "What the eye doesn't see..." he teased.

Robbie opened his book and began to read.

"Mrs E, there's a telephone call for you," Steven called from the conservatory.

"Enjoy the afternoon, boys." Jo checked that they'd everything they needed then ran across the lawn.

It was deliciously cool in the hotel as she hurried through to reception and picked up the phone.

"Thank you," she mouthed to Steven and he disappeared into the kitchen.

"Jo Edmonds, how can I help you?" "Hello,

Jo. How's that son of mine?"

A familiar voice waited for her to respond. Jo gripped the receiver. Her legs gave way and she reached blindly for the chair. Greg! Her exhusband. She felt winded and grabbed the desk.

"Where are you?" she said.

"That's no greeting after all these months, not far away as it happens," Greg laughed. Jo heard the rhythmic tick of the clock in the hall. Time seemed to stand still.

"I thought you were in Spain?"

"I was but I'm back now. I want to see Thomas, well both of you," Greg added.

"Well you can't come here," Jo shouted the words.

"Are you stopping me from seeing Thomas?" Greg sounded incredulous.

"No, but I don't want you here. You'll have to meet me somewhere else."

"Don't be so stupid." Greg raised his voice but obviously thought better of it and in a quieter tone continued.

"OK, what if I meet you at the Old Red Hen Tea Room tomorrow?"

Jo hadn't a clue where the Old Red Hen Tea Room was but was anxious to end the conversation. She needed time to think.

"I'll meet you there at two o'clock but if you're not there I won't wait."

"OK, I'll be on time and ..." Greg began, but Jo had put the phone down. She could scarcely believe that Greg was back.

Her heart was racing as she walked into the conservatory and watched her parents in the garden. Jean had joined George on the bench and he bounced his grandson up and down on his knee. Jo observed the happy scene and decided not to tell them about the phone call. George would like nothing better than to get hold of Greg and Jo feared for her father's health.

She'd better just get it over with and meet with Greg the following day.

Jo couldn't bear the thought of Greg having anything to do with the hotel and he certainly wasn't going to get a foot over the doorstep.

Steven walked past with a tray of cakes.

"Where's the Old Red Hen Tea Room, Steven?" Jo asked.

"Marland, Mrs E. It's alongside Pete Parks' garage, he leases it out. Can I get you anything? You look quite pale."

"No I'm fine, thank you."

Pete Parks' Garage had a tea room? Of course it did. She remembered that you could access it from the forecourt shop.

It was a great little stop-off, just off the motorway junction. Damn! Why had she agreed to meet Greg there? Pete Parks was bound to be about.

Damn you, Greg! Why did you have to come back?

24

Greg parked the Rover at the front of the garage and lit a cigarette. He opened the driver's window to rest his arm on the sill and casually flicked ash on the grass verge. He checked his watch - twenty minutes to two, he was early.

Greg tilted the rear-view mirror and looked at his reflection. His hair had grown long and was streaked with blonde from the hot Spanish sunshine. Estelle had wanted to cut it but Greg liked the look, it complemented his deep tan. He checked his watch again - still too early. He felt restless and took a last drag on the cigarette, then threw the stub out of the window. He closed the window, picked up his wallet from the passenger seat and climbed out of the car.

Pete Parks stood by a Land Cruiser in the showroom and folded his arms. He watched Greg loop a thumb in his jeans pocket, then tuck his wallet in the pocket of his faded pink shirt and stroll across the tarmac. The Rover that Pete had sold to Greg and Jo last year, looked dusty and scratched. Pete shook his head. It'd been a cracking motor but no doubt Greg had thrashed it as he travelled round Europe with his fancy piece.

Pete saw Greg hesitate and glance at his watch. He looked around, then opened the door to the tearoom and disappeared inside. Pete wondered what was going on. He stared out of the showroom windows to the road beyond and decided that Greg was meeting someone.

A few moments later Pete saw Jo's BMW turn off the roundabout and head to the rear of his garage. Pete smiled, his question answered. He hurried to the workshop at the back of the building where three of his mechanics were engaged in various motor repairs.

Pete ignored them and positioned himself in the shadows by an open door, which gave access to vehicle storage. Jo's car came into view and inched into a space between a recovery vehicle and cars waiting for MOTs.

Jo got out. She looked around then unfastened the safety belt on the child-seat in the rear of her car. She leaned in, scooped Thomas up and jiggling him on her hip, threw a bag over her shoulder and closed the door.

Pete found it hard to read her expression as she pulled dark glasses over her eyes and walked with purpose around the side of the building.

He rubbed his hands together and smiled.

He knew where he'd get a good view of the tearoom and rushed back into the shop.

Jo WAS nervous and clutched Thomas tightly as his chubby little legs kicked against her bare mid-drift. She tugged at her cerise angora shrug and realised that it was far too short. It didn't come anywhere near meeting the tight black jodhpur-style pants tucked into her leather riding boots. She stroked her son's smooth skin and straightened his white socks as his toes squirmed under her fingers.

"Piggy toes, Mumma." Thomas chortled.

"Not now, darling." Jo whispered. She pushed the door and stepped into the tea room. It was dark after the brightness outside. Jo hesitated and tried to focus on faces in the room.

GREG SPOTTED HER IMMEDIATELY.

Mesmerised, he couldn't move as he saw his wife and baby for the first time in the best part of a year. Completely floored, he felt as though he'd been punched in the stomach and gripped the edge of the table.

Jo looked incredible.

She'd lost at least two stones and short hair suited her face. She wasn't even wearing makeup. The child in her arms was a little boy – not the baby in a crib that Greg remembered. The blonde haired little chap was the image of himself and Greg felt a lump in his throat. Tears stung his eyes. Oh Christ, he was going to cry. What in God's name had he done?

He watched Jo lift her sunglasses and rest them on her shiny locks. She frowned and turned to leave.

"Jo!" Greg cried out. "Over here." He stood up. Jo saw Greg and walked over to his table.

"I didn't recognise you." she said.

"You've changed."

They stared at each other. Thomas put his head on his mother's shoulder. He pulled and kneaded her shrug and looked shyly at Greg.

"Sit down, sit down." Greg fumbled and dragged a chair out. Jo walked around the table and sat opposite.

"Erm, what will you have? What about Thomas? What shall I get?" Greg looked from one to the other. "What does he have?"

"He'll have some juice," Jo replied. She reached into her bag and produced a bottle. Thomas began to guzzle.

"He's beautiful, Jo," Greg whispered, he could feel tears welling up again as a waitress appeared.

"I'll have some tea thank you," Jo said.

"Will the little fella have a biscuit?" the waitress asked as she wrote Jo's order down and stared at Greg, who looked confused. He'd no idea what the little fellow would or wouldn't have.

"No, he's fine thank you very much," Jo said. "I've got a rusk for him but the big fella probably will."

"Er, just tea for me and maybe some scones," Greg dismissed the waitress and leaned over.

"I hardly recognised you. You look amazing."

"You've got long hair - it suits you."

"You've got short hair." They
stared at each other.

"Oh Christ, Jo, what have I done?" Greg felt tears roll down his face and he reached out. Jo pushed a box of napkins towards him as the waitress placed their tea and a plate of scones on the table.

"Where's Estelle?" Jo asked coldly.

Thomas let go of his bottle, his eyes drooped as Jo nestled him in her arms.

"Oh, she's erm..." Greg waved his hand then reached for a napkin and dried his eyes.

"What?" Jo asked sharply. She lifted the teacups off the tray and began to pour.

"She's in Butterly, we've rented a place for a bit," Greg mumbled. He pushed a plate and knife towards Jo, followed by butter, jam and scones.

"You're back to stay then?"

"Well yes, I suppose we, er I am." Greg looked up.

Jo shook her head in disbelief.

"Look, Jo, I've been a bloody idiot. And sitting on the beach in Spain I realised what a fool I was." Greg's words tumbled out. I should never have gone away and left you." He leaned in. "We needed this break and we'll be great when we get back together," he smiled encouragingly. "You need me, Jo - you can't do this on your own." Greg's words gushed. "I could be back with you tomorrow sorting everything out." He was out of breath and sat back.

Jo stared at Greg. She tried to remain calm as she listened to his outburst. She gripped her tea cup. Greg wanted to come back? Jo was gob-smacked.

The room had fallen quiet. Other diners seemed to be waiting for her response.

"Let's get this straight, Greg," Jo began quietly. "You disappear with that Spanish slapper and leave me high and dry with a baby barely weeks old," she leaned in, "then, after a sojourn around the continent, you find yourself sitting in the sun thinking about home?" Jo paused, her voice had become louder. Stunned diners hung off her words as she continued. "With the funds running low you suddenly think, 'I know, I'll get in touch with old Jo – she's always been a soft touch and she's no looker. She'll have me back in a flash. But in the meantime I'll keep Estelle on the go just in case Jo needs a bit of convincing…', "

Greg dragged his chair forward and looked around nervously, the whole tearoom was listening.

He put his hand up to stop Jo, but she was in full flow.

She slammed her tea cup down and Thomas woke up. He wriggled about on her knee but she held on tightly.

"Let's get this categorically clear once and for all," Jo said, "I would never take you back, no matter how bad things were and if you think you can dance into my life with your sunny smile and start upsetting everything I've worked my arse off for, you're very much mistaken!"

Pete Parks winced. He was under the counter, hidden from view.

"You can see Thomas but you must call ahead and agree times," Jo continued. "You're not to step a single flip-flopped foot over my threshold or I'll take you to court for maintenance and you won't know what day it is with the shit that'll stick to you!"

Thomas began to cry and Jo stood up. She was close to tears too. She thought of John Doherty and shot a parting blow.

"Christ, you're not even good in bed."

Pete Parks punched the air and grinned. He raised himself from beneath the counter as applause broke out. Several diners stood up when Jo pushed her chair back and headed blindly for the door. Greg stood too and crashed his chair to the floor.

"Come this way, Jo," Pete called out. He held the serving hatch and indicated that she should follow him. Jo hurried through the gap. Greg was furious and shouted after her.

"I'll fight you for custody! Don't think you've heard the last, you won't keep him."

Pete stepped forward. "Now, lad, best get on your way, eh?" he gripped Greg's shoulder.

"Oh piss off, Pete!" Greg snarled.

"Off you go." Pete shoved a dazed Greg out of the door. He was tempted to kick Greg's backside but resisted. Pete smiled at the customers. "Show's over folks."

Pete found Jo in the shop doorway.

She clutched Thomas and tried not to cry as Pete led her through the showroom into his office and closed the door. He gently pulled them into his arms. Jo had begun to sob and Thomas bawled too.

"There there, lass, it's over – don't upset yourself." Pete comforted her. Eventually Jo's sobs subsided. She untangled herself and Pete held Thomas while she searched for a tissue. Jo wiped her eyes, blew her nose and looked at Pete.

"Thank you, I needed a hug." She reached for Thomas and as he settled in her arms he stopped crying. "I'm so stupid. I shouldn't let Greg get to me, but I suppose it's just the shock that he's back and has the audacity to think he can come waltzing into my life and business." Jo tried to explain.

"No, lass, don't say anything. The man's a twat and he's realised his mistake. You'll be alright now you've got that lot off your chest." Pete gazed at her cleavage and smiled.

"Did I really say all that?" Jo sniffed.

"Aye, it'll make headlines in the Westmarland Tribune - 'Man Gets A Lot More Than Tea With His Scones!'. " They looked at each other and laughed.

"I'd better get back." Jo picked up her bag and slung it over her shoulder. "I don't know what came over me."

"Don't apologise, I'll always be here for you, I've told you that." Pete thought about her lovely firm body in his arms, her naked waist, and the smell of soft clean hair - a million miles from the acrid aroma of horses that he was used to at home. He opened the door and led her out to her car.

"Now don't forget - don't take any crap off him and I'm only on the end of the phone."

Pete watched Jo drive away. She waved and blew him a kiss and Pete reached out with his hand and cupped the air. He held it in a fist as if catching her kiss.

With a sigh Pete turned and went back to work.

"WELL I NEVER, WHAT A CHEEKY BUGGER." Hattie exclaimed in wonder.

Jo sat in reception. She'd placed a call to Hattie in Dublin and they discussed the meeting with Greg. Jo clutched the telephone to her ear and leaned back as she listened to Hattie rant on. Hattie couldn't believe that Greg had turned up like a bad penny. Jo however, was beginning to have feelings of remorse. Perhaps she shouldn't have been so horrible to Greg? But she was scared that he'd weasel his way back into her affections and knew that she could never trust him.

"And you end up in the arms of Pete Parks?" Hattie almost yelled.

"He was only consoling me. Just being a friend." Jo stood up and closed the office door. The radio in the kitchen blasted out Rick Astley's Never Goin' Give You Up! Sandra and Gerald sang along noisily.

"My arse," Hattie said, "I'll bet Pete Parks' hands were groping for all their worth."

"He was very kind, Hattie, don't try and twist it."

"Oh he'll twist it alright. He'll screw it right into you if he gets half a chance."

"Hattie!" Jo feigned shock. A heavenly smell of freshly baked scones reminded Jo that she was hungry.

"Anyway never mind me, how are you getting on with Bertie?" Jo kicked her shoes off, put her bare feet on the desk and admired the pink polish on her toenails. Paulie had assured her that Barbie Pink was 'utterly glam' this summer. Her aqua marine, wrap-around silk dress fell softly to one side, exposing tanned legs.

"Are you having a great time?"

"Well the boys love it," Hattie replied. "They run around like two wild things all day and Bertie lets them, says they need to get Irish air in their lungs."

"And what about you, what are you up to?" Jo tucked the receiver under her chin and filed a pink finger nail.

"I'm having a grand time." Hattie went on. "Bertie is as generous as can be and keeps inviting folk over to meet us. His house keeper seems to do everything for him, which is just as well as he's so disorganised." Hattie lowered her voice. "To be honest the house is crying out for a woman's touch. He's mental about his horses and spends all his time with them. I even went riding with him but I hate it. I couldn't walk for two days, felt like my backside was in a vice."

"Hah! Probably wasn't the horse that caused that. I bet you're shagging from dawn till dusk and all night too. Have I got to bring a stretcher when I meet you tomorrow?" Jo laughed.

"Well I wouldn't say I am going without, put it anyway you want to – Bertie certainly does."

"You're impossible, Hattie." Jo said. "So what are the plans today and what time is your flight back?" Hattie had extended her stay by a few days and was due home tomorrow.

"We're off to the beach in a bit. Bertie's organised a picnic. He's got the boys riding. I think I'll just sit in a deckchair and watch. Honest, Jo, he really seems to have accepted us and it is so beautiful here."

"Well, what about you help me with the shooting party then get yourselves back out there for the rest of the holidays?" Jo asked. "Crikey, you'll be getting married next. Have I got to go and buy a big hat?"

"Pah, I doubt I'll be a bride again but I have to say you never know. You can wear pink crochet and hoops and look like a toilet roll holder." Hattie giggled. "I'll be back tomorrow and I'll think about coming back here soon. He's even mentioning schools to me to go and look at, but I've got Mam to think about, Jo. I don't know how she'd be if I up sticks and move."

"Oh come on, Hattie. Take her with you; I'm sure Bertie has masses of room," Jo reassured. "Don't let that stop you." Jo stopped filing and admired her nails. "It sounds like it's working out for you and you want a life with Bertie. I know he does, that was obvious from the first time he saw you." Jo's stomach rumbled.

"I doubt Mam would move but it isn't as though Dublin is on the other side of the world."

"Exactly," Jo said. She heard the front door buzzer and whipped her legs off the desk. "I'll have to go, Hattie, someone's just come in. Have a safe flight and bring me back a lucky leprechaun. See you tomorrow."

Jo hung up and slipped her feet into a pair of suede pumps that matched her dress. She reached for a lipstick. With her back to the desk she peered in the mirror and smoothed Barbie Pink over her lips.

"Can I have afternoon tea for three?"

The world stopped and the lipstick fell to the floor. Hardly breathing, Jo slowly turned around and faced John Doherty.

"We're closed."

"You're not."

John put his head on one side and looked her up and down. He raised an eyebrow and grinned.

"We are." Jo felt naked under his scrutiny.

"Your sign says open?"

"Fuck."

"That'd be nice, with scones too? They smell delicious." His grin broadened and his beautiful blue eyes glinted as he waited for her reply. "In the Green Room?"

"Fuck."

"I'll take that as a yes." John leaned over the counter, scooped her chin and kissed her. His lips were warm and as they brushed her mouth, Jo's stomach did somersaults.

With a wink, he turned and strolled off to the Green Room where Rory and Pete Vardy had made themselves comfortable.

"Fuck!" Jo whispered to herself. "Fuck, fuck, fuckety fuck!"

25

Greg woke early. Estelle was asleep beside him, her long black hair poured over the white pillow like a slick of sticky oil. Greg shuddered. He slipped out of the double bed and picked up his discarded jeans and shirt, then crept out of the room.

Their rented flat was on the third floor of a town house in Butterly and overlooked the River Bevan. As he unlocked the main door and loped down the stairs, Greg pulled his tattered loafers over his bare feet and stepped out of the flat. He darted under an archway and began a brisk walk along the main road, which led to a stone bridge crossing the river. He hurried over to Butterly high street.

The town was deserted so early in the morning and Greg was hungry. He could smell bacon and eggs and his stomach rumbled as he opened the door of the Lemon Tree Café, where a few early risers tucked into hearty Westmarland breakfasts. Greg crossed the wooden floor and found a vacant seat by the window. A pretty young waitress took his order and as he watched her retreat to the kitchen he thought about Jo.

Yesterday had been a real shock. He'd expected to meet a tired, fraught and overworked Jo, ambling along in her scruffiest clothes. He certainly wasn't prepared for the gorgeous creature who had, in no uncertain terms, told him exactly what she thought of him. His game-plan was teetering.

Greg heaped two sugars into a mug of tea and stirred thoughtfully. He wondered what the hell to do now. Estelle had been furious with him when he'd eventually got back to the flat. She'd taken one look at his face and knew immediately that his meeting with Jo had knocked him sideways. Greg had tried to pacify her. He explained that he'd not been emotionally prepared to see Thomas and it had upset him, which was in a way true. The kid was his image and the cutest thing he could imagine.

Estelle's command of English wasn't great and she'd ranted in Spanish for ages, but he'd got the gist – she didn't want him anywhere near Jo.

What a bloody mess! Greg had been convinced that he'd be back with Jo within days and Estelle on a plane to Alicante. But his plan had back-fired. Although he'd kept Estelle in tow as a back-up, he wasn't too sure that it was such a good idea. It had enraged Jo. He pushed his half-finished breakfast to one side and reached in his shirt pocket for a cigarette.

"Do you want anything else?" The waitress placed an ashtray in front of him and picked up the plate. She gave him a coy smile and hovered.

"Not right now," Greg said and grinned, he couldn't help himself and a pretty girl was irresistible. But he had to think of a way of winning his wife back. He dragged heavily on the cigarette and blew smoke rings as he stared out of the window and contemplated the situation.

The hotel she'd opened looked great and from the talk around the place, it seemed to be doing alright. He was so angry with himself. Jo had wanted to buy that place ages ago when it was going for a song, and he'd dismissed it as too much like hard work. Why rock the boat when the pub was making a mint? Christ, he'd like to have his feet under the table now. He could see himself behind the bar - mixing cocktails for well-heeled guests and entertaining the residents, many of whom would be rich attractive women. He'd seen Jinny Atkinson go in yesterday. Now that was a pair of hips he wouldn't mind handling! The last year with Estelle had drained him. Living a five-star lifestyle had depleted most of his bank account and there was barely enough to put down on a bar on the Costas. Not that he was keen to do that. Long days and late nights were all well and good, but he didn't have Jo driving him and Estelle hadn't a clue when it came to business, or conversation for that matter; she was very immature. She'd learnt quickly in the bedroom but even that was becoming a bit of a bore.

Butterly was gradually coming to life, and as he looked out, Greg lit another cigarette and surveyed the busy street.

In the last few days he'd driven to Kirkton Sowerby several times and parked by the pub to watch the hotel. Yesterday there'd been some very flashy cars outside. Two men met got out of a Ferrari and met up with a guy who pulled up in a top of the range Mercedes. They'd spent a couple of hours sitting in the room to the left and seemed to be having a meeting. People came and went for meals and some were staying. He'd seen a young man, smartly dressed in shirt and bow tie assisting people with luggage. Jo must be raking it in!

Greg ground his cigarette out and put some money on the table. The waitress gave him a wave as he left the café. He flashed a smile and noted the name Christine on the plastic badge on her apron. No time for flirting now, Estelle would be wondering where he was. He sighed. She nagged all the time and wanted to go back to Spain, she hated the damp English flat. How things had changed in a year! He'd got to turn this round! Somehow he had to find a way to get back with Jo.

Greg quickened his step and thought about Thomas.

Being a good father would certainly help. How could she turn him away once she saw how much Thomas would want to be with his dad? He rubbed his hands together and began to smile. It was only a matter of time. He'd find a phone box and give her a ring, perhaps he could take Thomas out this afternoon? He hadn't a clue what to do with a small child but Estelle would know. Feeling happier than he had in several days, Greg set off in search of a telephone.

"I CAN'T BELIEVE IT." Hattie was aghast. Perched on her stool in reception she watched Jo wriggle uncomfortably on the office chair. "The bloody cheek," Hattie continued, "he calls in for afternoon tea, uses the

Green Room for a meeting and pisses off without so much as a, 'When can I take you out for dinner?', "

"Well he paid for the tea and said he would call me in a couple of days," Jo replied limply. She wished she hadn't said anything to Hattie about John Doherty's visit the day before. It'd been made worse by Jinny Atkinson who turned up as Pete Vardy left. John took Jinny into the Green Room and closed the door. At least Rory hadn't left them alone together but Jo wondered what the hell was going on. Jinny had avoided Jo and for once, wasn't rude and arrogant.

"Jo, he's a little shite and you'd do better to kick him into touch." Hattie was angry and tapped a pencil against her palm.

"What's he actually done wrong Hattie?" Jo said. "He's a typical man; he looked for an opportunity and took it. He doesn't owe me anything." The words choked in her throat as she remembered John's kiss when he leaned over the desk.

"He's playing with your affections and he knows it," Hattie snapped. "He's got you on a piece of string that he can reel in whenever he feels like it and it's time you cut it." Hattie jumped off the stool. "He's obviously doing the same with Jinny Atkinson, I almost feel sorry for the poor cow."

"You're right," Jo sighed. She hated to admit it and felt so inexperienced in these matters, she hadn't a clue how to handle things and knew she should listen to Hattie and tell him to get stuffed. She decided to change the subject.

"More important is the problem of Greg. Can you believe that he's living in Butterly with Estelle and wants to pick up with me again?" Jo pushed her chair back.

"I think you need to focus on your work." Hattie flicked through the diary. "If you want any distractions away from this place, go and have lunch with that nice Mark Pucker, he seems a decent sort."

"He phoned again last night."

"And?" Hattie raised her eyebrows.

"I told him I'd think about lunch on Thursday." Jo watched Hattie check the bookings. Thursday wasn't busy and she could easily slip out for a couple of hours.

"That's settled then." Hattie shoved Jo out of the way. "Now let's see what you've got sorted for this shoot. I can smell a title and a double-barrel at five paces and it looks like we're going to be wall-towall with them."

HATTIE WATCHED Jo as she walked away and hoped that she'd phone Mark Pucker. Anything to stop her thinking about John Doherty and that idiot Greg who looked intent on causing problems. Thank goodness George and Jean had gone home. Hattie knew Jo hadn't told her parents that she'd met up with Greg. George would be livid. She shook her head and sipped a coffee. It was cold and tasted terrible. She wrinkled her face in disgust and pushed it away to focus on the booking chart and diary.

They should be full but bookings were bleak. Hattie remembered a conversation she'd had with Bertie as they sat in the sunshine outside his local pub as they watched the boys kick a football about on the freshly cut grass.

"There are tough times ahead, Harriet." Bertie sipped from a glass of Guinness. "Mrs Thatcher isn't popular and she's doing nothing to stop the interest rates rising, property will crash if it continues."

He'd ordered a bowl of Dublin Bay prawns and shelled them as they chatted. Hattie sipped a cider and watched Bertie dip the fat pink prawns in warm garlic butter.

"The stock market's shaky too," Bertie said. "I've got rid of my shares, it's too risky. We're in for a rough ride."

Hattie wondered what Jo's borrowings were and hoped the business was taking enough to cover her overheads. Hattie could sense that Jo was worried about money. Jo kept a regular check on her bank account and paid the takings in as soon as she had any.

Hattie tapped a pencil against the desk. Thinking about Bertie gave her a warm glow. He was such a dear man. Bertie's love for her shone with each worshipful look and Hattie bathed in his adoration, she'd never felt so secure with a man.

He'd introduced her to his two brothers and their endless offspring and they'd all got along famously. Mrs Flannigan, Bertie's elderly housekeeper, seemed to approve and told Hattie that it was grand to see Bertie happy again; the boys brought new life to the farm - like a breath of fresh air she'd said. It was long overdue. In the decade since Oonagh had passed Bertie had been lonely. He rattled around in the big old house with just Mrs Flanningan for company and spent far too much time with his horses. Siobhan was fifteen when Oonagh died, still a child but suddenly an adult. Hattie had felt sad when she held a photo of Bertie's daughter in cap and gown on graduation day. He'd struggled to raise Siobhan on his own. She was a constant reminder of her mother. How alienated Siobhan must have been, Hattie thought, she could understand why the girl had buried her head in her books and left the farm at the first opportunity for university in Dublin. Hattie felt sorry for both father and daughter. Siobhan lived in California now, the trophy wife of an IT whiz kid who earned a fortune in Silicone Valley. Bertie rarely heard from her, other than duty calls twice a month. He'd visited them once and told Hattie that he'd felt totally out of his depth with the young movers and shakers. It was a world far removed from the gentle green pastures of home.

Hattie had made her mind up to go and live with Bertie. She'd told him at the airport, when they were saying their goodbyes. Tears had streamed down his cheeks.

"By God, Harriet you've made me the happiest man alive. I'll treat your boys as though they were my own and cherish you with all my heart."

He held her tightly, not wanting to let her go. The boys stood alongside.

"Come on you rascals, be good for your mammy." Bertie reached out and swung them both in the air. "I'll have a football pitch marked out in no time. Somehow I'll get to like Manchester United, like half the population of Ireland," he laughed as he hugged them.

When Hattie went through the gates, she had turned to wave and saw Bertie standing on his toes to get a last sight of them.

"I love you, Harriet!" Bertie shouted, oblivious to the stares of other passengers.

Hattie had blown him a kiss then hurried to board the plane.

His adorable face was imprinted on Hattie's mind and she glowed. She'd never felt like this in her whole life and could barely believe it was happening to her. To find love again when she least expected it. Hattie's life had never been so good. She smiled smugly to herself.

The phone rang, interrupting her thoughts.

"Kirkton House, can I help you?" Hattie smiled. "Yes, Mr Pucker, she's available – one moment and I'll put you through."

26

Jo held her face towards the sky, the sun was deliciously warm on her skin and she was glad that she'd worn a sleeveless dress and sandals.

The Shepherds Inn at Salkeld was busy.

Fell walkers took time out of their day and gathered to enjoy a hearty pub lunch. Children played on swings and ran around the village green, whilst their parents sat at benches with picnics and pints of local ale. Fine weather and school holidays had filled the area with day trippers and Jo hoped the hotel was equally as busy.

Mark Pucker placed glasses and a bottle on the table.

"What's this?" Jo stared at the champagne. She'd asked for a lager and lime.

"I couldn't buy you a beer," he replied. "You're definitely a champagne lady." He removed the cork and poured and they chinked glasses.

Jo wanted to tell him that he shouldn't have spent his money but didn't want to insult him. Mark seemed a decent sort. He was casually dressed today, in a short sleeved cotton shirt, jeans and trainers and as Jo sipped her drink, she watched him ease his tall frame onto the opposite bench. He leaned his beefy arms on the table and picked up the menu.

Mark had arrived at the hotel promptly at noon and found Jo in reception. She'd greeted him politely and told him she was hungry. It was a cue to leave. She didn't want the staff to see them and have a good gossip, but Hattie had appeared from nowhere and made a great fuss of Mark. She stood at the window and stuck her thumbs up as they drove away and Jo prayed that Mark hadn't seen Hattie's gesture. They'd driven through the village and out onto meandering lanes, surrounded by leafy hedgerows and lush fields. Farmers were haymaking and Mark opened a window.

"Do you mind?" he'd asked. Balmy air carried the scent of freshly cut hay into the car.

"No, it's lovely," Jo replied.

Mark had chatted politely. He told her that he'd worked for the American tobacco company since leaving university and as northern sales manager, was responsible for a large team. The company sponsored many sporting occasions from motor racing to darts championships and part of his job was to entertain their clients at these events. He loved his job but it kept him away from his kids – he had two children from a broken marriage. His wife lived with her new partner in Surrey and he spent many hours up and down the motorway. Jo had listened as he drove, she tried to concentrate but couldn't help hearing Hattie's words,

"Don't look at his cauliflower ears, you'll get used to them, all rugby players have them."

Jo was drawn to his ears. It was hard not to be, they seemed to dominate the sides of his head. Hattie said he was a nice man but Jo wasn't at all sure that she wanted a 'nice' man. Subconsciously she knew that a naughty man suited her far better. She wanted excitement in her life, not safety. She thought she'd had that with Greg and look where it'd got her! Great Dun Fell had appeared in the distance and Mark followed the sign for Salkeld. The village lay at the foot of the fell, with the pub on a rise overlooking the green. It was a chocolate box image complete with a duck pond and club-

house, where you could watch cricket on the green from the wooden veranda. They'd parked by the pub and found a table and seats outside.

"I expect you've noticed my ears," Mark sipped his drink and studied the menu. "I'll have cosmetic surgery when I stop playing rugby. I really should stop now, but it's hard to give up."

"I hadn't noticed," Jo lied.

He told her about his team in Darlington and playing for England under 21's when he was at university. His caps were proudly displayed under glass domes at home.

They ordered their food.

"I wasn't sure if a pub was ok," Mark looked anxious.

"Don't be daft. It's a real spoil to get away for a couple of hours," Jo said. Mr Knight from the Westmarland Trust Bank sat a few tables away with his wife. They both waved.

"You probably know everyone?"

"Not at all." Jo nodded politely at the Knights. "I hardly get out and any spare time is spent with Thomas. Kids grow so fast, as you know."

"Yes they do," Mark replied. "I hardly recognise mine if I don't see them for a few weeks."

Their meal arrived and Jo shook out a serviette. She looked at her food - a huge Yorkshire pudding filled with savoury mince.

"This is lovely. Thank you so much for asking me out."

"My pleasure, Jo, I hope it will be the first of many meals together." Mark raised his glass and tucked into his food.

"So has Perky Pucker asked you out again?"

Hattie sat at the table and watched Jo mash banana in a Beatrix Potter bowl then scoop some on a spoon.

"Yes, unfortunately, I wish he hadn't. I can't get my head around relationships." Jo made swooping noises like a plane and moved the spoon through the air. Thomas kicked his arms and legs and squealed with delight as it landed in his mouth. Pippa sat beside Jo and leaned against her legs.

"He wants me to go to the Gateshead Garden Festival next week. There's a 'Stars in Their Eyes Night.' His company is sponsoring it and he's one of the judges."

"Well you should go," Hattie replied. "Isn't Princess Anne opening the festival? Think of the conference business he'll bring." Hattie thought of the empty bedrooms and winter months to come.

"Let's get this shoot out of the way first and then I'll think about it. He knows I'm busy for the next few days and he's off to see his kids this weekend."

"Did you have a snog?"

"I just pecked him on the cheek and said goodbye."

"Very chaste I'm sure. Bit out of character for you."

Jo ignored the comment and scraped the bowl. Thomas squealed again and she managed to swoop the last of the banana into his eager mouth. She picked up a rusk, broke a piece off for Pippa and gave Thomas the rest.

"Greg rang again, you can't avoid him." Hattie scratched Pippa's head. "You'll have to let him have Thomas, even though you don't want to."

"I know," Jo sighed. She unfastened the safety strap on the high chair and lifted Thomas onto her knee.

Thomas chortled and began to suck on his rusk.

"He can come for him next week and take him out for a couple of hours. I'm not having Greg anywhere near while the shoot is here, he'll only poke his nose in." Jo bounced Thomas up and down.

"There's also the other matter..." Hattie sighed and shook her head.

John had called the previous day and asked for Jo. It was with great delight that Hattie informed him that Jo wasn't available; in fact Jo was away from the hotel having lunch with a male friend.

"He didn't sound too happy and really grilled me," Hattie chuckled. "I told him your friend was the MD of a tobacco company, played rugby at club level and was entertaining you in some style."

"The Shepherd's Inn?" Jo pulled a face. "Well that will put the lid on things. Did you have to elaborate so much?" Jo tried to hide her disappointment.

"He needs a reality check," Hattie was adamant.

Ann appeared from the kitchen, she held a beaker of warm milk and smiled when she saw Thomas.

"Shall I take the little darlin'?" Ann lifted Thomas off his mother's lap and cuddled him to her ample body. Thomas reached out for the drink and his rusk dropped to the floor.

"Jackanory's on the TV my precious, let's leave Mam to her work."

Ann held Thomas so that Jo could kiss him and they disappeared up the stairs for story time. Pippa followed, the sticky rusk gripped in her mouth.

"You're probably right, Hattie. I have to stop thinking about John." Jo sighed. "Anyway, far more important, are you going to get yourself off to Dorothy's for some country wear for Ireland?"

"You bet! I can't believe that I'll be shopping at The House of Osbourne," Hattie grinned. "Just think, I may even go and scare the silky drawers off our Vera and get some decent undies. That's if she's sober enough to serve me."

Hattie looked thoughtful and remembered Bertie's gift as they parted at Dublin airport. As she boarded the plane, Bertie tucked a folded cheque into her pocket and told her to spoil herself. When the flight took off Hattie retrieved it and to her utter astonishment saw that he'd made it out for a thousand pounds. It was more money that Hattie could imagine and combined with her winnings from the trotting she felt like all her Christmases had come at once. She was overwhelmed by Bertie's kindness and love.

"Just look at you, you're glowing," Jo laughed. "Bertie's brilliant for you and as soon as this shoot's over you must get straight back to him."

"I will, he phones me ten times a day. Let's get someone in to help you though. I'll not leave till I'm sure you'll be alright."

"Don't worry, Hattie. The way bookings look going forward, I'll be laying staff off not taking them on."

At last, Jo admitted her fears.

"Let's just get through this weekend shall we?" Jo said.

They looked at each other. So much had happened in the last few months.

"It'll all come right," Hattie tried to reassure Jo. "What's meant for you won't go past you." She picked up her pen and notepad. "Let's go and do another check-list for the royalty that's arriving tomorrow, we'll show them some real northern hospitality."

"And they can show us some southern money," Jo replied. "Let's get this show on the road!"

27

The shooting party guests were due to arrive at any time. Jo checked her watch against the clock on the hall table as it chimed four times, the pretty peal echoing through silent reception rooms.

She stood on the landing at the top of the stairs and looked out of the tall windows to the empty drive below. Soon it would be full of vehicles.

Behind her the bedrooms were prepared. Each had flowers, fruit, welcome cards and tins of freshly baked shortbreads alongside decanters of sherry. The bathrooms had extra towels on heated rails and fluffy white dressing gowns with complimentary slippers.

Jo drummed her fingers on the polished banister rail. She longed to straddle the smooth warm wood and whiz down the length, but instead, she trotted demurely down the stairs. The hotel would soon be full of affluent guests and Jo was acutely aware that one good shooting party could lead to many more and help the hotel's revenue. One thing was certain - they wouldn't survive the winter without them.

A heady perfume of roses, freesias and lilies greeted her; vases of carefully arranged flowers were in abundance. Jo walked into the bar where Steven was polishing glass flutes.

"All ready, Mrs E?"

"I hope so, Steven, they'll be here soon."

Jo marched past pedestal arrangements on either side of the Rose Room door and saw Hattie fiddling with Simon's bow tie.

"Any time now I reckon," Hattie called over her shoulder as she shoved Simon's chin up. The room was laid with one long central table where silver candelabras rose from mounds of pale yellow garden roses. "Beautiful!" Hattie said and patted Simon on the shoulder. "The room looks good too."

Vintage red wine from the Mulberry cellars had been decanted and stood alongside champagne and white wines that were chilling in large silver vats on the mahogany sideboard.

Jo felt sick in the pit of her stomach. She smoothed the crepe of her black suit.

The lining had been repaired after Hattie's exploits, but Jo had lost more weight and the suit was loose. She walked through to the bar and Hattie poured her a Cointreau. Jo silently picked it up and knocked it back gratefully.

"Action stations!" Steven shouted from the hallway.

Hattie and Jo looked at each other and Jo gulped.

"Teeth and tits out?" Hattie winked. Jo nodded and they hurried to the front door as two black Range Rovers crunched to a halt on the gravel. The twins were elbowing each other as they stared at the registration plates - Cider 1 and Cider 2.

"We've luggage, dogs and guns for Mr Mulberry and his brother," the drivers said. "They'll arrive shortly by separate vehicle."

"Thank you gentlemen," Jo smiled. "Your rooms are reserved at The Templars over the road."

Jo remembered that the landlord of The Templars had been uncharacteristically friendly when she'd made the booking.

Hattie explained to the chauffeurs that Steven would show them the courtyard to unload and Sandra and Gerald were waiting to take picnic hampers, which over the course of the weekend would be filled with food and drink to accompany the shoot.

Two handsome black Labradors sat calmly in the back of Cider 1 as Jo and Hattie watched the vehicles disappear under the archway leading to the courtyard.

"I hope Pippa's locked in the house." Jo looked anxious and bit her lip.

"They'll not give that mongrel a second glance." Hattie steered Jo back into the hotel.

"Do you think I should have got her a new lead?" Jo visualised Pippa's length of rope.

"A new pedigree couldn't help that one," Hattie said, "come on."

With drivers despatched and dogs in kennels, the twins took the Mulberry brothers' luggage to the front bedrooms. They deposited the leather trunks on wooden racks and placed gun cases from Holland & Holland safely in bureaus. Jo and Hattie waited by the front door for the next arrival.

"It's like Upstairs Downstairs," Hattie said as she watched the Range Rovers pull up outside the pub. "How good is this? Not only do you have No Vacancies on the board outside, but you'll soon have a fleet of amazing metal out there too. That'll set tongues wagging as folk drive past." Hattie folded her arms across her chest and leaned forward to watch the traffic beyond the gates.

A man in a pink shirt got out of a car in the pub car park and stared over at the hotel.

Hattie recognised him. Frigging Hell, not Greg! Hattie silently cursed. Jo had her back turned and was busy dead-heading geraniums in an urn by the door. Hattie glared at Greg and raised her middle finger.

A vehicle turned into the gates and Jo spun around.

"Here we go, bloody hell it's a Roller." Hattie stuck two fingers in her mouth and whistled down the corridor for the twins as a silver Rolls Royce purred to a stop by the front door. Yet another liveried chauffeur appeared and ran around to open the passenger doors.

Henry Mulberry climbed out of the car and stretched, his chauffeur held out a silk-lined jacket and Henry slipped it on. Another man appeared from the back of the car.

"Good afternoon, Mr Mulberry, we hope you had a pleasant journey." Jo held out her hand in welcome and Henry shook it warmly.

"Indeed we did, Mrs Edmonds, meet my brother Hugo."

His companion stepped forward. A younger version of Henry, Hugo was immaculately dressed in wheat-coloured corduroys, checked shirt, cashmere sweater and a red silk cravat.

"Our guests are in transit and should arrive shortly," Henry rubbed his hands.

"Of course, Mr Mulberry, would you like to freshen up after your journey? Simon and Steven will show you to your rooms. You might like tea and cakes when you're ready?"

"Or something a little stronger..." Hugo leaned in and Jo could feel his breath on her face.

"Are the dogs being attended to?" Henry ignored his brother.

"They're comfortable in their kennels, sir," Hattie chirped up. She bowed her head as though addressing royalty and seemed to dip at the knee. Jo looked at her incredulously, Hattie being reverent? Fortunately, the brothers appeared not to notice and Henry asked to see his dogs, Sefton and Oscar.

"Follow me, sir." Hattie curtsied again and led Henry off to the Kennels. Jo shook her head and followed Hugo, who'd wandered into the Green Room.

"Perhaps a snorter before everyone arrives?" Hugo said. He studied the paintings on the walls then looked at Jo. A leer crept across his shiny face.

"Of course, what can I get you?" Jo smiled.

"Now there's a thought." His eyes rested on her breasts. "Whisky and a dash for now old gal, make it a large one."

Jo forced another smile. Hugo's ruddy round cheeks bulged and she wondered if he rubbed cream in his skin to make them so rosy.

THE GUESTS ARRIVED over the next two hours and were soon familiar with the hotel. Jo and all the staff were kept busy, as luggage was whisked away and unpacked and numerous dogs deposited in the kennels where Alf was on hand to supervise arrangements.

"I hardly recognised you," Jo said.

They stood on the cobbled yard by the coach house. Alf looked immaculate in single pleat breeks, complete with gleaming buckle and shiny leather boots. He leaned over the dog-run and dug deep in the cartridge pocket of his tweed waistcoat, pulling out a handful of biscuits to feed to the pack.

"You'll be wantin' to marry me next." Alf gave Jo a cheeky smile.

"Bugger off, Alf" Jo suppressed a grin. "And make sure those dogs don't foul my lawns."

"I'll be over the road with the drivers having a pie and a pint." Alf doffed his cap, checked his watch and decided to go and meet the chauffeurs and brief them on timings for the following day.

Alf had been working all hours in preparation for this shoot and was pleased with the results. The red grouse he'd reared had been allowed to breed unmolested; they were fully mature and ready for the Home Counties set to enjoy a weekend's sport. Most likely with a lot of misses and cock-ups, Alf thought cynically as he stroked the heads of the agitated Spaniels and Labradors. When he was satisfied that the dogs were fed and comfortable, he headed for the pub.

As he approached the kitchen window Alf waved at Sandra and Gerald. He could see Judy was at the stillroom door, she grinned and wolf-whistled as he went by.

"Nice threads, Alf." Judy called out.

Alf felt his cheeks colour and hurried past before Judy noticed. She seemed to be smiling at him a lot these days. He made up his mind to pop back in a bit to let the dogs have a run in the meadow and perhaps have a word with her. In the meantime, there was a pint waiting.

Hattie appeared at the door; she pushed Judy out of the way and called out to Alf.

"If there's a fella by the pub in a poofy pink shirt clocking this place, warn him off, will you?"

"Who'd that be then?" Alf stopped.

"The twat who was married to Jo. I think he's got his sights set on her again."

"Sorted," Alf nodded.

Judy appeared behind Hattie's shoulder and Alf winked at her. With a spring in his step, headed off for the pub.

"Only two more to arrive and they won't be here till after dinner." Jo sat in reception and checked names off the booking chart.

"By heck there are some right posh pieces out there," Hattie said as she watched Jo write out bills on duplicated headed forms, then place one for each room in a concertina rack.

"It's a sea of yah'ing and braying, I'm amazed any of them knows what the other one's saying." Hattie shook her head.

"Will you help with drinks?" Jo asked. "The twins are run off their feet."

"I'll attend to it immediately, your Highness." Hattie jumped off her stool and straightened her blouse. The white fabric strained across her chest. She gave Jo a wink and disappeared into the cocktail bar.

Jo studied the evening's menu.

Cream of Leek Soup
or
Duck Terrine

Whitebait with Sauce Tartar

Medallions of Venison with Juniper and Redcurrant
Jus or
Fillet of Sea Bass with a Savoury Mousse, served on a bed of Spiced
Spinach

Sticky Toffee Pudding with Ice-cream
Summer Fruits in Raspberry Sauce

Westmarland Cheeses with Crisp Oatcakes

Coffee and Tiffin

She was relieved that she'd checked Hattie's typing for errors. The 'D' in the duck had begun life as an 'F' and Jo wondered if Hattie did it deliberately. She looked at the list of things to do for the shooting party. Simon needed help with the champagne and she must check that Sandra's canapés were ready. Henry wanted aperitifs at seven and dinner at eight and she must make sure that Kath had arrived to turn the guest's beds down and tidy their rooms. No doubt they'd all need fresh towels.

Jo filed the bar tabs into folders and glanced at the clock on the switchboard. It was nearly six-thirty. She picked up the menus as the phone rang.

"Good evening, Kirkton House Hotel," Jo said pleasantly.

"Not playing with rugby balls tonight?"

John Doherty's voice was prickly. Jo stifled a gasp and dropped the menus.

"Pub lunches aren't your style, Jo, don't lower your standards."

"Who on earth are you to tell me..." Jo sank onto the chair. Her pulse raced as she gripped the receiver.

"Ok, I'm sorry," John softened his tone. There was a long silence and neither spoke. Jo's hand shook. Had she just heard an apology? She closed her eyes and wondered where he was calling from.

"I've got a shooting party here for the weekend. I can't talk to you now," she said.

"I'm taking you out next week for a proper lunch, I want to spoil you." John's voice was gentle. "I'll call you in a couple of days. See you soon gorgeous." He hung up.

Jo stared at the receiver. Her heart threatened to burst through her ribcage.

"Seen a ghost?" Hattie stared at Jo. "Has Creepy in the Conservatory come back?" Jo seemed to be in a trance. "Who the hell was that?"

"Erm...wrong number."

"My arse. It wasn't anyone of Romany stock by any chance?" Hattie shook her head in disbelief.

"He wants to take me to lunch next week."

"Now there's a surprise, probably putting out a contract on a rugby player as we speak." Hattie banged the desk with her hand. "Come on, Jo, stir your stumps, you've got half of Kensington and Chelsea out here speaking a language I can't fathom." Hattie took the phone out of Jo's hand.

"I'm coming," Jo stood up. Put him out of your mind! She told herself angrily. But he'd called her gorgeous and he wanted to spoil her.

Jo's stomach did bunny hops and with an effort not to punch the air and whoop down the hallway, she followed Hattie to the Green Room.

28

The shoot departed for the moors after breakfast and Jo and Hattie sat at the table in the Rose Room, amongst the debris of the meal.

"What time did you eventually get to bed?" Hattie spoke with a mouth full of buttered toast.

"God knows," Jo replied. "Hugo bloody Mulberry is like a oneman-missile, charged-up and raring to launch." She reached for her coffee and yawned. "I spent the early hours being chased around the kitchen table, fending him off with a rolling pin." Jo watched Hattie spread marmalade on a croissant.

"Hmn… he had his hand up my skirt a couple of times during dinner." Hattie munched hungrily. "He's a letch."

The fleet of Range Rovers, Cider 1 to Cider 6 had cruised away from the hotel packed with hung-over residents. Old Johnny and several villagers had stood and watched from the opposite side of the road as the party set off.

Gerald and Marian's carefully prepared lunch was packed into wicker hampers, alongside bespoke wooden drinks cabinets in the back of the vehicles. At lunchtime on the moors the guests would dine on Hunters Stew from large flasks, with freshly baked rolls, followed by a savoury picnic loaf, fruit cake and cheese. The meal would conclude with coffee and chocolate tiffin. The first 'livener' of the day would begin with a brandy when they met Alf on the fell.

Jo put her feet up on a chair and cradled a glass of orange juice. She watched Judy snuff out tea lights from beneath a Georgian food warmer, then lift the lid to one side. Pippa nudged Judy's leg and drummed her tail against the cloth.

"Fancy some scrambled egg and bacon, Mrs E?" Judy asked. "It still looks alright and there's kidneys and mushrooms left," she held out a slice of bacon and Pippa snapped it up.

"God no, thanks though." Jo drank her juice. The thought of food made her queasy.

"You hit the Cointreau a bit hard last night?" Hattie said as she brushed crumbs off her mouth with the back of her hand.

"Yes I suppose I did," Jo replied. "It hardly seems to affect me anymore." Pippa placed her head on Jo's lap and glanced sideways at the warming tray and Jo stroked the dog rhythmically as she thought about the previous evening.

The place had been dripping in diamonds and pearls, as sophisticated couples appeared for dinner. The food had been delicious and everyone was complimentary about the menu. They'd been especially enthusiastic about the sea bass. Gerald had made a delicate sauce with fish stock and combined with Sandra's light mousse it had paid off. A toast had been made to the chef. Sandra was mortified when Jo told her that she was wanted in the dining room, but she changed her apron and bustled forward to acknowledge the drunken cheers, before returning to the kitchen flushed and happy. Gerald and Marion clapped their hands proudly.

Hattie interrupted Jo's thoughts.

"The food was great," Hattie said and pushed her plate to one side. Pippa switched allegiance and turned to Hattie's lap.

"Who'd have thought it?" Jo pondered.

"You did. You gave them a chance, no one bothered to before," Hattie looked at the left-over bacon and sautéed potatoes.

"Is there something going on between Arthur and Sandra?" Jo asked.

"Have you only just noticed?" Hattie took two strips of crisp and curling bacon and a spoonful of sautéed potato.

"Think of your hips," Jo said.

"Bertie likes the fuller figure." Hattie looked smug. She broke a piece of bacon rind and gave it to Pippa. "They've been an item for a bit now. Arthur runs her home when he's sure Gerald is safe in the caravan."

"Is he running Sandra back in the morning?"

"Let them have a bit of fun, you miserable devil, just because you're not being bonked senseless by the gypo."

"Hattie how can you say..."

Jo let her words hang in the air; she knew that Hattie was right. Everyone around her seemed to be pairing off. She'd even noticed Judy making eyes at Alf, but he did look very dapper in his finery.

Thinking of finery, Jo smiled as she thought about the guests that morning. The rain had lashed down as the cars were loaded. Barbour raincoats appeared to breed over an army of tweed and leather, with some very fetching combinations. Vibrant wool socks and a variety of head-gear peeped out. One female, Lady Malvern, tucked damp feathers into the band of her trilby.

The dogs had barked excitedly and drowned out conversation as Pippa stared longingly out of the house window. With her paws on the window-seat she'd howled as Sefton and Oscar were led across the drive.

Jo remembered the gun boxes on the gravel.

"Let's hope no one shoots anything other than birds." She wondered if the guests were experienced shots. "Did you see Lady Malvern this morning?" Jo asked Hattie. While the guests had dined the night before, Kath tidied the rooms and turned down beds. She'd placed a wrapped chocolate on each pillow.

"Did I..." Hattie laughed. "Her pearl earring was encrusted in chocolate." She shook her head. "She was out for the count last night, must have hit the pillow like a plank." The girls giggled.

"She'd drunk two bottles of Saint-Emilion before the end of the main course." Jo remembered Lady Malvern at breakfast.

"Morning m'dear's!" Lady Malvern had barked as she strode into the Rose Room. Thick lisle stockings rubbed against a heavy wool skirt. "Slept like a log." She swept past the staff who jumped back to stand to attention.

"Pissed as a fart," Hattie said. "She poured brandy in her tea."

"I think she was married to a Mulberry cousin."

"No wonder she's permanently pissed, with Hugo's roving hands." Hattie forked the last of the potato into her mouth.

"She was rambling about nannies," Jo looked thoughtful. "And Hugo kept banging on about uniforms, saying how much he liked them. I wonder if my black suit and stockings encouraged him?"

"Undoubtedly," Hattie dabbed her mouth with a serviette. "God help you if you were wearing a pair of Vera's big support pants, they'd be sure to turn him on."

"He leered over reception earlier, to whisper good morning," Jo shuddered. "He's got terrible breath."

"Be all those cigars," Hattie wrinkled her nose. She glared at an abandoned plate, where someone had rammed the butt of a cigar into a congealed egg yolk. They both shook their heads.

"Think of the money, Jo. Just think of the money."

"Hmm... I'm thinking." Jo stood up and opened the French doors. "At least the rain's stopped. We need some fresh air in here."

Pippa flew past Jo and bounded up the garden.

"For God's sake don't let her anywhere near those dogs," Jo said and thought of Sefton. "I don't know what's wrong with her. You don't suppose she's in season do you? She's seems demented at the moment." "Not the only one," Hattie mumbled.

"Are you going to get your fat bum off that chair and do some work?"

"Yes m'lady! Just as soon as I've put me big knickers on."

"Bertie's on the phone, Hattie." Judy called out. "I've told him we've got a load of VIPs in and you're taking very good care of them." "Oh shite, I've told him I'm very prim and proper now." Hattie ran to reception.

"Give him my love," Jo called. "Tell him I'm sending you back very soon."

Jo WATCHED Hattie retreat and wondered if she should start planning a wedding outfit? It wouldn't matter when it was; bookings were bleak over the next few months. The hotel should be full - autumn in Westmarland was usually busy.

She walked out to the garden and watched Pippa race around the top lawns, her nose glued to the ground tracing every scent. Jo had heard on the radio that morning that interest rates were going up again and property prices falling, she daren't think about her overdraft and hoped that the shoot takings would keep Mr Knight happy for a bit. She'd need to be very creative to drum up business over the next few months and knew that she must work on building conference business. More shooting parties would make things easier too.

"Pippa!" Jo called the dog. Pippa raised her head, ignored Jo and disappeared through the gate to the meadow. "You can stay out." Jo said crossly and hurried back to work.

THE GUESTS ARRIVED BACK in the late afternoon, bedraggled but happy from the wet and windy moor. They climbed out of the Range Rovers in search of hot baths and further sustenance.

"Lady Malvern is sitting on the drive," Hattie whispered. Hattie's arms were full of soaking raincoats. "I'm not going near; she's got a knife."

Jo shook her head in horror as they looked out of the side window.

Lady Malvern sat cross-legged on the gravel, in the rain, with a brace of grouse on her lap with more piled beside her. Feathers flew as she plucked the limp and lifeless birds and feathery down stuck to her mud encrusted face.

"It's like a scene from Ryan's Daughter..." Hattie muttered beneath armfuls of sodden wet wool. "I'll put this lot in the cellar to dry off before you put me up for Miss Wet T-Shirt." The tweeds clung to Hattie's thin blouse. Jo was tempted to ask Lady Malvern if she needed assistance but decided to send Simon.

"Like a lamb to the slaughter," Hattie giggled. She tugged at her blouse and watched Simon cross the gravel. Lady Malvern waved her knife perilously close to his face and indicated that she wanted a drink. Simon looked terrified and flew through the door to the bar. A voice boomed down the corridor.

"I say! Where's our Hostie?" Hugo Mulberry was in hot pursuit. Hattie and Jo dived into reception and crouched behind the desk.

"The Hostie with the Mostie! What?" Hugo stopped by reception.

"Too late," Hattie whispered and gave Jo a shove. Hugo Mulberry leaned over and waved an empty glass.

"Lost something, ladies?" his eyes glued to Hattie's damp blouse.

"You'll loose your friggin' eyeballs in a minute..." Hattie whispered under her breath. "Dropped our pencils," she beamed. "What can I get you sir?"

Hugo thrust his glass out. "Large Scotch, old gal."

"Large one it is." Hattie dumped the raincoats on the office chair, took the glass and disappeared. Hugo trotted behind her.

The shooting party took tea in the Green Room then retired to freshen up before dinner.

Jo went to get changed and was in the shower when Hattie interrupted her.

"The Spanish Love Machine's on the phone," Hattie said and held the shower curtain back. Jo gesticulated that she didn't want to take the call, but Hattie thrust the phone towards her. Jo grabbed it crossly and leapt out onto the bath mat. Hattie threw her a towel and with a smirk, disappeared.

"Hello?" Jo said.

"Hi, Babe, you busy?" Greg was on a charm offensive. Jo felt herself bristle as she heard his voice. His smooth words would have pleased her once, now she felt her hackles rise.

"What do you want, Greg?"

"Thought I'd drop by tomorrow, take the little man out for the afternoon. That's if you have no plans?" Greg waited for Jo to reply. Her thoughts went fast forward. The shoot would be out on the moor and the hotel quiet. It was as good a time as any.

"You can come for Thomas at two o'clock, but I want him back by six," Jo said. That gave her time to get Greg off the premises before the evening rush.

"Sure thing, Babe. You seem to have the place rocking, judging by the cars..."

Jo hung up, she didn't want a conversation with Greg. She looked at her face through the misted mirror. Why do I have to be so aggressive with him? She asked her reflection and wrapped the towel tightly around her damp body. She sighed and went to get ready for evening service.

GREG STARED AT THE PHONE. The line was dead - she'd hung up! He replaced the phone on its cradle and opened the heavy door of the telephone box then fumbled in his shirt pocket for a cigarette and flicked his lighter. As he blew smoke rings in the air and looked around the village green, he told himself that she must be busy. She usually held onto his every word.

But this new Jo was different and Greg felt uneasy.

He thought about an incident in the pub the previous day when a stranger had approached him. The man was dressed in shooting gear and seemed to know everyone. He'd nodded curtly then leaned over and spoke quietly into Greg's ear.

"You need to stay away from the lass over th'road."

"I beg your pardon?" Greg was startled.

"You heard. She's got a lot on and doesn't need the likes of you getting in the way." The man glared at Greg then turned and left.

Greg had downed his pint and pushed the glass forward for a refill. The landlord, who'd been chatty until then, pumped beer into the glass, took Greg's money then turned his back and began a conversation with a bunch of drivers staying at the pub.

Greg inhaled. This was going to be tricky. Clearly Jo had a following, not surprising as she employed half the village. Greg was used to getting his own way and felt depressed, he could usually charm his way out of most situations.

He thought about Estelle. She'd nagged all morning and complained that he never took her anywhere. In the end, he'd stormed out. How he longed to be back with Jo! To be comfortably ensconced in the hotel with a loving wife and son. What a bloody fool he'd been. Greg flicked the butt of his cigarette onto the grass verge and kicked out angrily. He was wearing flip-flops and swore as his foot connected with the metal frame of the phone box.

Cursing, he limped back to his car.

29

In The House of Beauty, Jo relaxed in a leather chair and watched an assistant pour coffee. Paulie was tinting Jo's hair and he leaned in to listen to the gossip whilst painting colour on to segregated locks, before folding them into strips of silver foil.

"Well I never…" he said and urged Jo to continue.

After three exhausting days and nights, Jo had finally despatched the shooting party. It had been mayhem. Staff flew about, fetching luggage and returning abandoned items to their clueless owners, who eventually stumbled into the chauffeur-driven vehicles.

The guests had enjoyed a raucous breakfast-come-brunch and Lady Malvern knocked back several brandies, before falling asleep on the plate of her half-finished Westmarland grill. Congealed egg yolk clung to her chocolate coated earring. Hugo Mulberry had a final feel of Hattie's ample behind and roared with laughter when she slapped his hand.

"I love a gal with spirit!"

Henry Mulberry stood in reception and settled the bills. He never flinched as Jo produced the total amount. He signed a Coutts cheque with flourish, then handed Jo an envelope of cash. It contained five hundred pounds, his gratuities for the staff.

"You've done us proud, thank you," Henry said. "We'll be back next year but I'm sure you'll see some of my guests well before then." He'd looked around and seemed to be searching for something. "Have you seen Sefton this morning?" Henry's Labrador was missing.

"I think you'll find him in the back of Cider 4." Jo had replied. She'd winced and hoped that Pippa wasn't in there too.

"THE BEDROOMS ARE BOMBED, PAULIE." Jo sighed and took a sip of coffee.

"Darling, I can imagine."

"None of them paid a scrap of attention to our no smoking policy and the place stinks of cigars. They were completely blotto for three days and there's such a mess everywhere."

Paulie shook his head.

"I've left the staff blitzing the place."

"It'll be sparkling when you get back," Paulie pursed his lips and folded the last foil. He patted her shoulder and disappeared.

Jo was exhausted but elated. The shoot was a great success and she'd been able to deposit a considerable sum into the bank which would take the pressure off for a week or two. Many of the guests had asked about future shoots. They belonged to various consortiums and were interested in shooting in the area. Alf would have no trouble in securing rights and had done a fine job with the supply of birds, ensuring that even the worst shot went home happy.

Paulie returned. He clicked his fingers and an assistant rushed forward to replenish Jo's coffee.

"Isn't Hugo Mulberry a Conservative MP?" Paulie asked as he checked Jo's hair.

"A true blue if ever you saw one."

"Very blue by the sound of things."

"Hands like an octopus, but my wine cellar is empty and the bar dry, it was worth every grope and grapple."

"What about Sefton?" Paulie raised his eyebrows. "Where on earth did you find him?" Jo closed her eyes.

SHE'D BEEN certain when she'd locked up the previous night that Pippa was alone in her box under the stairs. This morning however, two tired dogs slumbered happily together, their snores clearly audible when Jo flew into the lounge.

Pippa thumped her tail as she saw her mistress.

"Holy shite!" Hattie had exclaimed as she descended the stairs. "I wondered what the noise was." Hattie gathered her dressing gown and shook her head. "Their snores have been raising the roof. Sefton looks buggered."

"So   does   Pippa."

Neither dog moved.

"You'll have to get him out of there," Hattie whispered. They could hear voices from the restaurant. "Henry will have a heart attack if he sees his precious dog with a mongrel."

"Get dressed and find Alf," Jo hissed. "He's bound to be here, waiting for his tips."

Alf had immediately taken control.

"The Master's lookin' everywhere for this 'un." He clipped a lead onto Sefton's collar and tugged hard.

As the weary dog edged out of the box, Pippa howled.

"I'll get him in a vehicle and no one will be any the wiser," Alf said and furtively disappeared through the side door.

"WHAT A NAUGHTY GIRL!" Paulie clapped his hands to his face.

"Henry would have shot her if he'd found his precious Sefton anywhere near an unkempt mongrel, she's lucky to be alive," Jo shook her head.

"Is she in season?"

"Oh, who knows Paulie."

"Well I'm delighted that the weekend was a success for you, sweetheart, perhaps you'll pop into Mondi on your way home and treat yourself eh?"

"I might just do that," Jo said. "There's a lovely white crochet suit in the window."

"It's got your name on it, darling, but you need a hot date to go with it." Paulie blew a kiss and left Jo with a selection of magazines. "Ten more minutes," he called.

Jo turned the glossy pages. Her mind was a million miles away from the photos of a smiling Duke and Duchess of York who were celebrating the birth of their daughter, Princess Beatrice.

Jo thought about John.

He'd said he'd call and her heart skipped a beat as she remembered. She flicked a page and scanned the headline. Mrs Thatcher was visiting a navy patrol in the Gulf. Jo wished the Prime Minister would stay at home and sort out rising interest rates. She pushed the magazine to one side. John wouldn't phone and it was no good getting her hopes up. With a sigh, Jo reached for another magazine and studied the fashion pages.

"BY HECK, YOU'RE A NEW WOMAN." Hattie looked up from her paperwork as Jo stepped into reception and deposited several carrier bags.

"And you've been spending your ill-gotten gains?" Hattie looked at the bags with interest.

"It's exhausting keeping up appearances, Hattie." Jo slumped into a chair.

"Well it's not as exhausting as re-stocking and cleaning this place." Hattie drew a pencil line through a long list of jobs.

Jo leaned over to check. She could see that Hattie had completed all the orders and new supplies would soon be here.

"The phone's been ringing while you were out, and guess what?" Hattie said.

"What?"

"Mark Pucker's booked the Rose Room for a one-day conference on Thursday."

"God that was quick," Jo sat up. "I thought he was away with his kids."

"He is, but wants to get his team together and says it'll be handy to do it here."

"Well that's easy enough." Jo worked out what they would need. "Flip charts, boardroom seating, coffee, some lunch and afternoon tea."

"He's asked for a barbeque lunch in the garden."

"We can do that if the weather's still fine."

"I've told Gerald to wire-brush that old oil drum and Alf's rigged up a frame." Hattie was pleased with her improvised arrangements. "Is Greg having Thomas on Thursday?"

"He thinks he is, but he can think again," Jo snapped, she was furious with Greg. The day before, he'd returned Thomas two hours later than agreed and Jo had been frantic with worry, she'd visions of the child being whisked off to Spain. Greg had appeared at eight o'clock, just as the restaurant was getting busy and the shooting party about to sit down.

"Well I don't know what you expected, after the way you spoke to him." Hattie stifled a grin as she recalled the previous afternoon.

GREG HAD PULLED onto the drive at two o'clock precisely and parked by the house. Jo had Thomas in her arms and went to meet him. Ann followed behind carrying a bag that bulged with everything the child could possibly need for a few hours with his father, whilst Hattie dragged the buggy over the gravel and began to collapse it down.

Greg was charming as he greeted everyone. He wore a pale blue cotton shirt and printed on the fabric was a bikini-clad girl holding a beach ball. Around her smiling face was the motif, Lovers Do It Better In Espana!

Hattie nudged Ann as they watched Jo read the words. Her face was a picture.

"Lovers do it better in Espana?" Jo said incredulously. "You couldn't do it very well here, never mind bloody Spain!"

Greg's face turned puce and he was about to retort but Jo thrust a car seat into his arms. She handed Thomas to Ann, kissed his head and threw a parting shot. "Back by six and no later."

"Don't you think it was a bit harsh?" Hattie tried not to laugh as she remembered the incident. Greg had regained his composure quickly but Hattie knew he was furious.

"Oh he deserves it, Hattie." Jo looked perplexed. "I suppose it was a bit cruel though. But if he will wear such a stupid shirt." Hattie snapped the diary closed.

"Well I thought it was hilarious, he needs that smirk wiping off his smug face, but you can't blame him for being late. He had to get back at you somehow."

"I suppose not, I just hate the thought of him driving off with Thomas with Estelle only a few hundred yards away. He couldn't cope with Thomas on his own."

"Well you'll just have to get used to it." Hattie reached for her bag. "That sod I was married to doesn't come near my lads. At least Greg made an effort."

"I can't help but think there's an ulterior motive," Jo said. "Anyway, you've got Bertie now; he'll be a good influence for your boys." Jo watched Hattie's face light up.

"Aye, and talking of Bertie, I'm off to get some decent tackle, see you later." Hattie threw her bag over her shoulder and ran down the hallway.

Jo watched her go. Hattie was travelling to Ireland on Sunday and Bertie's money was burning a hole in her pocket. Hattie planned to be away for the rest of the school holidays but Jo knew it was unlikely she'd be back. Her new life was in Ireland.

"Shall I take over, Mrs E?" Judy appeared from the kitchen.

"Please, Judy." Jo glanced at her watch and began to gather her bags.

"Fancy a cup of tea before you disappear?"

"That would be lovely, thank you." Jo looked at Judy's neat new blouse and freshly washed hair, which softened her pretty face.

"You look nice. Is Alf on his way in by any chance?"

Judy blushed and hurried off to get the tea as the phone rang.

"Good afternoon, Kirkton House." Jo put the bags on a chair and reached for a pen.

"Hope you've got something sexy to wear on Thursday?" John Doherty whispered.

Jo's heart missed a beat and her eyes flew to the embossed Escada carrier bag, where the white crochet suit lay wrapped in layers of soft tissue.

"Underneath too," he teased. "I like the red lace best."

Jo sucked her stomach in and closed her eyes.

"I'll pick you up at twelve."

"Er, okay. I'll be ready." Jo's pulse raced.

"I take it you've ditched the rugby player?" John's voice had an edge.

"There's nothing to ditch." Jo crossed her fingers. Thursday? She thought and opened her eyes. Bugger! Mark was here with his conference.

"Good. I'll see you then." John hung up.

"Here's your tea, Mrs. E. Are you alright?" Judy asked. "You've gone all flushed."

"I'm fine Judy. It's very warm in here." She put the phone down and picked up the mug while Judy held the door.

"See you later, get some bookings in - we're going to need them soon."

Jo skipped past Judy. John was taking her out for lunch! She beamed as she headed off to try on her new suit.

HATTIE FLOORED the accelerator pedal and forced her old car into life. It chugged along the main road out of Kirkton Sowerby where the traffic was unusually light for an August afternoon. Even with the glorious weather, holiday makers seemed thin on the ground - people had begun to feel the pinch.

Hattie felt content.

For once, the worries weren't hers. She'd got a fantastic man who was going to spoil her rotten and make a home for her. They would be a proper family and Hattie couldn't wait.

She slowed as she approached the motorway, then drove onto the slip road and joined the fast-moving traffic. A green and red truck flashed its headlights to let her in. Betty Marie was embossed across its cabin.

Good old Eddie Stobart, Hattie thought as she held her hand up to thank the driver of the local fleet wagon, the most courteous drivers on the road.

Hattie was going to treat herself today. She was determined to buy at least one decent outfit, more if Dorothy had a sale on. She'd get a couple of pretty bras from Camille's too and wondered if Vera would be sober. Hattie planned her route around the shops, which included a trip to the boy's department in Hoopers and a nice dress for her mam, who was coming to visit Bertie's farm during the last week of their stay in Ireland.

She'd been amazed that her mother had agreed.

"There's no bus back from heaven our Harriet," her mother lit another cigarette from the butt she'd just finished. "I'll take me chances like you and get some memories under me belt, afore it's too late."

Hattie knew her mother loved her grandsons too much to be parted from them for long.

She sighed happily. It was all going to be fine for her family. If only it could work out well for Jo too. Hattie thought about Mark Pucker. He seemed keen but Hattie knew that it wasn't reciprocated and no amount of encouragement would make Jo see things differently. Not while John Doherty was on the scene. What was it with him? For the life of her, Hattie couldn't understand Jo's attraction. Hattie thought he was trouble in capital letters. But even Bertie had admitted a soft spot for John and he'd known him for years. Hattie would have to find out more and made a mental note to question Bertie when the opportunity next arose.

She thought about Greg who was a pain in the arse. He was trying to worm his way back in to Jo's affections and must have some money left from the settlement. Maybe he could help, Hattie thought.

But it would mean Jo taking him back and Hattie knew that would never do. What a bugger that the economy was struggling so badly. Jo had set up a cracking business which brought life to the village and everyone loved working at the hotel. All Jo needed was more customers. Hattie wracked her brains. She'd leave no stone unturned before she went away.

The sign for Carlisle loomed and Hattie slowed the car to make the turn. It rattled as she crunched through the gears. With any luck, she'd be driving something fancy soon.

Life couldn't get any better. Hattie sang to herself and with a grin from ear-to-ear, headed into Carlisle to make her purchases.

30

The conference was laid out in the Rose Room with a big square table in the middle. A flip chart stood by the back wall with a projector close by. Chairs were tucked in and blotters lined up, alongside pencils, water glasses and a dish of mints.

Jo moved around the table and straightened each setting then checked her watch, conscious that Mark would arrive at any moment. She walked over to the French windows where blooms of climbing roses hung heavy around the frame. Jo flung the doors open and inhaled the heady scent of the old English flower. The morning sun flooded the croquet lawn and swallows dive-bombed the crystal-clear water in the pond.

"It's beautiful," Mark stepped onto the patio and surprised her. He placed his briefcase down and touched Jo's arm. She turned and he kissed her cheek.

"Did you have a good journey?"

"Yes but the motorway was busy, it's going to be a long day." Mark pulled out a chair and sat down.

Penny appeared with a tray of coffee and a bacon sandwich.

"Will you join me?" Mark asked.

"Yes of course." Jo sat down and watched Mark pour a cup of coffee. He added hot frothy milk and pushed the cup towards her.

"How are you?" Mark smiled as Penny placed another cup on the table.

"Good thanks. I've just about recovered from our shooting party." Jo stirred the coffee. "They were a bunch of night owls."

"But lucrative?" Mark raised his eyebrows and bit into his sandwich. He dabbed at his mouth with a linen napkin.

"I certainly can't complain," Jo replied. "But you've got a busy day?" She nodded towards the Rose Room.

"Just a catch up with the troops, I need to fire them up a bit for the autumn, lots of new promotions coming on." He finished his sandwich and looked at the garden. "I could get you some big umbrellas to go out here." He studied the parasols dotted around.

"I'm trying to discourage smokers, not flash your logos all over the place," Jo laughed.

"We could make it worth your while," Mark said.

"Sponsorship too, don't tempt me." Jo stood. "You should have everything you need and Hattie will supervise lunch." She glanced at her watch again. Nearly nine o'clock. Three hours to go to her lunch date with John. Her stomach did a cartwheel.

"Have you got a busy day?"

"Lots of jobs today but I'll be back later." Jo crossed her fingers behind her back. Thankfully, delegates had started to arrive and distracted Mark.

"Just let Hattie know when you want anything," Jo said and left him to his conference.

"By HECK, we'll have to keep our wits about us today." Hattie flopped down on Jo's bed and knotted her hands behind her head as she watched Jo storm around the room.

"Why on earth did you tell Greg that he could come for Thomas at noon?" Jo threw her towel to one side and rubbed body lotion on her legs.

"I didn't think it would be a problem, I don't keep your personal diary." Hattie looked away as Jo glared at her. Hattie knew perfectly well that John was arriving at noon too.

"Whatever you do, make sure Mark is still in his conference. Don't break for lunch until at least one o'clock." Jo thrust her arms into a pale cream Rigby and Peller bra then stepped into matching lace knickers.

"It'll be like a theatrical farce if they all get sight of each other." Hattie suppressed a smile and watched Jo slip into the white crochet suit.

"Hattie, I trust you to keep them all at a distance," Jo implored. "Put John in the Green Room, Mark in the Rose Room, and Greg at the back door."

Jo applied her make up.

"We just need Passionate-Pete-Parks to do a reckie and RobertUnrequited-Love-Mann to turn up and we'll have a full house." Hattie giggled.

Jo shook her head and slipped into a pair of gold sandals.

"Beautiful," Hattie nodded. "Will we be seeing you again today?"

"Of course you will. I'm only going out for lunch."

"I don't think it'll be Macdonalds or a pub, I've a feeling you might be dining at a restaurant with rooms."

"Oh bog off, Hattie. Go and get some work done, I need to speak to Ann and make sure Greg brings Thomas back at six."

"Yes m'lady." Hattie slipped off the bed and doffed her brow, then moved backwards out of the room. Jo couldn't help but smile as she watched Hattie's performance.

"I'll fetch you a Cointreau!" Hattie called out.

Jo twirled in front of the mirror. Her suit was gorgeous. It was a perfect outfit for a summer day. She sprayed herself with perfume and took a final glance. You'll do. She nodded happily at her reflection.

HATTIE POURED Cointreau into a liqueur glass and placed the bottle back on the shelf. She heard the front door buzzer and lifted the bar hatch to step into the corridor.

John Doherty stood in the hall. He'd parked his gleaming Mercedes by the front door.

Hattie heard a rustle in the bar and turned around. Mark Pucker appeared from the Rose Room.

"Hattie, could we have some more coffee please?" Mark stared at the Cointreau.

"Of course, Mr Pucker, I'll just take this to a guest and be right with you." She placed the drink on a silver tray as Jo appeared in the doorway and bumped into Mark.

"You look lovely," Mark said.

"Erm, thanks. I have to see some suppliers." Jo crossed her fingers and gripped her clutch bag. She looked at Hattie who stared anxiously over Jo's shoulder. Greg had pulled up by the house and was heading across the gravel to the side door. Mark had his back to Hattie and didn't see her gesticulate as she drew a finger across her throat, pointed to the hallway and mouthed the word 'Greg!' Jo froze. Greg had opened the door and stepped in.

"Mrs E, there's a gentleman here to see you." Judy came into the bar, flushed from greeting John.

Hattie still had the tray in her hand and attempted to block the doorway. Mark turned and over Hattie's shoulder, saw two men collide in the hall. John and Greg politely apologised to each other.

"I'll bring your coffee straight away, Mr Pucker." Hattie urged Mark out of the bar.

Jo had disappeared.

"Greg, you need to go to the other door," Hattie said and smiled sweetly. "Thomas is in the house, not here."

Greg looked puzzled but retraced his steps.

"Mr Doherty! How nice to see you." Hattie gritted her teeth.

"Where is she?" John walked past Hattie. He went into the bar and saw Mark rejoin his colleagues.

The phone rang and Judy answered it.

"Yes, Mr Parks, a table for four tonight at seven o'clock, we'll keep that for you." Judy wrote the reservation in the diary.

Hattie swore under her breath and glared at John.

He studied her very carefully.

"Not a rugby convention by any chance?"

"God no, just salesmen from a chocolate company." Hattie forced a smile and waved John forward.

"I'll go and see where she's got to," Hattie said and encouraged John to return to the Green Room, but he stared out of the window and watched Greg take Thomas from Ann.

The front door opened and Hattie told Judy to see who was there.

Hattie heard a house phone ring. "Excuse me," she said to John and raced to reception where the switchboard lit up a call from Room Four. Hattie banged the tray down and the glass toppled, spilling some of the Cointreau.

Hattie picked up the phone.

"Is it safe?" Jo whispered.

"Where the hell are you?" Hattie hissed back.

"Hiding in Room Four, I panicked."

"For heaven's sake don't come down the back stairs. John's in the bar with Pucker on hover-mode and Greg is about to send out a search party for you. Leave it five minutes then take the main stairs. I'll get John in the Green Room." Hattie held her hand over the receiver and prayed that John hadn't heard her.

She looked up. John stood by the desk and stared at her.

"Have a seat in the Green Room," Hattie gulped. "She's just popped over the road. You'll catch her as she comes back in." John turned and walked down the corridor.

Hattie picked up the Cointreau and downed it in one gulp. She gasped as it burned her throat. She hated Cointreau!

"You alright, Hattie?" Judy leaned over the desk. "Not having a funny turn?"

Hattie had turned purple and her eyes watered as she began to cough.

"Is Mrs E on a date with the gorgeous Mr Doherty?" Judy wanted the gossip.

"Get some more coffee for the Rose Room and don't hang about," Hattie croaked, "I don't want that lot circulating."

"I'm just getting Mr Mann a coffee. He's in the Green Room talking to Mr Doherty."

"Holy Shite!" Hattie closed her eyes, held her burning throat and counted to ten. When she opened her eyes she saw Greg standing before her.

Judy waltzed past with coffee for Robert Mann and Mark stood by the bar door.

"Judy! Get the Rose Room coffee... Now! Your coffee is on the way, Mr Pucker." Hattie grabbed the tray.

"Hattie, is Jo around?" Greg asked. "I wanted to bring Thomas back a bit later..."

"Not now, Greg!" Hattie snapped and raced down the hall.

Jo appeared on the landing but Hattie held up a hand to stop her.

"Robert Mann!" Hattie mouthed and pointed to the Green Room. "Greg!" She nodded towards reception.

Jo stopped dead as Hattie surged into the Green Room where John and Robert sat in the bay window and chatted.

"Mr Doherty, your guest is ready," Hattie put the tray down in front of Robert.

John stood up. "Good to see you, Robert, enjoy your coffee."

"Good to see you too," Robert said and shook John's outstretched hand. "Shame Jo's not here, she's the only reason I've stopped by." Robert looked away.

John's eyes met Hattie's. She willed him not to speak as he walked past her to the hallway. Hattie followed and closed the Green Room door.

Jo was halfway down the stairs as Hattie manoeuvred herself into the hallway and prayed that Greg would stay put in reception.

Jo saw John and hurried down the stairs.

"Good to see the hotel's busy," he said.

"I'm hungry, shall we go?" Jo smiled and glided past.

"Don't let me stop you saying goodbye to anyone." John held the door.

Hattie visibly relaxed.

"Better get back to work, Hattie," John said. "You seem to have a lot to do." He looked at Greg who stood in the hallway and stared at Jo. John gave Greg a curt nod then followed Jo out of the hotel.

Robert stood by the Green Room window and watched John open the car door. Robert gazed longingly as Jo eased herself into the luxurious vehicle.

Hattie hurried Greg on his way and made sure that Judy had served coffee to the conference. She flopped onto the bar and let out a deep sigh, then reached for the Cointreau and poured a large measure.

"Bleedin' hell," Hattie shook her head as she slugged the drink back. "That was close!"

WISHAW BAY COUNTRY HOUSE HOTEL lay on the shores of Lake Ullswater. A private jetty stretched out onto the lake and was surrounded by twenty acres of immaculately maintained mature gardens. Luxurious accommodation in the main house was complimented by a further five guest cottages in the gardens. The restaurant was positioned to overlook the lake and had breathtaking views of the surrounding fells.

It was a stunning location for a romantic interlude and Jo absorbed the beauty of the place as they swept up the drive. A uniformed valet appeared as John pulled up by the front door.

"Good afternoon, Mr Doherty, madam." He held the door for Jo as she climbed out of the sports car and prayed that she hadn't flashed her knickers.

John tossed his keys to the valet. He took Jo's hand and they skipped up the steps to the hotel into a dark hallway leading through to the bar.

There was a conservatory on the right, with lounges to the left and large glass doors opened onto a patio which overlooked the lake. John spoke to the barman then turned and smiled at Jo.

"Shall we?"

They stepped outside into the warm sunshine, the panoramic view was breathtaking. A pair of cane armchairs with soft downy cushions were positioned either side of a table and parasol and they strolled over and sat down.

Within moments the barman was at their side. He fussed about with ice-cold glasses and a wine stand, then produced a bottle of Dom Perignon and deftly opened it.

John raised his glass. "To our lunch," he said.

Jo's stomach fluttered as his blue eyes gazed at her. She took a gulp of her drink to steady herself and the champagne bubbles exploded in her mouth as the delicious liquid crept down her throat and calmed her nerves.

"You look gorgeous," John smiled a lazy, sexy smile. Jo felt herself melt and was glad that she was sitting down; her body was weak with anticipation and happiness.

"Thank you," she said and took another sip of her drink.

A waiter appeared with a tray of canapés. He took great care to explain each one, then produced menus and spoke of the house specialities.

Jo's menu had no prices.

"Have you been here before?" she asked.

"No."

"They seem to know you."

"I phoned ahead."

John was immaculate in a light linen suit and pale blue shirt but he fiddled with his tie.

"I could do without this," he said and loosened the knot.

"They'll have a stroke if you go into the dining room without it."

Jo thought of the two wonderful old gentlemen who owned the hotel - etiquette was paramount in their establishment. They'd run it for decades and it was their life's work. The place was crammed full of expensive antiques and kitsch memorabilia and was admired the world over.

They ordered their lunch and enjoyed the atmosphere, as life on the lake gently floated by. A steamer full of tourists came into view and Jo heard a loud-speaker, as a guide described the famous hotel in detail. Passengers waved to the guests on the terrace and Jo found herself waving back, she felt so relaxed and happy.

John took her hand.

He gently rubbed his thumb along her skin as they watched the boats on the water.

Jo was in heaven.

"Lunch is served, sir."

They were led into the dining room to a table set in the bay window, which had privacy and a magnificent view. A waiter unfolded a napkin and placed it on Jo's knees.

"This is lovely, John, thank you," Jo said.

"Better than a pub lunch?" John grinned mischievously.

"Most definitely."

"You've made quite a hit in Kirkton Sowerby." He leaned back and studied Jo. "Robert's like a love-sick school boy."

"He's no such thing," she replied as a waiter used silver tongs to lift a bread roll from a basket.

"I take it that was your ex with your son?"

"Yes. He wants to see Thomas on a regular basis."

"And how do you feel about that?"

"Not very keen if I'm honest." She spread creamy butter on the light floury dough.

"Started doing conferences too?"

"Do we have to talk about work? It's so nice to be away from it for a few hours." Jo looked down at her plate.

John leaned over the table and put his fingers under Jo's chin. He tipped it upwards and gently stroked her skin; his fingers traced her cheek bones.

"No, gorgeous, we don't."

Two waiters stood by with the starters.

"Let's talk about all the places I would like to take you to and make love, starting with here and now." John leaned in and gently kissed her mouth.

Jo's heart fluttered as she responded.

After a few moments John sat back. The waiters moved forward and placed the plates on gold edged chargers.

Over the next few hours Jo enjoyed every second with John. He was the perfect partner – considerate, thoughtful and attentive to her every need as they ate their meal. It seemed natural to be so leisurely on such a perfect afternoon. John spoke a little about his business and background, but Jo felt it was like pulling teeth.

She learnt that he was from a large family and had tough times growing up.

He glossed over living arrangements with his siblings and changed the subject when she asked about school. He told her that he bought and sold property, mainly land deals, up and down the country. He enjoyed his cars but never held onto any - they were quite lucrative if you bought well and sold on to the right buyer. She asked about Pete Vardy and John explained that he'd known him since they were kids and Pete had since built up a huge car business.

Jo decided to ask about Jinny.

"She's just a friend, Jo. I've known Billy for years." John wouldn't be drawn.

They both ate fish as a main course and enjoyed a bottle of Chablis Grand Cru. Jo felt very mellow when they returned to their seats on the terrace for coffee. The afternoon had turned into evening. John moved closer, he laid his arm across the back of her chair and stroked her shoulder.

"Want a liqueur?" he asked.

"I'd love one but I'll fall asleep, I feel so relaxed."

"I've got something for you."

John pulled a small box out of his pocket and Jo looked up in surprise.

"You don't have to do that," she said and watched him put it on her knee.

"I want to. I'm happy when I'm with you," John smiled. "Go on, open it."

Jo held the little leather box and pressed a gold pin. It sprang open. A diamond sparkled back at her from its black velvet bed. It was mounted on a platinum chain.

"John, it's the most beautiful thing I've ever seen!" Jo gasped. "I couldn't possibly take it."

"Sshh…" He took the necklace from its box and placed it around Jo's neck. "Gorgeous. Just like you."

Jo was speechless and thought she was going to cry. She touched the stone and stared at John. God, he was so lovely. His blue eyes shone as his handsome face smiled back. Jo thought that she'd never been as happy as she was at that moment, sitting in the glorious sun, in a beautiful place with the man of her dreams. She leaned forward and threw her arms around him and he kissed her passionately.

"Mmn… I think we should get a room," John whispered as he nuzzled into Jo's hair.

Jo looked up.

A group of people appeared on the terrace and a waiter pointed in their direction.

"John, there's a policeman coming towards us."

Jo recognised the policeman. It was young Malcolm from Marland station, his parents lived in Butterly and he used to drink in the pub.

"Hello Jo," Malcolm began. He took his helmet off and held it under his arm.

"What is it, officer?" John asked, "Will you sit down?"

"Aye, I will," Malcolm replied, "thanks."

A waiter rushed forward with an additional chair. Malcolm looked at Jo and took a deep breath.

"Jo, I've bad news," he began. "It's to do with your friend, Hattie, I'm afraid. Judy told me you were here. I'm sorry to spoil your meal, but I think you need to be with her when we break it."

Jo's mouth was dry and she clutched her diamond. She began to pray and dreaded the words Malcolm was about to say.

"It's Bertie O'Reilly. He was killed this afternoon."

The breath sucked out of Jo's lungs and the table spun before her. She heard John gasp.

"There's no easy way of putting this I'm afraid. He was riding on the beach near his home and witnesses say something startled the horse and Bertie came off. It seems the horse kicked his head. The horse was in a terrible state, prancing and frothing and couldn't be controlled. It's all a bit of a mess."

Jo felt her world spin. Strong arms were around her and someone was holding a glass of iced water to her lips. She heard John's voice, as he held her.

"It's alright, officer, I'll get her back to the hotel. Hattie's on duty, we'll tell her, but I'd appreciate you being around to clarify things."

Jo gulped the water. Whatever was she doing? Hattie needed her! She had to get to her as quickly as possible. She stood up and saw John place a bundle of notes in the bill folder on the table. He shook Malcolm's hand and took Jo's. He led her to the car, which had been brought to the front of the hotel.

"Are you alright?" He glanced over as they sped through the lanes leading back to the main road.

"Yes, I think so."

"You've had a shock."

"So have you, he was your friend too."

Jo held John's hand and saw that his eyes were watery as tears dripped down his face.

"Hey, pull over, you can't drive like this." Jo handed him a tissue but John shook his head and kept going.

"The policeman's following us. We need to get things sorted." He began to punch numbers into the car phone.

Jo stared out of the window. She couldn't believe this was happening. One moment she was in paradise - a place Hattie had found too. Now she was speeding along on a mission to break terrible news.

News that would destroy Hattie's dreams and shatter her heart. You have to be strong, Jo! She braced herself and sat straight. Her time for crying could come later.

Hattie was the most important thing now.

THEY TURNED into the hotel gates and John switched off the engine. He turned to Jo.

"When we get out, I'll have Malcolm tell Judy and the staff. Get Hattie into the garden or a room somewhere quiet." John thought about Thomas, he didn't want the child to hear the upset that was to come. "We'll need to get her home and be with her when she breaks it to her kids and her mother. You must stay with her. Can Judy cope with the hotel?"

Jo thought ahead. They were quiet tonight. The conference should have finished and there were only a couple of rooms dining. Judy and Sandra could manage with whatever staff they needed.

They climbed out of the car as Malcolm parked his squad car discreetly by the archway.

"Ready?" John squeezed her hand.

"Yes, let's get on with it." Jo squeezed back. She braced herself for what was to come.

They went through the front door. Hattie hurried down the hallway to greet Jo.

"I thought I heard a car," Hattie smiled. "Nice timing, old Pucker has packed up, pissed off and paid his bill. He said he was sorry to miss you though." She glanced over Jo's shoulder and saw John.

"Shite, sorry..." Hattie lowered her voice. "Did you have a good time? Pete Parks is due in any minute for dinner." She glanced at her watch.

"Hattie, I need to talk to you. Come and sit down."

Jo took Hattie's arm and led her into the Green Room but Hattie had seen Malcolm in the porch, he was speaking to John.

She looked anxiously at Jo and grabbed her elbow. Hattie began to tremble. "What is it, Jo? Is it Mam?" Hattie said.

Jo felt Hattie's body slump and with great care she guided her to a sofa, then closed the door and went to sit beside her friend.

John heard the scream.

It was followed by terrible sobs. Simon rushed down the hallway; he saw the closed door and looked nervously at John.

"Fetch some brandy and two glasses, son. Better bring the bottle."

31

It seemed as though the whole of the county had turned out for the funeral and the weather was as sombre as the scene as a persistent drizzle fell from muddy grey skies.

Hattie and Jo walked slowly behind the cortege with Bertie's family and followed the black mourning carriage, harnessed to a single statuesque horse. Her ebony coat glistened as rain fell on the oily black surface and a plume of black feathers stood proud on her mane.

The church was ahead and as they approached, crowds of mourners bowed their heads. Jo linked Hattie's arm tightly through her own and gripped as the glass doors of the carriage were opened. Six men came forward and very gently, lifted Bertie's coffin onto their shoulders. With perfect timing, they began to make their way slowly through the churchyard. John was one of the bearers alongside Bertie's three brothers and a close friend. The coffin was lopsided as a sixth bearer towered above the others and Big Ken crouched to try and level his corner as they entered the church.

HATTIE WAS IN A DAZE. From the moment Jo had broken the terrible news, she'd been incapable of making any kind of decision. Her mam and Eileen Atkinson from over the road, had stepped in to take care of the boys. Hattie found it difficult to comfort her sons as they cried. They couldn't understand that they wouldn't be going to Ireland and would never see Bertie again. John had arranged transport for the funeral and Hattie vaguely remembered being put into a car alongside Jo, with Rory at the wheel as he drove them to the airport. Jo handled everything as they boarded and Rory had a hire car waiting at the other side.

In true Irish fashion, they'd gone straight to the house to pay their respects.

As Hattie got out of the car, she stared at Bertie's sturdy stone farmhouse, the scene of such happier times only a short while ago. All the curtains were drawn. She let Jo guide her along the gravel path and Bertie's elder brother greeted them at the front door.

Jo offered their condolences.

People sat everywhere, in the kitchen, the hallway and lounges, even the garden.

Tea and drinks were offered and sandwiches handed around. Mrs Flannigan met Hattie by the parlour where the body was laid out. She'd been the first to find Hattie's phone number when the accident happened and had insisted that the Garda tell Hattie straight away. Now, seeing Hattie, she rushed forward.

"'Tis a terrible business, so it is." She gripped Hattie's hand.

"Did he suffer at all?" Hattie whispered.

"Now don't you worry yourself with those thoughts," Mrs Flannigan replied. "It was instant, like turning out a light, may the good Lord be thanked."

Hattie closed her eyes. Her own light had been turned out forever from that fateful day. Mrs Flannigan gently opened the parlour door.

"Go on, girl. Say your goodbyes."

Hattie reached for Jo and gripped her hand, then let herself be led into the dimly lit room. The coffin was at the end, in the bay window

overlooking the coast. The curtains were drawn but Hattie saw them flutter gently by an open window.

" 'Tis to let his spirit out," Mrs Flannigan said.

A young woman sat by the coffin. She wore a smart black dress and gloves. A short net veil was clipped in her hair and partially covered her face, but they could see that she was the image of Bertie.

Hattie stumbled.

Jo caught her and Hattie felt herself being gently led forward.

"Siobhan?"

Hattie heard Jo make introductions.

Bertie's daughter stood up, she nodded curtly then moved to one side. A man about the same age as Siobhan emerged from the far end of the room. He was introduced as her husband. Hattie was almost on the point of collapse as Jo supported her and they moved forward. A mirror on the wall behind the coffin was covered over with a cloth. More Irish tradition.

They stared at the open coffin where Bertie lay. He wore a dark suit with a white shirt and black tie and was covered in a shroud from the waist down. His hands were laced across his chest and he held rosary beads between his fingers. His head was partially bandaged and the bruised skin surrounding the covered wound looked vicious against Bertie's sallow waxy complexion.

Hattie gasped and Jo gripped her more tightly but Hattie legs were folding and she felt Jo brace herself as she supported her.

"Oh my darling Bertie, your poor old face." Tears streamed down Hattie's cheeks. "He has such a dear face, such a dear, dear face…"

Hattie leaned forward and gently traced the bandages and stroked Bertie's cold injured cheek. She touched his eyes, gently stroking the closed lids.

"Goodnight, my darling. Thank you for loving me," Hattie whispered. Tears streamed down her face and dripped onto his jacket. She took a tissue from her sleeve and dabbed at the wet trail then touched two fingers to her lips and pressed them gently to Bertie's lips. With a sob, Hattie stepped away.

"He looks very peaceful," Hattie murmured and after what seemed like an eternity, turned to leave the room.

"Thank you for coming." Siobhan was terse as she held the door open.

Hattie put her coolness down to grief.

THE PRIEST SPOKE WARMLY of Bertie during the mass and two of Bertie's brothers said a few words and managed to raise a chuckle with the mourners.

The coffin was once again carried for the final journey to the church yard and as the mourners passed Bertie's house, the sun appeared from behind dark clouds and beamed down on the solid stone buildings.

Everyone stopped. The building was bathed in a soft golden light and they bowed their heads respectfully to Bertie's home.

Hattie stood bravely by the open grave, a few feet behind Siobhan and the family. Bertie was buried beside Oonagh and Hattie waited patiently as the family threw earth on the coffin. She carried a single red rose and as she stepped forward, Hattie kissed the flower then gently let it go. She closed her eyes as it fell onto the wooden box, then turned and wept in Jo's arms.

Everyone returned to Bertie's home, where food and drinks were served once more. The atmosphere was lighter and laughter could be heard as they approached. Hattie gripped Jo's arm.

"I don't want to go in."

"We'll just have one drink and make small talk."

Jo led them into the house where people remembered Hattie from her visit and were kind as they spoke of Bertie.

He'd told folk his intentions and how happy he was with Hattie and there was a great feeling of sympathy.

They searched for Siobhan but each time they got near her, she moved along. Jo knew that Siobhan was avoiding Hattie and was sure that Hattie knew it too.

"Jo, I don't want to be rude, but can we go?" Hattie said.

"Yes, of course we can."

Jo was keen to get out of the house herself. She knew that Hattie may well give Siobhan a mouthful if the atmosphere between them became any more strained. John was in the thick of it somewhere with the other men and they'd hardly seen him. She searched around for Rory and caught up with him in the kitchen. He stood by the table, talking to a pretty red-haired girl who was cutting a cake. "There you are, Rory, any chance of a lift to the airport?" Jo watched the girl thump Rory playfully on the arm.

"To be sure, anything to get away from this one." Rory crammed a piece of cake in his mouth. "I'll tell John you're off." He made a play of thumping the girl back as she wrapped a huge slab of cake in a napkin then pushed it in his pocket.

"Don't be leavin' it so long, big bro." She leaned over and hugged him and Jo saw the family resemblance as Rory hugged his sister.

Jo returned to find Hattie in the hallway and they stepped out into the front garden. The rain had stopped and weak sunshine warmed the damp air. Bertie's younger brother sat on a stone wall. He smoked a rolled-up cigarette and stood when he saw them.

"'Tis a terrible business, Harriet." He tossed the butt to one side and shook his head. "Bertie was happy with you and wanted you here." He took her hand. "I don't know what'll happen to the farm, 'tis all left to Siobhan, but you're always welcome in these parts, I hope you know that."

Jo thanked him for his kindness and Hattie allowed the brother to hug her.

"Don't I get a hug too?" A voice boomed out. Big Ken marched over the lawn and pulled Hattie into his arms. Safe in his secure embrace, Hattie finally broke down. She sobbed uncontrollably as Ken held her.

Jo stood back. She felt her own tears and tried to stay composed, even though she wanted to sob her eyes out too.

"Any hugs left for me?"

Jo felt warm breath on her neck as John's arms wrapped around her waist and he cuddled her. She melted into him and could smell the peat of malt whisky on his breath and a faint hint of expensive aftershave.

"Thanks for everything," Jo sighed.

"I'm flying back later. I'll stay on for a bit." John looked back at the house. The curtains were all open now and the parlour window closed.

"He was a good man," John said and hugged Jo.

She nestled her face in his shoulder and felt his warm skin, she wanted to sink into his strong arms forever.

"Cars ready," Rory called out. He had the back doors open and stood alongside to help the girls.

Hattie pulled away from Ken and blew her nose on his massive handkerchief. Jo reluctantly extricated herself from John and turned to say goodbye to Ken. She stood on her toes to peck his cheek. "It'll get better, girl," Ken smiled. "Give her time." John walked them to the car.

"I'll call you when I get back." He closed the doors then nodded to Rory. "Look after them."

Rory acknowledged the nod, climbed in and started the engine. Ken and John stood side by side and watched the girls drive away.

The farmhouse glowed in the late afternoon sun and as the car accelerated, they saw Bertie's horses in the meadow, swishing their tails as they lazily munched on the lush green pasture. Cattle with full udders meandered in an uneven line and stomped off to the milking shed, in the stone buildings behind the farmhouse.

Jo watched the scene grow smaller and the men turn and disappear into the house. Life goes on... she thought as she held Hattie's hand and watched Bertie's beloved home and countryside disappear from their world forever.

32

Pete Parks edged his car through the gates and leaned over the steering wheel to peer at the hotel. The place looked open, even though there were only a couple of cars outside - one of which was Jo's.

He pulled up at the front and eased himself carefully out of the driver's side. His leg was stiff and painful today. The damp weather always played havoc with his old racing injury. He tried not to limp as he opened the front door and let himself into the hallway. The place smelt of beeswax and a waft of fresh coffee drifted down the corridor. He followed it.

In the garden, Jo stood in a border and reached up. The best bloom was a couple of feet above her head and she was determined to pick it. If I put this on reception, it will bring me luck today... she superstitiously told herself. Goodness knows she needed a bit of luck. It had rained incessantly for days. The bedrooms were all empty and the post brought nothing but bills.

Jo clipped a rose and it fell to the path where Pippa sat and wagged her tail. Jo looked fondly at her dog. Pippa was clearly showing signs of pregnancy. More mouths to feed... Jo thought as she stood on a flat stone and leaned further towards the wall where climbing roses blossomed, their sodden heads heavy with rain. Jo stretched her arm and gripped the secateurs, ready to strike. She pulled the stem towards her but as she clipped, her foot slid off the stone and she stumbled into the muddy border.

"Damn!" Jo cursed and looked down at her red pumps. Sludge oozed over the suede and squelched into her toes. The rose had fallen, head down beside her feet. She bent to retrieve it and pricked her finger. "Blast!" She cried out. The rose's revenge was sharp.

"If it was a snake bite, I'd suck it out." Pete Parks crept beside her and Jo spun around.

"Blimey, Pete, do you have to sneak up on me?"

"Are you sinking?" Pete stared at Jo's feet, where mud covered the top of her pumps. He reached out to help her and Jo grabbed his hand but as she moved, she found herself stepping out of the soggy pumps and onto the path. Pippa began to dig and Pete reached down.

"Nothing that a good wash won't sort out," Pete said as he recovered the pumps. Pippa shook herself, sending particles of mud over his trousers.

"Got the kettle on?" Pete asked. "I could do with a coffee."

Jo glanced at the sky. Dark clouds threatened more rain and as big drops began to fall, she hurried over the lawn to the conservatory. Pete followed and placed the shoes on a mat inside the doorway.

"Do you want to sit in here while I fetch it?" Jo asked.

"Aye, can do." Pete sat on a Lloyd Loom sofa and made himself comfortable, a copy of the Farmers Weekly lay on the table and he began to read.

Jo stood barefoot in the stillroom and waited for the coffee to percolate. She rinsed mud from the petals of the rose and put it in a stem vase, then padded through the bar to put it on the desk in reception. The post had arrived with a large pile of menacing brown envelopes. Jo sighed and buried them under the desk, then returned to the stillroom and poured two mugs of coffee. As she heated milk, she wondered what had brought Pete to the hotel. She reached for a tin of shortbreads and returned to the conservatory, where heavy rain drummed on the roof and pelted against the windows.

"Are you sure you want to sit in here?" Jo asked as she put the tray on a table and pulled up a chair. Pete looked up from his newspaper and Pippa wagged her tail.

"Nothing wrong with a bit of rain," Pete said.

"Not in my line of work, I'm afraid." Jo pushed the coffee towards him. "Milk?"

Pete nodded and added two heaped spoons of sugar, then dunked a shortbread into the hot sweet liquid. Pippa sat beside him and put her head on his knee.

"Delicious," Pete smiled and folded the newspaper up. "Bit quiet is it?" He broke a piece of biscuit off and gave it to Pippa.

"Too quiet, September's been a disaster." Jo thought about the previous weeks. She'd dreamed of an Indian summer with last minute bookings filling the rooms and shooting parties stacked up after the success of the Mulberry shoot. But the opposite had happened. The rain had been incessant and the phone didn't ring.

They were now in the first week of October and things didn't look any better. Jinny had cancelled her September luncheon club, saying there were too many members unavailable and Mark Pucker had taken his team off to Majorca for some company bonding. Jo wondered why she hadn't heard from Mark and hoped that he'd book another conference soon.

Fortunately, with Alf's help, she'd two shoots booked for January and February but the coming weeks were a worry. There seemed to be an uncertainty in the air and everyone was reluctant to spend money. People weren't taking short breaks or holidays. Jo thought of her wage bill and wondered if she should be laying staff off.

"Bad business with Hattie." Pete reached for the shortbread tin. "How is she?" He bit into another buttery biscuit and flicked the crumbs off his dark blue sweater. Pippa snapped her head back to catch them.

"She's heartbroken." Jo sipped her coffee and stared out at the garden. "She won't go out of the house. Eileen Atkinson is taking the boys to school and Hattie's mother stays over to make sure they get something to eat, but Hattie is stuck in a chair in front of the television and won't move." Jo turned and looked at Pete. "I don't know what to do."

"It'll pass." He leaned forward and put his empty mug on the tray.

"I'm not so sure. She seems to have lost all her energy and drive, it's like her own life has been taken too."

"It's grief, give her time." Pete finished his coffee.

Jo put her mug down and began to tidy the tray but Pete grabbed her hand. She tried to pull away but he held on to it.

"As much as I'd like to be here for a social visit, I'm not," he said. "We were in for dinner the night Hattie got the news." Pete stared at her. Jo crossed her fingers with her free hand and prayed that they hadn't got food poisoning.

"Despite you not being here, we had a great night. You've got a grand place," Pete continued. Jo relaxed a little as he went on.

"The food was outstanding and your staff made us more than welcome. You've done a terrific job Jo. It's not your fault that the economy's struggling, but it'll get worse before it gets better if Mrs Thatcher has her way."

"So what should I do? I can't drag folk in here." Jo had managed to extract her hand and folded her arms stubbornly across her chest.

"You've got to hang onto it. There's a recession coming and the stock market will go tits-up anytime now. You've got to stick at it." Pete was adamant.

"I've thought about getting Robert in for a valuation, he always said a small chain would buy this sort of property in a flash. Maybe now would be a good time, at least it's had the renovation and is trading." Jo stared glumly out of the windows.

"Aye, snap it up for nowt as likely. Don't be doing that." Pete followed her gaze, the weather was still miserable. "A couple of years ago, I had a leak in the drains at the garage. We'd been leaking diesel into the town's drains for months. Hell of a fuss, the council threatened to sue me and the insurance wouldn't pay up. I nearly went under."

"What did you do?" Jo asked with interest.

"I hung on. Robbed Peter to pay Paul, fought the buggers off and battled it out. It was hard but I wasn't going to be beaten and you mustn't too – you've only just got this place off the ground."

"But I didn't see this lot coming," Jo stared at Pete. "My clients are affluent. This sort of crisis doesn't usually touch them."

"It does when their property's worth nowt, borrowings high and shares tumbling, they get hit worst."

"So what do I do?"

"I don't need to tell an intelligent girl like yourself what to do, Jo. I'm only saying you need to hang on with all your might. It'll pass."

Pete stood up. Jo sighed, it was easy for him to say but her bank account was well into overdraft and there was a VAT bill due. If only she could find a way of raising more capital.

"And don't be borrowing more." Pete read her mind. "Interest rates will kill you."

"Well, thanks for your thoughts." Jo stood up too. All very well him telling her to hang on, he wasn't faced with the daily calls from Mr Knight at the bank.

"I'll keep bringing folk in for dinner and do my bit," Pete smiled. "I take our staff, their partners and some customers out after Christmas. You can have that if you can entertain a hundred of us?" He raised his eyebrows and waited for Jo to reply. Jo focused. A hundred? She hadn't a clue how she'd do it but she wasn't going to turn it away.

"Consider that a firm booking, Pete. I'll get menus and details over to you."

"Make sure there's some music on, they like to get up and have a dance."

He moved towards the door and Jo went to follow him, stepping over Pippa who lay alongside the sofa. Pete glanced at Jo's feet.

"I'll just slip out of the back here and let you get on. You'll want to get cleaned up."

Jo looked down. Her toes were encrusted with dry mud.

"Thanks Pete..." she began but suddenly, he grabbed her and before she could twist away, his arms were around her and he kissed her passionately. His hands were strong and Jo was pinned in his vice-like grip. Furious, she twisted around, found her strength and shoved him away.

Pippa barked and jumped up.

"Pete!" She shouted and stumbled back. "Why do you have to spoil it? You're a married man."

"Aw, Jo, don't be mad, you can't blame me for trying." He had lipstick on his face and wiped it away with the back of his hand.

"Let's just keep it as friends, shall we." Jo thought of the hundred or so guests at Christmas and smiled. Two can play at your game, Pete sodding Parks! His eyes glinted in comprehension but he suddenly shuddered. Pippa had begun to howl and leaned against Jo's legs.

"Christ it's cold in here." Pete stood in the doorway and looked around. "You'd never think it was only September." He rubbed his arms and shook himself. "I feel as though someone just walked over my grave." He shivered.

Jo felt it too as an icy chill surrounded them, emanating from the doorway. Pippa was trembling.

"You'd better be off," Jo said.

Pete had turned pale and was eager to go. He blew warm breath on his hands, said goodbye and left with haste. Despite his limp, he ran around the side of the hotel to the car park at the front.

The Artic air froze Jo to the spot. Fear seized and she thought she heard someone whisper... Dance! Go! Jo shivered. Pippa had disappeared. What the hell was in this room? The last time she'd felt this presence, John Doherty had crept up and rescued her. A fresh blast of sub-zero air hit her and she slammed the door shut and ran out.

As she got to reception, she stopped. It was warm here. She gripped the desk and sat down. Pippa was under the desk, she no longer trembled and Jo put her feet on the dog's warm tummy and rubbed up and down.

Jo longed to put her head in her hands and sob. Everything seemed to be crumbling! Not just the business, but her heart too.

She'd not heard from John since the funeral. The rotten bastard hadn't so much as telephoned to see how she was, nor asked if Hattie was ok. Jo couldn't believe that he was such a shit but now, weeks later, she knew she'd got to accept it and it hurt more than she could explain.

They'd been so close. She thought of the beautiful diamond necklace on her dressing table which couldn't bring herself to wear. Perhaps she should pawn it and pay a few bills. Reluctantly, Jo had even started to be nice to Greg. He was now on a charm offensive and was taking Thomas out at least twice a week and adhered scrupulously to Jo's strict rule on timings. Oh, she thought, at this rate she'd be taking him back. Jo was sure Greg still had some money stashed, and it would at least sort her cash flow out for a bit. She was certain he'd dump Estelle in a flash if he could get his feet under the table here and the way Jo felt, she feared she may have to consider it. Or sell up. God what a mess!

Jo pushed her hair back from her face. This wouldn't do. She needed to get a grip and do something about bookings.

Pippa began to lick Jo's ankles and as Jo caressed the dog's head she thought about her business. Perhaps a theme night would get some punters in? If only Hattie was around. Jo longed for her sarcasm and sharp words. Hattie certainly wouldn't let Jo sit here feeling sorry for herself. Jo shook her head and forced herself to clear her thoughts. A theme night it would be! But what should they do? Chinese! Jo's brain spun into action as she thought about it. The only Chinese food in these parts came from a greasy takeaway in Marland. Jo felt sure she could sell the evening if she made it sound attractive. She'd make the Rose Room look like a pagoda. Jo turned the pages of the diary and chose a date. Friday the 23rd October, that would give them chance to advertise. She felt a little better.

The kitchen door opened and Judy peeped out.

"Cuppa, Mrs E?" Judy looked down at Pippa, who thumped her tail against the carpet.

"That would be lovely, Judy." Jo said and began to make notes for an advert to be placed in the Westmarland Tribune - an oriental banquet at a set price.

"You're deep in thought." Judy placed a mug on the desk and held out a biscuit for Pippa.

"What do you think about a Chinese night?"

"I think it's a great idea. Alf loves Chinese." Judy stopped. A blush spread over her neck and face.

"Better make sure he books a table then and brings some friends," Jo winked.

"Shall I tell Sandra and Gerald to start thinking about menus?" Judy sidestepped the subject of Alf.

"Yes get them on to it, give them something to do." Jo reached for the telephone. "Anything you can think of to get some bookings, Judy, anything at all." Jo dialled the number for the Westmarland Tribune and asked to be put through to classified adverts.

"Mrs E?" Judy said hesitantly. She looked puzzled as she stared at Jo's feet.

Jo glanced down. Dried mud had crumbled from her toes onto the carpet and Pippa licked biscuit crumbs from between the flecks of mud. Jo followed Judy's gaze.

"I can't afford shoes anymore, Judy. We need to do something!"

33

Greg sat at the window table in the Lemon Tree Café and lit another cigarette. It was his third of the morning. He sighed happily as he placed his lighter neatly on the packet then sat back, tilted his head and blew smoke rings towards the ceiling. Thoughtfully, he traced the edge of the pottery ashtray with his finger. Life had begun to improve.

The waitress recognised Greg. She flicked her blonde hair over one eye and gave him a sultry look. Then, pushing her chest out, leaned over and with a slow deliberate movement, reached across the table to change the ashtray. Greg's finger moved over her hand and gently touched her ring finger.

"Morning, Christine." he smiled, letting his finger linger on the bare skin.

"Anything else I can get you?" Christine left her hand on the ashtray.

"A coffee would be great – for now." Greg winked at the girl and saw her lick her lips suggestively as she moved away. Back of the net! Greg thought confidently. He watched her bottom sway in very tight blue jeans, then slide behind the counter. He thought about Jo's bottom. That used to sway too, but was considerably more pert these days and he longed to get his hands on it again. Well, he wouldn't have much longer to wait. The way things were going he reckoned he'd be in by Christmas.

Christine appeared with a mug of coffee and placed it before him.

"Sugar? Or are you sweet enough."

"I don't need any extras, sweetheart." Greg gave her what he considered to be his knicker-melting gaze. "Unless you're offering anything else that is?" He looked her up and down.

"Might be."

"Better write your number on the bill then." Greg picked up his coffee and licked his lips.

The café door opened and a man approached the counter.

"Chrissy, I want a cheese and pickle on white to go," he said and looked around. Alf recognised Greg and their eyes locked. "When you've finished wasting time with riff-raff that is."

Alf glared at Greg, who turned away and spooned several heaps of sugar into his coffee.

"Piss off, Alf." Christine retorted as she sailed past.

She went behind the counter and slapped thick slices of cheese between wedges of bread, then spooned two fat pickled onions from a jar and put it all in a paper bag.

She held her hand out. Alf placed several coins on her palm then grabbed the bag and marched past Greg. He glowered but Greg was focused on the sport pages of his newspaper. Alf stuffed the sandwich in his pocket and slammed the café door.

Greg looked up, relieved that Alf had gone without any fuss. He hadn't seen him since the incident in the pub and had kept clear of the place ever since. They'd all change their tune when he was ensconced in the hotel with all the creature comforts around him. He'd be the boss then and that mouthy gamekeeper would find himself out on his arse. Greg clicked his fingers and Christine appeared. He handed her a five pound note and waited for his change. It came back on a saucer with a number scrawled across a scrap of paper. Greg smiled, pocketed the receipt and left fifty pence.

"Be seeing you, sweetheart." Greg patted Christine's bottom and she giggled as he strode out of the cafe.

GREG WALKED up the main street of Butterly with a confident spring in his step. Things were going well with Thomas. The kid was high maintenance, but Estelle was always on hand and knew how to look after him.

It wasn't that Greg didn't enjoy seeing his son, he did. He just had more pressing matters on his mind.

Jo was at last, being civil to him. Greg had stepped into her house last week and made sure that he was overly gracious.

He'd looked around and complimented Jo on her great taste and comfortable home.

"I haven't actually done anything in here." She'd looked bemused. "All the investment went on the hotel. I just hope it was worth it."

Greg tactfully questioned Jo about business. He'd noticed fewer cars outside the hotel since the shoot and wondered if the imminent recession was affecting her. He asked if she'd borrow more money to see her through.

"Not a chance," she snapped back. "The banks have stopped lending and anyway the interest rates are too high, I just need to get people in here."

Jo was talking to him! Keep this up and she'll be weeping on your shoulder.

Greg imagined Jo so overcome with gratitude when he stepped in with the readies that she'd beg him to come back into her business and her bed.

Greg walked past the greengrocers and waved at Dick Littlefair who was stacking fruit and vegetables outside his shop. Dick waved back and continued with his display. At least the locals seem to be accepting him again Greg thought happily, as he crossed the road to the terrace of Alms houses on the hill.

Estelle appeared in one of the doors. She was surprised to see Greg and smiled. She turned back to the house and called out. "Goodbye, Miss Procter, I see you tomorrow."

Several elderly people lived in the houses and Estelle had set up a nice little business, cleaning their properties. Estelle closed the door and ran across the pavement to Greg. She linked his arm. It was unusual for him to meet her; he'd seemed very distant recently and she thought that he must be worrying about money. Greg had told her that his separation settlement had run out, he'd spent too much when they were travelling. Estelle was sure he had plenty left, but as she never saw it anymore she was pleased to get some work and have some money for herself. She was good and often got tips.

Sometimes the old people gave her things they no longer wanted. Her English had improved and now that Greg had Thomas a couple of times a week, he seemed a bit happier.

"Hey, Mr!" Estelle trotted along the pavement in a pair of mockcroc high heels, a gift from an employer. She thrust her cheek out and waited for Greg to kiss her. He ignored her and stared at her shoes.

"You no like?" She thrust her foot out and began to make circles to show off her high instep. "I got bag too." Estelle reached into a carrier bag and pulled out a matching clutch bag.

"Why do you have to bring all this crap home?" Greg shook his head, then took her arm and guided her down the hill. He felt a complete idiot as she clung on to him, tripping in her heels and moaning that she was tired and where was the car? Dick Littlefair stopped his stacking and looked up. Estelle wore skin tight leggings and a short crop top. Her thick black hair was pinned up and she'd painted her pouting lips crimson.

"Haven't I seen you dancing in West Side Story?" Dick said and grinned at Estelle as she blew him a kiss.

"Jesus, Estelle!" Greg hissed and glared at Estelle. "Not only do you look like a tart but do you have to behave like one?" He was furious and dragged her past the greengrocer, who shook his head and turned back to his work. Greg wished he'd picked her up in the car. All his good work would be undone at this rate. Estelle was a liability and he couldn't afford gossip. He'd already checked on flights to Spain and with any luck he'd be able to dispatch her back to her family sooner than he'd anticipated.

Thank God for the recession. If Jo didn't find bookings soon, she'd be begging him to come back. Greg smiled as he guided Estelle to the bridge over the River Bevan and made their way along the riverbank to their flat. It was only a matter of time.

Jo stopped the car on the roadside and unclipped her seat belt. She looked up at the house. The curtains were drawn and the front garden looked overgrown and unkempt. She stepped out onto the pavement as Pippa flew past and disappeared behind Hattie's garden wall, where next door's tabby cat sat basking in the sunshine.

Jo could no longer ignore the fact that Pippa was unmistakably pregnant. Until recently there hadn't been a sign, but in the last week or so her tummy had thickened and she looked like a fat pear-drop. At least I'll have time to look after her... Jo sighed as she thought of the empty bedrooms at the hotel.

Thomas woke up. He yawned as his mother lifted him gently from his car seat.

" 'Attie mumma!" Thomas pointed excitedly at the house. Jo kissed the top of his head, locked the car and walked up the pathway. She rang the bell but knew that Hattie wouldn't come to the door. She tried the handle. It gave and Jo opened the door and walked in.

"Anyone home?"

The house was in darkness but Jo could hear a television. She opened the door to the lounge. The curtains on the front window were closed but the blinds on the patio doors, overlooking the back garden, were open. Hattie lay on the sofa, her face inert as she watched the screen - an episode of Murder, She Wrote. She mumbled a greeting to Jo, but moved further down the sofa and turned her back on her visitors.

"How are you today?" Jo asked. The house smelt of Hattie's mother's cigarettes, stale and unwelcoming. Dust covered Hattie's collection of Lilliput Lane ornaments.

Jo moved to the patio doors and opened them.

"Damn dog will kill that cat one of these days," Hattie said. Jo could see Pippa whizzing around the back garden in hot pursuit of the tabby, who'd climbed onto the shed roof and was hissing viciously.

"Cup of tea?"

"No, nowt."

"Something to eat?"

"No, thank you."

"Fancy a walk and a bit of fresh air?" Jo sat on the arm of the sofa and looked at her friend. She wanted to put Thomas on the floor, but it was covered with dirty plates and overflowing ashtrays.

"I'm alright, Jo, just leave me alone."

"That I'm never going to do."

Jo reached her hand out and stroked Hattie's greasy hair away from her face. Hattie was wearing grubby pyjamas. She'd not been dressed for days.

"What can I do to help you?" Jo wished Hattie would get angry or shout or cry or do something to vent her anguish at losing Bertie. But this Hattie was alien to Jo and she didn't know how to handle her.

Hattie watched the television in a trance-like state while Jo began to collect dishes and carry them into the kitchen. Things were a bit better in there. Jo knew that Eileen Atkinson had been stocking the cupboards as Jo still had Hattie on the payroll and made sure Eileen had housekeeping money. Hattie's mam did her best to help but she was nearly seventy. Jo wondered how much money Hattie had left. Was the mortgage being covered? Jo was helping as much as she could but she had money troubles of her own and didn't know how long she could keep it up. She was worried about the boys too. How on earth was Hattie's grief affecting her kids? Jo had them over to the hotel several times a week after school and they liked being with Thomas and Ann, playing in the garden kicking a football around if the weather was fine, or games inside when it rained. But they had to come home and this is what they faced - a mother who could barely speak, and certainly didn't want to do anything other than lie on the sofa all day and night.

Jo's heart went out to Hattie and she knew that Bertie wouldn't want her to be like this. The whole house was sad and Jo felt helpless, but what could she do to make things better?

"Would you like a bath?" Jo asked. "I could stick some nice smellies in?"

Hattie didn't reply.

"Maybe we could get you out of those pyjamas into something clean? You might feel a bit better?" Jo said. Thomas was fidgety and tried to wriggle out of her arms. Pippa barked furiously at the cat.

"For Christ's sake, Jo!" Hattie shouted. She sat up and grabbed a cushion. "Can't you just leave me alone?" Hattie punched the cushion, then banged it down on the arm of the sofa and put her head on it. She grabbed the remote control and increased the volume on the television. Jo touched her arm but Hattie flinched away. Thomas began to cry and Hattie's neighbour yelled at Pippa to stop barking.

Jo stood up.

"Ok, if that's what you want, but I'll be back in a day or so and if there is anything that you do want, you just call me." Jo picked up the telephone and put it on the floor next to Hattie.

Hattie didn't look up.

With a sigh, Jo leaned down and kissed her on the forehead. "Anything at all – I'll be here."

Jo straightened the stained blanket that half covered Hattie then walked out of the living room. She looked back. Hattie hadn't moved and didn't seem to register Jo's departure. Jo felt tears in her eyes as she opened the front door and let herself out. She wondered what on earth she could do to get the old Hattie back again.

34

October began as quietly as September had ended. Bookings were thin on the ground and as the month progressed Jo was more worried than ever about her business. She'd taken to watching the news, where stories of the stock market in crisis brought panic to the nation's shareholders.

Jo discussed her fears with Robert and asked him for a valuation on the property. Robert knew the size of Jo's investment and thought she'd be foolish to put the hotel on the market.

"Currently, it's worth fifty percent less than its true value," Robert told her. "The bottom has fallen out of property. You've got to hang on, Jo, things will change, but it'll take a while."

"I'm not sure if I can." Jo thought about her overdraft and Mr Knight's never ending calls. "Have a think about it and make some subtle enquiries for me?"

If someone came along with a price to cover her debt, Jo felt sure she'd snap their hand off.

On a brighter note, she'd received a good response to the advert for the Chinese Evening and the restaurant was nearly full. Preparations were well under way.

Jo had sent the staff to the fancy-dress shop in Marland to hire suitable costumes. The twins would be dressed as Chinese Emperors and Judy and the girls all looked very pretty in silk cheongsams fitted silk dresses with coloured embroidery. Jo had found a Chinese supermarket in Carlisle and boxes of lights, lanterns, floating candles and fortune cookies were waiting to decorate the restaurant.

Pippa was listless and fretful and didn't stray far from her box. Jo had asked Martin, the vet next door, to have a look at her and in his opinion Pippa would be a mother any day now. He assured Jo that she wasn't to worry - a dog tended to get on with things. He told her that she would come down one morning and find a basket of puppies and a happy Pippa looking after them all.

Jo wasn't so sure.

Pippa was enormous and Jo tried to second guess what she might need for the birth. She'd asked Alf for his breeding expertise on the matter. He seemed to be spending a lot of time at the hotel these days, often coinciding with Judy sleeping over to cover Hattie's shifts. Jo was surrounded by breeding animals.

"The old lass will sort it out on her own," Alf said as he knelt by the box and gently stroked Pippa's swollen belly. Pippa lay back and tried to roll over. She gazed adoringly at Alf.

"Well I hope you'll help the old lass and me with the re-homing." Jo sat at the table with Thomas on her knee. They played with his farm animals.

"You'll have no trouble with these 'uns," Alf replied. "Pedigree father – they'll fly out." He stood up.

"I hope they do fly out, I'm no mid-wife." Jo said grumpily. She bounced a plastic pig over the table as Thomas made snorting noises. "Shouldn't she be hospitalised or something?"

"Nah, it'll be like shelling peas." Alf ruffled Thomas' mop of blonde hair with a calloused hand. "Don't worry, eh Tombo? Soon have some real animals to play with."

"Woof! 'Oof!" Thomas pointed towards Pippa and threw his pig in her box.

Jo woke early. She had no rush to get downstairs as there were only two residents and Judy was on an early shift. She listened to the baby alarm beside her bed and heard Ann with Thomas in his room, he'd woken and Ann gently fussed as she began his morning ritual. Jo turned the alarm off. She rolled over and flicked a switch on the bedside radio. A newsreader spoke solemnly.

"We are of course waiting for the stock markets to open around the world, but the day looks set to be one of the worst in financial history."

Jo sat up. What the hell had happened? She threw her legs over the side of the bed and turned the volume up. Various economic experts were adding their opinion to the radio debate and by the sound of things, monetary matters looked grim. Jo hurried to dress and decided that she'd call George in a bit and ask his opinion. Her dad would be glued to the news; no doubt his own shares were at risk...

THE DAY PROGRESSED AND, as everyone feared, the news didn't improve. The press called it Black Monday. The stock market had crashed and millions of pounds were lost. A sense of doom pervaded every new report, with tales of investors having lost everything.

Jo called her father.

"Are you alright dad?" she said.

"We've lost a bit, Jo, but nothing I'll miss," George replied. "I only ever dabbled. Some folk have lost the lot though. It's going to be tough for many." He asked about business and if she was coping. Jo made light of the lack of bookings and assured George that things were fine. She sighed as she put the phone down. Please God may things improve! She couldn't bring herself to tell George how bad it really was.

THE WEEK WENT BY SLOWLY. Pippa's appetite increased and Sandra took to preparing tasty delicacies of fresh fish and chicken for the grossly pregnant dog. A nervous Jo wondered how many puppies Pippa would have.

Bookings for the Chinese night had continued and they would now be using both restaurants. Perhaps folk need cheering up, Jo thought as she hung fairy lights and paper lanterns in the Rose Room on the morning of the event.

They'd decided to discount the bedrooms for anyone wishing to stay over and so far, half of the rooms were full. Jo felt a little brighter as she made final preparations, things seemed to have picked up.

The place had come alive again and Jo was surprised and pleased when Judy told her that Jinny Atkinson had booked her luncheon club for Christmas lunch in December. Mark Pucker had rung too and booked a conference day in November.

Jo sat in her dressing room and stared at her outfit. She'd chosen a sleeveless, calf-length tunic dress with a mandarin collar. It was a deep emerald blue silk with gold piping and felt wonderful against her skin. She carefully applied thick eyeliner and added an upward twist. Not particularly Chinese, more Bridget Bardot, she thought as she stood back and checked her appearance. It would have to do.

The phone rang.

"Mrs E, could you come down to reception please."

"I'm on my way, Judy, give me five minutes," Jo replied.

"Could you come straight down please, we're having a spot of bother." Judy sounded strange. Jo felt her heart miss a beat and wondered what on earth could have happened? She grabbed a red lipstick, smoothed some over her lips and raced down to reception.

At the desk, a head hung over the diary. It has very thick black hair, pulled into a bun at the nape of the neck, where two knitting needles poked out.

Jo stared in disbelief and Judy began to giggle.

"Taa Raa!" Hattie's head shot up and her face beamed from beneath the heavy wig. Jo gasped and felt a knot the size of a fist burst in her heart as tears poured down her face.

"Fuck me. It's Suzy Wong!" Hattie looked Jo up and down, then stood and threw her arms out. Jo almost vaulted the desk to get to her friend and they hugged each other tightly. Jo's tears saturated Hattie's wig, which had now slipped precariously to one side.

"I can't believe you're here!" Jo exclaimed. She was so thrilled to see Hattie.

"I thought it was time to get me finger out." Hattie turned to the mirror and straightened her wig. "You'll hardly pull this one off without me."

Jo was overjoyed. The day could not have got better.

"So what's to do?" Hattie asked and as she turned, she noticed that Jo was staring at her outfit. Hattie wore an odd mix of tight white wrap-over top, short black trousers and rubber flip flops. Jo recognised Hattie's mother's knitting needles stabbed into Hattie's hair in a cross shape.

"Well it was the best I could do," Hattie said. "They only had this wig left at the shop. Your lot have cleaned Fancy Pants out of Chinese gear. I had to improvise with our Tommy's Kung Foo kit." Hattie's breasts bulged out of the age eleven top and her legs were bare from the knee down. "I've put fake tan on me legs – don't look so precious, you're hardly Emelda bleedin' Marcos," Hattie retorted.

"She's not Chinese..." Jo began to giggle.

"Hadn't we better crack on?" Hattie snapped. "Shall I start pouring the Sake?" She opened the office door and pushed past Jo and Judy. "By the way – your mascara's run," Hattie called to Jo from the bar. "You look like a Panda, but perhaps that's intentional?"

SEVEN O'CLOCK. Everyone was ready to greet the guests. Delicious aromas came from the kitchen.

Guests were to be shown straight to their tables on arrival. Simon turned the stereo on and Chinese music piped out from speakers throughout the restaurant. Hattie drew back a red silk curtain that Jo had pinned to the entrance of the bar.

"Good job I'm here," she began as she poured out glasses of rice wine. "None of the raffle prizes were wrapped." "I told Judy to wrap them," Jo said.

"Well she left them on the side in the kitchen. Too busy gallivanting out the back with Alf. I've wrapped them now, they're on the piano." She pushed a glass towards Jo.

"Have you tried Gerald's wontons?" Hattie asked. Jo pulled a face as she sipped the wine. It tasted like creosote.

"Bloody delicious," Hattie sighed as she thought about the crisp batter parcels.

"Do you think black pudding was the right choice of filling?"

"Gives it a Northern touch, don't be so fussy."

The front door sounded and the staff rushed past them with trays of Sake.

"Looks like the cast of Madame Butterfly," Hattie chuckled. She watched the twins follow Judy and Penny. Penny had whitened her face and added rouge to her cheeks.

"Christ, shouldn't she live in the conservatory?" Hattie raised her eyebrows.

"Don't even joke about that," Jo downed the wine and shuddered.

The curtain lifted to one side and Peter Pigmy stuck his weasellike face around it.

"Where do you want me?" He was dressed in jeans, tucked into cowboy boots with spurs, a checked shirt and a shoestring tie, held in place with a banjo clip. Hattie opened her mouth in horror.

"It's a first," she cried out, "Westmarland's only Chinese Cowboy!"

"Piss off, Hattie," Peter snarled back and adjusted the large camera slung around his neck. "I'm shooting a hoedown straight after this. Where d'you want me?"

"Bottom of the Bevan," Hattie said. "Shouldn't you have a gun if you're going to a massacre?" She smirked in Peter's direction as Jo pushed her out of the way and told Peter to position himself in the hallway. He could photograph guests as they came in.

"I see your mother didn't get that acne cream I recommended," Hattie called after him.

Peter thrust his middle finger in the air as his spurs jangled as he sashayed down the corridor.

"Do you have to be so mean to him?"

"He's such a twat, thinks he's working for the glossies, the Tribune is hardly Hello Magazine."

Laughter came from the hallway.

Jo and Hattie turned to see Paulie and Robbie sail towards them as Simon made an announcement.

"The Emperor Hoisin Sauce and his Consort!" Simon called out and Paulie ducked under the red curtain and swept into the bar. He towered above the girls in a multi-coloured silk coat and magnificent headgear. Robbie looked equally as regal.

"Darlings!" Paulie squealed and embraced them both. "Let's have a toast to the evening," he raised his glass. "To Hattie – thank the Lord she's back with the living." He grimaced as he tasted the rice wine but continued, "I never thought I'd peel her off that vile sofa! She was drowning in Draylon."

Paulie gave Jo a conspiratorial wink and Jo realised who'd finally got Hattie going again. She winked back and mouthed a Thank You!

More guests had arrived and Alf led a party of eight lads from the pub, through to the restaurant. Heading them up as the War Lord Chin, Alf explained that they were his warriors taking a break from building the Great Wall. Jo and Hattie stood in amazement as they trooped into the dining room. They wore an assortment of old farming clothing and carried pitch forks and spades.

"More like The Worzels," Hattie commented as they watched the lads necking shots of Sake and cheering each other on. "Things could get messy," she said and shook her head.

The meal was a success. Course after course of delicacies poured from the kitchen, and each was greeted with enthusiasm by the more than merry diners. Alf admitted that the shredded duck had never flown anywhere near Peking and was swimming about on the Crowther estate pond a couple of days ago. Paulie was in raptures over the sweet and sour pork and declared that he simply had to have the recipe before he left the building.

Suzy played a medley of popular songs on the piano.

The wailing Chinese music tape had been wrenched from the stereo before the second course had begun.

"It's a great atmosphere Jo."

Hattie stood by the Rose Room doorway and watched the happy guests.

"Yes and it's made totally complete because you're here." Jo felt her eyes well-up again.

"Don't start. You'll have me going..." Hattie said. "It was time I got a grip." She looked around the room and her eyes rested on Paulie. "It took a bollocking from the Emperor to get me here though." She shook her head. "He told me you were going under and to get off my fat arse and help where helps needed, so here I am." She turned to Jo. "And Bertie wouldn't want me to leave you on your own. He'll be up there in his silk coat too, doing a jig and raising a glass," she smiled. "Come on – we've a raffle to draw."

Hattie picked up a spoon and banged it on a glass bowl and Jo announced that if everyone would like to get their tickets ready, the raffle was about to be drawn. Hattie had folded the raffle tickets into a silver ice bucket and she asked one of the guests to select the first ticket. Jo called out the number and a guest in the panel room pagoda held up her ticket with delight. Jo selected one of the wrapped prizes from the pile on the piano and handed it to her. The guest unwrapped a box of chocolates whilst returning to her seat and was greeted with loud applause. The second ticket was drawn and another happy diner received a bottle of red wine. The third ticket went to one of the lads on Alf's table. He beamed as he felt a glass bottle through the paper and began to unwrap it.

"Are you takin' the piss?" a voice bellowed.

Jo and Hattie spun around and saw the lad holding up a halfempty bottle of soy-sauce. Its rim was crusty and congealed matter stuck to the neck of the bottle.

"Fuck!" Hattie whispered. "I was talking to Sandra - I must've wrapped up her ingredients." She dived through the swing door to the wine cellar and came out with a bottle of Blue Nun.

"Just a little joke," Jo called out. She managed to retrieve the situation but glared at Hattie as the lad grabbed the wine.

"No offence taken," he grinned back.

The raffle continued and unwilling to risk the soy-sauce incident happening again, Jo made a point of feeling each prize as it left the top of the piano. On the final prize, she hesitated before handing it out.

"It feels like a tube," she hissed to Hattie.

"That's all right – its body lotion," Hattie whispered back.

Paulie swept forward with his winning ticket and claimed the prize. He flounced back to his chair to cheers of "All Hail the Mighty Emperor!" from Alf's table.

"And his Queen!" Paulie replied looking lovingly at Robbie as he handed him the prize.

"They'll love it," Hattie referred to the body lotion and Jo sighed with relief.

Suzy began to thump out Elvis numbers and the staff pulled back tables to enable the guests to dance.

The evening was a triumph. Hattie and Simon were glued to the bar for the rest of the night and served until well after closing time, as guests partied after the meal. The staff flew around and Gerald stepped into the still-room which was a mass of dirty china and pots.

"Soon have this lot sorted, Mrs E." Gerald assured Jo and instructed the part-time students to get stuck in. Jo took drinks into the kitchen and placed the tray on Sandra's spotless table.

"Good night eh?" Sandra smacked her lips together as she tasted her pint of ale.

"Brilliant, Sandra, the food was fantastic." Jo picked up a wonton and bit into it. "These are very good."

"Aye we'll make something of the lad yet," Sandra smiled at Gerald. He blushed but looked pleased as he sipped a shandy. Arthur had joined him. He wore a rubber apron and was carefully drying glasses. He waved when he saw Jo.

"Sorry about the ingredients getting mixed up in the raffle," Sandra gulped the pint back.

"Well at least it was only one that went wrong, I can't blame Hattie – I'm too pleased that she's back."

"What's that about me?" Hattie appeared from the bar and flopped on the table.

"Talking about you not to you," Sandra said and swept the glasses off the table. "Clear off. We've got a full house of breakfasts tomorrow and I need to get finished." Sandra glanced fondly at Arthur and shooed them away.

"I'll get on with the bills." Hattie headed off to reception.

Jo looked at her watch and decided to slip to the ladies room. She returned to reception and leaned on the desk as Hattie prepared guest accounts.

"I'll check the restaurant and make sure the stragglers are happy. It's time Elvis left the building," Jo said as she watched Hattie.

"Paulie was doing a Chinese version of Little Richard last time I looked and it wasn't going down too well with the Worzels. Pitchforks and handbags at dawn..." Hattie mumbled as she totted up the bills.

"I thought Paulie was very good about the mix up with the body lotion." Jo poked Hattie on the shoulder.

"Alright, I'm sorry." Hattie hung her head. "I honestly didn't wrap up that half-empty tube of tomato puree on purpose." She looked up at Jo and they both began to giggle.

The front door buzzer sounded and Hattie turned her head. "Who can that be?"

"Probably a taxi, I'll go and see."

A man stood with his back to the corridor and as Jo approached he turned around.

"Nice get up," John Doherty looked Jo up and down.

Jo's heart crashed through her chest. "You have to be joking," she stammered.

"Not at this time of night." John glanced at his Rolex.

Jo could barely speak. She felt a wave of pleasure which quickly turned into a storm of anger. He was so flippant!

"Still serving?" John asked.

"No."

"Got a room?"

"No chance. We're full."

"Come on, Jo, we need to talk," John stepped towards her but she moved away.

"I'm sure the North Westmarland Hotel will have a room; you should try there." Jo was adamant, her face set.

John watched her for a few moments.

"OK, fair enough," he succumbed. "But come and have a coffee with me in the morning, I need to talk to you."

"I don't want to talk to you ever again." Jo coolly replied then turned and walked down the corridor.

She tried to keep control - it was so hard to send him on his way! She felt her heart pulling her back, but somehow stayed resolute and kept walking.

"Jo!" John called after her.

"What?" she snapped back.

"Your dress is caught in your knickers."

Jo grabbed at the hem of her dress. Sure enough, it was embedded in the waistband of her large flesh-coloured control pants.

"Fuck!" she exclaimed as the front door closed behind John.

35

"Oh Lord, Hattie, just look at them." Jo lay on the floor in her lounge. Her blue silk dress was crumpled and stained and tears streamed down her tired and unkempt face. She reached into the mound of blankets under the stairs and stroked Pippa's head lovingly. "You're a beautiful girl," Jo cooed as Pippa nuzzled her hand. The dog licked the bodies of eight squirming puppies vying for position on her swollen nipples.

Hattie handed Jo a glass of champagne and smiled. It'd been a long night and even longer morning...

CONTRARY TO MARTIN'S assurances that Pippa would 'get on with it' the vet had been wrong and Jo and Hattie had spent the whole night chasing around after the dog.

Pippa had managed to slope into the panel room when Hattie was locking up and Jo was alerted by the dog's plaintive howls. Screaming for Hattie to bring hot water and towels, Jo sank to her knees and tried to coax Pippa out from under the tables and chairs. She wanted to lead the dog back to the comfort of her warm box but Pippa was having none of it. Panting heavily, she darted away from Jo and made it as difficult as possible to let anyone near her, then proceeded to intermittently pop puppies out as she travelled around the room.

Jo was almost hysterical.

"Call an ambulance!" she screamed as Hattie dashed in with armfuls of towels and told her not to be so bleedin' stupid. The dog was doing what dogs did.

"Oh my God, Hattie there's one wriggling by the coal scuttle!" Jo crawled along the floor and gently scooped the minute puppy onto her palm. "It's so tiny," she whispered. "Oh heck, what do we do?"

"Give it here." Hattie crawled behind Jo and took the puppy. She tucked it in her cleavage. "I'll keep the little bugger warm till his mam's ready for him."

By dawn they'd managed to cordon Pippa off and get her back into the house.

She'd had five puppies.

Jo BREATHED a sigh of relief as Pippa stepped into her box and snuggled down on the soft, clean blankets.

Hattie made a cup of tea and handed one to Jo as they watched the puppies wriggle like maggots.

"Why isn't she feeding them?" Jo looked worried.

"I don't know," Hattie replied. "I think we should put them somewhere separate or she'll crush them, she looks restless."

"It's no good, Hattie, go and wake Martin up." Jo elbowed Hattie.

"Watch me outfit!" Hattie hissed as tea slopped onto the remnants of last night's fancy dress gear.

"Never mind that – get over there and wake him up." Jo shooed Hattie away and reached into the box to separate the puppies from an anguished Pippa.

A few moments later, Martin appeared in his pyjamas.

"Thank God you're here." Jo stood up and moved back to allow Martin access to the box.

"I could hardly refuse. It's not often you have one of the Crankies banging your door down in the middle of the night." He glared at Hattie then taking his stethoscope, knelt down and began to examine Pippa. Jo pulled Hattie back as she took a swinging kick at Martin's behind.

"There's at least three more to come." Martin stood up. "Give the others formula milk until she's ready to feed." He took a tin and pipettes out of his leather case. "Call me if she struggles but please try and leave it till at least lunchtime." He glared at Hattie, then turned on his slippers and marched out of the room.

Ann was leaning over the banisters.

"Want any help?" She trotted down the stairs. "Gosh they're beautiful. Alf will be delighted, a collie and lab mix – perfect for the farmers." She picked up one of the puppies and stroked it.

"Sod Alf," Hattie said and nudged Ann. "Can you show Mother Theresa here how to feed these little blighters?"

Ann went into the kitchen and put the kettle on. She made up the formula, let it cool then drew it up into five tiny pipettes. She took a puppy in one hand and fed it from a pipette in the other.

"Look, he's hungry. Come on, Hattie – get busy." Jo had returned to the box and was back on her stomach stroking Pippa.

As Martin had predicted three more puppies were born during the morning.

Hattie tidied the box for the little family and put clean blankets down. Sandra crept in with some finely minced chicken and gravy for the new mother and watched with pleasure as Pippa gobbled it down. Gerald brought two brand new shiny dog bowls wrapped in paw-marked gift paper, with a card from Arthur and himself. Judy knelt with a pen and pad and began to make a note of names, she wanted to order name tags for their collars. Old Johnny knocked at the window and handed them huge bunch of roses. The last of this year's blooms, he whispered.

Jo was in raptures over the eight magnificent puppies that squirmed before her. She watched in awe as they gravitated to Pippa and began to feed. Ann handed Thomas to Jo and they all sat around the box watching the new arrivals.

"Uppies Muma! 'Oof!" Thomas stared in wonder.

The kitchen door opened and Alf banged into the room. He placed planks of wood on the floor, beside a hammer and nails.

"You'll need a whelping box." Alf too knelt down and stared at Pippa's brood. "Bonny," he spoke softly and smiled. "Little beauties, all black like their dad." He thought fondly of Sefton.

Jo handed Thomas to Ann then moved away from the box.

She stood up and looked around.

Things were tough right now, she thought to herself and knew in her heart that the business was a struggle which had a knock-on effect on them all. But she was safe in her lovely home with new life happily being nourished and everyone helping in their way. Jo looked over at Hattie. Minus the wig, Hattie's hair was flattened to her head and her body burst out of the ill-fitting outfit that she still wore.

Hattie looked up and caught Jo's eye. She smiled and held out her hand.

"Bertie loved dogs," Hattie spoke quietly. "He had a soft spot for old Pippa." Tears moistened her eyes.

"Then we'd better call our first-born Bertie." Jo took Hattie's hand.

They looked down at the sleeping form of puppy Bertie, who they'd found beside the coal scuttle and kept warm in Hattie's bra. He was lying on his back with his paws in the air, his soft pink tummy exposed to the world. Hattie chuckled.

"Aye," she whispered "And doesn't he just look like him." She squeezed Jo's hand.

Jo touched Judy's shoulder. "Open some champagne and take it through to the kitchen – I want everyone to toast this little lot." She looked fondly at a snoring Pippa. "Could you bring a bottle in here for me and Hattie? I think our new arrivals need some peace and quiet but thank you all for everything..."

"You simply cannot beat the taste of bubbly." Jo lay on the floor with Hattie comatose beside her. Both stared up at the ceiling.

"We ought to get out of these mucky clothes," Hattie eventually said.

"Yes and get a couple of hours sleep. The weekend could be busy."

The weather had improved and the sun shone like lozenges through the leaded windows of the house. It danced across the carpet to the whelping box where Pippa licked her puppies. They began to squeal, feeding time again! The girls sat up and Jo knocked over the empty bottle.

"Shit, we've drunk it all."

"I think we deserved it." Hattie shook her head. "I'm off for a shower." She stood up unsteadily and began to climb the stairs.

"What time is it?" Jo looked anxiously at the wall clock. It had stopped.

"Why?" Hattie held onto the banister. Please God, may Jo not remember that trouble with a capital T had arrived last night and asked her to meet him this very morning. "It's well after lunchtime," Hattie said. She crossed her fingers and disappeared up the stairs.

Jo crawled to her knees and looked into Pippa's box. The dog appeared content as the puppies began to feed again.

"Well I've buggered that up, Pippa," Jo whispered. She stroked the tiny bodies and thought about John. He'd have checked out of the North Westmarland Hotel by now and Jo doubted if she'd ever see him again. But maybe that was for the best? If he'd really wanted to speak to her he would have phoned or called in this morning. Jo sighed. Her heart hurt and felt as if a cold steel was being twisted through it. Come on Jo – get over it! You've a business to run.

She stood and straightened her dress then followed Hattie.

"I hope you haven't had all the hot water," Jo said.

Hattie stepped into the shower. She closed her eyes and looked heavenward. There is a God – thank you Bertie! She whispered to the ceiling. Jo hadn't mentioned John.

Smiling to herself, Hattie picked up a tube of Jo's most expensive shower cream and liberally squeezed it all over her body, then luxuriated in the hot jets of rejuvenating water that poured down.

GREG WAS happy as he drove along the main road and contemplated the day. He was picking Thomas up for the afternoon and with any luck, he'd see Jo and continue his charm offensive.

He felt she was ready for it. Black Monday will have hit her hard. No one was spending any money - even the pub had been empty last night. Greg contemplated a few carefully chosen words of wit and charm and planned his approach. Subtle hints that his bank account was healthy should work and he'd be home and dry in no time. He thought that Jo must be having sleepless nights with all those overheads. Anyway, the place was too posh by far, no wonder she was struggling.

Greg dug in his pocket and pulled out a cigarette. He fumbled with his lighter, lit the cigarette and dragged deeply. His plan was to make the hotel one big pub, serving decent bar meals with a kid's play area in the back - they'd make a mint! Never mind fancy bedrooms, he'd rent the rooms out as bed-sitters. He'd heard that Heaven Holiday Parks had planning in for a site in Marland Forest, there'd be staff from all over wanting rooms. Greg thought that the land at the back of the hotel was ideal for grazing too - think what the travellers would pay in Fair Week.

He pulled into the hotel gates and noticed a red Ferrai. He'd seen it before and whistled in awe as he parked his car, it was some piece of metal and must be worth a fortune. A man came out of the front door and Greg thought he looked angry as he got in the Ferrai, slammed the door and roared away. There were several cars on the car park but Greg couldn't see Jo's BMW, it was probably at the back.

As he crossed the gravel he flicked his cigarette into the shrubbery and stepped on some biscuits, which on close inspection he recognised as fortune cookies. He kicked them away and knocked on the side door. Ann hurried to let him in.

"I can't get Thomas away from the puppies," she said, "you'd better come in."

Greg stepped into the lounge and saw Thomas gripping a wooden structure under the stairs. He peeped over the top.

"'Uppies Daddy."

Greg followed the child's gaze. He wasn't one for animals and couldn't understand why Jo had taken a mongrel in. Now it had produced a litter, she must be mad.

Thomas bounced up and down and pointed into the box. The kid was adorable. Dressed in pale blue striped dungarees, yellow shirt and socks, Greg couldn't imagine that lot coming from Mothercare. That would stop too. No point in lashing out on designer stuff when the kid would only be in it for five minutes.

Ann reassured Thomas that the puppies needed to sleep and he could wake them up when he got back.

"Jo around?" Greg asked casually. Sow the first seed…

"She's gone to the cash and carry." Hattie's voice boomed down the stairs. Greg jumped back.

"We were busy last night. She's gone to stock up."

"Are you busy?" Greg looked incredulous.

"Heaving," Hattie replied and came to a stop in front of Greg. "You ready for the off?"

She turned and grabbed the pushchair from behind the table and started to push it in his direction. Fearing that she would break his legs, Greg darted away and took Thomas from Ann.

"Back at six," Hattie ordered and watched Ann load the pushchair with kit bag, coat and rabbit toy.

Greg glared at her. Well it wouldn't last he thought angrily and strapped Thomas into the car.

HATTIE SAT IN RECEPTION. She'd taken several bookings that afternoon and the restaurant was half full tonight, she hoped things were picking up for Jo.

She hadn't realised how bad it'd been. But Hattie wasn't a fool and knew that an unopened VAT demand was buried under a pile of stationery with many more brown envelopes.

They'd have to get it sorted, Jo couldn't ignore this lot. At least the weather was better; they'd done lots of afternoon teas and folk were coming through the doors.

Hattie read the telephone message Judy had recorded that morning. John Doherty called for Mrs E at 10.15 and again at 12 noon. Bang in the middle of birthing, not a chance! Hattie screwed up the message and put it in the bin.

She couldn't bear the thought of Jo having her heart broken, not after all that she'd done for Hattie.

Hattie sat back in her chair and rocked up and down. She thought about Bertie, who'd liked John enormously but warned Hattie that he'd never settle with Jo. Hattie didn't know why and Bertie wouldn't be drawn, but if those were Bertie's thoughts on the matter, then it was good enough for Hattie. Come hell or high water, she wasn't having Jo upset even if she did light up like a Christmas tree the minute John came within her radar.

John had called in just after lunch. Judy couldn't wait to tell Hattie that the red car was here again and Mr Gorgeous was asking for Jo. Thank God Jo had gone to the cash and carry. Then there was that idiot Greg. He was getting far too cocky now that he was allowed in the house and Hattie had no doubt that Estelle's days would be numbered if Greg saw a chink of light past the pushchair.

The phone rang. Peter Gavmin wanted to book a table for himself, his good lady and the Manns. Eight o'clock would be perfect. She wrote it down as the phone rang again.

"Now then, Harriet." Pete Parks spoke warmly. "Good to hear you're back in the saddle." Hattie rolled her eyes and picked up a pen.

"A table tonight?" Hattie asked and drew her chair under the desk as she studied the restaurant diary.

"Aye, a table for six and make sure Sandra's got t-bones on the menu," Pete said.

"It will be our pleasure." Hattie replaced the phone and made a note to increase the price of steak that evening.

JO AND HATTIE sat in reception and counted the day's takings. Jo couldn't believe it! They'd had a fantastic day, and with the Chinese night added to it, she couldn't wait to get to the bank on Monday and get Mr Knight off her back.

"Another Cointreau?" Hattie yawned.

"No thanks. I'm knackered." Jo started to yawn too. She looked at the clock on the switchboard, one in the morning! She rubbed her eyes wearily and thought longingly of her bed. No doubt the puppies would keep her awake with their squealing and she'd need to change their blankets.

"The Gavmins were lively." Hattie looked at their bill. They'd drunk several bottles of wine between them.

Robert had been positively mellow, even being pleasant to Lady Miriam, who had to be supported by both himself and Peter as they all fell into a taxi.

"Hmn. I thought he was drunk to be honest." Jo frowned as she remembered Robert's words. He'd pulled her to one side in the cloak room and pinned her to the wall.

"Jo, I have to speak to you," Robert said, his face inches from hers. "You're mad to even think of selling this place and I'm not at all happy about making any enquiries."

Jo had tried to push him away but he'd moved her hands to one side.

"I've told you things will improve – look how busy you are tonight." Robert had urged.

"It's just a one-off Robert, the press are painting a very gloomy picture and winter is coming."

"Well if you need to sell so badly, why don't you offer it to John Doherty?" Robert snarled. "He'd have cash on the table and the place turned into a housing estate before you could say One Flew Over Fair Hill! You're mad! Someone like him would make a killing and you've done all the hard work. Take my advice and stay put!" He'd glared at her, his face red and angry.

"Robert, I know you're concerned but this is my decision." Jo had pushed him away. She didn't like to see him like this.

"Yes, Jo, it is," Robert said maliciously. "John was at the North Westmarland Hotel today, you could have discussed it with him, if you can get past Jinny Atkinson; they were very chummy when I saw them."

His parting shot had shocked Jo and she was speechless as she watched Robert returned to the Gavmins.

Jo was mortified. John was such a rotten bastard! Talk about having your cake and eating it... He'd had the audacity to ask Jo to go and see him and all the time he's cosied up with Jinny bloody Atkinson!

Jo stood up. Hattie was locking the bar. Jo felt tense and was seething with anger as she thought about John.

"I will have that Cointreau." she told Hattie. "Remind me to cancel Jinny Atkinson's Christmas party, she can find another venue for her cronies."

Hattie reached for the bottle. She knew better than question Jo's motives but something had happened and no doubt it involved the Romany Romeo.

Hattie poured a large measure into a glass. With a sigh, she pushed it across the bar and watched Jo take a swig. Just as things seemed better, he was like a curse. Hattie reached for a glass and poured out a beer.

"To better days?" She raised her glass.

"To much better days." Jo chinked Hattie's glass and downed the rest of her drink.

36

Christmas was around the corner and Jo could hardly believe it. November had flown by and December had crept up before she knew it.

Where had the year gone? To her relief, trade had improved but the country seemed to be in the doldrums with an overall feeling of hard times ahead.

She'd had to change the business. People weren't taking holidays and the weekend breaks and autumnal get-a-ways - so popular in Westmarland, were none existent. Conferences, shoots and seasonal menus would now hopefully get them through the winter.

Following the success of Mark Pucker's first conference, Jo had contacted many companies and offered them facilities with overnight packages for their delegates. It had paid off. She could undercut the larger hotels and offer good value in luxury surroundings for small sales teams. The location was perfect, being a ten-minute drive from the motorway and on a major route. They'd picked up eight new companies who'd hopefully re-book once they had experienced the Kirkton House package.

Mark Pucker had visited again with his troops and during a break in his meeting he'd pulled Jo to one side.

"Jo, I've been meaning to talk to you." They sat in the conservatory and Jo waited to hear him out.

"I'm sorry that I haven't been in touch. I had a wonderful meal with you that day and wanted to see you again."

Jo murmured that she knew he'd been very busy. She prayed that he wasn't going to ask her out again and crossed her fingers in her lap.

Hattie interrupted them and asked if they'd like some coffee. Jo had to force herself to keep a straight face, as Hattie stood behind Mark and drew large ears in the air. Completely unaware, Mark looked uncomfortable as he began to speak.

Hattie remained behind Mark and looked puzzled. She pulled a face as he began.

"The thing is, I took the troops to Majorca as a reward for hitting targets and I caught up with an old friend." Mark looked away. "Sarah used to work for me years ago as a John Player Special promotions girl on the Embassy circuits," Mark continued, avoiding Jo's gaze.

"She married and moved out to Majorca but her husband had a heart attack and sadly died. I didn't know until she met up with us on this trip, she'd heard we were out there."

Jo uncrossed her fingers, things were going well.

"I know that I'd mentioned seeing you, and I'd wanted to take you to the Gateshead Garden Festival, but Sarah and I, well..." He looked embarrassed.

"You've got together." Jo made it easy for him. She was absolutely delighted but thought she'd better not show it too much. "I understand, Mark. Well, I think I do – I had wondered why you didn't ask me out again..." She wasn't going to make it too easy for him.

"I know and I'm very sorry." He looked up, in some discomfort. "But it just sort of happened and she's met the kids and..." he trailed off.

Didn't waste any bloody time! Jo felt rather miffed. "Well naturally I'm upset." She looked down at her hands, unable to meet his eye.

Jo looked up as Hattie made a thumbs-up sign in the air and indicated that Jo should keep it going.

"I had hoped that there might be something special between us." Jo put her head down again. Hattie was making signs of a long nose and mouthing the word Pinocchio!

"Oh God, Jo, I'm so sorry." Mark reached for her hand. "It was just one of those things, our eyes met again and I just knew that Sarah was the girl for me. I really don't want to see you upset."

Hattie played an imaginary violin. Jo didn't think she could keep this going much longer.

"That's all right, Mark." She stood up and Hattie leapt back. "I am upset but time will heal."

Mark jumped to his feet and put a consoling hand on her shoulder.

"At least you'll come here sometimes for your conferences and we can be friends." Jo sniffed and took a tissue from her pocket.

Hattie's palm shot up from the doorway. Perhaps Jo was going too far.

"Of course I will." Mark patted Jo on the back. "In fact I'll get them booked ahead every month for next year."

Jo nodded, seemingly unable to speak and rushed from the conservatory.

Hattie sat in reception with a calculator.

"Played a blinder, thought you might have gone over the top but he fell for it." She wrote a figure down on a piece of paper and pushed it over to Jo. "That's what his conferences are worth next year, that'll sort a few VAT bills out. Cast iron bookings - bank manager's wet dream."

"Bloody hell, you don't help. I nearly lost it with the nose." Jo's eyes lit up as she read the figure.

"Time you played them at their own game," Hattie snorted. "Grieving widow? My arse... The troops were on an away-day and sexy Sarah could smell a sales manager's salary, no wonder she whipped out her old John Player kit - tight white shorts and knee high plastic boots? He's hardly going to put up with puppies pissing in his briefcase and your long hours. No contest..." She tapped a pencil on the desk. "Fancy a brew?"

It was time to get the Christmas decorations out and make the hotel feel festive. Judy knelt on the stairs and passed boxes to the twins.

Jo was submerged in the cupboards under the eaves of her house. She could just about stand up and shuffled the boxes across the dusty floor. Judy heard her curse every time she banged her head on a beam.

Christmas! Judy was so excited. She loved everything about Christmas, her mum always made a big thing of it with tons of decorations and mountains of food and this year was going to be extra special. Not only did Judy have all the frenzy of the hotel and Christmas parties to look forward to, but she was getting engaged! Alf had proposed to her and they planned to announce their engagement on Christmas Eve.

Judy could hardly contain her happiness. She never imagined being married to a game keeper and a successful one at that. Alf told her that he had a fair sum put away in savings and to start thinking about where she wanted to live, as they'd be able to put a decent deposit down. Judy fantasised about a little stone cottage with roses around the door, at the end of a long drive in the forest. Two black Labradors sat on the steps. She could even see a pram outside in the sunshine.

"Wake up, Judy," Jo called out, "it's piling up in here." Judy shook herself out of her daydream and leaned forward into the cupboard.

"Careful with that one, it's got the shiny balls and breakables," Jo said.

Simon appeared at the dog-leg of the stairs. He had a silver garland on his neck and a glass Father Christmas hanging off each ear.

"Don't let Mrs E see you," Judy giggled. "She's just said there are lots of breakables." Judy pulled the boxes carefully away from the doorway and handed them to Simon.

"Is Alf on the way with those trees?" Jo asked, her voice muffled.

"Yes, he said he'd be here by lunchtime."

Alf had been sent to select four of the finest trees he could find from the Marland estate. He was doing quite a trade in Christmas trees and all the greengrocers had their orders with him.

Judy knew he'd bring only the best for the hotel.

A tall one to go out the front and another in the garden then two twelve-footers, for the Red Room and Green Room. Judy smiled to herself. It would look like fairy-land!

Hattie bustled through the hallway and searched around for the twins. Where was everyone?

Penny came out from the kitchen.

"They're sorting out the old decorations from the pub," Penny explained and pointed to the Panel Room restaurant. "They've put it all in there."

Hattie peered in and pulled a face as she looked at the heap of dusty boxes. That lot will need some brightening up! Good job she'd been to the pound shop and cash and carry on her way in.

"Tell Simon to get the boxes out of my car," she told Penny and marched into the kitchen.

"By 'eck Sandra something smells delicious." Hattie leaned across the table and picked up a mince pie. Sandra swiped at her hand with a ladle.

"Don't begrudge a poor old spinster her only pleasure." Hattie stuffed the pie in her mouth.

Gerald stood by marble counter and rolled out a square of honeycoloured mixture. A rack of biscuits cooled on the window sill beside him. When Sandra's back was turned, he thrust one over to Hattie and she slipped it in her pocket.

"What's Santa Claus putting in your stocking then?" Hattie asked Sandra mischievously. "Or should I say Santa Arthur?" "I'm

not biting," Sandra retorted without turning.

Gerald giggled.

"There's those that'd say romance was in the air and Christmas is a time for gold rings and not just the five in the song," Hattie teased.

"Well it wouldn't surprise me if one will be going Judy's way," Sandra replied.

Gerald pushed another biscuit over the table to Hattie but Sandra had seen him and she clipped him on the ear with her wooden spoon.

"It'll come off your wages!" Sandra bellowed.

"Judy?" Hattie exclaimed. "Well I never, mind she has been tripping the light fandango with Marland's answer to Lady Chatterley's Lover for some time." She paused and bit into the biscuit. "A wedding... great, we could do with a good knees-up."

"Who's having a knees-up?" Jo came into the kitchen. Her hair was covered in cob-webs and she had black dust smeared all over her face.

"Going out?" Hattie said as she brushed crumbs off her mouth.

Jo glared at Hattie.

"Did you get the fairy lights?" Jo asked.

"I most certainly did and a few other novelties that will bring a touch of class and elegance to the place." Hattie marched through the still-room and Jo followed behind.

The twins had unloaded Hattie's car and an assortment of boxes and bags tumbled off chairs in the panel room. Jo stared at the pile of Christmas items. She reached into a bag and pulled out a two-foot high garden gnome wearing a tired Santa suit and grubby white beard. "It lights up." Hattie looked pleased.

Jo flung it to one side and dug further into the bag. She'd found a paper garland of Snow White and the Seven Dwarfs. Snow White resembled and ageing old crone.

"What do you expect from the pound shop?" Hattie bristled as Jo crumpled the chain into a ball. "I've got some lovely items at bargain prices - no need to be so critical."

"Did you get the fairy lights?"

"Yes, hundreds of the bloody things, I got them from Cleators, so don't be worrying that the place is going to ignite." Hattie reached down and produced a large bag. Cleator's Superior Electrical Supplies was embossed on its side. "Cost a friggin' fortune."

"Does none of you do nowt but gossip round here?"

Alf marched into panel room and Jo stared at his trail of muddy footprints. Alf looked at the pile of decorations.

"You'll need something to hang this lot on." Alf indicated to the twins that they should follow him. He had four Christmas trees on the back of his truck. The muddy prints made a return journey.

"Thomas!" Ann's voice cried out from the house, as little fingers inched around the panel room door and a giggling Thomas fell into the room.

Eight bounding puppies flew past.

"Uppies Mamma!" He pulled himself to his feet and toddled over to Jo's legs. She scooped her son into her arms.

"Dirty Mumma…" Thomas poked a podgy finger across Jo's face and held it out. It was black. She put his finger in her mouth and licked it clean while Ann scrambled on the floor trying to round the puppies up. They were now six weeks old and full of energy and inquisitiveness.

Jo smiled. It was like having eight more children, but she adored each and every one.

The twins held two and tickled their tummies.

"Have you got homes for them all?" Simon asked.

"Yes, we have." Jo looked sad. She thought how easy it had been to find good homes for Pippa's brood. Alf had instigated the whole procedure and assured every interested party that the lineage was impeccable. He'd chosen two males for himself. One bitch was going to the twins' mother, who'd fallen in love the moment she clapped eyes on it. Martin next door wanted one and another was going up to Ann's family farm in Marland. Phillip and Helen Campbell in the village had pleaded for a male and Marion the part-time cook said she'd like the last bitch; it would be good company for her. That left one - the fattest and naughtiest of the bunch - little Bertie would be staying with Jo and Pippa. The pups were due to have their injections that week and would depart soon after.

One of the boxes of decorations moved. They stared down and watched it shuffle across the floor. It stopped and a little black nose peeped out. Pippa appeared from the doorway and searched for her pups. She moved over to the box and nudged it to one side. Bertie sat underneath surrounded by Christmas nativity pieces. He had something small and pink in his mouth.

"Baby!" Thomas cried out and pointed.

Jo closed her eyes. Bertie was chewing on Baby Jesus.

"Baby dead!" Thomas giggled as Jo thrust him into Ann's arms and bent down to pick the pup up. Hattie smiled as she smoothed out her Snow-White decoration.

"If no one else wants this, I'll take it home."

THE TREES WENT up that afternoon and everyone watched the lights being turned on at the front.

Old Johnny brushed up leaves and stopped to watch. The late afternoon sky was inky and dark and as the lights sprung into life, they all clapped their hands – it looked magical! Draped with gold and red garlands, the tree had a large sparkling glass star at the top.

"My fairy would have looked much better," Hattie grumbled.

Jo winced as she thought about the plastic horror Hattie had purchased from the pound shop. It had a gross gaping red hole for a mouth and enormous breasts and would have sat comfortably on a shelf in a sex shop.

"Why don't you put it on your tree at home?"

"Aye, I might just do that." Hattie flounced back into the hotel.

The trees in the front reception rooms were dressed with red and gold ornaments and they'd wrapped tartan ribbon on fir cone garlands for the stairs and along the fireplaces. Bunches of holly with bright red berries framed pictures and dark green candles stood tall on mantelpieces.

Jo thought it all looked very festive, she was pleased with their efforts and wandered through to her house to shower before evening service.

They had their first Christmas party that night. Jim from the sorting office and Mystic Myra had organised the Post Office workers in Marland. They would dine in the Panel Room, which now resembled a grotto and was decorated with Christmas ribbons, garlands and bright crackers. A welcoming log fire glowed in the grate.

Jo climbed the stairs to her bedroom. The house was quiet. Ann had taken Thomas over to Marland to play with Hattie's boys.

She sat down and looked at her face in the dressing-room mirror. The old mirror had a lovely frame but the glass was bevelled and Jo rubbed the smoky surface as she leaned in to inspect herself more closely. The mirror was one of Robert's 'finds' and Jo loved it, even though the gilt border was peeling off.

She rubbed cleanser into her skin and thought about Robert. He'd been mortified after his outburst and had stopped by to apologise. He said he was ashamed of his behaviour. Jo thought he was going over the top, but knew that a drunk always regrets his actions. Robert justified his concern and said he didn't want her to move away. Jo had made light of it and Robert promised to do as she'd asked and keep his ear to the ground.

The phone rang.

"Mrs E – there's an overseas call for you," Judy said excitedly. Jo thanked her and wondered who could be calling from abroad. She held the phone in one hand and picked up a cotton wool ball in the other.

"Hello?" she said brightly.

"Decided to speak to me then?" John Doherty sounded like he was in the next room.

Jo held the receiver out and stared at it in shock. Her hand shook.

"Pardon?"

"I waited all morning, left you two messages," John said. "I came in to too, but you gave me the cold shoulder."

"I did not!" Jo was indignant. What messages? No one had told her he'd called in?

"Well it doesn't matter now. You think I'm a complete shit and you're right – I am." His voice softened.

"Does it matter what I think?" Jo didn't know what to say.

"Well I think the world of you - that's the trouble."

"I don't understand?" Jo moved the cotton ball mechanically across her face.

"Don't you? Surely you've worked it out by now?" John sounded surprised. "Bertie must have explained to Hattie. How is she by the way?" he sidetracked.

"She's doing well but what do you mean, Bertie explained what?" Jo had the sudden fear that John was married.

"Why I can't see you."

"You're married."

"I was Jo, a long time ago."

"And now..."

"She died, with my son. We were just kids."

He was very quiet. Jo stopped cleaning her face, the cotton ball had turned to a muddy mess.

"I'm sorry," she spoke gently. "But if it was a long time ago, why can't you see me now?"

"You really don't know do you?" he sighed deeply. "I'm a gypsy," he calmly stated. "A true blooded Romany gypsy, I'm born of pure stock and am the oldest son in our family."

"What's that got to do with us?" She was baffled.

"I grew up in a Vardo – a travelling horse drawn caravan. As kids, we slept by the roadside and at night and my mother cooked over an open fire. Usually a pigs-head stew in an iron pot." He paused. "Do you want me to go on?"

"Of course I do."

"My mother got sick of travelling and my dad bought some land and rented it to other gypsy families, we lived in a caravan community but I missed out on school and never learnt to read or write."

Jo thought about the cash John always used to pay his bills – wads of it, never a cheque book or bank card in sight.

"I grew up learning to fight, bare knuckle boxing to please the old man." John paused. "He was a scrap dealer but dabbled in antiques, he was quite good at it. But he liked the horses too and always gambled his money away. I should have worked with him on the antiques, but I wanted something better and liked the land, I was good at buying at auction. Cars too – I seem to have the knack. Rory does the contracts, he's a brilliant lawyer and I trust him with everything. He watches my back."

Jo thought about Rory, settling John's bill, hiring cars, running around for him – probably of Irish gypsy stock. Their blood bonded them together.

"But you could learn to read and write?"

"Oh I have, I'm not that stupid, but it's harder when you're older."

"But I still don't understand." Jo shook her head, it didn't make any sense.

"The old man has been ill for years. His heart isn't strong and he lost a fortune including the home. The family was penniless, so I support them. Most of them work for me," he added. "I've eight brothers and sisters and god knows how many in-laws, nephews and nieces."

"Is your mother still alive?"

"Yes and she lives in comfort, no more Vardos for her, although sometimes I think she'd prefer one."

"So what's the problem?" Jo asked. "Why haven't you married again? I thought gypsies made as many babies as they could?"

"As I've said, I married at sixteen – I didn't know Jenny but our parents pushed us together, the marriage was arranged, it's how things are done. When she died in childbirth, it was as though there was a curse on me. To lose them both meant I was cursed. It's how we think, what the family said."

Jo listened, she'd never heard anything so foolish, but she tried to make sense of what he was saying.

"Since then I've had to prove myself," John spoke softly. "Show them that I wasn't cursed, that I could make something of myself. And I have and I'm proud of my roots. But …" he hesitated. "I can never marry a non-gypsy, a gorger, it would kill my parents, they'd disown me and my family would never approve of me marrying outside." He stopped.

Jo could hear waves, crashing in the background.

"Where are you?" she asked.

"In Spain, sitting by a beach bar."

Not bloody Spain! Jo thought angrily. She shoved at the pot of cleanser and it fell to the floor, the contents oozing over the carpet. Jo ignored it. She was furious and couldn't understand his logic! Surely his parents would be proud of what he'd achieved? Dear Lord, he supported them all after all, how could they possibly deny him his happiness? It was 1987 for God's sake! Surely the old gypsy ways and customs were dying out. What the hell did it matter?

"I know you don't understand." John spoke quietly. "I just wanted you to know why I've kept my distance."

Jo's stomach churned. She felt sick, surely he couldn't mean this?

"You blew me away, Jo. At first it was a bit of fun, but lunch by the lake was magical and I fell in love with you. Then watching you care for Hattie and your compassion at the funeral, seeing how you've built up your business, you're a great mother too. I could go on and on."

"So what are you saying?" Jo felt a sob at the back of her throat.

"It's over," he sighed. "I can't mess you about or string you along – you deserve better. That's what I wanted to tell you to your face. But I wanted you to know that I love you. I love you, Jo."

Jo stared at her muddy face in the mirror. Oh, Christ! Just when she'd been so angry with him! Now he told her that he loved her but could never see her again. This is just crazy! Surely she could speak to his family... Meet with his parents? Make them understand?

"John! Listen to me..." She gripped the phone, she had to make him realise...

The connection was lost.

"JOHN!" she screamed.

The line was dead.

Jo closed her eyes and placed the phone on its cradle as her tears dripped onto the dressing table. She picked up the diamond necklace and stroked the dazzling stone. A shudder tore through her body and Jo felt pain like she'd never known before. She put her head in her hands and wept.

37

"I want to look like the fairy off the top of the Christmas tree," Hattie said as she leaned forward and turned the heating up in Jo's car.

"Not the pound shop fairy I hope?" Jo carefully pulled out of the hotel gates and turned onto the main road. The weather was treacherous.

"I want sparkles and sequins and a plunging neckline."

"So more 'Come Dancing' than restaurant hostess?" Jo flicked the wipers on as sleet lashed against the windscreen.

"Never mind restaurant hostess," Hattie replied "It's a Gala Ball we're having and I intend to look the part."

The girls were heading to Carlisle. An appointment had been made with Dorothy Osbourne and she had instructions to find them both something fabulous to wear for the party on New Years' Eve.

Jo had decided to have a big bash to celebrate the end of the year. Pete Park's booking for a hundred had convinced her that she needed to hire a marquee, she could never accommodate them all in the restaurant. If she was having a marquee, why not have a decent size and sell more tickets for the event? So, a marquee had been booked. It would completely cover the croquet lawn, with a tunnel from the conservatory and there would be proper flooring and heating.

It had cost a fortune.

"I hope you know what you're taking on with this do." Hattie stuck a toffee in her mouth. "The band is two hundred and fifty quid alone and what if it blows a gale and the tent takes off?"

Good old Hattie, ever the optimist, Jo thought as she navigated the icy road. Pete Parks' party had nearly covered the costs. He'd paid upfront for the tickets and wine for his guests. God Bless him... Jo thought.

Tickets were on sale and she hoped they'd sell another two hundred.

It was a huge event for the village.

Additional toilet facilities had been hired with cloakrooms and a catering tent, which would all be situated in the courtyard.

Extra staff, china and glassware were coming from an agency in Carlisle and they'd have a separate bar as a late licence had been approved.

Jo was excited.

"To be honest, Hattie, if we only break even I'll be happy." She concentrated on the slippery road surface. "This is a bit of a thank you to everyone. I can't believe how things have picked up in the last month or so and everyone has been so supportive."

"Sell all the tickets and you should make a packet," Hattie replied and thought of the advert in the Tribune last week.

Celebrate the New Year at Kirkton House Gala Ball
Join us in our festive marquee
Champagne Reception
Sumptuous Buffet & Licensed Bar
Dancing to the Cumberland Quartet
7.30pm for 8pm
Carriages at 2 am Black Tie

"I don't know what folk will make of Black Tie – they only wear one round here when there's a funeral," Hattie said.

"Nonsense," Jo replied. "It's a chance to dress up and have a bit of fun. I'm sure everyone will enter into the spirit."

"Well let's hope Dorothy finds you a grander outfit than Jinny." Hattie sucked her toffee and turned the heater up to its highest setting.

Jo gritted her teeth, mention of Jinny's name made her seethe with rage. She had eventually backed down and carried on with the booking for Jinny's Christmas lunch party. After all, Hattie had pointed out, Jinny's money was as good as anyone else's so why turn it away? At the party Jinny had strutted about the place and rudely ignored Jo.

Jo had bitten her tongue.

Hattie stuck an extra fifty pounds on the bar bill, hoping that it might ease Jo's pain, but she knew the real reason for Jo's anguish, a certain gypsy by the name of John.

Hattie was aware that John had phoned. Judy couldn't contain her excitement about a call from Spain and had told all the staff. Jo barely spoke for two days and in the end Hattie sat her down and demanded that Jo talk about it. The whole tale spilled out as Jo sobbed and dabbed at her eyes.

But Hattie had understood John's reasoning; it wasn't so strange really. Genuine gypsy folk had odd customs and Bertie had told her of many, Hattie could see why John had cut Jo off. There was one thing she couldn't understand though, what had Jinny to do with all this? John seemed to be more than friendly with her. The more they discussed it, the angrier Jo became, she was sure he was lying to her and making excuses.

Hattie sighed and undid another toffee. At least Jo seemed to have pulled herself together now. She said she'd chalk it down to experience and they'd vowed never to mention his name again.

Dorothy was welcoming as Jo and Hattie bustled out of the freezing weather into the The House of Osbourne.

"Ladies, what a pleasure it is to see you both."

She ushered them into the warmth and comfort of her business and beckoned to her daughter, "Vicky, get the Bristol Cream out," she said as Jo and Hattie relaxed on a velvet couch.

The girls sipped their sherry and gradually thawed out.

"Now I must settle with you for six tickets to your ball." Dorothy produced her cheque book and signed with a flourish. "Myself and my new partner and Vicky and her young man, are joining Vera and her husband Victor. It's my treat." Dorothy gave the cheque to Hattie, who tucked it in her bag.

"When you're ready ladies, shall we go through?" Dorothy guided them both into separate fitting rooms.

Vicky assisted Hattie, who appeared in one outfit after another and danced around in front of the full-length mirrors.

"What do you think of this, Jo?" she twirled in an emerald green sheath that plunged at the neck and fell softly to her knees.

"Not really a fairy is it?" Jo smiled.

"Fuck the fairy – this is divine," Hattie exclaimed. "Wrap it up, Mrs O!"

Dorothy had prepared one single outfit for Jo.

It hung on a padded hanger in her dressing room and Jo stared in awe at the full-length dress. A deep red velvet bodice, laced at the back with soft marabou feathers off the shoulder and a scarlet silk skirt falling into a fishtail train.

"I'm not so sure, Dorothy, it looks terribly tight." Jo touched the lacing and frowned. "The colour will clash with my hair."

"Shall we just slip it on, dear?" Dorothy helped Jo. She laced the bodice then held out a pair of scarlet silk court shoes.

"Try these too, come out when you're ready."

Hattie was still twirling and selected various evening bags against her dress. Dorothy chose a clutch bag that matched perfectly.

Jo stepped out and they both turned.

"Holy Mother of Mary..." Hattie gasped and dropped the bag.

"Walk around and see how you feel in it, have a look in these mirrors." Dorothy stood to one side so that Jo could see her image.

It was incredible. The dress fitted like a glove and gave Jo a perfect hour-glass figure. The colour warmed her skin and toned the highlights in her hair.

"It's fabulous, Dorothy." Jo whispered.

"I'm beginning to feel like one of the Ugly Sisters..." Hattie stared at Jo's dress.

"Don't be so silly, you look beautiful." Jo pulled Hattie to her side and they stared at their reflections.

"Well, Cinders," Hattie smiled. "You most certainly shall go to the ball."

"Put them on my account, Dorothy." Jo turned to Hattie and smiled. "Now if we could just find a couple of Prince Charmings…"

GREG WASN'T HAPPY. Things were definitely not going to plan. The hotel seemed to be having a mini-boom and he couldn't even park there some days when he went to collect Thomas.

He sat at the kitchen table in the flat and with a sigh, opened the Westmarland Tribune.

The local rag was full of the same old rubbish - best cake at the Women's Institute, a prize cup for award winning long-horn cattle at the agricultural show, Mrs Parks grinning foolishly as she collected a horse event rosette. Greg yawned and flicked idly through the paper.

Celebrate the New Year, Kirkton House Gala Ball…

What was this? Greg read on and became angry as he digested the advert. A Ball? What the hell was she doing now? Dancing? Late bar?

He closed his eyes as he imagined the till ringing all night. The odds were narrowing. Didn't she know there was a recession out there? As if anyone was going to spend that sort of money on a night out in the middle of a village with some naff pork pie buffet and a few paper chains and crackers!

Greg pushed the paper away.

Estelle was out at work. She'd picked up an evening job at the Butterly Arms Hotel where the owner said it was good to have someone bi-lingual on the staff.

Greg couldn't for the life of him see that there was much call for Spanish conversation in Butterly but she was bringing in a tidy amount these days.

He stared at the shiny shoes piled by the bedroom door and a new coat on the peg. Makeup was strewn over the dresser.

Greg thought about Jo.

She was pleasant these days but never spent any time with him, she seemed too busy and his attempts at conversation went in vain.

It was all backfiring.

He pulled the paper towards him. An idea began to form. New Years' Eve - what better time to romance someone? Everyone went daft on New Years' Eve and made promises as the clock struck twelve. He searched the advert for the price of the tickets. They weren't cheap. He'd get Estelle to order some for the Butterly Arms. Hattie would say they were full if he called the hotel. The price of a new frock and a night out should encourage Estelle to sort it out. He wondered where he could hire a dinner suit and returned to the paper to scan the classifieds.

ROBERT UNLOCKED HIS OFFICE DOOR. He turned the radiator up by his desk and sat down in his comfortable old leather Captain's chair. He remembered that his secretary was on holiday for two weeks. They seemed to take so much time off over Christmas these days; it would be the New Year before she was back. Still, there wasn't a great deal happening in the property market, it wasn't as though he'd miss her.

But he'd certainly miss Jo.

Robert stared at a letter on top of the pile on his desk. The header read Capital Country Houses, Small & Exclusive Properties. Robert sighed. The offer was too good to be true.

It was twice what he'd expected and he wished he'd never contacted his friend in Capital's acquisition department. Roger had been more than interested when Robert told him the name of his client.

"Jo Edmonds?" Roger said and asked Robert for details.

"Didn't she buy Kirkton House about a year ago? Pipped us to the post, I hear she got it for a song?"

"Well, now she's thinking of selling it." Robert bit his lip as he explained.

"Big old place too much for her?" Roger asked. "Expect it's falling down."

"On the contrary!" Robert bristled. "It's booming, despite the recession, she has a well-heeled bunch tripping through the doors and the place is quite magnificent."

Robert visualised the busy restaurant and elegant surroundings as Roger took notes - he assured Robert he'd get back to him as soon as possible and asked Robert to give Capital first refusal.

And now Robert had an offer on the table. Jo would be crazy not to accept this, it would set her up for the rest of her life. He reluctantly reached for the telephone and with a heavy heart, dialled her number.

ALF AND JUDY walked along the high street in Marland. Judy linked her arm through Alf's and cuddled into the thick, warm tweed. The sleet was horrible and she was pleased that she had a hood on her coat and wellies on her feet.

They stopped outside Braithwaite the Jewellers and stared at scores of gleaming rings.

Judy knew which one she wanted.

"Let's get in and see what they've got," Alf said and looked down at the two damp dogs by his heel. They sat on the wet pavement in their training harnesses and looked up adoringly at their master.

"Do you think it will be alright to take Sefton and Caesar in?" Judy reached down to pick the puppies up. She handed Sefton to Alf. "Course it will," Alf said and tucked Sefton into the pocket of his shooting jacket.

He reached for Caesar and put him in the opposite side. The puppies snuggled into the warm lining and their heads poked out of the flaps.

The sales assistant could instantly spot a couple about to get engaged. He gushed over and admired the dogs, then pulled out two chairs.

Alf and Judy sat down.

"Have you given any thought to the style of ring for Madam?" He tapped long thin fingers on the glass counter.

Judy told him what she wanted and with a quick flick he produced a velvet cloth and a tray of rings. She pointed to a small ruby set in old gold.

"Don't you want a diamond?" Alf looked at the antique ring.

"Well, I like rubies and…" Judy hesitated. She didn't want to tell Alf that she thought diamonds and rubies would be too expensive, rubies were her favourite after all.

"Well I like diamonds, somethin' proper on your finger." He looked up. The sales assistant nodded and disappeared into the back of the shop. He returned moments later with a leather box.

"This has only just come in," he said. "It came from an inheritance sale, an estate in Scotland. There's a whole collection of precious items from the former Lady of the House but you may be interested in this ring." He unclipped the fastening.

A beautiful ruby set in white gold, surrounded by small diamonds, sparkled. Judy gasped and Alf's eyes lit up. The assistant took it out of the box and placed it on Judy's finger.

It fitted perfectly.

Judy turned to Alf. She had tears in the corner of her eyes.

"How much?" Alf asked. The assistant wrote a figure down on a piece of paper and discreetly handed it to Alf. Alf's face was deadpan.

"Take twenty percent off and you've got a deal."

"I couldn't possibly go that low, sir." The assistant motioned to Judy's hand. "And it does look so wonderful on madam's finger." "That's th'offer." Alf was adamant. Judy looked nervously from one to the other. The dogs seemed to be watching too.

"Well I suppose I could…"

"That's a deal then." Alf held out his hand and crunched the assistant's bony fingers.

Judy flung her arms around Alf's neck. She could hardly believe it! Alf placed a large pile of notes on the counter as the assistant, flexing his crushed fingers, wrote out a bill of sale and gift wrapped the ring in its pretty little box. He sighed as he tied the ribbon.

It was Christmas after all.

38

At last, Christmas Eve! Jo flopped down on a chair beside the Red Room fire and raised her glass to George.

"Here's wishing you a happy Christmas, Dad."

"Thank you, love, and a very happy Christmas to you too."

George smiled as he looked at his daughter and took a sip of his malt whisky. He stroked Nipper, who was curled up on his knee.

Their glasses sparkled in the glowing fire light and fairy lights on the tree twinkled above piles of wrapped gifts.

The hotel was closed for three days.

Jo had decided to have a family Christmas and her parents had arrived that afternoon. Ann had gone home to her family in Marland and Jean was bathing Thomas. Pippa stretched out in front of the fire with a sleepy little Bertie snuggled beside her. Hattie, her mother and the boys would arrive at any moment.

The staff had worked hard throughout December and could now all enjoy Christmas with their families. Sandra and her mother were having Arthur and Gerald over for Christmas lunch and Gerald was cooking for them all on Boxing Day. He'd been planning the menu carefully and was going to roast a joint of pork with all the trimmings. Trevor Pigmy dropped it off when he delivered Jo's Christmas turkey. "May I wish you the compliments of the season, Mrs Edmonds," Trevor had said. His head shone under the bright kitchen light, the black hair slicked into place. Add a few cherries and he'd look like a Christmas pudding, Jo thought as she admired the size and quality of the bird, now spread-eagled on the kitchen table. They'd be eating turkey for weeks.

Alf and Judy had been over that afternoon and proudly showed off the engagement ring. Judy glowed and Jo was delighted for them. She'd bought an engagement gift and watched with apprehension as they opened it.

"His & Her bathrobes, how lovely!" Judy clapped her hands. "Look Alf, the pockets are deep enough for Sefton and Caesar."

Alf examined the items. He wasn't sure that he approved, there was nothing wrong with his flannel nightshirt.

They celebrated the engagement with champagne and Old Johnny, who'd been sweeping snow off the front door step, came in to toast the happy couple. He'd declined champagne and had a measure of whisky with George.

Jo sipped her drink and stared into the flickering flames. Robert had told her about the offer from Capital Country Houses. It was simply too good to refuse. Jo could hardly believe that they wanted the hotel so badly, but Robert said the group was looking to the future. The location was perfect for their chain. When the recession was over they would build at least forty more bedrooms and the garden could easily take a large extension, possibly a leisure club too. Jo sighed. She didn't know how she was going to tell everyone, especially Hattie, but it would have to wait until after the New Years' Party, she didn't want anything to spoil that. She'd told Robert that she'd agree in principle but he wasn't to breathe a word until the New Year.

"Problems, love?" George was watching Jo.

"No, Dad, not at all." She sat up and finished her drink. "I was just thinking what a strange year it has been, so up and down." Surely her dad would be pleased that she'd clear such a big profit? He'd be the first person she'd break the news to in the New Year.

"At least you're finishing on a high, the party sounds great."

George held his glass out and Jo topped it up from a decanter on the coffee table. "Too much excitement for your mum and me, but we'll be with you in spirit.

"I hope it's a success, Dad. It's costing a bomb."

The door opened and Jean came in with a sleepy Thomas on her shoulder. She peeled him off and handed him to Jo. Thomas wore a red sleep-suit trimmed in white with a hood. Pretty embroidery across the front read Santa's Little Helper.

Jo took the tired child and stood by the Christmas tree. "Look at all the pretty lights, Thomas."

His eyes were wide as he sucked on his thumb. She walked over to the fireplace where a plate with a carrot and mince pie, sat next to a small glass of Cointreau.

"Roodof." Thomas pointed at the carrot. "Santa!" He pointed to the Cointreau. Jo looked over his head at George.

"Santa has a sweet tooth." George winked.

A car pulled up on the drive and they heard the doors slam and footsteps crunch.

"That sounds like Aunty Hattie, here go to Gran for a moment." Jo handed Thomas over to Jean.

Hattie's car was splayed at an angle by the front door and the boys carried black bin liners, filled with presents.

Hattie's mother flicked a cigarette into the border then hurried into the porch. Hattie followed with their cases.

It was freezing and as Jo looked out she could see that the trees were white with frost.

"Bleedin' hell, I hope you've got that fire on." Hattie shivered as she shook herself in the doorway. The boys raced past her and pulled their grandmother into the Red Room to see the tree.

"Happy Christmas to you too." Jo took Hattie's coat.

Hattie paused and looked at her reflection in the hall mirror. She ran her fingers through her hair and glanced down at the nativity scene on the table. Mary, Joseph and the Three Kings huddled around a crib containing a knarled baby Jesus.

She turned to face Jo.

"Are you alright?" Jo asked. "You look like something's bothering you."

"You're selling up, aren't you?" Hattie said.

Jo was shocked.

"How did you know?"

"Call it intuition, or maybe an Irish angel?" Hattie stared at Jo's anxious face. "Don't look so panic-stricken, I'd do exactly the same in your shoes."

Hattie linked Jo's arm. "I won't tell anyone, let's get the party over first eh? By the sound of things, they've made you an offer you'd be bloody mental to refuse." She raised her eyebrows and looked around. "I'm not half going to miss it though." She looked fondly at Jo. "Happy Christmas, Jo, you deserve it."

"Thank you, Hattie and so do you. Happy Christmas."

39

The weather stayed bitterly cold and although the village resembled a pretty Christmas card scene, with banks of snow sweeping across the green and icicles hanging from hedgerows, Jo was worried that it might affect the party. The marquee company assured Jo that their generators could function at temperatures as low as minus twenty degrees and they'd never had a problem. But as the party got closer, Jo began to worry about everything.

The marquee was erected three days before the event and a team of men spent a day securing it down and laying the flooring.

Hattie watched with interest. The main person in charge was a man called Maurice, a cousin of Arthur's, who was a stickler for detail and placed each piece with precision. He stood up as Hattie handed him a mug of tea.

"I hope that floor is strong." She nodded at his work. "There'll be plenty of bodies jigging about on it."

"It'll take an aircraft landing by the time I've finished with it." Maurice smiled and sipped his tea. He was a well-muscled man with a weathered complexion. Hattie smiled back then continued her inspection of the marquee.

"Looks like a circus tent," she commented as she gazed at the pointed ceiling. Chairs were stacked in groups of ten and table bases and tops rested against them. A stage was set at the top end, opposite the entrance.

"Give us a twirl." Jo called out as she walked towards Hattie. She carried a pile of chair covers and matching ribbon tie-backs. Hattie skipped across the floor and spun herself round on one foot. She tripped and fell, landing on her bottom by Maurice.

"I hope that's just your practice run." He offered his hand.

"Very funny." Hattie scrambled to her feet. "I've got bleedin' splinters where I've no right to have splinters," she grumbled.

"Need a hand to get them out?" Maurice gave her a wink.

Hattie grabbed his empty mug and stomped away.

Sandra, Gerald and Marian had the immense task of creating a grand buffet for three hundred hungry revellers. They'd been hard at it since they returned from their Christmas days off and with only one day to go, were working round the clock.

In the days before New Years' Eve, Jo had restricted restaurant meals to residents only, to take the pressure off the kitchen, but there was still a massive amount of work to be done. In the marquee, guests would be seated at circular tables and in turn help themselves from the buffet. Starters and desserts would be served by the waiting team, supervised by Judy who was currently in the catering tent with a clipboard, busy ticking china, utensils and glassware off her lists as it was delivered and stored.

Car parking seemed to be in order. Pete Parks had organised two coaches to bring his guests to the party and taxi numbers had been given to everyone when they booked their tickets. Phillip Campbell had a seven-seater jeep and would ferry guests over from the village green, where the police had suggested additional parking. Martin next door offered his large driveway and Old Johnny was busy getting notices ready. The hotel was fully booked, the bedrooms having sold quickly and with the overflow, the pub too now had a No Vacancies sign outside.

The phone rang constantly.

Hattie glued herself to reception and monitored all the calls from the florist, the brewery, the wine merchant and numerous suppliers who confirmed what time they would be delivering or setting up. People still called asking for last minute tickets, but the event had been sold out for over a week and Jo couldn't increase the numbers.

NEW YEARS EVE morning began with another hard frost. Jo woke early and threw her bedroom window open. She breathed in the crisp cold air and gazed at the garden below, where the top of the marquee was almost as tall as her window. It stretched out before her like a shimmering silver screen, as the sun's winter rays reflected across the large expanse of canvas. Jo wanted to leap out of her window and bounce over it like an acrobat on a huge trampoline.

"Don't jump!" Hattie called out as she came through the bedroom door with a tray of tea. She placed it on the table by Jo's bed then gathered her housecoat around her and climbed under the duvet.

"Shut the bleedin' window and get us a cup of tea, my fingers are too numb to grip the pot."

Jo closed the window and poured.

"There's nothing like the first cup of the day," Hattie mumbled and cradled a mug in her hands. She sank deep into the warm bed.

"Well this is it." Jo shoved Hattie to one side and climbed in beside her. "I'm really excited."

"Been a funny old year, hasn't it?" Hattie was thoughtful. "I don't just mean with Bertie dying and I'm not going on about that or I'll get upset." She sipped her tea. "But you did a hell of a lot this year and you changed my life when you offered me a job."

"I don't know how I would have done it without you, Hattie." Jo said.

"Ah rubbish, you'll always be fine. By the way, you mustn't think folk don't know about the offer." She looked over at Jo. "There's been surveyors taking photos and Peter Gavmin was pissed in the Templars the other night and said he'd have a big conveyancing job soon. Folk aren't daft. They'll soon put two and two together and be worried about their jobs."

"Oh bugger!" Jo was furious. "It's supposed to be confidential. Capital Country Houses have no right to have surveyors sneaking about and I'll kill Peter Gavmin."

"Never trust a fat man with round eyes," Hattie muttered.

"The staff have nothing to worry about – quite the opposite if Capital get planning permission for another forty bedrooms." "It'll be like a Travel Lodge." Hattie sunk deeper into the bed.

"Anyway," Jo gave Hattie a nudge. "We've got tons to do and a party to get organised, move your fat arse."

"It's curvy and cuddly," Hattie retorted. "Wait till I strut my stuff in that green dress tonight, Westmarland Wives better watch out."

Hattie leapt out of bed and headed for the shower. As she went through Jo's dressing room she stopped and looked at their dresses hanging on the wardrobe. Jo's red creation was a stunner, even on the hanger. Hattie started to hum Chris De Burgh's hit song Lady In Red... Never can forget, the way you look tonight... If only Jo had someone special to dance with.

Hattie wondered what Gypsy John was up to.

No doubt married at long last and organising a Romany revelry to bring in the New Year. Well bloody good luck to him! She thought angrily and stomped into the bathroom.

FOR THE LAST TWO DAYS, households throughout the county had been gearing themselves up for this evening's frivolity. The Atkinsons had arranged to have a drinks reception at home, for their party of twenty family and friends and Billy had two mini buses laid on to take them all to the hotel.

Paulie was rushed off his feet in the salon with local ladies wanting upswept styles like Princess Diana, to go with cocktail dresses that had been resurrected from the back of dusty closets, camphor bags removed and mothballs brushed out of silk and taffeta ensembles.

Jo had visited the salon the day before for a cut and highlights.

"Everyone's talking about the Ball, sweetie, it's the hottest ticket in town," Paulie said as he spun in a frenzy, cutting and tinting two clients at once. They had London friends arriving in time for the party and Robbie was meeting the afternoon train.

"Make sure we've got the best table." Paulie watched Jo's reflection in the mirror, then leaned over and whispered in her ear. "A little bird
has told me that you may be sprouting wings?"

Jo couldn't hold his gaze.

"You mustn't believe what you hear, you gossip too much," she said and shook out a magazine, then began to take interest in Mrs Thatcher's visit with Falkland war veterans. She felt guilty that she couldn't tell Paulie the truth.

"Well it's none of my business I'm sure." Paulie pulled a face and flounced off to another client.

As Jo walked back to her car she saw Dougie Cannon wiping down his fish counter. He called out to her.

"We're looking forward to the party, Mrs Edmonds. We've a table booked with Arthur Harrison and Sandra's mam. Annie's got a new dress." Dougie wrung out his cloth and beamed. Jo called back that she was looking forward to seeing them too and as she headed back to the hotel she wondered if Arthur's relationship with Sandra was about to develop further.

PETER GAVMIN WAS NURSING the mother of all hangovers that ran from one day into the next. Christmas was a time when he could drink in abundance, his office being closed for two weeks.

Like Robert, things were quiet over the festive period but Peter was relishing the thought that Kirkton House would soon change hands, Robert had told him in confidence and Peter was certain he'd handle the legalities.

That would be a nice little earner for the New Year. He was travelling by taxi to the event tonight with Isabel, Robert and Miriam. Dick Littlefair, the greengrocer and his wife, were sharing their table alongside Trevor and Prue Pigmy.

Peter rubbed his hands together, it was always good to socialise with his clients. He looked at his watch, three o'clock - no harm in having a livener, he'd get a couple or so ahead of the others and get rid of this hang-over. Hair of the dog and all that, he thought as he poured himself a large scotch.

Linda and Kath stood by the mirror in Margaret's bedroom and complimented each other on their smart get-ups. They wore black dresses, which they normally wore for the church choir, and had added white lace collars. It was a nice change from their normal chambermaid's gear.

They pulled on warm coats, said goodbye to Margaret's husband and walked together through the snowy village to the hotel. The trio were to oversee the cloakroom and would have three hundred coats to take responsibility for. They decided how to store tickets and pin the corresponding numbers on coats, scarves, brollies and hats.

Mr Knight from the bank and his good lady wife were staying with their friends the Capsticks, who lived in the village. Capsticks Carpets had supplied the hotel in the refurbishment and the close friends had arranged for Phillip Campbell to transport them all to the hotel at seven twenty-five sharp. Mr Knight was looking forward to the evening. He'd had the unpleasant task of monitoring Jo's overdraft and it had been stressful.

Left to him, he wouldn't have bothered her, but head office at the Westmarland Trust Bank had very strict rules.

Thankfully, she'd ridden through her little storm and was now on track. Although he'd heard that she may be selling up. That would be a great pity as he'd always enjoyed having her as a client.

Jo WATCHED the band unload their instruments and set their equipment up on the stage. Casually dressed in jeans and trainers, they'd asked for a changing room and Hattie had instructed them to use the staff room.

Agency staff had arrived and Judy showed them what to do as she handed out long black aprons with Kirkton House embroidered on the bib. They looked smart in crisp white shirts and black trousers. Simon, Steven and Penny would each take charge of a team. Bottles of champagne in huge plastic boxes were chilling in mountains of ice and Hattie supervised the brewery staff as they set up the bar.

In the catering tent Sandra had the starters stacked on tall plate racks, a medley of seafood or game terrine was carefully plated, covered and ready to go.

Thank God we don't have to wash this lot up... Jo thought. The catering company who hired the china offered that service and Jo had taken advantage of it.

Sandra was focussed as she supervised last minute details of the meal. Sumptuous joints of meat were ready to be carved at the buffet table and salads and savouries were piled high in huge serving dishes, with dozens of different accompaniments to the lavish spread. Gerald and Marian ran around as Sandra barked out her final instructions.

IN THE TOWN-HOUSE flat in Butterly, Estelle dressed very carefully. She was every inch a Spanish Flamenco dancer tonight, in her tightly fitted Salsa-style dress with a thigh-high split. Fancy combs and a mantilla looked splendid in her hair.

Greg hunted for cuff links and thrust his wrists out so that Estelle could fasten them.

He had to admit, she looked stunning.

Her glossy black hair was piled high on her head and she towered above him in black stilettos. Estelle leaned into a mirror and painted her full lips with a scarlet lipstick.

"Your hair too long in that suit." Estelle frowned as she watched his reflection. "Look stupid."

Greg lifted his locks off the collar of his dinner suit. She was right; it was far too casual for this penguin look.

"Tie it back." Estelle tossed one of her elastic hair bands over to him. Greg caught the band and looked at her with surprise. She was very bossy recently and her command of English was improving by the day. He combed his hair into a pony tail and twisted it into the band.

"Better." Estelle walked confidently past. She towered over him in her high heels.

Greg sighed as he liberally applied Jo's favourite aftershave. Not for much longer!

40

The clock on the hall table chimed seven o'clock. Jo and Hattie kneeled on the window seat on the first-floor landing and looked out of the long window to the driveway below where snow was falling in soft spongy blobs on the gravel.

The 'A' board on the verge was covered in a large poster which read —

GALA BALL TONIGHT!

Stationed by the door, the twins waited to greet guests, take tickets and direct them to the marquee. They looked handsome in their black dinner suits with tartan bow ties and matching cummerbunds.

Jo took a deep breath. Her stomach lurched like a bouncing ball. There was nothing more she could do to prepare and the scene was now set for the party.

Hattie pointed to a vehicle making its way across the village.

"It looks like Phillip has started all ready," Hattie said. They could see bright balloons bouncing from the roof-rack of Phillip Campbell's jeep. The words SHUFFLE BUS in Old Johnny's bold print were emblazed across the bonnet.

"Shouldn't that read Shuttle?" Hattie asked.

"Yes, but we won't dwell on it." Jo smiled.

Hattie and Jo turned and faced each other. Both were resplendent in their party outfits.

"God we look good!" Hattie said as she thrust her shoulders back and pushed her chest forward. Jo fiddled nervously with her diamond necklace; she'd decided to wear it at the last minute.

"Come on Cinders – you shall go to the ball." Hattie held out her arm and Jo took it, then they both slowly descended the stairs. "Feels like a scene from Gone with the Wind," Hattie whispered as they negotiated the turn in the stairway. "You make a good Scarlett O'Hara in that get up." She held onto the banister. "You go first."

Jo lifted the front of her dress. As she began her descent, the fishtail skirt fanned out behind her and the red silk rippled over the stairs.

The Gavmin party had arrived and were being greeted by the twins. They looked up as Jo and Hattie appeared on the staircase. Peter wolf whistled and Robert's jaw dropped. Lady Miriam scowled and tugged at Robert's sleeve.

"You're making a fool of yourself!" she hissed.

"Quite frankly my dear – I don't give a damn."

Robert gazed at Jo with complete adoration. She looked absolutely beautiful in her red gown.

"Good evening everybody." Jo smiled warmly and welcomed the guests.

Penny came forward to take them through to the marquee.

"There's trouble there." Hattie nodded at the retreating backs.

Lady Miriam's head bounced as she told Robert off and Peter Gavmin swayed from side to side. He was half-cut already and Jo wondered who else he might have indiscreetly told her news to.

Taxis and cars arrived in quick succession and Judy came forward with her team to greet the guests and guide them through to the marquee. Jo and Hattie followed and stopped at reception where Suzy, pretty in her prom dress, sat behind the desk and manned the phone. She smiled as she saw them. Hattie leaned over, she pulled out a glass of Cointreau from under the counter and handed it to Jo. "You're usual bracer madam."

"Thanks Hattie." Jo let out a deep breath. "I need this." She tossed the liquid back and shuddered. "Right, let's get this party started!"

THE MARQUEE LOOKED MAGNIFICENT. The red carpeted tunnel was lined with little silver lights and opened to a stunningly decorated room.

A dark canopied ceiling of fairy lights twinkled like stars. Pillars were covered with winter foliage and tied with tartan bows, while festive swags, draped in huge loops, hung around the sides of the room. The tables were set with white linen and crystal, with central arrangements of poinsettias and gold candles. Chairs had red covers and were trimmed with tartan ribbon, draped to the floor.

The guests mingled as staff circulated with champagne cocktails and canapés. Piped music played softly in the background.

Hattie shot off to supervise the bar, where several men had gathered and were ordering pints of beer.

Jo moved around the room and greeted her guests. The seating plan seemed to be working and slowly but surely everyone settled at their tables. Pete Parks crept up and gave her bottom a squeeze.

"You're lookin' bonny." He breathed onto her neck. Jo wanted to step back and impale him to the floor with her heel, but she turned and smiled sweetly. He needn't think he could pull any sexual favours in return for the booking. Mrs Parks, head to toe in acres of creased taffeta, waved to her.

"I hope everything's alright for your party?" Jo said and waved to his wife.

"Aye, all set for a good night. The place looks grand." Pete touched her arm and whispered "I hear you're leaving, it's not true surely?" Pete looked concerned but before Jo had time to reply he was summoned to his table. With a nod, he moved away.

There was an excited buzz of expectation as everyone took their seats and began to pull the festive crackers that lay beside each place setting. With party hats at jaunty angles, guests laughed and exchanged key rings, whistles and corny jokes.

It was nearly eight o'clock and Jo was anxious to formally start the evening. She knew that Jinny and Billy Atkinson's party were all seated but their hosts were nowhere to be seen.

Jo paced nervously down the hall to see if the Atkinson's needed anything. They were in the Green Room but the door was closed.

As she approached she heard raised voices.

"How much!" Billy yelled. "You stupid, stupid bitch!" He shouted the words out.

Jo reeled back, Billy was furious! Jinny was mumbling and Jo couldn't make out what she was saying but Jinny seemed to be crying. Jo decided not to intervene and headed back to the party.

As Jo entered the marquee, Judy took her place in line with the staff and indicated that they were ready. Jo took a deep breath and swept across the floor, then nervously walked up the steps to the stage.

The Cumberland Quartet were checking their equipment and tuning up. Jeans and trainers abandoned, the band looked classy in smart dinner jackets, drainpipe trousers and shoe string ties. More like the high school hop... Jo thought as they welcomed her onto the stage and handed her the microphone.

"Ladies and gentlemen." she began. The audience shushed each other and someone rattled a spoon against a glass.

"Thank you." Jo smiled. "I'd like to say a very good evening to you all and thank you for joining us here tonight, to celebrate the start of the New Year."

She looked around the room. Annie Cannon sipped an orange juice, whilst Dougie drained his pint and indicated to Arthur that he was ready for a refill. Sandra's mother sipped gin and bitter lemon and smiled up at Jo.

"It's absolutely wonderful to see so many familiar faces." Jo continued. "I'm sure that we're going to have a great night."

Peter Gavmin banged the table with his empty scotch glass and cried out, "Hear, hear!"

"We have a delicious meal for you to enjoy." Jo glanced towards the catering doorway where Sandra stood ready.

Jo looked around the room. Greg and Estelle sat with a party from the Butterly Arms Hotel and Greg lifted his glass and waved. Jo was horrified - did Greg have a pony tail? Jo's eyes met Hattie's. Hattie nodded towards Greg and mouthed the word "Wanker."

Jo quickly composed herself and continued. "After dinner we'd like you to relax and dance the night away to the fabulous Cumberland Quartet." She turned and introduced the band and they all took a bow as the guests whooped and cheered.

"We have a great raffle tonight and all proceeds will go to the Marland Dogs Home." Jo looked at Alf and he raised his glass. "Many of you know that our local gamekeeper is patron of the charity, so please dig deep. There are some super prizes."

"Any tomato puree?" Paulie squealed from across the room as Robbie smiled with their smart London guests.

"Then of course, just before midnight we'll join with the band and countdown to the New Year." Everyone cheered. "So please enjoy yourselves and have a wonderful evening." Jo stepped down from the stage.

"Well done." Hattie said and handed Jo a Cointreau as staff glided around the room in a well-executed service and Sandra and Gerald, in starched whites and tall chefs hats, took their places behind the buffet and began to carve from huge joints of meat.

Jinny and Billy Atkinson finally joined their party. Jinny moved elegantly across the floor and Jo looked at her in wonder.

No one would know that a few moments ago she'd been bawling her eyes out! Jinny wore a black sequinned ankle-length dress, cut low at the back. Diamond clusters twinkled on her ears.

"Not a patch on you," Hattie whispered as she poured a pint of ale for Maurice. He handed over a ten-pound note.

"Take one for yourself." Maurice smiled.

"Don't mind if I do." Hattie beamed back.

With the main courses finished, Judy synchronised the team and desserts followed. Christmas Pudding with fudge and brandy sauce, Lemon Tart and Westmarland Cheeses.

Jo stood in the catering marquee surveying the activity and felt proud of her staff. Sandra, Gerald and Marian checked each plate as it left their kitchen. Jo wanted to hug them all. Who would have thought that their modest little team could pull this off!

The band took to the stage and announced that dancing was about to begin. There was a loud cheer and as people took their partners for the first dance, Jo slipped away. She needed to check her makeup and decided to use the ladies room in the hallway. As she reached the door open she heard female voices.

Jo paused.

"Did you see her face?" a woman giggled.

"Aye, covered in slap but you could see she'd been crying."

"Billy's gone ballistic, threatened to divorce her!" They both gasped. "Once a gambler always a gambler."

"But I've heard she's no more funds coming in."

Jo could hear the women spraying perfume from the complimentary bottles.

"Some gypo's been bailing her out. She told him she was buying horses with Billy's approval, but the pikey's found out that she's been gambling it away and has called in the loan..."

The words trailed away but their impact hit Jo like a blow and she staggered back. She groped her way into reception.

"You alright, Mrs E?" Suzy stood up and motioned for Jo to sit down.

"I'll be fine, Suzy." Jo fell into the chair and stared at the desk as the words sank in. He's been lending her money! Jo couldn't believe it!

Minutes ticked by. The door opened and a glass of Cointreau appeared.

"I heard you needed this." Hattie said. Jo looked up gratefully.

"You'll never believe what I've just heard," Jo said and repeated the conversation.

"Friggin hell," Hattie chuckled. "And all the time you thought he was bonkin' her! It seems our Jinny's been leading everyone a merry dance." They both shook their heads.

"It doesn't change anything, Hattie. He doesn't want me." Jo finished the Cointreau. "He'll be married by now, making things right with his parents."

"He probably will." Hattie sighed and picked up the empty glass. "Come on, get back to your party, it's going brilliantly out there and there's a tale Old Johnny's telling that I think you should hear."

THE MARQUEE WAS in full swing and the Cumbrian Quartet in their stride, as they belted out boogie tunes to a packed dance floor. Estelle danced with the landlord of the Butterly Arms Hotel and as she strutted her stuff she threw her head back and laughed.

"Her mantilla runneth over," Hattie said as they watched Estelle jive and spin around the floor. Her long legs kicked out and thick glossy hair tumbled from the decorative combs. Greg leaned against a pillar and flirted with Christine Harrison from the Lemon Tree Café.

"That's Arthur's niece," Hattie explained. "She's a right little raver by all accounts."

Greg looked up and saw Jo watching him. He abandoned Christine and hurried to Jo's side.

"I'll get back to the bar," Hattie said and glanced at Greg. "That a dead rat on your neck?" She smiled sweetly and disappeared.

Greg glared at hattie but composed himself and turned his charm on Jo. "You look absolutely amazing." He stroked her arm. "That's a lovely necklace." Greg didn't remember it and frowned.

Jo touched the diamond. She couldn't believe that she'd briefly considered taking Greg back a few weeks ago. She supposed she ought to be nice to him, it was Christmas.

"Thomas enjoys his time with you. You've been very good with him."

"I love that little fella." Greg looked misty-eyed and Jo hoped he wasn't going to cry.

Greg took a deep breath. It was now or never.

"Just knowing that it's only a matter of time before we're all a proper family, keeps me going." Greg eyes were pleading.

Jo thought she'd misheard as he went on.

"I know you've been going through some difficult times emotionally and financially and... I've decided to help you." Greg leaned in so that Jo could hear him over the music.

"What are you saying, Greg?" Jo was confused.

"I've still got plenty of money and I'll put it in the business when we get back together. With winter set in, I suggest that happens soon." He stood back and reached for Jo's hand then gave his most engaging smile.

Jo could see Christine hovering in the background.

"I think we should get back together again, I'm ready to move in with you and our son. I know that's what you want." Greg laced his fingers through Jo's and pulled her to him.

Jo was horrified.

The scene in the Red Rooster Café flashed through her mind surely he hadn't forgotten what she'd said to him? She hadn't changed her mind! Jo removed her hand and gently pushed Greg away.

It's Christmas be nice... "I'm very flattered, Greg, and it's very sweet of you, but getting together again is not an option." She stood firm.

Greg looked shocked. Surely she didn't mean it?

"You're a great dad and you can see Thomas whenever you want, but not as a family with me, that's not going to happen." Jo began to move away and Greg looked like he was about to burst into tears. "What about that drink you promised me?" Christine tugged on his arm.

Jo made her exit.

"Marvelous party, darling!" Dorothy Osbourne bellowed as she sashayed past. The Cumberland Quartet cranked out Rock Around The Clock and Jo was wide-eyed as she watched Dorothy's partner. She was immaculately dressed in a pin-striped suit and spats, and spun Dorothy round before throwing her over her shoulder in a wellpractised jive move. Jo smiled as the two ladies stole the show on the dance floor.

"Love the garlands, I've got those at home!" Dorothy gasped and pointed to the bar where a crumpled Snow White and the Seven Dwarfs hung over the optics.

Hattie grinned and gave a wave.

Wine flowed as staff began a table service for drinks. Jo noted that lots of champagne had been ordered for midnight, she hoped that she'd ordered enough and went to check on stocks in the cellar. As she passed through the conservatory she saw Old Johnny and his wife sitting quietly in the corner.

Old Johnny beckoned her over. "I want to ask thee a question." Jo gathered her skirt and squeezed into a cane chair.

"Have you felt 'owt strange in 'ere?" Old Johnny asked.

"Yes I have." Jo looked at the doorway. "There's an icy chill sometimes by the door and I feel terrified when I stand next to it. Even Pippa cowers away."

"Well we can explain that to thee..." Old Johnny lit a fresh pipe and nodded to his wife. She looked at Jo and started to explain his tale.

"In 1730 the family who owned Kirkton House, bought a slave named Abraham to the property," she began. "They were prosperous from the slave trade in Whitehaven and a sugar cane plantation in Jamaica. The family thought it would be a novelty to have a slave to work for them in Westmarland and Abraham was set to work on the large garden."

Old Johnny puffed on his pipe and nodded his head as his wife continued.

"Abraham liked to dance and was badly homesick. In his home village in Africa, he danced all the time and he took to dancing around the garden at Kirkton House, to remind himself of home.
Most of the time he forgot to do his jobs." Old
Johnny shook his head.

"The family became impatient and forbade him to dance - after all, he was here to work. But without his dancing Abraham became more and more depressed. He told the cook that he'd put an African curse on the house and his masters and he'd forever haunt the place." She stopped and looked at the doorway.

Jo felt cold.

"Early one morning he tied a rope over the lintel in that doorway and hung himself in despair."

Old Johnny shook his head and Jo shivered.

"His masters felt so guilty about his death that they decided to lay him to rest in the garden and folklore says he's buried under the croquet lawn."

Jo rubbed her arms, she was freezing. "But what was the curse?" she asked.

Old Johnny's wife smiled and continued. "He told the cook that only a thousand footsteps dancing on his grave would let his soul rest."

Old Johnny knocked his pipe on the ashtray as Jo let his words sink in. They could hear music from the marquee and the sound of people dancing. The room began to feel warm and Jo threw her head back and laughed. Old Johnny and his wife joined in with her.

"I think we should drink to Abraham." Jo beamed and signalled to Simon, who was passing with a tray of champagne.

Jo took three glasses.

"To Abraham," she toasted. "May your dancing soul finally find peace..." She whispered the words and looked out to the marquee, where three hundred folk danced ecstatically round the floor.

"To Abraham!" Old Johnny and his wife raised their glasses and looked out at the moon-lit night.

MIDNIGHT APPROACHED. Jo stood by the entrance and watched Mrs Brough and Ivan do the jitterbug. Her blue perm bobbed up and down as they bounced around.

Hattie hurried from behind the bar to join Jo.

"The jungle drums are beating..." Hattie whispered.

"Please don't use that expression." Jo thought of poor Abraham.

"Alright then Chinese whispers!" Hattie snapped.

"We had enough of those a couple of months ago..."

"Folk think you're leaving." Hattie was serious. "They're expecting an announcement at midnight. You'll have to tell them Jo and now's the perfect time."

Hattie was right.

It was wrong of Jo to wait, she felt like she was deceiving everyone. At least she could assure the staff of their jobs with the new owners and that the place would continue as a hotel. It was a beginning not an ending. She'd explain it that way. She braced herself.

"Need a Cointreau?"

"Nope. I need a clear head." Jo took a deep breath.

"Good luck," Hattie called after her and watched Jo walk across the dance floor.

Hattie looked at the clock – five minutes to twelve. The room became silent as guests watched Jo walk up the steps and stride across the stage. The music came to a discreet end and Jo reached for the microphone.

"Ladies and gentlemen," she began nervously, "it's nearly midnight and I hope you're all having a wonderful evening." She looked around, "I know that I am."

The room was quiet. A pot crashed in the kitchen and Sandra could be heard yelling at the staff to be quiet.

"This last year has been a real merry-go-round for me." Jo felt their eyes bore into her as they hung off her every word. She heard Peter Gavmin cough and as she glanced over he smiled with anticipation.

"We began with the enormous task of putting this lovely old place back together..."

Jo paused and looked around. Pete Parks winked and did a thumbs-up. Paulie and Robbie stood arm-in-arm shaking their heads sadly. Judy and Alf held hands.

"You all helped me so much," Jo said. "You pulled out all the stops and made sure that we'd open on time."

She felt a choke in her voice. Sandra wrung a tea towel in whiteknuckled hands and Arthur put his arm around her shoulder.

"And when we did open our doors, you supported me. You came and dined and bought all your friends and recommended us all over the county."

Hattie wiped her eyes with a hanky. "The autumn was tough..."

Mr Knight took a swig of his drink.

"I had a bit of a panic, and we were very saddened by the loss of a dear friend..."

The twins put their arms around Hattie.

Jo took a deep breath. She had to tell them.

"And I know that there's been a lot of speculation in the last week or so about my future here."

She put her shoulders back and stared at the faces before her. They waited patiently for confirmation of her news. Jo looked around the room and felt an overpowering wave of kindness, these people weren't just customers and employees - they were her friends!

She gripped the microphone and looked at the clock, it was almost midnight.

"And I've come to a decision..."

Everyone waited for her news. Robert hung his head, he couldn't look at Jo.

"I've no intention of moving anywhere!" Jo announced. "Kirkton House is my home and you all feel like family to me, so here's to 1988 and another great year!"

A huge cheer broke out as the news sank in. Peter Gavmin groaned and made his way to the bar and Jo handed the microphone to the band leader and he began a countdown to the New Year.

"Ten, nine, eight!" Everyone joined in. "Three, two, one!"

The cheer raised the roof of the marquee as balloons fell and poppers exploded and everyone kissed and hugged each other. The band began to play and as Jo left the stage she was pulled into the middle of the floor. Someone shouted out,

"Three cheers for Jo! Hip hip hurrah!" Everyone joined in and followed it up with, 'For She's a Jolly Good Fellow.'

Across the room, Maurice asked Hattie to dance.

The party continued and as a squiffy Vera, supported by husband Victor, led a conga around the room, Jo made her escape.

She went through to reception where Judy and Suzy made out bills and counted money. Judy packed a pile of notes into a metal box and locked it in the safe.

"It's a great party, Mrs E," she said.

"I couldn't have done it without you all, you've been brilliant."

"We're so relieved that you're not going." Judy looked tearful. "It would never have been the same without you." Jo waved her hand in dismissal.

"Have you heard that Arthur has proposed?" Judy clapped her hands together. "And Sandra's said yes!"

"Oh how marvellous! A joint wedding?" Jo grinned at Judy.

"Hattie looks like she's copped off too," Suzy said.

"He's very fit and owns a flooring business," Judy beamed. The girls discussed Maurice's merits as they filed the bills. "Did you know that Estelle is moving in with landlord of the Butterly Arms?" Judy watched Jo's reaction.

"What?" Jo's eyes widened as she digested all this information and shook her head. The night was full of surprises! And to think that she'd started the year longing for Greg to come back.

Jo suddenly felt exhausted.

The party pulsed in the distance, laughter and music echoed from the marquee and Jo decided to step away. She was in need of a few quiet moments.

She left the girls to it and wandered down the hallway.

Jo stood at the door of the hotel and gazed out at the inky, snow laden sky. In the distance, the band struck up Auld Lang Syne and she imagined the revellers joining hands as they sung their hearts out and promised eternal friendship tonight and evermore.

The beginning of 1987 had been life-changing and now, as it rolled over into a new year, Jo made another monumental decision.

It was freezing. She should have put a jacket over her gown but Jo was unaware of the cold as she watched the snow begin to fall. She wondered where her gypsy was, what night sky would he be watching?

The snow came down in a sudden flurry and Jo held her face up to the heavens as the giant flakes caressed her skin. The temperature had dropped and Jo felt the bitter cold.

She stirred herself and noticed that the Christmas tree by the door bowed, its branches looked heavy and as Jo glanced at the top where a full-breasted plastic fairy leaned to one side, her open mouth full of snow. Good old Hattie!

A car approached in the distance.

Jo saw dimmed headlights as the car made its way slowly through the oncoming blizzard. Who could it be? She rubbed her hands up and down her arms to try and get warm.

The engine stopped and the head-lights went out.

Who on earth was travelling in this weather? Perhaps they needed a room? You couldn't get near the hotel for cars parked along the verges, but the Kirkton House Hotel sign still glowed under the yellow lamp.

Jo peered into the darkness but snow blurred her vision. No one was there. She shivered and decided to go back in, her dress would be ruined.

As she turned, a figure, huddled into an overcoat, appeared at the gate.

"Are you alright?" Jo called out.

A man came into view, his head down as he entered the driveway and Jo tried to make out a face. Perhaps he needed the breakdown service?

"Do you need any help?"

The figure got closer. Something was familiar and Jo strained to see who it was. She caught her breath, was she dreaming… Could it be?

John came towards her.

"Jo! Whatever are you doing out here?"

He tried to run across the icy drive and stumbled. Jo raced forward and tripped too, falling into his arms. John's blue eyes gazed at her with total adoration and Jo melted with joy as he wrenched at the buttons of his coat to wrap the warm cashmere tightly around her trembling body.

"You're frozen," he whispered. "Get inside." He took her hand and they fell into the porch.

"What are you doing here?" Jo hardly dared ask.

"Shh..." John put his finger on her lips. He dug into his pocket and reaching for her left hand, gently pushed a diamond ring onto her finger.

"Jo, will you marry me?" Jo
gasped.

Wide-eyed, she stared at the ring - it matched the necklace perfectly.

"But what about your family?"

"They'll get over it." John was serious.

"But what about Romany tradition and never marrying out?"

"It's time to change."

"But where will we live?"

"In a Vardo at the back of your garden." John smiled and tilted her chin.

Jo was lost for words as he kissed her.

"I take it that's a yes?"

Jo nodded and gazed at the diamond. "I'm good at pig's head stew," she said.

"Well that's alright then." John closed his eyes and hugged her to him. He never wanted to let her go again.

"Let's go and tell Hattie."

Hand-in-hand, they walked down the hall and out to the marquee, where the party was in full swing. Guests toasted each other as the band began a Highland fling and everyone took to the floor. Hattie whirled past with Maurice and nearly fell over when she saw Jo.

Hattie stopped and stared at them, then shook her head and began to smile. She turned to the band and caught the eye of the lead singer. The music ended abruptly and everyone looked around to see why.

The singer picked up the microphone and started to sing:

"Never seen you look so lovely as you look tonight..."

John took Jo's hand. Her diamond ring flashed under the spotlight as he led her to the floor.

"Lady in Red..."

The guests began to clap.

"I'll never forget..."

The clapping built into a thunderous round of applause.

"The way you look tonight..."

Jo's romance with the gypsy began with his first kiss. She'd never forgotten it and never would, as he kissed her again and again and again...

* * *

Read *Coffee Tea the Caribbean & Me* to find out what happened next...

ALSO BY CAROLINE JAMES

If you enjoyed reading Coffee Tea the Gypsy & Me find out what happened next. Catch up with Hattie, Jo and many more characters in...

Coffee Tea the Caribbean & Me

Coffee Tea the Chef & Me

Jungle Rock

The Best Boomerville Hotel

Boomerville at Ballymegille

Hattie Goes to Hollywood

The Spa Break

* * *

REVIEWS

We'd love to hear if you enjoyed reading *Coffee Tea The Gypsy & Me*. Reviews are hugely important to an author. Please take a moment to leave a comment on either Amazon or Goodreads.

With love and happy reading

Caroline

CAROLINE JAMES

Caroline James was born in Cheshire and wanted to be a writer from an early age. She trained, however, in the catering trade and worked both at home and abroad. Caroline has owned and run many related businesses and cookery is a passion, alongside her writing, combining her love of the hospitality industry and romantic fiction. She is a member of the Romantic Novelist's Association and the Society of Women's Writers & Journalists and contributes short stories and food related articles for many magazines. As a guest speaker, she appears at events throughout the country and on cruise ships. Caroline can often be found with her nose in a book and hand in a box of chocolates and when not doing either, likes to write, climb mountains and contemplate life.

CONTACT

To find out more about Caroline James, please contact her on any of the links below:

Facebook: Caroline James Author
Twitter: @carolinejames12
Web: www.carolinejamesauthor.co.uk
Amazon: Caroline James Author

Printed in Great Britain
by Amazon

34140806R00199